FOES

A Novel

MARY JOHNSTON

Foes

Mary Johnston

© 1st World Library, 2007
PO Box 2211
Fairfield, IA 52556
www.1stworldlibrary.com
First Edition

LCCN: 2007927842

Softcover ISBN: 978-1-4218-4559-3
Hardcover ISBN: 978-1-4218-4475-6
eBook ISBN: 978-1-4218-4643-9

Purchase *"Foes"*
as a traditional bound book at:
www.1stWorldLibrary.com/purchase.asp?ISBN=978-1-4218-4559-3

1st World Library is a literary, educational organization
dedicated to:

- Creating a free internet library of downloadable ebooks

- Hosting writing competitions and offering book
publishing scholarships.

Interested in more 1st World Library books?
contact: literacy@1stworldlibrary.com
Check us out at: www.1stworldlibrary.com

1ˢᵗ World Library Literary Society

Giving Back to the World

"If you want to work on the core problem, it's early school literacy."

- James Barksdale, former CEO of Netscape

"No skill is more crucial to the future of a child, or to a democratic and prosperous society, than literacy."

- Los Angeles Times

"Literacy... means far more than learning how to read and write... The aim is to transmit... knowledge and promote social participation."

- UNESCO

"Literacy is not a luxury, it is a right and a responsibility. If our world is to meet the challenges of the twenty-first century we must harness the energy and creativity of all our citizens."

- President Bill Clinton

"Parents should be encouraged to read to their children, and teachers should be equipped with all available techniques for teaching literacy, so the varying needs and capacities of individual kids can be taken into account."

- Hugh Mackay

CHAPTER I

Said Mother Binning: "Whiles I spin and whiles I dream. A bonny day like this I look."

English Strickland, tutor at Glenfernie House, looked, too, at the feathery glen, vivid in June sunshine. The ash-tree before Mother Binning's cot overhung a pool of the little river. Below, the water brawled and leaped from ledge to ledge, but here at the head of the glen it ran smooth and still. A rose-bush grew by the door and a hen and her chicks crossed in the sun. English Strickland, who had been fishing, sat on the door-stone and talked to Mother Binning, sitting within with her wheel beside her.

"What is it, Mother, to have the second sight?"

"It's to see behind the here and now. Why're ye asking?"

"I wish I could buy it or slave for it!" said Strickland. "Over and over again I really need to see behind the here and now!"

"Aye. It's needed mair really than folk think. It's no' to be had by buying nor slaving. How are the laird and the leddy?"

"Why, well. Tell me," said Strickland, "some of the things you've seen with second sight."

"It taks inner ears for inner things."

"How do you know I haven't them?"

"Maybe 'tis so. Ye're liked well enough."

Mother Binning looked at the dappling water and the June trees and the bright blue sky. It was a day to loosen tongue.

"I'll tell you ane thing I saw. It's mair than twenty years since James Stewart, that was son of him who fled, wad get Scotland and England again intil his hand. So the laddie came frae overseas, and made stir and trouble enough, I tell ye!... Now I'll show you what I saw, I that was a young woman then, and washing my wean's claes in the water there. The month was September, and the year seventeen fifteen. Mind you, nane hereabouts knew yet of thae goings-on!... I sat back on my heels, with Jock's sark in my hand, and a lav'rock was singing, and whiles I listened the pool grew still. And first it was blue glass under blue sky, and I sat caught. And then it was curled cloud or milk, and then it was nae color at all. And then I *saw*, and 'twas as though what I saw was around me. There was a town nane like Glenfernie, and a country of mountains, and a water no' like this one. There pressed a thrang of folk, and they were Hieland men and Lowland men, but mair Hieland than Lowland, and there were chiefs and chieftains and Lowland lords, and there were pipers. I heard naught, but it was as though bright shadows were around me. There was a height like a Good People's mount, and a braw fine-clad lord speaking and reading frae a paper, and by him a surpliced man to gie a

Mary Johnston

prayer, and there was a banner pole, and it went up high, and it had a gowd ball atop. The braw lord stopped speaking, and all the Hielandmen and Lowlandmen drew and held up and brandished their claymores and swords. The flash ran around like the levin. I kenned that they shouted, all thae gay shadows! I saw the pipers' cheeks fill with wind, and the bags of the pipes fill. Then ane drew on a fine silken rope, and up the pole there went a braw silken banner, and it sailed out in the wind. And there was mair shouting and brandishing. But what think ye might next befall? That gowden ball, gowden like the sun before it drops, that topped the pole, it fell! I marked it fall, and the heads dodge, and it rolled upon the ground.... And then all went out like a candle that you blaw upon. I was kneeling by the water, and Jock's sark in my hand, and the lav'rock singing, and that was all."

"I have heard tell of that," said Strickland. "It was near Braemar."

"And that's mony a lang league frae here! Sax days, and we had news of the rising, with the gathering at Braemar. And said he wha told us, 'The gilt ball fell frae the standard pole, and there's nane to think that a good omen!' But I *saw* it," said Mother Binning. She turned her wheel, a woman not yet old and with a large, tranquil comeliness. "What I see makes fine company!"

Strickland plucked a rose and smelled it. "This country is fuller of such things than is England that I come from."

"Aye. It's a grand country." She continued to spin. The tutor looked at the sun. It was time to be going if he wished another hour with the stream. He took up his rod and book and rose from the door-step. Mother Binning glanced aside from her wheel.

"How gaes things with the lad at the House?"

"Alexander or James?"

"The one ye call Alexander."

"That is his name."

"I think that he's had ithers. That's a lad of mony lives!"

Strickland, halting by the rose-bush, looked at Mother Binning. "I suppose we call it 'wisdom' when two feel alike. Now that's just what I feel about Alexander Jardine! It's just feeling without rationality."

"Eh?"

"There isn't any reason in it."

"I dinna know about 'reason.' There's *being* in it."

The tutor made as if to speak further, then, with a shake of his head, thought better of it. Thirty-five years old, he had been a tutor since he was twenty, dwelling, in all, in four or five more or less considerable houses and families. Experience, adding itself to innate good sense, had made him slow to discuss idiosyncrasies of patrons or pupils. Strong perplexity or strong feeling might sometimes drive him, but ordinarily he kept a rein on speech. Now he looked around him.

"What high summer, lovely weather!"

"Oh aye! It's bonny. Will ye be gaeing, since ye have na mair to say?"

English Strickland laughed and said good-by to Mother Binning and went. The ash-tree, the hazels that fringed the water, a point of mossy rock, hid the cot. The drone of the wheel no longer reached his ears. It was as though all that had sunk into the earth. Here was only the deep, the green, and lonely glen. He found a pool that invited, cast, and awaited the speckled victim. In the morning he had had fair luck, but now nothing.... The water showed no more diamonds, the lower slopes of the converging hills grew a deep and slumbrous green. Above was the gold, shoulder and crest powdered with it, unearthly, uplifted. Strickland ceased his fishing. The light moved slowly upward; the trees, the crag-heads, melted into heaven; while the lower glen lay in lengths of shadow, in jade and amethyst. A whispering breeze sprang up, cool as the water sliding by. Strickland put up his fisherman's gear and moved homeward, down the stream.

He had a very considerable way to go. The glen path, narrow and rough, went up and down, still following the water. Hazel and birch, oak and pine, overhung and darkened it. Bosses of rock thrust themselves forward, patched with lichen and moss, seamed and fringed with fern and heath. Roots of trees, huge and twisted, spread and clutched like guardian serpents. In places where rock had fallen the earth seemed to gape. In the shadow it looked a gnome world—a gnome or a dragon world. Then upon ledge or bank showed bells or disks or petaled suns of June flowers, rose and golden, white and azure, while overhead was heard the evening song of birds alike calm and merry, and through a cleft in the hills poured the ruddy, comfortable sun.

The walls declined in height, sloped farther back. The path grew broader; the water no longer fell roaring, but ran sedately between pebbled beaches. The scene grew wider, the mouth of the glen was reached. He came out into a sunset world of dale and moor and mountain-heads afar. There were fields of grain, and blue waving feathers from chimneys of cottage and farm-house. In the distance showed a village, one street climbing a hill, and atop a church with a spire piercing the clear east. The stream widened, flowing thin over a pebbly bed. The sun was not yet down. It painted a glory in the west and set lanes and streets of gold over the hills and made the little river like Pactolus. Strickland approached a farm-house, prosperous and venerable, mended and neat. Thatched, long, white, and low, behind it barns and outbuildings, it stood tree-guarded, amid fields of young corn. Beyond it swelled a long moorside; in front slipped the still stream.

There were stepping-stones across the stream. Two young girls, coming toward the house, had set foot upon these. Strickland, halting in the shadow of hazels and young aspens, watched them as they crossed. Their step was free and light; they came with a kind of hardy grace, elastic, poised, and very young, homeward from some visit on this holiday. The tutor knew them to be Elspeth and Gilian Barrow, granddaughters of Jarvis Barrow of White Farm. The elder might have been fifteen, the younger thirteen years. They wore their holiday dresses. Elspeth had a green silken snood, and Gilian a blue. Elspeth sang as she stepped from stone to stone:

> "But I will get a bonny boat,
> And I will sail the sea,
> For I maun gang to Love Gregor,
> Since he canna come hame to me—"

They did not see Strickland where he stood by the hazels. He let them go by, watching them with a quiet pleasure. They took the upward-running lane. Hawthorns in bloom hid them; they were gone like young deer. Strickland, crossing the stream, went his own way.

The country became more open, with, at this hour, a dreamlike depth and hush. Down went the sun, but a glow held and wrapped the earth in hues of faery. When he had walked a mile and more he saw before him Glenfernie House. In the modern and used moiety seventy years old, in the ancient keep and ruin of a tower three hundred, it crowned—the ancient and the latter-day—a craggy hill set with dark woods, and behind it came up like a wonder lantern, like a bubble of pearl, the full moon.

CHAPTER II

The tutor, in his own room, put down his fisherman's rod and bag. The chamber was a small one, set high up, with two deep windows tying the interior to the yet rosy west and the clearer, paler south. Strickland stood a moment, then went out at door and down three steps and along a passageway to two doors, one closed, the other open. He tapped upon the latter.

"James!"

A boy of fourteen, tall and fair, with a flushed, merry face, crossed the room and opened the door more widely. "Oh, aye, Mr. Strickland, I'm in!"

"Is Alexander?"

"Not yet. I haven't seen him. I was at the village with Dandie Saunderson."

"Do you know what he did with himself?"

"Not precisely."

"I see. Well, it's nearly supper-time."

Back in his own quarters, the tutor made such changes as were needed, and finally stood forth in a comely suit of brown, with silver-buckled shoes, stock and cravat of fine cambric, and a tie-wig. Midway in his toilet he stopped to light two candles. These showed, in the smallest of mirrors, set of wig and cravat, and between the two a thoughtful, cheerful, rather handsome countenance.

He had left the door ajar so that he might hear, if he presently returned, his eldest pupil. But he heard only James go clattering down the passage and the stair. Strickland, blowing out his candles, left his room to the prolonged June twilight and the climbing moon.

The stairway down, from landing to landing, lay in shadow, but as he approached the hall he caught the firelight. The laird had a London guest who might find a chill in June nights so near the north. The blazing wood showed forth the chief Glenfernie gathering-place, wide and deep, with a great chimneypiece and walls of black oak, and hung thereon some old pieces of armor and old weapons. There was a table spread for supper, and a servant went about with a long candle-lighter, lighting candles. A collie and a hound lay upon the hearth. Between them stood Mrs. Jardine, a tall, fair woman of forty and more, with gray eyes, strong nose, and humorous mouth.

"Light them all, Davie! It'll be dark then by London houses."

Davie showed an old servant's familiarity. "He wasna sae grand when he left auld Scotland thirty years since! I'm thinking he might remember when he had nae candles ava in his auld hoose."

"Well, he'll have candles enough in his new hall."

Davie lit the last candle. "They say that he is sinfu' rich!"

"Rich enough to buy Black Hill," said Mrs. Jardine, and turned to the fire. The tutor joined her there. He had for her liking and admiration, and she for him almost a motherly affection. Now she smiled as he came up.

"Did you have good fishing?"

"Only fair."

"Mr. Jardine and Mr. Touris have just returned. They rode to Black Hill. Have you seen Alexander?"

"No. I asked Jamie—"

"So did I. But he could not tell."

"He may have gone over the moor and been belated. Bran is with him."

"Yes.... He's a solitary one, with a thousand in himself!"

"You're the second woman," remarked Strickland, "who's said that to-day," and told her of Mother Binning.

Mrs. Jardine pushed back a fallen ember with the toe of her shoe. "I don't know whether she sees or only thinks she sees. Some do the tane and some do the tither. Here's the laird."

Two men entered together—a large man and a small man. The first, great of height and girth, was plainly dressed; the last, seeming slighter by contrast than he actually was, wore fine cloth, silken hose, gold buckles to his shoes, and a full wig. The first had a massive, somewhat saturnine countenance, the last a shrewd, narrow one. The first had a long stride and a wide reach from thumb to little finger, the last a short step and a cupped hand. William Jardine, laird of Glenfernie, led the way to the fire.

"The ford was swollen. Mr. Touris got a little wet and chilled."

"Ah, the fire is good!" said Mr. Touris. "They do not burn wood like this in London!"

"You will burn it at Black Hill. I hope that you like it better and better?"

"It has possibilities, ma'am. Undoubtedly," said Mr. Touris, the Scots adventurer for fortune, set up as merchant-trader in London, making his fortune by "interloping" voyages to India, but now shareholder and part and lot of the East India Company—"undoubtedly the place has possibilities." He warmed his hands. "Well, it would taste good to come back to Scotland—!" His words might have been finished out, "and laird it, rich and influential, where once I went forth, cadet of a good family, but poorer than a church mouse!"

Mrs. Jardine made a murmur of hope that he *would* come back to Scotland. But the laird looked with a kind of large gloom at the reflection of fire and candle in battered breastplate and morion and crossed pikes.

Supper was brought in by two maids, Eppie and Phemie, and with them came old Lauchlinson, the butler. Mrs. Jardine placed herself behind the silver urn, and Mr.

Touris was given the seat nearest the fire. The boy James appeared, and with him the daughter of the house, Alice, a girl of twelve, bonny and merry.

"Where is Alexander?" asked the laird.

Strickland answered. "He is not in yet, sir. I fancy that he walked to the far moor. Bran is with him."

"He's a wanderer!" said the laird. "But he ought to keep hours."

"That's a fine youth!" quoth Mr. Touris, drinking tea. "I marked him yesterday, casting the bar. Very strong—a powerful frame like yours, Glenfernie! When is he going to college?"

"This coming year. I have kept him by me late," said the laird, broodingly. "I like my bairns at home."

"Aye, but the young will not stay as they used to! They will be voyaging," said the guest. "They build outlandish craft and forthfare, no matter what you cry to them!" His voice had a mordant note. "I know. I've got one myself—a nephew, not a son. But I am his guardian and he's in my house, and it is the same. If I buy Black Hill, Glenfernie, I hope that your son and my nephew may be friends. They're about of an age."

The listening Jamie spoke from beyond Strickland. "What's your nephew's name, sir?"

"Ian. Ian Rullock. His father's mother was a Highland lady, near kinswoman to Gordon of Huntley." Mr. Touris was again speaking to his host. "As a laddie, before his father's death (his mother, my sister, died at his birth), he was much with those troublous northern kin. His father took him, too, in England, here and there among the Tory crowd. But I've had him since he was twelve and am carrying him on in the straight Whig path."

"And in the true Presbyterian religion?"

"Why, as to that," said Mr. Touris, "his father was of the Church Episcopal in Scotland. I trust that we are all Christians, Glenfernie!"

The laird made a dissenting sound. "I kenned," he said, and his voice held a grating gibe, "that you had left the Kirk."

Mr. Archibald Touris sipped his tea. "I did not leave it so far, Glenfernie, that I cannot return! In England, for business reasons, I found it wiser to live as lived the most that I served. Naaman was permitted to bow himself in the house of Rimmon."

"You are not Naaman," answered the laird. "Moreover, I hold that Naaman sinned!"

Mrs. Jardine would make a diversion. "Mr. Jardine, will you have sugar to your tea? Mr. Strickland says the great pine is blown down, this side the glen. The *Mercury* brings us news of the great world, Mr. Touris, but I dare say you can give us more?"

"The chief news, ma'am, is that we want war with Spain and Walpole won't give it to us. But we'll have it—British trade must have it or lower her colors to the Dons! France, too—"

Supper went on, with abundant and good food and drink.

The laird sat silent. Strickland gave Mrs. Jardine yeoman aid. Jamie and Alice now listened to the elders, now in an undertone discoursed their own affairs. Mr. Touris talked, large trader talk, sprinkled with terms of commerce and Indian policy. Supper over, all rose. The table was cleared, wine and glasses brought and set upon it, between the candles. The young folk vanished. Bright as was the night, the air carried an edge. Mr. Touris, standing by the fire, warmed himself and took snuff. Strickland, who had left the hall, returned and placed her embroidery frame for Mrs. Jardine.

"Is Alexander in yet?"

"Not yet."

She began to work in cross-stitch upon a wreath of tulips and roses. The tutor took his book and withdrew to the table and the candles thereon. The laird came and dropped his great form upon the settle. He held silence a few moments, then began to speak.

"I am fifty years old. I was a bairn just talking and toddling about the year the Stewart fled and King William came to England. My father had Campbell blood in him and was a friend of Argyle's. The estate of Glenfernie was not to him then, but his uncle held it and had an heir of his body. My father was poor save in stanchness to the liberties of Kirk and kingdom. My mother was a minister's daughter, and she and her father and mother were among the persecuted for the sake of the true Reformed and Covenanted Church of Scotland. My mother had a burn in her cheek. It was put there, when she was a young lass, by order of Grierson of Lagg. She was set among those to be sold into the plantations in America. A kinsman who had power lifted her from that bog, but much she suffered before she was freed.... When I was little and sat upon her knee I would put my forefinger in that mark. 'It's a seal, laddie,' she would say. 'Sealed to Christ and His true Kirk!' But when I was bigger I only wanted to meet Grierson of Lagg, and grieved that he was dead and gone and that Satan, not I, had the handling of him. My grandfather and mother.... My grandfather was among the outed ministers in Galloway. Thrust from his church and his parish, he preached upon the moors—yea, to juniper and whin-bush and the whaups that flew and nested! Then the persecuted men, women and bairns, gathered there, and he preached to them. Aye, and he was at Bothwell Bridge. Claverhouse's men took him, and he lay for some months in the Edinburgh tolbooth, and then by Council and justiciary was condemned to be hanged. And so he was hanged at the cross of Edinburgh. And what he said before he died was '*With what measure ye mete, it shall be measured to you*' ... My grandmother, for hearing preaching in the fields and for sheltering the distressed for the Covenant's sake, was sent with other godly women to the Bass Rock. There in cold and heat, in hunger and sickness, she bided for two years. When at last they let her body forth her mind was found to be broken.... My father and mother married and lived, until Glenfernie came to him, at Windygarth. I was born at Windygarth. My grandmother lived with us. I was twelve years old before she went from earth. It was all her pleasure to be forth from the house—any house, for she called them all prisons. So I was sent to ramble with her. Out of doors, with the harmless things of earth, she was wise enough— and good company. The old of this countryside remember us, going here and there.... I used to think, 'If I had been living then, I would not have let those things happen!' And I dreamed of taking coin, and of dropping the same coin into the hands that gave.... And so, the other having served your turn, Touris, you will change back to the true Kirk?"

Mr. Touris handled his snuff-box, considered the chasing upon the gold lid. "Those were sore happenings, Glenfernie, but they're past! I make no wonder that, being you, you feel as you do. But the world's in a mood, if I may say it, not to take so hardly religious differences. I trust that I am as religious as another—but my family was always moderate there. In matters political the world's as hot as ever—but there, too, it is my instinct to ca' canny. But if you talk of trade"—he tapped his snuff-box—"I will match you, Glenfernie! If there's wrong, pay it back! Hold to your principles! But do it cannily. Smile when there's smart, and get your own again by being supple. In the end you'll demand—and get—a higher interest. Prosper at your enemy's cost, and take repayment for your hurt sugared and spiced!"

"I'll not do it so!" said Glenfernie. "But I would take my stand at the crag's edge and cry to Grierson of Lagg, 'You or I go down!'"

Mr. Touris brushed the snuff from his ruffles. "It's a great century! We're growing enlightened."

With a movement of her fingers Mrs. Jardine helped to roll from her lap a ball of rosy wool. "Mr. Jardine, will you give me that? Had you heard that Abercrombie's cows were lifted?"

"Aye, I heard. What is it, Holdfast?"

Both dogs had raised their heads.

"Bran is outside," said Strickland.

Mary Johnston

As he spoke the door opened and there came in a youth of seventeen, tall and well-built, with clothing that testified to an encounter alike with brier and bog. The hound Bran followed him. He blinked at the lights and the fire, then with a gesture of deprecation crossed the hall to the stairway. His mother spoke after him.

"Davie will set you something to eat."

He answered, "I do not want anything," then, five steps up, paused and turned his head. "I stopped at White Farm, and they gave me supper." He was gone, running up the stairs, and Bran with him.

The laird of Glenfernie shaded his eyes and looked at the fire. Mrs. Jardine, working upon the gold streak in a tulip, held her needle suspended and sat for a moment with unseeing gaze, then resumed the bright wreath. The tutor began to think again of Mother Binning, and, following this, of the stepping-stones at White Farm, and Elspeth and Gilian Barrow balanced above the stream of gold. Mr. Touris put up his snuff-box.

"That's a fine youth! I should say that he took after you, Glenfernie. But it's hard to tell whom the young take after!"

CHAPTER III

The school-room at Glenfernie gave upon the hill's steepest, most craglike face. A door opened on a hand's-breadth of level turf across from which rose the broken and ruined wall that once had surrounded the keep. Ivy overgrew this; below a wide and ragged breach a pine had set its roots in the hillside. Its top rose bushy above the stones. Beyond the opening, one saw from the school-room, as through a window, field and stream and moor, hill and dale. The school-room had been some old storehouse or office. It was stone walled and floored, with three small windows and a fireplace. Now it contained a long table with a bench and three or four chairs, a desk and shelves for books. One door opened upon the little green and the wall; a second gave access to a courtyard and the rear of the new house.

Here on a sunny, still August forenoon Strickland and the three Jardines went through the educational routine. The ages of the pupils were not sufficiently near together to allow of a massed instruction. The three made three classes. Jamie and Alice worked in the school-room, under Strickland's eye. But Alexander had or took a wider freedom. It was his wont to prepare his task much where he pleased, coming to the room for recitation or for colloquy upon this or that aspect of knowledge and the attainment thereof. The irregularity mattered the less as the eldest Jardine combined with a passion for personal liberty and out of doors a passion for knowledge. Moreover, he liked and trusted Strickland. He would go far, but not far enough to strain the tutor's patience. His father and mother and all about Glenfernie knew his way and in a measure acquiesced. He had managed to obtain for himself range. Young as he was, his indrawing, outpushing force was considerable, and was on the way, Strickland thought, to increase in power. The tutor had for this pupil a mixed feeling. The one constant in it was interest. He was to him like a deep lake, clear enough to see that there was something at the bottom that cast conflicting lights and hints of shape. It might be a lump of gold, or a coil of roots which would send up a water-lily, or it might be something different. He had a feeling that the depths themselves hardly knew. Or there might be two things of two natures down there in the lake....

Strickland set Alice to translating a French fable, and Jamie to reconsidering a neglected page of ancient history. Looking through the west window, he saw that Alexander had taken his geometry out through the great rent in the wall. Book and student perched beneath the pine-tree, in a crook made by rock and brown root, overhanging the autumn world. Strickland at his own desk dipped quill into ink-well and continued a letter to a friend in England. The minutes went by. From the courtyard came a subdued, cheerful household clack and murmur, voices of men and maids, with once Mrs. Jardine's genial, vigorous tones, and once the laird's deep bell note, calling to his dogs. On the western side fell only the sough of the breeze in the pine.

Jamie ceased the clocklike motion of his body to and fro over the difficult lesson. "I never understood just what were the Erinnys, sir?"

"The Erinnys?" Strickland laid down the pen and turned in his chair. "I'll have to think a moment, to get it straight for you, Jamie.... The Erinnys are the Fates as avengers. They are the vengeance-demanding part of ourselves objectified, supernaturalized, and named. Of old, where injury was done, the Erinnys were at hand to pull the roof down upon the head of the injurer. Their office was to provide unerringly sword for sword, bitter cup for bitter cup. They never forgot, they always avenged, though sometimes they took years to do it. They esteemed themselves, and were esteemed, essential to the moral order. They are the dark and bitter extreme of justice, given power by the imagination.... Do you think that you know the chapter now?"

Jamie achieved his recitation, and then was set to mathematics. The tutor's quill drove on across the page. He looked up.

"Mr. Touris has come to Black Hill?"

Jamie and Alice worshiped interruptions.

"He has twenty carriers bringing fine things all the time—"

"Mother is going to take me when she goes to see Mrs. Alison, his sister—"

"He is going to spend money and make friends—"

"Mother says Mrs. Alison was most bonny when she was young, but England may have spoiled her—"

"The minister told the laird that Mr. Touris put fifty

pounds in the plate—"

Strickland held up his hand, and the scholars, sighing, returned to work. *Buzz, buzz!* went the bees outside the window. The sun climbed high. Alexander shut his geometry and came through the break in the wall and across the span of green to the school-room.

"That's done, Mr. Strickland."

Strickland looked at the paper that his eldest pupil put before him. "Yes, that is correct. Do you want, this morning, to take up the reading?"

"I had as well, I suppose."

"If you go to Edinburgh—if you do as your father wishes and apply yourself to the law—you will need to read well and to speak well. You do not do badly, but not well enough. So, let's begin!" He put out his hand and drew from the bookshelf a volume bearing the title, *The Treasury of Orators*. "Try what you please."

Alexander took the book and moved to the unoccupied window. Here he half sat, half stood, the morning light flowing in upon him. He opened the volume and read, with a questioning inflection, the title beneath his eyes, "'The Cranes of Ibycus'?"

"Yes," assented Strickland. "That is a short, graphic thing."

Alexander read:

"Ibycus, who sang of love, material and divine, in Rhegium and in Samos, would wander forth in the world and make his lyre sound now by the sea and now in the mountain. Wheresoever he went he was clad in the favor of all who loved song. He became a wandering minstrel-poet. The shepherd loved him, and the fisher; the trader and the mechanic sighed when he sang; the soldier and the king felt him at their hearts. The old returned in their thoughts to youth, young men and maidens trembled in heavenly sound and light. You would think that all the world loved Ibycus.

"Corinth, the jeweled city, planned her chariot-races and her festival of song. The strong, the star-eyed young men, traveled to Corinth from mainland and from island, and those inner athletes and starry ones, the poets, traveled. Great feasting was to be in Corinth, and contests of strength and flights of song, and in the theater, representation of gods and men. Ibycus, the wandering poet, would go to Corinth, there perhaps to receive a crown.

"Ibycus, loved of all who love song, traveled alone, but not alone. Yet shepherds, or women with their pitchers at the spring, saw but a poet with a staff and a lyre. Now he was found upon the highroad, and now the country paths drew him, and the solemn woods where men most easily find God. And so he approached Corinth.

"The day was calm and bright, with a lofty, blue, and stainless sky. The heart of Ibycus grew warm, and there seemed a brighter light within the light cast by the sun. Flower and plant and tree and all living things seemed to him to be glistening and singing, and to have for him, as he for them, a loving friendship. And, looking up to the sky, he saw, drawn out stringwise, a flight of cranes, addressed to Egypt. And between his heart and them ran, like a rippling path that the sun sends across the sea, a stream of good-will and understanding. They seemed a part of himself, winged in the blue heaven, and aware of the part of him that trod earth, that was entering the grave and shadowy wood that neighbored Corinth.

"The cranes vanished from overhead, the sky arched without stain. Ibycus, the sacred poet, with his staff and his lyre, went on into the wood. Now the light faded and there was green gloom, like the depths of Father Sea.

"Now robbers lay masked in the wood—"

Jamie and Alice sat very still, listening. Strickland kept his eyes on the reading youth.

"Now robbers lay masked in the wood—violent men and treacherous, watching for the unwary, to take from them goods and, if they resisted, life. In a dark place they lay in wait, and from thence they sprang upon Ibycus. 'What hast thou? Part it from thyself and leave it with us!'

"Ibycus, who could sing of the wars of the Greeks and the Trojans no less well than of the joys of young love, made stand, held close to him his lyre, but raised on high his staff of oak. Then from behind one struck him with a keen knife, and he sank, and lay in his blood. The place was the edge of a glade, where the trees thinned away and the sky might be seen overhead. And now, across the blue heaven, came a second line of the south-ward-going cranes. They flew low, they flapped their wings, and the wood heard their crying. Then Ibycus the poet raised his arms to his brothers the birds. 'Ye cranes, flying between earth and heaven, avenge shed blood, as is right!'

"Hoarse screamed the cranes flying overhead. Ibycus the poet closed his eyes, pressed his lips to Mother Earth, and died. The cranes screamed again, circling the wood, then in a long line sailed southward through the blue air until they might neither be heard nor seen. The robbers stared after them. They laughed, but without mirth. Then, stooping to the body of Ibycus, they would have rifled it when, hearing a sudden sound of men's voices entering the wood, they took violent fright and fled."

Strickland looked still at the reader. Alexander had straightened himself. He was speaking rather than reading. His voice had intensities and shadows. His brows had drawn together, his eyes glowed, and he stood with nostrils somewhat distended. The emotion that he plainly showed seemed to gather about the injury done and the appeal of Ibycus. The earlier Ibycus had not seemed greatly to interest him. Strickland was used to stormy youth, to its passional moments, sudden glows, burnings, sympathies, defiances, lurid shows of effects with the causes largely unapparent. It was his trade to know youth, and he had a psychologist's interest. He said now to himself, "There is something in his character that connects itself with, that responds to, the idea of vengeance." There came into his memory the laird's talk, the evening of Mr. Touris's visit, in June. Glenfernie, who would have wrestled with Grierson of Lagg at the edge of the pit; Glenfernie's mother and father, who might have had much the same feeling; their forebears beyond them with like sensations toward the Griersons of their day.... The long line of them—the long line of mankind—injured and injurers....

"Travelers through the wood, whose voices the robbers heard, found Ibycus the poet lying upon the ground, ravished of life. It chanced that he had been known of them, known and loved. Great mourning arose, and vain search for them who had done this wrong. But those strong, wicked ones were gone, fled from their haunts, fled from the wood afar to Corinth, for the god Pan had thrown against them a pine cone. So the travelers took the body of Ibycus and bore it with them to Corinth.

"A poet had been slain upon the threshold of the house of song. Sacred blood had spattered the white robes of a queen dressed for jubilee. Evil unreturned to its doers must darken the sunshine of the famous days. Corinth uttered a cry of lamentation and wrath. 'Where are the ill-doers, the spillers of blood, that we may spill their blood and avenge Ibycus, showing the gods that we are their helpers?' But those robbers and murderers might not be found. And the body of Ibycus was consumed upon a funeral pyre.

"The festival hours went by in Corinth. And now began to fill the amphitheater where might find room a host for number like the acorns of Dodona. The throng was huge, the sound that it made like the shock of ocean. Around, tier above tier, swept the rows, and for roof there was the blue and sunny air. Then the voice of the sea hushed, for now entered the many-numbered chorus. Slow-circling, it sang of mighty Fate: 'For every word shall have its echo, and every deed shall see its face. The word shall say, "Is it my echo?" and the deed shall say, "Is it my face?"'—

"The chorus passes, singing. The voices die, there falls a silence, sent as it were from inner space. The open sky is above the amphitheater. And now there comes, from north to south, sailing that sea above, high, but not so high that their shape is indistinguishable, a long flight of cranes. Heads move, eyes are raised, but none know why that interest is so keen, so still. Then from out the throng rises, struck with forgetfulness of gathered Corinth and of its own reasons for being dumb as is the stone, a man's voice, and the fear that Pan gives ran yet around in that voice. 'See, brother, see! The cranes of Ibycus!'

"'Ibycus!' The crowd about those men pressed in upon them. 'What do you know of Ibycus?' And great Pan drove them to show in their faces what they knew. So Corinth took—"

Alexander Jardine shut the book and, leaving the window, dropped it upon the table. His hand shook, his face was convulsed. "I've read as far as needs be. Those things strike me like hammers!" With suddenness he turned and was gone.

Strickland was aware that he might not return that day to the school-room, perhaps not to the house. He went out of the west door and across the grassy space to the gap in the wall, through which he disappeared. Beyond was the rough descent to wood and stream.

Jamie spoke: "He's a queer body! He says he thinks that he lived a long time ago, and then a shorter time ago, and then now. He says that some days he sees it all come up in a kind of dark desert."

Alice put in her word, "Mother says he's many in one, and that the many and one don't yet recognize each other."

"Your mother is a wise woman," said the tutor. "Let me see how the work goes."

The pine-tree, outside the wall, overhung a rude natural stairway of stony ledge and outcropping root with patches of moss and heath. Down this went Alexander into a cool dimness of fir and oak and birch, watered by a little stream. He kneeled by this, he cooled face and hands in the water, then flung himself beneath a tree and, burying his head in his arms, lay still. The waves within subsided, sank to a long, deep swell, then from that to quiet. The door that wind and tide had beaten open shut again. Alexander lay without thinking, without overmuch feeling. At last, turning, he opened his eyes upon the tree-tops and the August sky. The door was shut upon tales of injury and revenge. Between boy and man, he lay in a yearning stillness, colors and sounds and dim poetic strains his ministers of grace. This lasted for a time, then he rose, first to a sitting posture, then to his feet. Crows flew through the wood; he had a glimpse of yellow fields and purple heath. He set forth upon one of the long rambles which were a prized part of life.

An hour or so later he stopped at a cotter's, some miles from home. An old man and a woman gave him an oat cake and a drink of home-brewed. He was fond of folk like these—at home with them and they with him. There was no need to make talk, but he sat and looked at the marigolds while the woman moved about and the old man wove rushes into mats. From here he took to the hills and walked awhile with a shepherd numbering his sheep. Finally, in mid-afternoon, he found himself upon a heath, bare of trees, lifted and purple.

He sat down amid the warm bloom; he lay down. Within was youth's blind tumult and longing, a passioning for he knew not what. "I wish that there were great things in my life. I wish that I were a discoverer, sailing like Columbus. I wish that I had a friend—"

He fell into a day-dream, lapped there in warm purple waves, hearing the bees' interminable murmur. He faced, across a narrow vale, an abrupt, curiously shaped hill, dark with outstanding granite and with fir-trees. Where at the eastern end it broke away, where at its base the vale widened, shone among the lively green of elms turrets and chimneys of a large house. "Black Hill—Black Hill—Black Hill...."

A youth of about his own age came up the path from the vale. Alexander, lying amid the heath, caught at some distance the whole figure, but as he approached lost him. Then, near at hand, the head rose above the brow of the ridge. It was a handsome head, with a cap and feather, with gold-brown hair lightly clustering, and a countenance of spirit and daring with something subtle rubbed in. Head, shoulders, a supple figure, not so tall nor so largely made as was Glenfernie's heir, all came upon the purple hilltop.

CHAPTER IV

Alexander raised himself from his couch in the heather.

"Good day!" said the new-comer.

"Good day!"

The youth stood beside him. "I am Ian Rullock."

"I am Alexander Jardine."

"Of Glenfernie?"

"Aye, you've got it."

"Then we're the neighbors that are to be friends."

"If we are to be we are to be.... I want a friend.... I don't know if you're the one that is to answer."

The other dropped beside him upon the heath. "I saw you walking along the hilltop. So when you did not come on I thought I'd climb and meet you. This is a lonely, miserable country!"

Alexander was moved to defend. "There are more

miserable! It's got its points."

"I don't see them. I want London!"

"That's Babylon.—It's your own country. You're evening it with England!"

"No, I'm not. But you can't deny that it's poor."

"There's one of its sons, named Touris, that is not poor!"

Rullock rose upon one knee. "The wise man gets rich and the fool stays poor. Do you want to be friends or do you want to fight?"

Alexander clasped his hands behind his head and lay back upon the earth. "No, I do not want to fight—not now! I wouldn't fight you, anyhow, for standing up for one to whom you're beholden."

Silence fell between them, each having eyes upon the other. Something drew each to each, something repelled each from each. It was a question, between those forces, which would gain. Alexander did not feel strange with Ian, nor Ian with Alexander. It was as though they had met before. But how they had met and why, and where and when, and what that meeting had entailed and meant, was hidden from their gaze. The attractive increased over the repellent. Ian spoke.

"There's none down there but my uncle and his sister, my aunt. Come on down and let me show you the place."

"I do not care if I do." He rose, and the two went along the hilltop and down the path.

Ian was the readier in talk. "I am going soon to Edinburgh—to college."

"I'm going, too. The first of the year. I am going to try if I can stand the law."

"I want to be a soldier."

"I don't know what I want.... I want to journey—and journey—and journey ... with a book along."

"Do you like books?"

"Aye, fine!"

"I like them right well. Are there any pretty girls around here?"

"I don't know. I don't like girls."

"I like them at times, in their places. You must wrestle bravely, you're so strong in the shoulder and long in the arm!"

"You're not so big, but you look strong yourself."

Each measured the other with his eyes. Friendship was already here. It was as though hand had fitted into glove.

"What is your dog named?"

"Hector."

"Mine's Bran. You come to Glenfernie to-morrow and I'll show you a place that's all mine. It's the room in the old keep. I've books there and apples and nuts and curiosities.

There's a big fireplace, and my father's let me build a furnace besides, and I've kettles and crucibles and pans and vials—"

"What for?"

Alexander paused and gazed at Ian, then gave into his keeping the great secret. "Alchemy. I'm trying to change lead into gold."

Ian thrilled. "I'll come! I'll ride over. I've a beautiful mare."

"It's not eight miles—"

"I'll come. We're just in at Black Hill, you see, and I've had no time to make a place like that! But I'll show you my room. Here's the park gate."

They walked up an avenue overarched by elms, to a house old but not so old, once half-ruinous, but now mended and being mended, enlarged, and decorated, the aim a spacious place alike venerable and modern. Workmen yet swarmed about it. The whole presented a busy, cheerful aspect—a gracious one, also, for under a monster elm before the terrace was found the master and owner, Mr. Archibald Touris. He greeted the youths with a manner meant to exhibit the expansive heart of a country gentleman.

"You've found each other out, have you? Why, you look born to be friends! That's as it should be.—And what, Alexander, do you think of Black Hill?"

"It looks finely a rich man's place, sir."

Mr. Touris laughed at his country bluntness, but did not take the tribute amiss. "Not so rich—not so mighty rich. But enough, enough! If Ian here behaves himself he'll have enough!" A master workman called him away. He went with a large wave of the hand. "Make yourself at home, Alexander! Take him, Ian, to see your aunt Alison." He was gone with the workman.

"I'll take you there presently," said Ian. "I'm fond of Aunt Alison—you'll like her, too—but she'll keep. Let's go see my mare Fatima, and then my room."

Fatima was a most beautiful young, snowy Arabian. Alexander sighed with delight when they led her out from her stable and she walked about with Ian beside her, and when presently Ian mounted she curveted and caracoled. Ian and she suited each other. Indefinably, there was about him, too, something Eastern. The two went to and fro, the mare's hoofs striking music from the flags. Behind them ran a gray range of buildings overtopped by bushy willows. Alexander sat on a stone bench, hugged his knees, and felt true love for the sight. Ian had come to him like a gift from the blue.

Ian dismounted, and they watched Fatima disappear into her stall. "Come now and see the house."

The house was large and cumbered with furniture too much and too rich for the Scotch countryside. Ian's room had a great, rich bed and a dressing-table that drew from Alexander a whistle, contemplative and scornful. But there were other matters besides luxury of couch and toilet. Slung against the wall appeared a fine carbine, the pistols and sword of Ian's father, and a wonderful long, twisted, and damascened knife or dirk—creese, Ian called it—that had come in some trading-ship of his uncle's. And he had books in a small closet room, and a picture that the two stood before.

"Where did you get it?"

"There was an Italian who owed my uncle a debt. He had no money, so he gave him this. He said that it was painted a long time ago and that it was very fine."

"What is it?"

"It is a Bible piece. This is a city of refuge. This is a sinner fleeing to it, and here behind him is the avenger of blood. You can't see, it is so dark. There!" He drew the window-curtain quite aside. A flood of light came in and washed the picture.

"I see. What is it doing here?"

"I don't know. I liked it. I suppose Aunt Alison thought it might hang here."

"I like to see pictures in my mind. But things like that poison me! Let's see the rest of the house."

They went again through Ian's room. Coming to a fine carved ambry, he hesitated, then stood still. "I'm going to show you something else! I show it to you because I trust you. It's like your telling me about your making gold out of lead." He opened a door of the ambry, pulled out a drawer, and, pressing some spring, revealed a narrow, secret shelf. His hand went into the dimness and came out bearing a silver goblet. This he set carefully upon a neighboring table, and looked at Alexander somewhat aslant out of long, golden-brown eyes.

"It's a bonny goblet," said Alexander. "Why do you keep it like that?"

Ian looked around him. "Years and years ago my father, who is dead now, was in France. There was a banquet at Saint-Germain. *A very great person* gave it and was in presence himself. All the gentlemen his guests drank a toast for which the finest wine was poured in especial goblets. Afterward each was given for a token the cup from which he drank.... Before he died my father gave me this. But of course I have to keep it secret. My uncle and all the world around here are Whigs!"

"James Stewart!" quoth Alexander. "Humph!"

"Remember that you have not seen it," said Ian, "and that I never said aught to you but *King George, King George!*" With that he restored the goblet to the secret shelf, put back the drawer, and shut the ambry door. "Friends trust one another in little and big.—Now let's go see Aunt Alison."

They went in silence along a corridor where every footfall was subdued in India matting. Alexander spoke once:

"I fccl all through me that we're friends. But you're a terrible fool there!"

"I am not," said Ian. His voice carried the truth of his own feeling. "I am like my father and mother and the chieftains my kin, and I have been with certain kings ever since there were kings. Others think otherwise, but I've got my rights!"

With that they came to the open door of a room. A voice spoke from within:

"Ian!"

Ian crossed the threshold. "May we come in, Aunt Alison? It's Alexander Jardine of Glenfernie."

A tall, three-leaved screen pictured with pagodas, palms, and macaws stood between the door and the rest of the room. "Come, of course!" said the voice behind this.

Passing the last pagoda edge, the two entered a white-paneled parlor where a lady in dove-gray muslin overlooked the unpacking of fine china. She turned in the great chair where she sat. "I am truly glad to see Alexander Jardine!" When he went up to her she took his two hands in hers. "I remember your mother and how fine a lassie she was! Good mind and good heart—"

"We've heard of you, too," answered Alexander. He looked at her in frank admiration, *Eh, but you're bonny!* written in his gaze.

Mrs. Alison, as they called her, was something more than bonny. She had loveliness. More than that, she breathed a cleanliness of spirit, a lucid peace, a fibered self-mastery passing into light. Alexander did not analyze his feeling for her, but it was presently one of great liking. Now she sat in her great chair while the maids went on with the unpacking, and questioned him about Glenfernie and all the family and life there. She was slight, not tall, with hair prematurely white, needing no powder. She sat and talked with her hand upon Ian. While she talked she glanced from the one youth to the other. At last she said:

"Alexander Jardine, I love Ian dearly. He needs and will need love—great love. If you are going to be friends, remember that love is bottomless.—And now go, the two of you, for the day is getting on."

They passed again the macaw-and-pagoda screen and left the paneled room. The August light struck slant and gold. The two quitted the house and crossed the terrace into the avenue without again encountering the master of the place.

"I will go with you to the top of the hill," said Ian. They climbed the ridge that was like a purple cloud. "I'll come to Glenfernie to-morrow or the next day."

"Yes, come! I'm fond of Jamie, but he's three years younger than I."

"You've got a sister?"

"Alice? She's only twelve. You come. I've been wanting somebody."

"So have I. I'm lonelier than you."

They came to the level top of the heath. The sun rode low; the shadow of the hill stretched at their feet, out over path and harvest-field.

"Good-by, then!"

"Good-by!"

Ian stood still. Alexander, homeward bound, dropped over the crest. The earth wave hid from him Black Hill, house and all. But, looking back, he could still see Ian against the sky. Then Ian sank, too. Alexander strode on toward Glenfernie. He went whistling, in expanded, golden spirits. Ian—and Ian—and Ian! Going through a grove of oaks, blackbirds flew overhead, among and above the branches. *The cranes of Ibycus!* The phrase flashed into mind. "I wonder why things like that disturb me so!... I wonder if there's any bottom or top to living anyhow!... I wonder—!" He looked at the birds and at the violet evening light at play in the old wood. The phrase went out of his mind. He left the remnant of the forest and was presently upon open moor. He whistled again, loud and clear, and strode on happily. Ian—and Ian—and Ian!

Mary Johnston

CHAPTER V

The House of Glenfernie and the House of Touris became friends. A round of country festivities, capped by a great party at Black Hill, wrought bonds of acquaintanceship for and with the Scots family returned after long abode in England. Archibald Touris spent money with a cautious freedom. He set a table and poured a wine better by half than might be found elsewhere. He kept good horses and good dogs. Laborers who worked for him praised him; he proved a not ungenerous landlord. Where he recognized obligations he met them punctually. He had large merchant virtues, no less than the accompanying limitations. He returned to the Church of Scotland.

The laird of Glenfernie and the laird of Black Hill found constitutional impediments to their being more friendly than need be. Each was polite to the other to a certain point, then the one glowered and the other scoffed. It ended in a painstaking keeping of distance between them, a task which, when they were in company, fell often to Mrs. Jardine. She did it with tact, with a twist of her large, humorous mouth toward Strickland if he were by. Admirable as she was, it was curious to see the difference between her method, if method there were, and that of Mrs. Alison. The latter showed no effort, but where she was there fell harmony. William Jardine liked her, liked to be in the room with her. His great frame and her slight one, his rough, massive, somewhat unshaped personality and her exquisite clearness contrasted finely enough. Her brother, who understood her very little, yet had for her an odd, appealing affection, strange in one who had so positively settled what was life and the needs of life. It was his habit to speak of her as though she were more helplessly dependent even than other women. But at times there might be seen who was more truly the dependent.

August passed into September, September into brown October. Alexander and Ian were almost continually in company. The attraction between them was so great that it appeared as though it must stretch backward into some unknown seam of time. If they had differences, these apparently only served in themselves to keep them revolving the one about the other. They might almost quarrel, but never enough to drag their two orbs apart, breaking and rending from the common center. The sun might go down upon a kind of wrath, but it rose on hearts with the difference forgotten. Their very unlikenesses pricked each on to seek himself in the other.

They were going to Edinburgh after Christmas, to be students there, to grow to be men. Here at home, upon the eve of their going, rein upon them was slackened. They would so soon be independent of home discipline that that independence was to a degree already allowed. Black Hill did not often question Ian's comings and goings, nor Glenfernie Alexander's. The school-room saw the latter some part of each morning. For the rest of the day he might be almost anywhere with Ian, at Glenfernie, or at Black Hill, or on the road between, or in the country roundabout.

William Jardine, chancing to be one day at Black Hill,

watched from Mrs. Alison's parlor the two going down the avenue, the dogs at their heels. "It's a fair David and Jonathan business!"

"David needed Jonathan, and Jonathan David."

"Had Jonathan lived, ma'am, and the two come to conflict about the kingdom, what then, and where would have flown the friendship?"

"It would have flown on high, I suppose, and waited for them until they had grown wings to mount to it."

"Oh," said the laird, "you're one I can follow only a little way!"

Ian and Alexander felt only that the earth about them was bright and warm.

On a brown-and-gold day the two found themselves in the village of Glenfernie. Ian had spent the night with Alexander—for some reason there was school holiday—the two were now abroad early in the day. The village sent its one street, its few poor lanes, up a bare hillside to the church atop. Poor and rude enough, it had yet to-day its cheerful air. High voices called, flaxen-haired children pottered about, a mill-wheel creaked at the foot of the hill, iron clanged in the smithy a little higher, the drovers' rough laughter burst from the tavern midway, and at the height the kirk was seeing a wedding. The air had a tang of cooled wine, the sky was blue.

Ian and Alexander, coming over the hill, reached the kirk in time to see emerge the married pair with their kin and friends. The two stood with a rabble of children and boys beneath the yew-trees by the gate. The yellow-haired bride in her finery, the yellow-haired groom in his, the dressed and festive following, stepped from the kirkyard to some waiting carts and horses. The most mounted and took place, the procession put itself into motion with clatter and laughter. The children and boys ran after to where the road dipped over the hill. A cluster of village folk turned the long, descending street. In passing they spoke to Alexander and Ian.

"Who was married?—Jock Wilson and Janet Macraw, o' Langmuir."

The two lounged against the kirkyard wall, beneath the yews.

"*Marry!* That's a strange, terrible, useless word to me!"

"I don't know...."

"Yes, it is!... Ian, do you ever think that you've lived before?"

"I don't know. I'm living now!"

"Well, I think that we all lived before. I think that the same things happen again—"

"Well, let them—some of them!" said Ian. "Come along, if we're going through the glen."

They left the kirkyard for the village street. Here they sauntered, friends with the whole. They looked in at the tavern upon the drovers, they watched the blacksmith and his helper. The red iron rang, the sparks flew. At the foot of the hill flowed the stream and stood the mill. The wheel turned, the water diamonds dropped in sheets.

Mary Johnston

Their busy, idle day took them on; they were now in bare, heathy country with the breathing, winey air. Presently White Farm could be seen among aspens, and beyond it the wooded mouth of the glen. Some one, whistling, turned an elbow of the hill and caught up with the two. It proved to be one several years their senior, a young man in the holiday dress of a prosperous farmer. He whistled clearly an old border air and walked without dragging or clumsiness. Coming up, he ceased his whistling.

"Good day, the both of ye!"

"It's Robin Greenlaw," said Alexander, "from Little-farm.—You've been to the wedding, Robin?"

"Aye. Janet's some kind of a cousin. It's a braw day for a wedding! You've got with you the new laird's nephew?— And how are you liking Black Hill?"

"I like it."

"I suppose you miss grandeurs abune what ye've got there. I have a liking myself," said Greenlaw, "for grandeurs, though we've none at all at Littlefarm! That is to say, none that's just obvious. Are you going to White Farm?"

Alexander answered: "I've a message from my father for Mr. Barrow. But after that we're going through the glen. Will you come along?"

"I would," said Greenlaw, seriously, "if I had not on my best. But I know how you, Alexander Jardine, take the devil's counsel about setting foot in places bad for good clothes! So I'll give myself the pleasure some other time. And so good day!" He turned into a path that took him presently out of sight and sound.

"He's a fine one!" said Alexander. "I like him."

"Who is he?"

"White Farm's great-nephew. Littlefarm was parted from White Farm. It's over yonder where you see the water shining."

"He's free-mannered enough!"

"That's you and England! He's got as good a pedigree as any, and a notion of what's a man, besides. He's been to Glasgow to school, too. I like folk like that."

"I like them as well as you!" said Ian. "That is, with reservations of them I cannot like. I'm Scots, too."

Alexander laughed. They came down to the water and the stepping-stones before White Farm. The house faced them, long and low, white among trees from which the leaves were falling. Alexander and Ian crossed upon the stones, and beyond the fringing hazels the dogs came to meet them.

Jarvis Barrow had all the appearance of a figure from that Old Testament in which he was learned. He might have been a prophet's right-hand man, he might have been the prophet himself. He stood, at sixty-five, lean and strong, gray-haired, but with decrepitude far away. Elder of the kirk, sternly religious, able at his own affairs, he read his Bible and prospered in his earthly living. Now he listened to the laird's message, nodding his head, but saying little. His staff was in his hand; he was on his way to kirk session; tell the laird that the account was correct. He stood without his door as though he waited for the youths to give good day and depart. Alexander had made a movement in this direction when from beyond Jarvis Barrow came a woman's voice. It belonged to Jenny Barrow, the farmer's unmarried daughter, who kept house for him.

"Father, do you gae on, and let the young gentlemen bide a wee and rest their banes and tell a puir woman wha never gaes onywhere the news!"

"Then do ye sit awhile, laddies, with the womenfolk," said Jarvis Barrow. "But give me pardon if I go, for I canna keep the kirk waiting."

He was gone, staff and gray plaid and a collie with him. Jenny, his daughter, appeared in the door.

"Come in, Mr. Alexander, and you, too, sir, and have a crack with us! We're in the dairy-room, Elspeth and Gilian and me."

She was a woman of forty, raw-boned but not unhandsome, good-natured, capable, too, but with more heart than head. It was a saying with her that she had brains enough foi kirk on the Sabbath and a warm house the week round. Everybody knew Jenny Barrow and liked well enough bread of her baking.

The room to which she led Ian and Alexander had its floor level with the turf without the open door. The sun flooded it. There came from within the sound, up and down, of a churn, and a voice singing:

"O laddie, will ye gie to me
A ribbon for my fairing?"

CHAPTER VI

It grew that Ian was telling stories of cities—of London and of Paris, for he had been there, and of Rome, for he had been there. He had seen kings and queens, he had seen the Pope—

"Lord save us!" ejaculated Jenny Barrow.

He leaned against the dairy wall and the sun fell over him, and he looked something finer and more golden than often came that way. Young Gilian at the churn stood with parted lips, the long dasher still in her hands. This was as good as stories of elves, pixies, fays, men of peace and all! Elspeth let the milk-pans be and sat beside them on the long bench, and, with hands folded in her lap, looked with brown eyes many a league away. Neither Elspeth nor Gilian was without book learning. Behind them and before them were long visits to scholar kindred in a city in the north and fit schooling there. London and Paris and Rome.... Foreign lands and the great world. And this was a glittering young eagle that had sailed and seen!

Alexander gazed with delight upon Ian spreading triumphant wings. This was his friend. There was nothing finer than continuously to come upon praiseworthiness in your friend!

"And a beautiful lady came by who was the king's favorite—"

"Gude guide us! The limmer!"

"And she was walking on rose-colored velvet and her slippers had diamonds worked in them. Snow was on the ground outside and poor folk were freezing, but she carried over each arm a garland of roses as though it were June—"

Jenny Barrow raised her hands. "She'll sit yet in the cauld blast, in the sinner's shift!"

"And after a time there walked in the king, and the courtiers behind him like the tail of a peacock—"

They had a happy hour in the White Farm dairy. At last Jenny and the girls set for the two cold meat and bannocks and ale. And still at table Ian was the shining one. The sun was at noon and so was his mood.

"You're fey!" said Alexander, at last.

"Na, na!" spoke Jenny. "But, oh, he's the bonny lad!"

The dinner was eaten. It was time to be going.

"Shut your book of stories!" said Alexander. "We're for the Kelpie's Pool, and that's not just a step from here!"

Elspeth raised her brown eyes. "Why will you go to the Kelpie's Pool? That's a drear water!"

"I want to show it to him. He's never seen it."

"It's drear!" said Elspeth. "A drear, wanrestfu' place!"

But Ian and Alexander must go. The aunt and nieces accompanied them to the door, stood and watched them forth, down the bank and into the path that ran to the glen. Looking back, the youths saw them there—Elspeth and Gilian and their aunt Jenny. Then the aspens came between and hid them and the white house and all.

"They're bonny lasses!" said Ian.

"Aye. They're so."

"But, oh, man! you should see Miss Delafield of Tower Place in Surrey!"

"Is she so bonny?"

"She's more than bonny. She's beautiful and high-born and an heiress. When I'm a colonel of dragoons—"

"Are you going to be a colonel of dragoons?"

"Something like that. You talk of thinking that you were this and that in the past. Well, I was a fighting-man!"

"We're all fighting-men. It's only what we fight and how."

"Well, say that I had been a chief, and they lifted me on their shields and called me king, the very next day I should have made her queen!"

"You think like a ballad. And, oh, man, you talk mickle of the lasses!"

Ian looked at him with long, narrow, dark-gold eyes.

"They're found in ballads," he said.

Alexander just paused in his stride. "Humph! that's true!..."

They entered the glen. The stream began to brawl; on either hand the hills closed in, towering high. Some of the trees were bare, but to most yet clung the red-brown or the gold-brown dress. The pines showed hard, green, and dead in the shadow; in the sunlight, fine, green-gold, and alive. The fallen leaves, moved by foot or by breeze, made a light, dry, talking sound. The white birch stems clustered and leaned; patches of bright-green moss ran between the drifts of leaves. The sides of the hills came close together, grew fearfully steep. Crags appeared, and fern-crowded fissures and roots of trees like knots of frozen serpents. The glen narrowed and deepened; the water sang with a loud, rough voice.

Alexander loved this place. He had known it in childhood, often straying this way with the laird, or with Sandy the shepherd, or Davie from the house. When he was older he began to come alone. Soon he came often alone, learned every stick and stone and contour, effect of light and streak of gloom. As idle or as purposeful as the wind, he knew the glen from top to bottom. He knew the voice of the stream and the straining clutch of the roots over the broken crag. He had lain on all the beds of leaf and moss, and talked with every creeping or flying or running thing. Sometimes he read a book here, sometimes he pictured the world, or built fantastic stages, and among fantastic others acted himself a fantastic part. Sometimes with a blind turning within he looked for himself. He had his own thoughts of God here, of God and the Kirk and the devil. Often, too, he neither read, dreamed, nor thought. He might lie an hour, still, passive, receptive. The trees and the clouds, crag life, bird life, and flower life, life of water, earth, and air, came inside. He was so used to his own silence in the glen that when he walked through it with others he kept it still. Slightly taciturn everywhere, he was actively so here. The path narrowing, he and Ian must go in single file. Leading, Alexander traveled in silence, and Ian, behind, not familiar with the place, must mind his steps, and so fell silent, too. Here and there, now and then, Alexander halted. These were recesses, or it might be projecting platforms of rock, that he liked. Below, the stream made still pools, or moved in eddies, or leaped with an innumerable hurrying noise from level to level. Or again there held a reach of quiet water, and the glen-sides were soft with weeping birch, and there showed a wider arch of still blue sky. Alexander stood and looked. Ian, behind him, was glad of the pause. The place dizzied him who for years had been away from hill and mountain, pass and torrent. Yet he would by no means tell Alexander so. He would keep up with him.

There was a mile of this glen, and now the going was worse and now it was better. Three-fourths of the way through they came to an opening in the rock, over which, from a shelf above, fell a curtain of brier.

"See!" said Alexander, and, parting the stems, showed a veritable cavern. "Come in—sit down! The Kelpie's Pool is out of the glen, but they say that there's a bogle wons here, too."

They sat down upon the rocky floor strewn with dead leaves. Through the dropped curtain they saw the world brokenly; the light in the cave was sunken and dim, the air cold. Ian drew his shoulders together.

"Here's a grand place for robbers, wraiths, or dragons!"

"Robbers, wraiths, or dragons, or just quiet dead leaves and ourselves. Look here—!" He showed a heap of short fagots in a corner. "I put these here the last time I came." Dragging them into the middle of the rock chamber, he swept up with them the dead leaves, then took from a great pouch that he carried on his rambles a box with flint and steel. He struck a spark upon dry moss and in a moment had a fire. "Is not that beautiful?"

The smoke mounted to the top of the cavern, curled there or passed out into the glen through the briers that dropped like a portcullis. The fagots crackled in the flame, the light danced, the warmth was pleasant. So was the sense of adventure and of *solitude a deux*. They stretched themselves beside the flame. Alexander produced from his pouch four small red-cheeked apples. They ate and talked, with between their words silences of deep content. They were two comrade hunters of long ago, cavemen who had dispossessed bear or wolf, who might presently with a sharpened bone and some red pigment draw bison and deer in procession upon the cave wall.—They were skin-clad hillmen, shag-haired, with strange, rude weapons, in hiding here after hard fighting with a disciplined, conquering foe who had swords and shining breastplates and crested helmets.—They were fellow-soldiers of that conquering tide, Romans of a band that kept the Wall, proud, with talk of camps and Caesars.—They were knights of Arthur's table sent by Merlin on some magic quest.—They were Crusaders, and this cavern an Eastern, desert cave.—They were men who rose with Wallace, must hide in caves from Edward Longshanks.—They were outlaws.—They were wizards—good wizards who caused flowers to bloom in winter for the unhappy, and made gold here for those who must be ransomed, and fed themselves with secret bread. The fire roared—they were happy, Ian and Alexander.

At last the fagots were burned out. The half-murk that at first was mystery and enchantment began to put on somberness and melancholy. They rose from the rocky floor and extinguished the brands with their feet. But now they had this cavern in common and must arrange it for their next coming. Going outside, they gathered dead and fallen wood, broke it into right lengths, and, carrying it within, heaped it in the corner. With a bough of pine they swept the floor, then, leaving the treasure hold, dropped the curtain of brier in place. They were not so old but that there was yet the young boy in them; he hugged himself over this cave of Robin Hood and swart magician. But now they left it and went on whistling through the glen:

Gie ye give ane, then I'll give twa,
For sae the store increases!

The sides of the glen fell back, grew lower. The leap of the water was not so marked; there were long pools of quiet. Their path had been a mounting one; they were now on higher earth, near the plateau or watershed that marked the top of the glen. The bright sky arched overhead, the sun shone strongly, the air moved in currents without violence.

"You see where that smoke comes up between trees? That's Mother Binning's cot."

"Who's she?"

"She's a wise auld wife. She's a scryer. That's her ash-tree."

Their path brought them by the hut and its bit of garden. Jock Binning, that was Mother Binning's crippled son, sat fishing in the stream. Mother Binning had been working in the garden, but when she saw the figures on the path below she took her distaff and sat on the bench in the sun. When they came by she raised her voice.

"Mr. Alexander, how are the laird and the leddy?"

"They're very well, Mother."

"Ye'll be gaeing sune to Edinburgh? Wha may be this laddie?"

"It is Ian Rullock, of Black Hill."

"Sae the baith o' ye are gaeing to Edinburgh? Will ye be friends there?"

"That we will!"

"Hech, sirs!" Mother Binning drew a thread from her distaff. The two were about to travel on when she stopped them again with a gesture. "Dinna mak sic haste! There's time enough behind us, and time enough before us. And it's a strange warld, and a large, and an auld! Sit ye and crack a bit with an auld wife by the road."

But they had dallied at White Farm and in the cave, and Alexander was in haste.

"We cannot stop now, Mother. We're bound for the Kelpie's Pool."

"And why do ye gae there? That's a drear, wanrestfu' place!" said Mother Binning.

"Ian has not seen it yet. I want to show it to him."

Mother Binning turned her distaff slowly. "Eh, then, if ye maun gae, gae!... We're a' ane! There's the kelpie pool for a'."

"We'll stop a bit on the way back," said Alexander. He spoke in a wheedling, kindly voice, for he and Mother Binning were good friends.

"Do that then," she said. "I hae a hansel o' coffee by me. I'll mak twa cups, for I'll warrant that ye'll baith need it!"

The air was indeed growing colder when the two came at last upon the moor that ran down to the Kelpie's Pool. Furze and moss and ling, a wild country stretched around without trees or house or moving form. The bare sunshine took on a remote, a cool and foreign, aspect. The small singing of the wind in whin and heather came from a thin, eery world. Down below them they saw the dark little tarn, the Kelpie's Pool. It was very clear, but dark, with a bottom of peat. Around it grew rushes and a few low willows. The two sat upon an outcropping of stone and gazed down upon it.

"It's a gey lonely place," said Alexander. "Now I like it as well or better than I do the cave, and now I would leave it far behind me!"

"I like the cave best. This is a creepy place."

"Once I let myself out at Glenfernie without any knowing and came here by night."

Ian felt emulation. "Oh, I would do that, too, if there was any need! Did you see anything?"

"Do you mean the kelpie?"

"Yes."

"No. I saw something—once. But that time I wanted to see how the stars looked in the water."

Ian looked at the water, that lay like a round mirror, and then to the vast shell of the sky above. He, too, had love of beauty—a more sensuous love than Alexander's, but love. This shared perception made one of the bonds between them.

"It was as still—much stiller than it is to-day! The air was clear and the night dark and grand. I looked down, and there was the Northern Crown, clasp and all."

Ian in imagination saw it, too. They sat, chin on knees, upon the moorside above the Kelpie's Pool. The water was faintly crisped, the reeds and willow boughs just stirred.

"But the kelpie—did you ever see that?"

"Sometimes it is seen as a water-horse, sometimes as a demon. I never saw anything like that but once. I never told any one about it. It may have been just one of those willows, after all. But I thought I saw a woman."

"Go on!"

"There was a great mist that day and it was hard to see. Sometimes you could not see—it was just rolling waves of gray. So I stumbled down, and I was in the rushes before I knew that I had come to them. It was spring and the pool was full, and the water plashed and came over my foot. It was like something holding my ankles.... And then I saw her—if it was not the willow. She was like a fair woman with dark hair unsnooded. She looked at me as though she would mock me, and I thought she laughed—and then the mist rolled down and over, and I could not see the hills nor the water nor scarce the reeds I was in. So I lifted my feet from the sucking water and got away.... I do not know if it was the kelpie's daughter or the willow—but if it was the willow it could look like a human—or an unhuman—body!"

Ian gazed at the pool. He had many advantages over Alexander, he knew, but the latter had this curious daring. He did more things with himself and of himself than did he, Ian. There was that in Ian that did not like this, that was jealous of being surpassed. And there was that in Ian that would not directly display this feeling, that would provide it, indeed, with all kinds of masks, but would, with certainty, act from that spurring, though intricate enough might be the path between the stimulus and the act.

"It is deep?"

"Aye. Almost bottomless, you would think, and cold as winter."

"Let us go swimming."

"The day's getting late and it's growing cold. However, if you want to—"

Ian did not greatly want to. But if Alexander could be so indifferent, he could be determined and ardent. "What's a little mirk and cold? I want to say I've swum in it." He began to unbutton his waistcoat.

They stripped, left their clothes in the stone's keeping, and ran down the moorside. The light played over their bodies, unblemished, smooth, and healthfully colored, clean-lined and rightly spare. They had beautiful postures and movements when they stood, when they ran; a youthful and austere grace as of Spartan youth plunging down to the icy Eurotas. The earth around lay as stripped as they; the naked, ineffable blue ether held them as it did all things; the wandering air broke against them in invisible surf. They ran down the long slope of the moor, parted the reeds, and dived to meet their own reflections. The water was most truly deep and cold. They struck out, they swam to the middle of the pool, they turned upon their backs and looked up to the blue zenith, then, turning again, with strong arm strokes they sent the wave over each other. They rounded the pool under the twisted willows, beside the shaking reeds; they swam across and across.

Alexander looked at the sun that was deep in the western quarter. "Time to be out and going!" He swam to the edge of the pool, but before he should draw himself out stopped to look up at a willow above him, the one that he thought he might, in the mist, have taken for the kelpie's daughter. It was of a height that, seen at a little distance, might even a tall woman. It put out two broken, shortened branches like arms.... He lost himself in the study of possibilities, balanced among the reeds that sighed around. He could not decide, so at last he shook himself from that consideration, and, pushing into shallow water, stepped from the pool. He had taken a few steps up the moor ere with suddenness he felt that Ian was not with him. He turned. Ian was yet out in the middle ring of the tarn. The light struck upon his head. Then he dived under—or seemed to dive under. He was long in coming up; and when he did so it was in the same place and his backward-drawn face had a strangeness.

"Ian!"

Ian sank again.

"He's crampit!" Alexander flashed like a thrown brand down the way he had mounted and across the strip of weeds, and in again to the steel-dark water. "I'm coming!" He gained to his fellow, caught him ere he sank the third time.

Dragged from the Kelpie's Pool, Ian lay upon the moor. Alexander, bringing with haste the clothes from the stone above, knelt beside him, rubbed and kneaded the life into him. He opened his eyes.

"Alexander—!"

Alexander rubbed with vigor. "I'm here. Eh, lad, but you gave me a fright!"

In another five minutes he sat up. "I'm—I'm all right now. Let's get our things on and go."

They dressed, Alexander helping Ian. The blood came slowly back into the latter's cheek; he walked, but he shivered yet.

"Let's go get Mother Binning's coffee!" said Alexander. "Come, I'll put my arm about you so." They went thus up the moor and across, and then down to the trees, the stream, and the glen. "There's the smoke from her chimney! You may have both cups and lie by the fire till you're warm. Mercy me! how lonely the cave would have been if you had drowned!"

They got down to the flowing water.

"I'm all right now!" said Ian. He released himself, but before he did so he turned in Alexander's arm, put his own arm around the other's neck, and kissed him. "You saved my life. Let's be friends forever!"

"That's what we are," said Alexander, "friends forever."

"You've proved it to me; one day I'll prove it to you!"

"We don't need proofs. We just know that we like each other, and that's all there is about it!"

"Yes, it's that way," said Ian, and so they came to Mother Binning's cot, the fire, and the coffee.

CHAPTER VII

Upon a quiet, gray December afternoon, nine years and more from the June day when he had fished in the glen and Mother Binning had told him of her vision of the Jacobite gathering at Braemar, English Strickland, walking for exercise to the village and back, found himself overtaken by Mr. M'Nab, the minister who in his white manse dwelt by the white kirk on the top of the windy hill. This was, by every earthly canon, a good man, but a stern and unsupple. He had not been long in this parish, and he was sweeping with a strong, new besom. The old minister, to his mind, had been Erastian and lax, weak in doctrine and in discipline of the fold. Mr. M'Nab meant not to be weak. He loathed sin and would compel the sinner also to loathe it. Now he came up, tall and darkly clad, and in his Calvinistic hand his Bible.

"Gude day, sir!"

"Good day, Mr. M'Nab!" The two went on side by side. The day was very still, the sky an even gray, snow being prepared. "You saw the laird?"

"Aye. He's verra low."

"He'll not recover I think. It's been a slow failing for two years—ever since Mrs. Jardine's death."

"She was dead before I came to this kirk. But once, when I was a young man, I stayed awhile in these parts. I remember her."

"She was the best of women."

"So they said. But she had not that grip upon religion that the laird has!"

"Maybe not."

Mr. M'Nab directed his glance upon the Glenfernie tutor. He did not think that this Englishman, either, had much grip upon religion. He determined, at the first opportunity, to call his attention to that fact and to strive to teach his fingers how to clasp. He had a craving thirst for the saving of souls, and to draw one whole from Laodicea was next best to lifting from Babylon. But to-day the laird and his spiritual concerns had the field.

"He comes, by the mother's side, at least, of godly stock. His mother's father was martyred for the faith in the auld persecuting time. His grandmother wearied her mind away in prison. His mother suffered much when she was a lassie."

"It's small wonder that he has nursed bitterness," said Strickland. "He must have drunk in terror and hate with her milk.... He conquered the terror."

"'*Do not I hate them, O Lord, that hate thee? and am not I grieved with those that rise up against thee? I hate them with perfect hatred; I count them my enemies.*'—What else should his heart do but burn with a righteous wrath?"

Strickland sighed, looking at the quiet gray hills and the vast, still web of cloud above. "It's come to be a withering fire, hunting fuel everywhere! I remember when he held it in bounds, even when for a time it seemed to die out. But of late years it has got the better of him. At last, I think, it is devouring himself."

M'Nab made a dissenting sound. "He has got the implicit belief in God that I see sair lack of elsewhere! He holds fast to God."

"Aye. The God who slays the Amalekites."

M'Nab turned his wintry glance upon him. "And is not that God?"

The other looked at the hill and at the vast, quiet, gray field of cloud. "Perhaps!... Let's talk of something else. I am too tired to argue. I sat up with him last night."

The minister would have preferred to continue to discuss the character of Deity. He turned heavily. "I was in company, not long ago, with some gentlemen who were wondering why you stayed on at Glenfernie House. They said that you had good offers elsewhere—much better than with a Scots laird."

"I promised Mrs. Jardine that I would stay."

"While the laird lived?"

"No, not just that—though I think that she would have liked me to do so. But so long as the laird would keep Jamie with him at home."

"What will he do now—Jamie?"

"He has set his heart on the army. He's strong of body, with a kind of big, happy-go-luckiness—"

A horseman came up behind them. It proved to be Robin Greenlaw, of Littlefarm. He checked his gray and exchanged greetings with the minister and the tutor. "How does the laird find himself the day?" he asked Strickland.

"No better, I think, Mr. Greenlaw."

"I'm sorry. It's the end, I jalouse! Is Mr. Alexander come?"

"We look for him to-morrow."

"The land and the folk'll be blithe to see him—if it was not for the occasion of his coming! If there's aught a body can do for any at Glenfernie—?"

"Every one has been as good as gold, Greenlaw. But you know there's not much at the last that can be done—"

"No. We all pass, and they that bide can but make the dirge. But I'll be obliged if you'll say to Mr. Alexander that if there *is* aught " He gathered up the reins. "It will be snowing presently. I always thought that I'd like to part on a day like this, gray and quiet, with all the color and the shouting lifted elsewhere." He was gone, trotting before them on his big horse.

Strickland and the minister looked after him. "There's one to be liked no little!" said Strickland.

But Mr. M'Nab's answering tone was wintry yet. "He makes mair songs than he listens to sermons! Jarvis Barrow, that's a strong witness, should have had another sort of great-nephew! And so he that will be laird comes home to-morrow? It's little that he has been at home of late years."

"Yes, little."

The manse with the kirk beyond rose before them, drawn against the pallid sky. "A wanderer to and fro in the earth, and I doubt not—though we do not hear much of it—an eater of husks!—Will you not come in, Mr. Strickland?"

"Another time, Mr. M'Nab. I've an errand in the village.— Touching Alexander Jardine. I suppose that the whole sense-bound world might be called by a world farther on an eater of husks. But I know naught to justify any especial application of the phrase to him. I know, indeed, a good deal quite to the contrary. You are, it seems to me, something less than charitable—"

M'Nab regarded him with an earnest, narrow, wintry look. "I would not wish to deserve that epithet, Mr. Strickland. But the world is evil, and Satan stands close at the ear of the young, both the poor and them of place and world's gear! So I doubt not that he eats the husks. I doubt not, either, that the Lord has a rod for him, as for us all, that will drive him, willy-nilly, home. So I'll say good day, sir. To-morrow I'll go again to the laird, and so every day until his summons comes."

They parted at the manse door. The world was gray, the snow swiftening its approach. Strickland, passing the kirk, kept on down the one village street. All and any who were out of doors spoke to him, asking how did the laird. Some asked if "the young laird" had come.

In the shop where he made his purchase the woman who

sold would have kept him talking an hour: "Wad the laird last the week? Wad he make friends before he died with Mr. Touris of Black Hill with whom he had the great quarrel three years since? Eh, sirs! and he never set foot again in Touris House, nor Mr. Touris in his!—Wad Mr. Jamie gae now to Edinburgh or on his travels, that had been at home sae lang because the laird wadna part with him?—Wad Miss Alice, that was as bonny as a rose and mair friendly than the gowans on a June lea, just bide on at the house with her aunt, Mrs. Grizel, that came when the leddy died? Wad—"

Strickland smiled. "You must just come up to the house, Mrs. Macmurdo, and have a talk with Mrs. Grizel.—I hope the laird may last the week."

"You're a close ane!" thought the disappointed Mrs. Macmurdo. Aloud she said, "Aweel, sir, Mr. Alexander that will be laird is coming hame frae foreign parts?"

"Yes."

"Sic a wanderer as he has been! But there!" said Mrs. Macmurdo, "ony that saw him when he was a laddie gaeing here and gaeing there by his lane-some, glen and brae and muir, might ha' said, 'Ye're a wanderer—and as sune as ye may ye'll wander farther!'"

"You're quite right, Mrs. Macmurdo," said Strickland, and took his parcel from her.

"A wanderer and a seeker!" Mrs. Macmurdo was loth to let him go. "And his great friend is still Captain Ian Rullock?"

"Yes, still."

Mrs. Macmurdo reluctantly opened the shop door. "Aweel, sir, if ye maun gae.—There'll be snaw the night, I'm thinking! Do ye stop at the inn? There's twa-three sogers in town."

Strickland had not meant to stop. But, coming to the Jardine Arms and glancing through the window, he saw by the light of the fire in the common room four men in red coats sitting at table, drinking. He felt jaded and depressed, needing distraction from the gray chill day and the laird's dying. Curiosity faintly stretched herself. He turned into the inn, took a seat by a corner table, and called for a bottle of wine. In addition to the soldiers the room had a handful of others—farmers, a lawyer's clerk from Stirling, a petty officer of the excise, and two or three village nondescripts. From this group there now disengaged himself Robin Greenlaw, who came across to Strickland's table.

"Sit down and have a glass with me," said the latter. "Who are they?"

"A recruiting party," answered Greenlaw, accepting the invitation. "I like to hear their talk! I'll listen, drinking your wine and thanking you, sir! and riding home I'll make a song about them."

He sat with his arm over the chair-back, his right hand now lifting and now lowering the wine-glass. He had a look of strength and inner pleasure that rested and refreshed.

"What are they saying now?" asked Strickland.

The soldiers made the center of attention. More or less all in the room harkened to their talk, disconnected, obscure, idle, and boisterous as much of it was. The revenue officer, by virtue of being also the king's paid man, had claimed comrade's right and was drinking with them and putting questions. He was so obliging as to ask these in a round tone of voice and to repeat on the same note the information gathered.

"Recruits for the King's army, fighting King Louis on the river Main.—Where's that?—It's in Germany. Our King and the Hanoverians and the King of Prussia and the Queen of Austria are fighting the King of France.—Aye, of course ye know that, neighbors, being intelligent Scots folk, but recapitulation is na out of order!"

"Ask them what's thought of the Hanoverians." It was the lawyer's clerk's question. Thereupon rose some noisy difference of opinion among the drinking redcoats. The excise man finally reported. "They're na English, nor Scots, nor even Irish. But they're liked weel enough! They're good fighters. Oh, aye, when ye march and fight alangside them, they're good enough! They're his Majesty's cousins. God save King George!"

The recruiting party banged with tankards upon the table. One of the number put a question of his own. He had a look half pedant, half bully, and he spoke with a one-quarter-drunken, owllike solemnity.

"I may take it from the look of things that there are none hereabouts but good Whigs and upholders of govern-ment? No Tories—no damned black Jacobites?"

The excise man hemmed. "Why, ye see we're no sae muckle far from Hielands and Hielandmen, and it's known what they are, chief, chieftain, and clan—saving always the duke and every Campbell! And I wadna say that there are not, here and there, this side the Hielands, an auld family with leanings the auld way, and even a few gentlemen who were *out* in the 'fifteen. But the maist of us, gentle and simple, are up and down Whig and Kirk and reigning House.—Na, na! when we drink to the King we dinna pass the glass over the water!"

A dark, thin soldier put in his word, well garnished with oaths. "Now that there's war up and down and so many of us are going out of the country, there's a saying that the Pretender may e'en sail across from France and beat a drum and give a shout! Then there'll be a sorting—"

"Them that would rise wouldn't be enough to make a graveyard ghost to frighten with!"

"You're mistaken there. They'll frighten ye all right when they answer the drum! I'm thinking there's some in the army would answer it!"

"Then they'll be hanged, drawn, and quartered!" averred the corporal. "Who are ye thinking would do that?"

"I'm not precisely knowing. But there are some with King George were brought up on the hope of King James!"

More liquor appeared upon the table, was poured and drunk. The talk grew professional. The King's shilling, and the advantage of taking it, came solely upon the board, and who might or might not 'list from this dale and the bordering hills. Strickland and Robin Greenlaw left their corner.

"I must get back to the house."

"And I to Littlefarm."

They went out together. There were few in the street. The snow was beginning to fall. Greenlaw untied his horse.

"I hope that we're not facing another 'fifteen! *'Scotland's ain Stewarts, and Break the Union!'* It sounds well, but it's not in the line of progression. What does Captain Ian Rullock think about it?"

"I don't know. He hasn't been here, you know, for a long while."

"That's true. He and Mr. Alexander are still like brothers?"

"Like brothers."

Greenlaw mounted his horse. "Well, he's a bonny man, but he's got a piece of the demon in him! So have I, I ken very well, and so, doubtless, has he who will be Glenfernie, and all the rest of us—"

"I sit down to supper with mine very often," said Strickland.

"Oh yes, he's common—the demon! But somehow I could find him in Ian Rullock, though all covered up with gold. But doubtless," said Greenlaw, debonairly, "it would be the much of the fellow in me that would recognize much in another!" He put his gray into motion. "Good day, sir!" He was gone, disappearing down the long street, into the snow that was now falling like a veil.

Strickland turned homeward. The snow fell fast and thick in large white flakes. Glenfernie House rose before him, crowning the craggy hill, the modern building and the remnant of the old castle, not a great place, but an ancient, settled, and rooted, part of a land poor but not without grandeur, not without a rhythm attained between grandeur and homeliness. The road swept around and up between leafless trees and green cone-bearing ones. The snow was whitening the branches, the snow wrapped house and landscape in its veil. It broke, in part it obliterated, line and modeling; the whole seemed on the point of dissolving into a vast and silent unity. "Like a dying man," thought Strickland. He came upon the narrow level space about the house, passed the great cedar planted by a pilgrim laird the year of Flodden Field, and entered by a door in the southern face.

Davie met him. "Eh, sir, Mr. Alexander's come!"

"Come!"

"Aye, just! An hour past, riding Black Alan, with Tam Dickson behind on Whitefoot, and weary enough thae horses looked! Mr. Alexander wad ha' gane without bite or sup to the laird's room, but he's lying asleep. So now he's gane to his ain auld room for a bit of rest. Haith, sir," said Davie, "but he's like the auld laird when he was twenty-eight!"

CHAPTER VIII

Strickland went, to the hall, where he found Alice.

"Come to the fire! I've been watching the snow, but it is so white and thick and still it fair frightens me! Davie told you that Alexander has come?"

"Yes. From Edinburgh to-day."

"Yes. He left London as soon as he had our letters."

She stood opposite him, a bright and bonny lass, with a look of her mother, but with more beauty. The light from the burning logs deepened the gold in her hair, as the warmth made more vivid the rose of her cheek. She owned a warm and laughing heart, a natural goodness. Strickland, who had watched and taught her since she was a slip of a child, had for her a great fondness.

Jamie entered the hall. "Father's awake now, but Aunt Grizel and Tibbie Ross will not tell him Alexander's come until they've given him something to eat." He came to the fire and stood, his blue eyes glinting light. "It's fine to see Alexander! The whole place feels different!"

"You've got a fine love for Alexander," said Strickland.

So long had he lived with the Jardines of Glenfernie that they had grown like own folk to him, and he to them. He looked very kindly at the young man, handsome, big, flushed with feeling. He did not say, "Now you'll be going, Jamie, and he'll be staying," but the thought was in mind, and presently Alice gave it voice.

"He says that he has seen his earth, and that now he means to be a long time at home."

Davie appeared. "Mr. Alexander has gone to the laird's room. Mrs. Grizel wad have ye all come, too, sae be ye move saftly and sit dumb."

The three went. The laird's room was large and somewhat grimly bare. When his wife died he would have taken out every luxury. But a great fire burned on the hearth and gave a touch of redemption. A couch, too, had been brought in for the watcher at night, and a great flowered chair. In this now sat Mrs. Grizel Kerr, a pleasant, elderly, comely body, noted for her housewifery and her garden of herbs. Behind her, out of a shadowy corner, gleamed the white mutch of Tibbie Ross, the best nurse in that countryside. Jamie and Alice took two chairs that had been set for them near the bed. Strickland moved to the recess of a window. Outside the snow fell in very large flakes, large and many, straight and steady, there being no wind.

In a chair drawn close to the great bed, on a line with the sick man's hand lying on the coverlet, sat the heir of Glenfernie. He sat leaning forward, with one hand near the hand of his father. The laird's eyes were closed. He had been given a stimulant and he now lay gathering his powers that were not far from this life's frontier. The curtains of the bed had been drawn quite back; propped by pillows into a half-sitting posture, he was plain to all in the room, in the ruddy light of the fire. A clock upon the wall ticked, ticked. Those in the room sat very still.

The laird drew a determined breath and opened his eyes. "Alexander!"

"Father!"

"You look like myself sitting there, and yet not myself. I am going to die."

"If that's your will, father."

"Aye, it's my will, for I've made it mine. I can't talk much. We'll talk at times and sit still between. Are you going to stay with me to-night?"

"Indeed I am, father. Right here beside you."

"Well, I've missed you. But you had to have your wanderings and your life of men. I understood that."

"You've been most good to me. It is in my heart and in the tears of my eyes."

"I did not grudge the siller. And I've had a pride in you, Alexander. Now you'll be the laird. Now let's sit quiet a bit."

The snow fell, the fire burned, the clock ticked. He spoke again. "It's before an eye inside that you'll be a wanderer and a goer about yet—within and without, my laddie, within and without! Do not forget, though, to hold the old place together that so many Jardines have been born in, and to care for the tenant bodies and the old folk—and there's your brother and sister."

"I will forget nothing that you say, father."

"I have kept that to say on top of my mind.... The old place and the tenant bodies and old folk, and your brother and sister. I have your word, and so," said the laird, "that's done and may drift by.—Grizel, I wad sleep a bit. Let him go and come again."

His eyes closed. Alexander rose from the chair beside him. Coming to Alice, he put his arm around her, and with Jamie at his other hand the three went from the room. Strickland tarried a moment to consult with Mrs. Grizel.

"The doctor comes to-morrow?"

"Aye. Tibbie thinks him a bit stronger."

"I will watch to-night with Alexander."

"Hoot, man! ye maun be weary enough yourself!" said Mrs. Grizel.

"No, I am not. I will sleep awhile after supper, and come in about ten. So you and Tibbie may get one good night."

Some hours later, in the room that had been his since his first coming to Glenfernie, he gazed out of window before turning to go down-stairs. The snow had ceased to fall, and out of a great streaming floe of clouds looked a half-moon. Under it lay wan hill and plain. The clouds were all of a size and vast in number, a herd of the upper air. The wind drove them, not like a shepherd, but like a wolf at their heels. The moon seemed the shepherd, laboring for control. Then the clouds themselves seemed the wolves, and the moon a traveler against whom they leaped, who was thrown among them, and rose again.... Then the moon was a soul, struggling with the wrack and wave of things.

Strickland went down the old, winding Glenfernie stair, and came at last to the laird's room. Tibbie Ross opened the door to him, and he saw it all in low firelight and made ready for the night. The laird lay propped as before in the great bed, but seemed asleep. Alexander sat before the fire, elbows upon knees and chin in hand, brooding over the red coals. Tibbie murmured a direction or two and showed wine and bread set in the deep window. Then with a courtesy and a breathed, "Gie ye gude night, sirs!" she was forth to her own rest. The door closed softly behind her. Strickland stepped as softly to the chair beyond Alexander. The couch was spread for the watchers' alternate use, if so they chose; on a table burned shaded candles. Strickland had a book in his pocket. Sitting down, he produced this, for he would not seem to watch the man by the fire.

Alexander Jardine, large and strong of frame, with a countenance massive and thoughtful for so young a man, bronzed, with well-turned features, gazed steadily into the red hollows where the light played, withdrew and played again. Strickland tried to read, but the sense of the other's presence affected him, came between his mind and the page. Involuntarily he began to occupy himself with Alexander and to picture his life away from Glenfernie, away, too, from Edinburgh and Scotland. It was now six years since, definitely, he had given up the law, throwing himself, as it were, on the laird's mercy both for long and wide travel, and for life among books other than those indicated for advocates. The laird had let him go his gait—the laird with Mrs. Jardine a little before him. The Jardine fortune was not a great one, but there was enough for an heir who showed no inclination to live and to travel *en prince*, who in certain ways was nearer the ascetic than the spendthrift.... Before Strickland's mind, strolling dreamily, came pictures of far back, of years ago, of long since. A by-wind had brought to the tutor then certain curious bits of knowledge. Alexander, a student in Edinburgh, had lived for some time upon half of his allowance in order to accommodate Ian Rullock with the other half, the latter being in a crisis of quarrel with his uncle, who, when he quarreled, used always, where he could, the money screw. Strickland had listened to his Edinburgh informant, but had never divulged the news given. No more had he told another bit, floated to him again by that ancient Edinburgh friend and gossip, who had young cousins at college and listened to their talk. It pertained to a time a little before that of the shared income. This time it had been shared blood. Strickland, sitting with his book in the quiet room, saw in imagination the students' chambers in Edinburgh, and the little throng of very young men, flushed with wine and with youth, making friendships, and talking of friendships made, and dubbing Alexander Damon and Ian Pythias. Then more wine and a bravura passage. Damon and Pythias opening each a vein with some convenient dagger, smearing into the wound some drops of the other's blood, and going home each with a tourniquet above the right wrist.... Well, that was years ago—and youth loved such passages!

Alexander, by the fire, stooped to put back a coal that had fallen upon the oak boards, then sank again into his reverie. Strickland read a paragraph without any especial comprehension, after which he found himself again by the stream of Alexander's life. That friendship with Ian

Rullock utterly held, he believed. Well, Ian Rullock, too, seemed somehow a great personage. Very different from Alexander, and yet somehow large to match.... Where had Alexander been after Edinburgh—where had he not been? Very often Ian was with him, but sometimes and for months he would seem to have been alone. Glenfernie might receive letters from Germany, from Italy or Egypt, or from further yet to the east. He had been alone this year, for Ian was now the King's man and with his regiment, Strickland supposed, wherever that might be. Alexander had written from Buda-Pesth, from Erfurt, from Amsterdam, from London. Now he sat here at Glenfernie, looking into the fire. Strickland, who liked books of travel, wondered what he saw of old cities, grave or gay, of ruined temples, sphinxes, monuments, grass-grown battle-fields, and ships at sea, storied lands, peoples, individual men and women. He had wayfared long; he must have had many an adventure. He had been from childhood a learner. His touch upon a book spoke of adeptship in that world.... Well, here he was, and what would he do now, when he was laird? Strickland lost himself in speculation. Little or naught had ever been in Alexander's letters about women.

The white ash fell, the clock ticked, the wind went around the house with a faint, banshee crying. The figure by the fire rested there, silent, still, and brooding. Strickland observed with some wonder its power of long, concentrated thinking. It sat there, not visibly tense, seemingly relaxed, yet as evidently looking into some place of inner motion, wider and swifter than that of the night world about it. Strickland tried to read. The clock hand moved toward midnight.

The laird spoke from the great bed. "Alexander—"

"I am here, father." Alexander rose and went to the sick man's side. "You slept finely! And here we have food for you, and drops to give you strength—"

The laird swallowed the drops and a spoonful or two of broth. "There. Now I want to talk. Aye, I am strong enough. I feel stronger. I am strong. It hurts me more to check me. Is that the wind blowing?"

"Yes. It is a wild night."

"It is singing. I could almost pick out the words. Alexander, there's a quarrel I have with Touris of Black Hill. I have no wish to make it up. He did me a wrong and is a sinner in many ways. But his sister is different. If you see her tell her that I aye liked her."

"Would it make you happier to be reconciled to Mr. Touris?"

"No, it would not! You were never a canting one, Alexander! Let that be. Anger is anger, and it's weakness to gainsay it! That is," said the laird, "when it's just—and this is just. Alexander, my bonny man—"

"I'm here, father."

"I've been lying here, gaeing up and down in my thoughts, a bairn again with my grandmither, gaeing up and down the braes and by the glen. I want to say somewhat to you. When you see an adder set your heel upon it! When a wolf goes by take your firelock and after him! When a denier and a cheat is near you tell the world as much and help to set the snare! Where there are betrayers and persecutors hunt the wild plant shall make a cup like their ain!" He fell to coughing, coughing more and more violently.

Strickland rose and came to the bedside, and the two watchers gave him water and wine to drink, and would have had him, when the fit was over, cease from all speech. He shook them off.

"Alexander, ye're like me. Ye're mair like me than any think! Where ye find your Grierson of Lagg, clench with him—clench—Alexander!"

He coughed, lifting himself in their arms. A blood-vessel broke. Tibbie Ross, answering the calling, hurried in. "Gude with us! it's the end!" Mrs. Grizel came, wrapped in a great flowered bed-gown. In a few minutes all was over. Strickland and Alexander laid him straight that had been the laird.

CHAPTER IX

The month was May. The laird of Glenfernie, who had walked to the Kelpie's Pool, now came down the glen. Mother Binning was yet in her cot, though an older woman now and somewhat broken.

"Oh aye, my bonny man! All things die and all things live. To and fro gaes the shuttle!"

Glenfernie sat on the door-stone. She took all the news he could bring, and had her own questions to put.

"How's the house and all in it?"

"Well."

"Ye've got a bonny sister! Whom will she marry? There's Abercrombie and Fleming and Ferguson."

"I do not know. The one she likes the best."

"And when will ye be marrying yourself?"

"I am not going to marry, Mother. I would marry Wisdom, if I could!"

"Hoot! she stays single! Do ye love the hunt of Wisdom so?"

"Aye, I do. But it's a long, long chase—and to tell you the truth, at times I think she's just a wraith! And at times I am lazy and would just sit in the sun and be a fool."

"Like to-day?"

"Like to-day. And so," said Alexander, rising, "as I feel that way, I'll e'en be going on!"

"I'm thinking that maist of the wise have inner tokens by which they ken the fule. I was ne'er afraid of folly," said Mother Binning. "It's good growing stuff!"

Glenfernie laughed and left her and the drone of her wheel. A clucking hen and her brood, the cot and its ash-tree, sank from sight. A little longer and he reached the middle glen where the banks approached and the full stream rushed with a manifold sound. Here was the curtain of brier masking the cave that he had shared with Ian. He drew it aside and entered. So much smaller was the place than it had seemed in boyhood! Twice since they came to be men had he been here with Ian, and they had smiled over their cavern, but felt for it a tenderness. In a corner lay the fagots that, the last time, they had gathered with laughter and left here against outlaws' needs. Ian! He pictured Ian with his soldiers.

Outside the cavern, the air came about him like a cloud of fragrance. As he went down the glen, into its softer sweeps, this increased, as did the song of birds. The primrose was strewn about in disks of pale gold, the white thorn lifted great bouquets, the bluebell touched the heart. A lark sang in the sky, linnet and cuckoo at hand, in the wood at the top of the glen cooed the doves. The water rippled by the leaning birches, the wild bees went from flower to flower. The sky was all sapphire, the air a perfumed ocean. So beautiful rang the spring that it was like a bell in the heart, in the blood. The laird of Glenfernie, coming to a great natural chair of sun-warmed rock, sat down to listen. All was of a sweetness, poignant, intense. But in the very act of recognizing this, there came upon him an old mood of melancholy, an inner mist and chill, a gray languor and wanting. The very bourgeoning and blossoming about him seemed to draw light from him, not give light. "I brought the Kelpie's Pool back with me," he thought. He shut his eyes, leaning his head against the stone, at last with a sideward movement burying it in his folded arms. "More life—more! What was a great current goes sluggish and landbound. Where again is the open sea—the more—the boundless? Where again—where again?"

He sat for an hour by the wild, singing stream. It drenched him, the loved place and the sweet season, with its thousand store of beauties. Its infinite number of touches brought at last response. The vague crying and longing of nature hushed before a present lullaby. At last he rose and went on with the calling stream.

The narrow path, set about with living green, with the spangly flowers, and between the branches fragments of the blue lift as clear as glass, led down the glen, widening now to hill and dale. Softening and widening, the world laughed in May. The stream grew broad and tranquil, with grassy shores overhung by green boughs. Here and there the bank extended into the flood a little grassy cape edged with violets. Alexander, following the spiral of the path, came upon the view of such a spot as this. It lay just before him, a little below his road. The stream washed its fairy beach. From the new grass rose a blooming thorn-tree; beneath this knelt a girl and, resting upon her hands, looked at her face in the water.

The laird of Glenfernie stood still. A drooping birch hid him; his step had been upon moss and was not heard. The face and form upon the bank, the face in the water, showed no consciousness of any human neighbor. The face was that of a woman of perhaps twenty-four. The hair was brown, the eyes brown. The head was beautifully placed on a round, smooth throat. With a wide forehead, with great width between the eyes, the face tapered to a small round chin. The mouth and under the eyes smiled in a thousand different ways. The beauty that was there was subtle, not discoverable by every one.—The girl settled back upon the grass beneath the thorn-tree. She was very near Glenfernie; he could see the rise and fall of her bosom beneath her blue print gown. It was Elspeth Barrow—he knew her now, though he had not seen her for a long time. She sat still, her brown eyes raised to building birds in the thorn-tree. Then she began herself to sing, clear and sweet.

"A lad and a lass met ower the brae;
They blushed rose-red, but they said nae word—
The woodbine fair and the milk-white slae:—
And frae one to the other gaed a silver bird,
A silver bird.

"A man set his Wish all odds before,
With sword, with pen, and with gold he stirred
Till the Wish and he met on a conquered shore,
And frae one to the other gaed an ebon bird,
An ebon bird.

"God looked on a man and said: "Tis time!

The broken mends, clear flows the blurred.
You and I are two worlds that rhyme!'
And frae one to the other gaed a golden bird,
A golden bird."

She sang it through, then sat entirely still against the stem of the thorn, while about her lips played that faint, unapproachable, glamouring smile. Her hands touched the grass to either side her body; her slender, blue-clad figure, the all of her, smote him like some god's line of poetry.

There was in the laird of Glenfernie's nature an empty palace. It had been built through ages and every wind of pleasure and pain had blown about it. Then it had slowly come about that the winds of pain had increased upon the winds of pleasure. The mind closed the door of the palace and the nature inclined to turn from it. It was there, but a sea mist hid it, and a tall thorn-hedge, and a web stretched across its idle gates. It had hardly come, in this life, into Glenfernie's waking mind that it was there at all.

Now with a suddenness every door clanged open. The mist parted, the thorn-wood sank, the web was torn. The palace stood, shining like home, and it was he who was afar, in the mist and the wood, and the web of idleness and oblivion in shreds about him. Set in the throne-room, upon the throne, he saw the queen.

His mood, that May day, had given the moment, and wide circumstance had met it. Now the hand was in the glove, the statue in the niche, the bow upon the string, the spark in the tinder, the sea through the dike. Now what had reached being must take its course.

He felt that so fatally that he did not think of resistance.... Elspeth, upon the grassy cape, beneath the blooming thorn, heard steps down the glen path, and turned her eyes to see the young laird moving between the birch stems. Now he was level with the holding; now he spoke to her, lifting his hat. She answered, with the smile beneath her eyes:

"Aye, Glenfernie, it's a braw day!"

"May I come into the fairy country and sit awhile and visit?"

"Aye." She welcomed him to a hillock of green rising from the water's edge. "It *is* fairyland, and these are the broad seas around, and I know if I came here by night I should find the Good People before me!" She looked at him with friendliness, half shy, half frank. "It is the best of weather for wandering."

"Are you fond of that, too? Do you go up and down alone?"

"By my lee-lane when Gilian's not here. She's in Aberdeen now, where live our mother's folk."

"I have not seen you for years."

"I mind the last time. Your mother lay ill. One evening at sunset Mr. Ian Rullock and you came to White Farm."

"It must have been after sunset. It must have been dark."

"Back of that you and he came from Edinburgh one time. We were down by the wishing-green, Robin Greenlaw and Gilian and I and three or four other lads and lassies. Do you remember? Mr. Rullock would have us dance, and we all took hands—you, too—and went around the ash-tree as though it were a May-pole. We changed hands, one with another, and danced upon the green. Then you and he got upon your horses and rode away. He was riding the white mare Fatima. But oh," said Elspeth, "then came grandfather, who had seen us from the reaped field, and he blamed us sair and put no to our playing! He gave word to the minister, and Sunday the sermon dealt with the ill women of Scripture. Back of that—"

"Back of that—"

"There was the day the two of you would go to the Kelpie's Pool." Elspeth's eyes enlarged and darkened. "The next morn we heard—Jock Binning told us—that Mr. Ian had nearly drowned."

"Almost ten years ago. Once—twice—thrice in ten years. How idly were they spent, those years!"

"Oh," cried Elspeth, "they say that you have been to world's end and have gotten great learning!"

"One comes home from all that to find world's end and great learning."

Elspeth leaned from him, back against the thorn-tree. She looked somewhat disquietedly, somewhat questioningly, at this new laird. Glenfernie, in his turn, laid upon himself both hands of control. He thought:

"Do not peril all—do not peril all—with haste and frightening!"

He sat upon the green hillock and talked of country news. She met him with this and that ... White Farm affairs, Littlefarm.

"Robin," said Alexander, "manages so well that he'll grow wealthy!"

"Oh no! He manages well, but he'll never grow wealthy outside! But inside he has great riches."

"Does she love him, then?" It poured fear into his heart. A magician with a sword—with a great, evil, written-upon creese like that hanging at Black Hill—was here before the palace.

"Do you love him?" asked Alexander, and asked it with so straight a simplicity that Elspeth Barrow took no offense.

She looked at him, and those strange smiles played about her lips. "Robin is a fairy man," she said. "He has ower little of struggle save with his rhymes," and left him to make what he could of that.

"She is heart-free," he thought, but still he feared and boded.

Elspeth rose from the grass, stepped from beneath the blooming tree. "I must be going. It wears toward noon."

Together they left the flower-set cape. The laird of Glenfernie looked back upon it.

"Heaven sent a sample down. You come here when you wish? You walk about with the spring and summer days?"

"Aye, when my work's done. Gilian and I love the greenwood."

He gave her the narrow path, but kept beside her on stone and dead leaves and mossy root. Though he was so large of frame, he moved with a practised, habitual ease, as far as might be from any savor of clumsiness. He had magnetism, and to-day he drew like a planet in glow. Now he looked at the woman beside him, and now he looked straight ahead with kindled eyes.

Elspeth walked with slightly quickened breath, with knitted brows. The laird of Glenfernie was above her in station, though go to the ancestors and blood was equal enough! It carried appeal to a young woman's vanity, to be walking so, to feel that the laird liked well enough to be where he was. She liked him, too. Glenfernie House was talked of, talked of, by village and farm and cot, talked of, talked of, year by year—all the Jardines, their virtues and their vices, what they said and what they did. She had heard, ever since she was a bairn, that continual comment, like a little prattling burn running winter and summer through the dale. So she knew much that was true of Alexander Jardine, but likewise entertained a sufficient amount of misapprehension and romancing. Out of it all came, however, for the dale, and for the women at White Farm who listened to the burn's voice, a sense of trustworthiness. Elspeth, walking by Glenfernie, felt kindness for him. If, also, there ran a tremor of feeling that it was very fair to be Elspeth Barrow and walking so, she was young and it was natural. But beyond that was a sense, vague, unexplained to herself, but disturbing. There was feeling in him that was not in her. She was aware of it as she might be aware of a gathering storm, though the brain received as yet no clear message. She felt, struggling with that diffused kindness and young vanity, something like discomfort and fear. So her mood was complex enough, unharmonized, parted between opposing currents. She was a riddle to herself.

But Glenfernie walked in a great simplicity of faeryland

or heaven. She did not love Robin Greenlaw; she was not so young a lass, with a rose in her cheek for every one; she was come so far without mating because she had snow in her heart! The palace gleamed, the palace shone. All the music of earth—of the world—poured through. The sun had drunk up the mist, time had eaten the thorn-wood, the spider at the gate had vanished into chaos and old night.

CHAPTER X

The cows and sheep and work-horses, the dogs, the barn-yard fowls, the very hives of bees at White Farm, seemed to know well enough that it was the Sabbath. The flowers knew it that edged the kitchen garden, the cherry-tree knew it by the southern wall. The sunshine knew it, wearing its calm Sunday best. Sights and sounds attuned themselves.

The White Farm family was home from kirk. Jenny Barrow and Elspeth put away hood and wide hat of straw, slipped from and shook out and folded on the shelf Sunday gowns and kerchiefs. Then each donned a clean print and a less fine kerchief and came forth to direct and aid the two cotter lasses who served at White Farm. These by now had off their kirk things, but they marked Sunday still by keeping shoes and stockings. Menie and Merran, Elspeth and Jenny, set the yesterday-prepared dinner cold upon the table, drew the ale, and placed chairs and stools. Two men, Thomas and Willy, father and son, who drove the plow, sowed and reaped, for White Farm, came from the barn. They were yet Sunday-clad, with very clean, shining faces. "Call father, Elspeth!" directed Jenny, and set on the table a honeycomb.

Elspeth went without the door. Before the house grew a

great fir-tree that had a bench built around it. Here, in fine weather, in rest hours and on Sunday, might be looked for Jarvis Barrow. It was his habit to take the far side of the tree, with the trunk between him and the house. So there spread before him the running river, the dale and moor, and at last the piled hills. Here he sat, leaning hands upon a great stick shaped like a crook, his Bible open upon his knees. It was a great book, large of print, read over in every part, but opening most easily among the prophets. No cry, no denunciation, no longing, no judgment from Isaiah to Malachi, but was known to the elder of the kirk. Now he sat here, in his Sunday dress, with the Bible. At a little distance, on the round bench, sat Robin Greenlaw. The old man read sternly, concentratedly on; the young one looked at the purple mountain-heads. Elspeth came around the tree.

"Grandfather, dinner is ready.—Robin! we didn't know that you were here—"

"I went the way around to speak with the laird. Then I thought, 'I will eat at White Farm—'"

"You're welcome!—Grandfather, let me take the Book."

"No," said the old man, and bore it himself withindoors. Spare and unbent of frame, threescore and ten and five, and able yet at the plow-stilts, rigid of will, servant to the darker Calvinism, starving where he might human pride and human affections, and yet with much of both to starve, he moved and spoke with slow authority, looked a patriarch and ruled his holding. When presently he came to table in the clean, sanded room with the sunlight on the wall and floor, and when, standing, he said the long, the earnest grace, it might have been taken that here, in the Scotch farm-house, was at least a minor prophet. The grace was long, a true wrestling in prayer. Ended, a decent pause was made, then all took place, Jarvis Barrow and his daughter and granddaughter, Robin Greenlaw, Thomas and Willy, Menie and Merran. The cold meat, the bread, and other food were passed from hand to hand, the ale poured. The Sunday hush, the Sunday voices, continued to hold. Jarvis Barrow would have no laughter and idle clashes at his table on the Lord's day. Menie and Merran and Willy kept a stolid air, with only now and then a sidelong half-smile or nudging request for this or that. Elspeth ate little, sat with her brown eyes fixed out of the window. Robin Greenlaw ate heartily enough, but he had an air distrait, and once or twice he frowned. But Jenny Barrow could not long keep still and incurious, even upon the Sabbath day.

"Eh, Robin, what was your crack with the laird?"

"He wants to buy Warlock for James Jardine. He's got his ensign's commission to go fight the French."

"Eh, he'll be a bonny lad on Warlock! I thought you wadna sell him?"

"I'll sell to Glenfernie."

The farmer spoke from the head of the table. "I'll na hae talk, Robin, of buying and selling on the day! It clinks like the money-changers and sellers of doves."

Thomas, his helper, raised his head from a plate of cold mutton. "Glenfernie was na at kirk. He's na the kirkkeeper his father was. Na, na!"

"Na," said the farmer. "Bairns dinna walk nowadays in parents' ways."

Willy had a bit of news he would fain get in. "Nae doot Glenfernie's brave, but he wadna be a sodger, either! I was gaeing alang wi' the yowes, and there was he and Drummielaw riding and gabbing. Sae there cam on a skirling and jumping wind and rain, and we a' gat under a tree, the yowes and the dogs and Glenfernie and Drummielaw and me. Then we changed gude day and they went on gabbing. And 'Nae,' says Glenfernie, 'I am nae lawyer and I am nae sodger. Jamie wad be the last, but brithers may love and yet be thinking far apairt. The best friend I hae in the warld is a sodger, but I'm thinking I hae lost the knack o' fechting. When you lose the taste you lose the knack.'"

"I's fearing," said Thomas, "that he's lost the taste o' releegion!"

"Eh," exclaimed Jenny Barrow, "but he's a bonny big man! He came by yestreen, and I thought, 'For a' there is sae muckle o' ye, ye look as though ye walked on air!'"

Thomas groaned. "Muckle tae be saved, muckle tae be lost!"

Jarvis Barrow spoke from the head of the table. "If fowk canna talk on the Sabbath o' spiritual things, maybe they can mak shift to haud the tongue in their chafts! I wad think that what we saw and heard the day wad put ye ower the burn frae vain converse!"

Thomas nodded approval.

"Aweel—" began Jenny, but did not find just the words with which to continue.

Elspeth, turning ever so slightly in her chair, looked

farther off to the hills and summer clouds. A slow wave of color came over her face and throat. Menie and Merran looked sidelong each at the other, then their blue eyes fell to their plates. But Willy almost audibly smacked his lips.

"Gude keep us! the meenister gaed thae sinners their licks!"

"A sair sight, but an eedifying!" said Thomas.

Robin Greenlaw pushed back his chair. He saw the inside of the kirk again, and two miserable, loutish, lawless lovers standing for public discipline. His color rose. "Aye, it was a sair sight," he said, abruptly, made a pause, then went on with the impetuousness of a burn unlocked from winter ice. "If I should say just what I think, I suppose, uncle, that I could not come here again! So I'll e'en say only that I think that was a sair sight and that I felt great shame and pity for all sinners. So, feeling it for all, I felt it for Mallie and Jock, standing there an hour, first on one foot and then on the other, to be gloated at and rebukit, and for the minister doing the rebuking, and for the kirkful all gloating, and thinking, 'Lord, not such are we!' and for Robin Greenlaw who often enough himself takes wildfire for true light! I say I think it was sair sight and sair doing—"

Barrow's hand came down upon the table. "Robin Greenlaw!"

"You need not thunder at me, sir. I'm done! I did not mean to make such a clatter, for in this house what clatter makes any difference? It's the sinner makes the clatter, and it's just promptly sunk and lost in godliness!"

The old man and the young turned in their chairs, faced

each other. They looked somewhat alike, and in the heart of each was fondness for the other. Greenlaw, eye to eye with the patriarch, felt his wrath going.

"Eh, uncle, I did not mean to hurt the Sunday!"

Jarvis Barrow spoke with the look and the weight of a prophet in Israel. "What is your quarrel about, and for what are ye flyting against the kirk and the minister and the kirkkeepers? Are ye wanting that twa sinners, having sinned, should hae their sin for secret and sweet to their aneselves, gilded and pairfumed and excused and unnamed? Are ye wanting that nane should know, and the plague should live without the doctor and without the mark upon the door? Or are ye thinking that it is nae plague at all, nae sin, and nae blame? Then ye be atheist, Robin Greenlaw, and ye gae indeed frae my door, and wad gae were ye na my nephew, but my son!" He gathered force. "Elder of the kirk, I sit here, and I tell ye that were it my ain flesh and blood that did evil, my stick and my plaid I wad take and ower the moor I wad gae to tell manse and parish that Sin, the wolf, had crept into the fauld! And I wad see thae folly-crammed and sinfu' sauls, that had let him in and had his bite, set for shame and shawing and warning and example before the conger-gation, and I wad say to the minister, 'Lift voice against them and spare not!' And I wad be there the day and in my seat, though my heart o' flesh was like to break!" His hand fell again heavily upon the board. "Sae weak and womanish is thae time we live in!" He flashed at his great-nephew. "Sae poetical! It wasna sae when the Malignants drove us and we fled to the hills and were fed on the muirs with the word of the Lord! It wasna sae in the time when Gawin Elliot that Glenfernie draws frae was hanged for gieing us that word! Then gin a sin-blasted ane was found amang us, his road indeed was shawn him! Aye, were't man or woman! *'For while they be folded together as thorns, and while they are drunken as drunkards, they shall be devoured as stubble fully dry!'"*

He pushed back his heavy chair; he rose from table and went forth, tall, ancient, gray, armored in belief. They heard him take his Bible from where it lay, and knew that he was back under the fir-tree, facing from the house toward moor and hill and mountain.

"Eh-h," groaned Thomas, "the elder is a mighty witness!"

The family at White Farm ate in silence. Elspeth slipped from her place.

"Where are ye gaeing, hinny?" asked Jenny. "Ye hae eaten naething."

"I've finished," said Elspeth. "I'm going to afternoon kirk, and I'll be getting ready."

She went into the room that she shared with Gilian and shut the door. Robin looked after her.

"When is Gilian coming home?"

"Naebody knows. She is sae weel at Aberdeen! They write that she is a great student and is liked abune a', and they clamor to keep her.—Are ye gaeing to second kirk, Robin?"

"I do not think so. But I'll walk over the moor with you."

The meal ended. Thomas and Willy went forth to the barn. Menie and Merran began to clear the table. They were not going to second kirk, and so the work was left to their hand. Jenny bustled to get on again her Sunday gear. She would not have missed, for a pretty, afternoon kirk and all the neighbors who were twice-goers. It was fair and theater and promenade and kirk to her in one—though of course she only said "kirk."

They walked over the moor, Jarvis Barrow and Jenny and Robin and Elspeth. And at a crossing path they came upon a figure seated on a stone and found it to be that of the laird of Glenfernie.

"Gude day, Glenfernie!"

"Good day, White Farm!"

He joined himself to them. For a moment he and Robin Greenlaw were together.

"Do you know what I hear them calling you?" quoth the latter. "I hear them say 'The wandering laird!'"

Alexander smiled. "That's not so bad a name!"

He walked now beside Jarvis Barrow. The old man's stride was hardly shortened by age. The two kept ahead of the two women, Greenlaw, Thomas, and the sheep-dog Sandy.

"It's a bonny day, White Farm!"

"Aye, it's bonny eneuch, Glenfernie. Are ye for kirk?"

"Maybe so, maybe not. I take much of my kirk out of doors. Moors make grand kirks. That has a sound, has it not, of heathenish brass cymbals?"

"It hae."

"All the same, I honor every kirk that stands sincere."

"Wasna your father sincere? Why gae ye not in his steps?"

"Maybe I do.... Yes, he was sincere. I trust that I am so, too. I would be."

"Why gae ye not in his steps, then?"

"All buildings are not alike and yet they may be built sincerely."

"Ye're wrong! Ye'll see it one day. Ye'll come round to your father's steps, only ye'll tread them deeper! Ye've got it in you, to the far back. I hear good o' ye, and I hear ill o' ye."

"Belike."

"Ye've traveled. See if ye can travel out of the ring of God!"

"What is the ring of God? If it is as large as I think it is," said Glenfernie, "I'll not travel out of it."

He looked out over moor and moss. There breathed about him something that gave the old man wonder. "Hae ye gold-mines and jewels, Glenfernie? Hae the King made ye Minister?"

The wandering laird laughed. "Better than that, White Farm, better than that!" He was tempted then and there to say: "I love your granddaughter Elspeth. I love Elspeth!"

It was his intention to say something like this as soon as might be to White Farm. "I love Elspeth and Elspeth loves me. So we would marry, White Farm, and she be lady beside the laird at Glenfernie." But he could not say it yet, because he did not know if Elspeth loved him. He was in a condition of hope, but very humbly so, far from assurance. He never did Elspeth the indignity of thinking that a lesser thing than love might lead her to Glenfernie House. If she came she would come because she loved—not else.

They left the moor, passed through the hollow of the stream and by the mill, and began to climb the village street. Folk looked out of door or window upon them; kirk-goers astir, dressed in their best, with regulated step and mouth and eyes set aright, gave the correct greeting, neither more nor less. If the afternoon breeze, if a little runlet of water going down the street, chose to murmur: "The laird is thick with White Farm! What makes the laird so thick with White Farm?" that was breeze or runlet's doing.

They passed the bare, gaunt manse and came to the kirkyard with the dark, low stones over the generations dead. But the grass was vivid, and the daisies bloomed, and even the yew-trees had some kind of peacock sheen, while the sky overhead burnt essential sapphire. Even the white of the lark held a friendly tinge as of rose petals mixed somehow with it. And the bell that was ending its ringing, if it was solemn, was also silver-sweet. Glenfernie determined that he would go to church. He entered with the White Farm folk and he sat with them, leaving the laird's high-walled, curtained pew without human tenancy. Mrs. Grizel came but to morning sermon. Alice was with a kinswoman of rank in a great house near Edinburgh, submitting, not without enjoyment, to certain fine filings and polishings and lacquerings and contacts. Jamie, who would be a soldier and fight the French, had his commission and was gone this past week to Carlisle, to his regiment. English Strickland was yet at Glenfernie House. Between him and the laird held much liking and respect. Tutor no longer, he stayed on as secretary and right-hand man. But Strickland was not at church.

The white cavern, bare and chill, with small, deep windows looking out upon the hills of June, was but sparely set out with folk. Afternoon was not morning. Nor was there again the disciplinary vision of the forenoon. The sinners were not set the second time for a gazing-stock. It was just usual afternoon kirk. The prayer was made, the psalm was sung, Mr. M'Nab preached a strong if wintry sermon. Jarvis Barrow, white-headed, strong-featured, intent, sat as in some tower over against Jerusalem, considering the foes that beset her. Beside him sat his daughter Jenny, in striped petticoat and plain overgown, blue kerchief, and hat of straw. Next to Jenny was Elspeth in a dim-green stuff, thin, besprent with small flowers, a fine white kerchief, and a wider straw hat. Robin Greenlaw sat beside Elspeth, and the laird by Greenlaw. Half the congregation thought with variations:

"Wha ever heard of the laird's not being in his ain place? He and White Farm and Littlefarm maun be well acquaint'! He's foreign, amaist, and gangs his ain gait!"

Glenfernie, who had broken the conventions, sat in a profound carelessness of that. The kirk was not gray to him to-day, though he had thought it so on other days, nor bare, nor chill. June was without, but June was more within. He also prayed, though his unuttered words ran in and out between the minister's uttered ones. Under the wintry sermon he built a dream and it glowed like jewels.

At the psalm, standing, he heard Elspeth's clear voice praising God, and his heart lifted on that beam of song until it was as though it came to Heaven.

"Lord, thou hast been our dwelling-place
In generations all.
Before thou ever hadst brought forth
The mountains great or small,
Ere ever thou hadst formed the earth
And all the world abroad,
Ev'n thou from everlasting art
To everlasting God."

"Love, love, love!" cried Glenfernie's heart. His nature did with might what its hand found to do, and now, having turned to love between man and woman, it loved with a huge, deep, pulsing, world-old strength. He heard Elspeth, he felt Elspeth only; he but wished to blend with her and go on with her forever from the heaven to heaven which, blended so, they would make.

"... As with an overflowing flood
Thou carriest them away;
They like a sleep are, like the grass
That grows at morn are they.
At morn it flourishes and grows,
Cut down at ev'n doth fade—"

"Not grass of the field, O Lord," cried Glenfernie's heart, "but the forest of oaks, but the stars that hold for aye, one to the other—"

CHAPTER XI

The glen was dressed in June, at its height of green movement and song. Alexander and Elspeth walked there and turned aside through a miniature pass down which flowed a stream in miniature to join the larger flood. This cleft led them to a green hollow masked by the main wall of the glen, a fairy place, hidden and lone. Seven times had the two been in company since that morning of the flower-sprinkled cape and the thorn-tree. First stood a chance meeting upon the moor, Elspeth walking from the village with a basket upon her arm and the laird riding home after business in the nearest considerable town. He dismounted; he walked beside her to the stepping-stones before the farm. The second time he went to White Farm, and she and Jenny, with Merran to help, were laying linen to bleach upon the sun-washed hillside. He had stayed an hour, and though he was not alone with her, yet he might look at her, listen to her. She was not a chatterer; she worked or stood, almost as silent as a master painter's subtle picture stepped out of its frame, or as Pygmalion's statue-maid, flushing with life, but as yet tongue-holden. Yet she said certain things, and they were to him all music and wit. The third time had been by the wishing-green. That was but for a moment, but he counted it great gain.

"Here," she said, "was where we danced! Mr. Ian Rullock

and you and Robin and the rest of us. Don't you remember? It was evening and there was a fleet of gold clouds in the sky. It is so near the house. I walk here when I have a glint of time."

The fourth time, riding Black Alan, he had stopped at the door and talked with Jarvis Barrow. He was thirsty and had asked for water, and Jenny had called, "Elspeth, bring the laird a cup frae the well!" She had brought it, and, taking it from her, all the romance of the world had seemed to him to close them round, to bear them to some great and fair and deep and passionate place. The fifth time had been the day when he went to kirk with White Farm and listened to her voice in the psalm. The sixth time had been again upon the moor. The seventh time was this. He had come down through the glen as he had done before. He had no reason to suppose that this day more than another he would find her, but there, half a mile from White Farm, he came upon her, standing, watching a lintwhite's nest. They walked together, and when that little, right-angled, infant fellow of the glen opened to them they turned and followed its bright rivulet to the green hidden hollow.

The earth lay warm and dry, clad with short turf. They sat down beneath an oak-tree. None would come this way; they had to themselves a bright span of time and place. Elspeth looked at him with brown, friendly eyes. Each time she met him her eyes grew more kind; more and more she liked the laird. Something fluttered in her nature; like a bird in a room with many windows and all but one closed, it turned now this way, now that, seeking the open lattice. There was the lovely world—which way to it? And the window that in a dream had seemed to her to open was mayhap closed, and another that she had not noted mayhap opening.... But Glenfernie, winged, was in that world, and now all that he desired was that the bright bird should fly to him there. But until to-day patience and caution and much humility had kept him from direct speech. He knew that she had not loved, as he had done, at once. He had set himself to win her to love him. But so great was his passion that now he thought:

"Surely not one, but two as one, make this terrible and happy furnace!" He thought, "I will speak now," and then delayed over the words.

"This is a bonny, wee place!" said Elspeth. "Did you never hear the old folks tell that your great-grandmother, that was among the persecuted, loved it? When your father was a laddie they often used to sit here, the two of them. They were great wanderers together."

"I never heard it," said Alexander. "Almost it seems too bright...."

They sat in silence, but the train of thought started went on with Glenfernie:

"But perhaps she never went so far as the Kelpie's Pool."

"The Kelpie's Pool!... I do not like that place! Tell me, Glenfernie, wonders of travel."

"What shall I tell you?"

"Tell me of the East. Tell me what like is the Sea of Galilee."

Glenfernie talked, since Elspeth bade him talk. He talked of what he had seen and known, and that brought him, with the aid of questions from the woman listening, to talk of himself. "I had a strange kind of youth.... So many dim, struggling longings, dreams, aspirings!—but I think they may be always there with youth."

"Yes, they are," said Elspeth.

"We talked of the Kelpie's Pool. Something like that was the strangeness with me. Black rifts and whirlpools and dead tarns within me, opening up now and again, lifted as by a trembling of the earth, coming up from the past! Angers and broodings, and things seen in flashes—then all gone as the lightning goes, and the mind does not hold what was shown.... I became a man and it ceased. Sometimes I know that in sleep or dream I have been beside a kelpie pool. But I think the better part of me has drained them where they lay under open sky." He laughed, put his hands over his face for a moment, then, dropping them, whistled to the blackbirds aloft in the oak-tree.

"And now?"

"Now there is clean fire in me!" He turned to her; he drew himself nearer over the sward. "Elspeth, Elspeth, Elspeth! do not tell me that you do not know that I love you!"

"Love me—love me?" answered Elspeth. She rose from her earthen chair; she moved as if to leave the place; then she stood still. "Perhaps a part of me knew and a part did not know.... I will try to be honest, for you are honest, Glenfernie! Yes, I knew, but I would not let myself perceive and think and say that I knew.... And now what will I say?"

"Say that you love me! Say that you love and will marry me!"

"I like you and I trust you, but I feel no more, Glenfernie, I feel no more!"

"It may grow, Elspeth—"

Elspeth moved to the stem of the oak beneath which they had been seated. She raised her arm and rested it against the bark, then laid her forehead upon the warm molded flesh in the blue print sleeve. For some moments she stayed so, with hidden face, unmoving against the bole of the tree, like a relief done of old by some wonderful artist. The laird of Glenfernie, watching her, felt, such was his passion, the whole of earth and sky, the whole of time, draw to just this point, hang on just her movement and her word.

"Elspeth!" he cried at last. "Elspeth!"

Elspeth turned, but she stood yet against the tree. Now both arms were lifted; she had for a moment the appearance of one who hung upon the tree. Her eyes were wet, tears were upon her cheek. She shook them off, then left the oak and came a step or two toward him. "There is something in my brain and heart that tells me what love is. When I love I shall love hard.... I have had fancies.... But, like yours, Glenfernie, their times are outgrown and gone by.... It's clear to try. I like you so much! but I do not love now—and I'll not wed and come to Glenfernie House until I do."

"'It's clear to try,' you said."

Elspeth looked at him long. "If it is there, even little and far away, I'll try to bend my steps the way shall bring it nearer. But, oh, Glenfernie, it may be that there is naught upon the road!"

"Will you journey to look for it? That's all I ask now. Will you journey to look for it?"

"Yes, I may promise that. And I do not know," said Elspeth, wonderingly, "what keeps me from thinking I'll meet it." She sat down among the oak roots. "Let us rest a bit, and say no word, and then go home."

The sunlight filled the hollow, the wimpling burn took the blue of the sky, the breeze whispered among the oak leaves. The two sat and gazed at the day, at the grass, at the little thorn-trees and hazels that ringed the place around. They sat very still, seeking composure. She gained it first.

"When will your sister be coming home?"

"It is not settled. Glenfernie House was sad of late years. She ought to have the life and brightness that she's getting now."

"And will you travel no more?"

He saw as in a lightning glare that she pictured no change for him beyond such as being laird would make. He was glad when the flash went and he could forget what it had of destructive and desolating. He would drag hope down from the sky above the sky of lightnings. He spoke.

"There were duties now to be taken up. I could not stay away all nor most nor much of the time. I saw that. But I could study here, and once in a while run somewhere over the earth.... But now I would stay in this dale till I die! Unless you were with me—the two of us going to see the sights of the earth, and then returning home—going and returning—going and returning—and both a great sweetness—"

"Oh!" breathed Elspeth. She put her hands again over her eyes, and she saw, unrolling, a great fair life *if—if—*She rose to her feet. "Let us go! It grows late. They'll miss me."

They came into the glen and so went down with the stream to the open land and to White Farm.

"Where hae you been?" asked Jenny. "Here was father hame frae the shearing with his eyes blurred, speiring for you to read to him!"

"I was walking by the glen and the laird came down through, so we made here together. Where is grandfather?"

"He wadna sit waiting. He's gane to walk on the muir. Will ye na bide, Glenfernie?"

But the laird would not stay. It was wearing toward sunset. Menie, withindoors, called Jenny. The latter turned away. Glenfernie spoke to Elspeth.

"If I find your grandfather on the moor I shall speak of this that is between us. Do not look so troubled! 'If' or 'if not' it is better to tell. So you will not be plagued. And, anyhow, it is the wise folks' road."

Back came Jenny. "Has he gane? I had for him a tass of wine and a bit of cake."

The moor lay like a stiffened billow of the sea, green with purple glints. The clear western sky was ruddy gold, the sun's great ball approaching the horizon. But when it dipped the short June night would know little dark in this northern land. The air struck most fresh and pure. Glenfernie came presently upon the old farmer, found him seated upon a bit of bank, his gray plaid about him, his crook-like stick planted before him, his eyes upon the western sea of glory. The younger man stopped beside him, settled down upon the bank, and gazed with the elder into the ocean of colored air.

"Ae gowden floor as though it were glass," said Jarvis Barrow. "Ae gowden floor and ae river named of Life, passing the greatness of Orinoco or Amazon. And the tree of life for the healing of the nations. And a' the trees that ever leafed or flowered, ta'en together, but ae withered twig to that!"

Glenfernie gazed with him. "I do not doubt that there will come a day when we'll walk over the plains of the sun—the flesh of our body then as gauze, moved at will where we please and swift as thought—inner and outer motion keeping time with the beat and rhythm of that *where we are*—"

"The young do not speak the auld tongue."

"Tongues alter with the rest."

Silence fell while the sun reddened, going nearer to the mountain brow. The young man and the old, the farmer and the laird, sat still. The air struck more freshly, stronger, coming from the sea. Far off a horn was blown, a dog barked.

"Will ye be hame now for gude, Glenfernie? Lairds should bide in their ain houses if the land is to have any gude of them."

"I wish to stay, White Farm, the greatest part of the year round. I want to speak to you very seriously. Think back a moment to my father and mother, and to my forebears farther back yet. As they had faults, and yet had a longing to do the right and struggled toward it over thick and thin, so I believe I may say of myself. That is, I struggle toward it," said Alexander, "though I'm not so sure of the thick and thin."

"Your mither wasna your father's kind. She had always her smile to the side and her japes, and she looked to the warld. Not that she didna mean to do weel in it! She did. But I couldna just see clear the seal in her forehead."

"That was because you did not look close enough," said Alexander. "It was there."

"I didna mind your uphawding your mither. Aweel, what did ye have to say?"

The laird turned full to him. "White Farm, you were once a young man. You loved and married. So do I love, so would I marry! The woman I love does not yet love me, but she has, I think, some liking.—I bide in hope. I would speak to you about it, as is right."

"Wha is she?"

"Your granddaughter Elspeth."

Silence, while the shadows of the trees in the vale below grew longer and longer. Then said White Farm:

"She isna what they call your equal in station. And she

has nae tocher or as good as nane."

"For the last I have enough for us both. For the first the springs of Barrow and Jardine, back in Time's mountains, are much the same. Scotland's not the country to bother overmuch if the one stream goes, in a certain place, through a good farm, and the other by a not over-rich laird's house."

"Are ye Whig and Kirk like your father?"

"I am Whig—until something more to the dawn than that comes up. For the Kirk ... I will tell truth and say that I have my inner differences. But they do not lean toward Pope or prelate.... I am Christian, where Christ is taken very universally—the higher Self, the mounting Wisdom of us all.... Some high things you and I may view differently, but I believe that there are high things."

"And seek them?"

"And seek them."

"You always had the air to me," vouchsafed White Farm, "of one wha hunted gowd elsewhaur than in the earthly mine." He looked at the red west, and drew his plaid about him, and took firmer clutch upon his staff. "But the lassie does not love you?"

"My trust is that she may come to do so."

The elder got to his feet. Alexander rose also.

"It's coming night! Ye will be gaeing on over the muir to the House?"

"Yes. Then, sir, I may come to White Farm, or meet her when I may, and have my chance?"

"Aye. If so be I hear nae great thing against ye. If so be ye're reasonable. If so be that in no way do ye try to hurt the lassie."

"I'll be reasonable," said the laird of Glenfernie. "And I'd not hurt Elspeth if I could!" His face shone, his voice was a deep and happy music. He was so bound, so at the feet of Elspeth, that he could not but believe in joy and fortune. The sun had dipped; the land lay dusk, but the sky was a rose. There was a skimming of swallows overhead, a singing of the wind in the ling. He walked with White Farm to the foot of the moor, then said good night and turned toward his own house.

CHAPTER XII

Two days later Alexander rode to Black Hill. There had been in the night a storm with thunder and lightning, wind and rain. Huge, ragged banks of clouds yet hung sullen in the air, though with lakes of blue between and shafts of sun. The road was wet and shone. Now Black Alan must pick his way, and now there held long stretches of easy going. The old laird's quarrel with Mr. Archibald Touris was not the young laird's. The old laird's liking for Mrs. Alison was strongly the young laird's. Glenfernie, in the months since his father's death, had ridden often enough to Black Hill. Now as he journeyed, together with the summer and melody of his thoughts Elspeth-toward, he was holding with himself a cogitation upon the subject of Ian and Ian's last letter. He rode easily a powerful steed, needing to be strong for so strongly built a horseman. His riding-dress was blue; he wore his own hair, unpowdered and gathered in a ribbon beneath a three-cornered hat. There was perplexity and trouble, too, in the Ian complex, but for all that he rode with the color and sparkle of happiness in his face. In his gray eyes light played to great depths.

Black Hill appeared before him, the dark pine and crag of the hill itself, and below that the house with its far-stretching, well-planted policy. He passed the gates, rode under the green elm boughs of the avenue, and was presently before the porch of the house. A man presented himself to take Black Alan.

"Aye, sir, there's company. Mr. Touris and Mrs. Alison are with them in the gardens."

Glenfernie went there, passing by a terrace walk around the house. Going under the windows of the room that was yet Ian's when he came home. Ian still in his mind, he recovered strongly the look of that room the day Ian had taken him there, in boyhood, when they first met. Out of that vividness started a nucleus more vivid yet—the picture in the book-closet of the city of refuge, and the silver goblet drawn from the hidden shelf of the aumry. The recaptured moment lost shape and color, returned to the infinite past. He turned the corner of the house and came into the gardens that Mr. Touris had had laid out after the French style.

Here by the fountain he discovered the retired merchant, and with him a guest, an old trade connection, now a power in the East India Company. The laird of Black Hill, a little more withered, a little more stooped than of old, but still fluent, caustic, and with now and then to the surface a vague, cold froth of insincerity, made up much to this magnate of commerce. He stood on his own heath, or by his own fountain, but his neck had in it a deferential crook. Lacs—rupees—factories—rajahs—ships—cottons —the words fell like the tinkle of a golden fountain. Listening to these two stood, with his hands behind his back, Mr. Wotherspoon, Black Hill's lawyer and man of business down from Edinburgh. At a little distance Mrs. Alison showed her roses to the wife of the East India man and to a kinsman, Mr. Munro Touris, from Inverness way.

Mr. Touris addressed himself with his careful smile to Alexander. "Good day, Glenfernie! This, Mr. Goodworth, is a good neighbor of mine, Mr. Jardine of Glenfernie. Alexander, Mr. Goodworth is art and part of the East India. You have met Mr. Wotherspoon before, I think? There are Alison and Mrs. Goodworth and Munro Touris by the roses."

Glenfernie went over to the roses. Mrs. Alison, smiling upon him, presented him to Mrs. Goodworth, a dark, bright, black-eyed, talkative lady. He and Munro Touris nodded to each other. The laird of Black Hill, the India merchant, and the lawyer now joined them, and all strolled together along the very wide and straight graveled path. The talk was chiefly upheld by Black Hill and the great trader, with the lawyer putting in now and again a shrewd word, and the trader's wife making aside to Mrs. Alison an embroidery of comment. There had now been left trade in excelsis and host and guests were upon the state of the country, an unpopular war, and fall of ministers. Came in phrases compounded to meet Jacobite complications and dangers. The Pretender—the Pretender and his son—French aid—French army that might be sent to Scotland—position of defense—rumors everywhere you go—disaffected and Stewart-mad—.Munro Touris had a biting word to say upon the Highland chiefs. The lawyer talked of certain Lowland lords and gentlemen. Mr. Touris vented a bitter gibe. He had a black look in his small, sunken eyes. Alexander, reading him, knew that he thought of Ian. In a moment the whole conversation had dragged that way. Mrs. Goodworth spoke with vivacity.

"Lord, sir! I hope that your nephew, now that he wears the King's coat, has left off talking as he did when he was a boy! He showed his Highland strain with a warrant! You would have thought that he had been *out* himself thirty years ago!"

Her husband checked her. "You have not seen him since he was sixteen. Boys like that have wild notions of romance and devotion. They change when they're older."

The lawyer took the word. "Captain Rullock doubtless buried all that years ago. His wearing the King's coat hauds for proof."

Munro Touris had been college-mate in Edinburgh. "He watered all that gunpowder in him years ago, did he not, Glenfernie?"

"'To water gunpowder—to shut off danger.' That's a good figure of yours, Munro!" said Alexander. Munro, who had been thought dull in the old days, flushed with pleasure.

They had come to a kind of summer-house overrun with roses. Mr. Archibald Touris stopped short and, with his back to this structure, faced the company with him, brought thus to a halt. He looked at them with a carefully composed countenance.

"I am sure, Munro, that Ian Rullock 'watered the gun-powder,' as you cleverly say. Boys, ma'am"—to Mrs. Goodworth—"are, as your husband remarks, romantic simpletons. No one takes them and their views of life seriously. Certainly not their political views! When they come men they laugh themselves. They are not boys then; they are men. Which is, as it were, the preface to what I might as well tell you. My nephew has resigned his captaincy and quitted the army. Apparently he has come to feel that soldiering is not, after all, the life he prefers. It may be that he will take to the law, or he may wander and then laird it when I am gone. Or if he is very wise—I meant to speak to you of this in private, Goodworth—he might be furnished with shares and ventures in the East India. He has great abilities."

"Well, India's the field!" said the London merchant, placidly. "If a man has the mind and the will he may make and keep and flourish and taste power—"

"Left the King's forces!" cried Munro Touris. "Why—! And will he be coming to Black Hill, sir?"

"Yes. Next week. We have," said Mr. Touris, and though he tried he could not keep the saturnine out of his voice— "we have some things to talk over."

As he spoke he moved from before the summer-house into a cross-path, and the others followed him and his Company magnate. The Edinburgh lawyer and Glenfernie found themselves together. The former lagged a step and held the younger man back with him; he dropped his voice

"I've not been three hours in the house. I've had no talk with Mr. Touris. What's all this about? I know that you and his nephew are as close as brothers—not that brothers are always close!"

"He writes only that he is tired of martial life. He has the soldier in him, but he has much besides. That 'much besides' often steps in to change a man's profession."

"Well, I hope you'll persuade him to see the old gunpowder very damp! I remember that, as a very young man, he talked imprudently. But he has been," said the lawyer, "far and wide since those days."

"Yes, far and wide."

Mr. Wotherspoon with a long forefinger turned a crimson rose seen in profile full toward him. "I met him—once—when I was in London a year ago. I had not seen him for years." He let the rose swing back. "He has a magnificence! Do you know I study a good deal? They say that so do you. I have an inclination toward fifteenth-century Italian. I should place him there." He spoke absently, still staring at the rose. "A dash—not an ill dash, of course—of what you might call the Borgia ... good and evil tied into a sultry, thunderous splendor."

Glenfernie bent a keen look upon him out of gray eyes. "An enemy might describe him so, perhaps. I can see that such a one might do so."

"Ah, you're his friend!"

"Yes."

"Well," said Mr. Wotherspoon, straightening himself from the contemplation of the roses, "there's no greater thing than to have a steadfast friend!"

It seemed that an expedition had been planned, for a servant now appeared to say that coach and horses were at the door. Mr. Touris explained:

"I've engaged to show Mr. and Mrs. Goodworth our considerable town. Mr. Wotherspoon, too, has a moment's business there. Alison will not come, but Munro Touris rides along. Will you come, too, Glenfernie? We'll have a bit of dinner at the 'Glorious Occasion.'"

"No, thank you. I have to get home presently. But I'll stay a little and talk to Mrs. Alison, if I may."

"Ah, you may!" said Mrs. Alison.

From the porch they watched the coach and four away, with Munro Touris following on a strong and ugly bay mare. The elm boughs of the avenue hid the whole. The cloud continents and islands were dissolving into the air ocean, the sun lay in strong beams, the water drops were drying from leaf and blade. Mrs. Alison and Alexander moved through the great hall and down a corridor to a little parlor that was hers alone. They entered it. It gave, through an open door and two windows set wide, upon a small, choice garden and one wide-spreading, noble, ancient tree. Glenfernie entered as one who knew the place, but upon whom, at every coming, it struck with freshness and liking. The room itself was most simple.

"I like," said Alexander, "our spare, clean, precise Scotch parlors. But this is to me like a fine, small prioress's room in a convent of learned saints!"

His old friend laughed. "Very little learned, very little saintly, not at all prior! Let us sit in the doorway, smell the lavender, and hear the linnets in the tree."

She took the chair he pushed forward. He sat upon the door-step at her feet.

"Concerning Ian," she said. "What do you make out of it all?"

"I make out that I hope he'll not involve himself in some French and Tory mad attempt!"

"What do his letters say?"

"They speak by indirection. Moreover, they're at present few and short.... We shall see when he comes!"

"Do you think that he will tell you all?"

Alexander's gray eyes glanced at her as earlier they had glanced at Mr. Wotherspoon. "I do not think that we keep much from each other!... No, of course you are right! If there is anything that in honor he cannot tell, or that I— with my pledges, such as they are, in another urn—may not hear, we shall find silences. I pin my trust to there being nothing, after all!"

"The old wreath withered, and a new one better woven and more evergreen—"

"I do not know.... I said just now that Ian and I kept little from each other. In an exceeding great measure that is true. But there are huge lands in every nature where even the oldest, closest, sworn friend does not walk. It must be so. Friendship is not falsified nor betrayed by its being so."

"Not at all!" said Mrs. Alison. "True friend or lover loves that sense of the unplumbed, of the infinite, in the cared-for one. To do else would be to deny the unplumbed, the infinite, in himself, and so the matching, the equaling, the *oneing* of love!" She leaned forward in her chair; she regarded the small, fragrant garden where every sweet and olden flower seemed to bloom. "Now let us leave Ian, and old, stanch, trusted, and trusting friendship. It is part of oneness—it will be cared for!" She turned her bright, calm gaze upon him. "What other realm have you come into, Alexander? It was plain the last time that you were here, but I did not speak of it—it is plain to-day!" She laughed. She had a silver, sweet, and merry laugh. "My dear, there is a bloom and joy, a *vivification* about you that may be felt ten feet away!" She looked at him with affection and now seriously. "I know, I think, the look of one who comes into spiritual treasures. This is that and not that. It is the wilderness of lovely flowers—hardly quite the music of the spheres! It is not the mountain height, but the waving, leafy, lower slopes—and yet we pass on to the height by those slopes! Are you in love, Alexander?"

"You guess so much!" he said. "You have guessed that, too. I do not care! I am glad that the sun shines through me."

"You must be happy in your love! Who is she?"

"Elspeth Barrow, the granddaughter of Jarvis Barrow of White Farm.... You say that I must be happy in my love. The Lord of Heaven knows that I am! and yet she is not yet sure that she loves me in her turn. One might say that I had great uncertainty of bliss. But I love so strongly that I have no strength of disbelief in me!"

"Elspeth Barrow!"

"My old friend—the unworldliest, the better-worldliest soul I know—do not you join in that hue and cry about world's gear and position! To be Barrow is as good as to be Jardine. Elspeth is Elspeth."

"Oh, I know why I made exclamation! Just the old, dull earthy surprise! Wait for me a moment, Alexander." She put her hands before her eyes, then, dropping them, sat with her gaze upon the great tree shot through with light from the clearing sky. "I see her now. At first I could not disentangle her and Gilian, for they were always together.

I have not seen them often—just three or four times to remember, perhaps. But in April I chanced for some reason to go to White Farm.... I see her now! Yes, she has beauty, though it would not strike many with the edge of the sword.... Yes, I see—about the mouth and the eyes and the set of the head. It's subtle—it's like some pictures I remember in Italy. And intelligence is there. Enchantment ... the more real, perhaps, for not being the most obvious.... So you are enchained, witched, held by the great sorceress!... Elspeth is only one of her little names— her great name is just love—love between man and woman.... Oh yes, the whole of the sweetness is distilled into one honey-drop—the whole giant thing is shortened into one image—the whole heaven and earth slip silkenly into one banner, and you would die for it! You see, my dear," said Mrs. Alison, who had never married, "I loved one who died. I know."

Glenfernie took her hand and kissed it. "Nothing is loss to you—nothing! For me, I am more darkly made. So I hope to God I'll not lose Elspeth!"

Her tears, that were hardly of grief, dropped upon his bent head. "Eh, my laddie! the old love is there in the midst of the wide love. But the larger controls.... Well, enough of that! And do you mean that you have asked Elspeth to marry you—and that she does not know her own heart?"

They talked, sitting before the fragrant garden, in the little room that was tranquil, blissful, and recluse. At last he rose.

"I must go."

They went out through the garden to the wicket that

parted her demesne from the formal, wide pleasure-sweeps. He stopped for a moment under the great tree.

"In a fortnight or so I must go to Edinburgh to see Renwick about that land. And it is in my mind to travel from there to London for a few weeks. There are two or three persons whom I know who could put a stout shoulder to the wheel of Jamie's prospects. Word of mouth is better with them than would be letters. Jamie is at Windsor. I could take him with me here or there—give him, doubtless, a little help."

"You are a world-man," said his friend, "which is quite different from a worldly man! Come or go as you will, still all is your garden that you cultivate.... Now you are thinking again of Elspeth!"

"Perhaps if for a month or two I plague her not, then when I come again she may have a greater knowledge of herself. Perhaps it is more generous to be absent for a time—"

"I see that you will not doubt—that you cannot doubt—that in the end she loves you!"

"Is it arrogance, self-love, and ignorance if I think that? Or is it knowledge? I think it, and I cannot and will not else!"

They came to the wicket, and stood there a moment ere going on by the terrace to the front of the house. The day was now clear and vivid, soft and bright. The birds sang in a long ecstasy, the flowers bloomed as though all life must be put into June, the droning bees went about with the steadiest preoccupation. Alexander looked about him.

"The earth is drunk with sweetness, and I see now how great joy is sib to great pain!" He shook himself. "Come back to earth and daylight, Alexander Jardine!" He put a hand, large, strong, and shapely, over Mrs. Alison's slender ivory one. "She, too, has long fingers, though her hand is brown. But it is an artist hand—a picture hand—a thoughtful hand."

Mrs. Alison laughed, but her eyes were tender over him. "Oh, man! what a great forest—what an ever-rising song—is this same thing you're feeling! And so old—and so fire-new!" They walked along the terrace to the porch. "They're bringing you Black Alan to ride away upon. But you'll come again as soon as Ian's here?"

"Yes, of course. You may be assured that if he is free of that Stewart coil—or if he is in it only so deep that he may yet free himself—I shall say all that I can to keep him free or to urge him forth. Not for much would I see Ian take ship in that attempt!"

"No!... I have been reading the Book of Daniel. Do you know what Ian is like to me? He is like some great lord—a prince or governor—in the court maybe of Belshazzar, or Darius the Mede, or Cyrus the Persian—in that hot and stately land of golden images and old rivers and the sound of the cornet, flute, harp, sackbut, psaltery, and dulcimer and all kinds of music. He must serve his tyrant—and yet Daniel, kneeling in his house, in his chamber, with the windows open toward Jerusalem, might hear a cry to hold his name in his prayers.... What strange thoughts we have of ourselves, and of those nearest and dearest!"

"Mr. Wotherspoon says that he is fifteenth-century Italian. You have both done a proper bit of characterization! But I," said Alexander, "I know another great territory of Ian."

"I know that, Glenfernie! And so do I know other good realms of Ian. Yet that was what I thought when I read Daniel. And I had the thought, too, that those old people were capable of great friendships."

Black Alan was waiting. Glenfernie mounted, said good-by again; the green boughs of the elm-trees took him and his steed.

CHAPTER XIII

Ian forestalled Alexander, riding to Glenfernie House the morning after his arrival at Black Hill. "Let us go," he said, "where we can talk at ease! The old, alchemical room?"

They crossed the grass-grown court to the keep, entered and went up the broken stair to the stone-walled chamber that took up the second floor, that looked out of loophole windows north, south, east, and west. The day was high summer, bright and hot. Strong light and less strong light came in beams from the four quarters and made in the large place a conflict of light and shadow. The fireplace was great enough for Gog and Magog to have warmed themselves thereby. Around, in an orderly litter, yet stood on table or bench or shelf many of the matters that Alexander had gathered there in his boyhood. In one corner was the furnace that when he was sixteen his father had let him build. More recent was the oaken table in the middle of the room, two deep chairs, and shelves with many books. After the warmth of the sun the place presented a grave, cool, brown harbor.

The two, entering, had each an arm over the other's shoulder. Where they were known their friendship was famed. Youth and manhood, they had been together when it was possible. When it was not so the thought of each outtraveled separation. Their differences, their varied colors of being, seemed but to bind them closer. They entered this room like David and Jonathan.

Ian also was tall, but not so largely made as was the other. Lithe, embrowned, with gold-bronze hair and eyes, knit of a piece, moving as by one undulation, there was something in him not like the Scot, something foreign, exotic. Sometimes Alexander called him "Saracen"—a finding of the imagination that dated from old days upon the moor above the Kelpie's Pool when they read together the *Faery Queen*. The other day, at Black Hill, this ancient fancy had played through Alexander's mind while Mr. Wotherspoon talked of Italy, and Mrs. Alison of Babylonish lords.... The point was that he relished Paynim knight and Renaissance noble and prince of Babylon. Let Ian seem or be all that, and richer yet! Still there would be Ian, outside of all circles drawn.

In the room that he called the "alchemical," Ian, disengaging himself, turned and put both hands on Alexander's shoulders. "Thou Old Steadfast!" he cried. "God knows how glad I am to see thee!"

Alexander laughed. "Not more glad than I am at the sight of you! What's the tidings?"

"What should they be? I am tired of being King George's soldier!"

"So that you are tired of being any little king of this earth's soldier!"

"Why, I think I am—"

"Kings 'over the water' included, Ian?"

"Kings without kingdoms? Well," said Ian, "they don't amount to much, do they?"

"They do not." The two moved together to the table and the chairs by it. "You are free of them, Ian?"

"What is it to be free of them?"

"Well, to be plain, out of the Stewart cark and moil! Pretender, Chevalier de St. George, or uncrowned king— let it drift away like the dead leaf it is!"

"A dead leaf. Is it a dead leaf?... I wonder!... But you are usually right, old Steadfast!"

"I see that you will not tell me plainly."

"Are you so anxious? There is nothing to be anxious about."

"Nothing.... What is 'nothing'?"

Ian drummed upon the table and whistled "Lillibullero." "Something—nothing. Nothing—something! Old Stead-fast, you are a sight for sair een! They say you make the best of lairds! Every cotter sings of just ways!"

"My father was a good laird. I would not shatter the tradition. Come with me to Edinburgh and London, on that journey I wrote you of!"

"No. I want to sink into the summer green and not raise my head from some old poetry book! I have been marching and countermarching until I am tired. As for what you have in your mind, don't fash yourself about it! I will say that, at the moment, I think it *is* a dead leaf.... Of course, should the Pope's staff unexpectedly begin to bud and flower—! But it mayn't—indeed, it only looks at present smooth and polished and dead.... I left the army because, naturally, I didn't want to be there in case—just in case—the staff budded. Heigho! It is the truth. You need not look troubled," said Ian.

His friend must rest with that. He did so, and put that matter aside. At any rate, things stood there better than he had feared. "I shall be gone a month or two. But you'll still be here when I come home?"

"As far as I know I'll be here through the summer. I have no plans.... If the leaf remains dry and dead, what should you say to taking ship at Leith in September for Holland? Amsterdam—then Antwerp—then the Rhine. We might see the great Frederick—push farther and look at the Queen of Hungary."

"No, I may not. I look to be a home-staying laird."

They sat with the table between them, and the light from the four sides of the room rippled and crossed over them. Books were on the table, folios and volumes in less.

"The home-staying laird—the full scholar—at last the writer—the master ... it is a good fortune!"

As Ian spoke he stretched his arms, he leaned back in his chair and regarded the room, the fireplace, the little furnace, and the shelves ranged with the quaint, makeshift apparatuses of boyhood. He looked at the green boughs without the loophole windows and at the crossing lights and shadows, and the brown books upon the brown table, and at last, under somewhat lowered lids, at Alexander. What moved in the bottom of his mind it would be hard to say. He thought that he loved the man sitting over against him, and so, surely, to some great amount he did. But somewhere, in the thousand valleys behind them, he had stayed in an inn of malice and had carried hence poison in a vial as small as a single cell. What suddenly made that past to burn and set it in the present it were hard to say. A spark perhaps of envy or of jealousy, or a movement of contempt for Alexander's "fortune." But he looked at his friend with half-closed eyes, and under the sea of consciousness crawled, half-blind, half-asleep, a willingness for Glenfernie to find some thorn in life. The wish did not come to consciousness. It was far down. He thought of himself as steel true to Alexander. And in a moment the old love drew again. He put out his hands across the board. "When are we going to see Mother Binning and to light the fire in the cave?... There are not many like you, Alexander! I'm glad to get back."

"I'm glad to have you back, old sworn-fellow, old Saracen!"

They clasped hands. Gray eyes and brown eyes with gold flecks met in a gaze that was as steady with the one as with the other. It was Alexander who first loosened handclasp.

They talked of affairs, particular and general, of Ian's late proceedings and the lairdship of Alexander, of men and places that they knew away from this countryside. Ian watched the other as they talked. Whatever there was that had moved, down there in the abyss, was asleep again.

"Old Steadfast, you are ruddy and joyous! How long since I was here, in the winter? Four months? Well, you've changed. What is it?... Is it love? Are you in love?"

"If I am—" Glenfernie rose and paced the room. Coming to one of the narrow windows, he stood and looked out and down upon bank and brae and wood and field and moor. He returned to the table. "I'll tell you about it."

He told. Ian sat and listened. The light played about him, shook gold dots and lines over his green coat, over his hands, his faintly smiling face, his head held straight and high. He was so well to look at, so "magnificent"! Alexander spoke with the eloquence of a possessing passion, and Ian listened and felt himself to be the sympathizing friend. Even the profound, unreasonable, unhumorous idealism of old Steadfast had its quaint, Utopian appeal. He was going to marry the farmer's granddaughter, though he might, undoubtedly, marry better.... Ian listened, questioned, summed up:

"I have always been the worldly-wise one! Is there any use in my talking now of worldly wisdom?"

"No use at all."

"Then I won't!... Old Alexander the Great, are you happy?"

"If she gives me her love."

Ian dismissed that with a wave of his hand. "Oh, I think she'll give it, dear simpleton!" He looked at Glenfernie now with genial affection. "Well, on the whole, and balancing one thing against another, I think that I want you to be happy!"

Alexander laughed at that minification. "And my

happiness is big enough—or if I get it it will be big enough—not in the least to disturb our friendship country, Ian!"

"I'll believe that, too. Our relations are old and rooted."

"Old and rooted."

"So I wish you joy.... And I remember when you thought you would not marry!"

"Oh—memories! I'm sweeping them away! I'm beginning again!... I hold fast the memory of friendship. I hold fast the memory that somehow, in this form or that, I must have loved her from the beginning of things!" He rose and moved about the room. Going to the fireplace, he leaned his forehead against the stone and looked down at the laid, not kindled, wood. He turned and came back to Ian. "The world seems to me all good."

Ian laughed at him, half in raillery, but half in a flood of kindness. If what had stirred had been ancient betrayal, alive and vital one knew not when, now again it was dead, dead. He rose, he put his arm again about Alexander's shoulder. "Glenfernie! Glenfernie! you're in deep! Well, I hope the world will stay heaven, e'en for your sake!"

They left the old room with its hauntings of a boy's search for gold, with, back of that, who might know what hauntings of ancient times and fortress doings, violences and agonies, subduings, revivings, cark and care and light struggling through, dark nights and waited-for dawns! They went down the stair and out of the keep. Late June flamed around them.

Ian stayed another hour or two ere he rode back to Black

Hill. With Glenfernie he went over Glenfernie House, the known, familiar rooms. They went to the school-room together and out through the breach in the old castle wall, and sat among the pine roots, and looked down through leafy tree-tops to the glint of water. When, in the sun-washed house and narrow garden and grassy court, they came upon men and women they stopped and spoke, and all was friendly and merry as it should be in a land of good folk. Ian had his crack with Davie, with Eppie and Phemie and old Lauchlinson and others. They sat for a few minutes with Mrs. Grizel where, in a most house-wifely corner, she measured currants and bargained with pickers of cherries. Strickland they came upon in the book-room. With the Jardines and this gentleman the sense of employed and employee had long ago passed into a larger inclusion. He and the young laird talked and worked together as members of one family. Now there was some converse among the three, and then the two left Strickland in the cool, dusky room. Outside the house June flamed again. For a while they paced up and down under the trees in the narrow garden atop the craggy height. Then Ian mounted Fatima, who all these years was kept for him at Black Hill.

"You'll come over to-morrow?"

"Yes."

Glenfernie watched him down the steep-descending, winding road, and thought of many roads that, good company, he and Ian had traveled together.

This was the middle of the day. In the afternoon he walked to White Farm.... It was sunset when he turned his face homeward. He looked back and saw Elspeth at the stepping-stones, in a clear flame of golden sky and golden water. She had seemed kind; he walked on air, his hand in Hope's. Hope had well-nigh the look of Assurance. He was going away because it was promised and arranged for and he must go. But he was coming again—he was coming again.

A golden moon rose through the clear east. He was in no hurry to reach Glenfernie House. The aching, panting bliss that he felt, the energy compressed, held back, straining at the leash, wanted night and isolation. So it could better dream of day and the clasp of that other that with him would make one. Now he walked and now stood, his eyes upon the mounting orb or the greater stars that it could not dim, and now he stretched himself in the summer heath. At last, not far from midnight, he came to that face of Glenfernie Hill below the old wall, to the home stream and the bit of thick wood where once, in boyhood, he had lain with covered face under the trees and little by little had put from his mind "The Cranes of Ibycus." The moonlight was all broken here. Shafts of black and white lay inextricably crossed and mingled. Alexander passed through the little wood and climbed, with the secure step of old habit, the steep, rough path to the pine without the wall, there stooped and came through the broken wall to the moon-silvered court, and so to the door left open for him.

CHAPTER XIV

The laird of Glenfernie was away to Edinburgh on Black Alan, Tam Dickson with him on Whitefoot. Ian Rullock riding Fatima, behind him a Black Hill groom on an iron-gray, came over the moor to the head of the glen. Ian checked the mare. Behind him rolled the moor, with the hollow where lay, water in a deep jade cup, the Kelpie's Pool. Before him struck down the green feathered cleft, opening out at last into the vale. He could see the water there, and a silver gleam that was White Farm. He sat for a minute, pondering whether he should ride back the way he had come or, giving Fatima to Peter Lindsay, walk through the glen. He looked at his watch, looked, too, at a heap of clouds along the western horizon. The gleam in the vale at last decided him. He left the saddle.

"Take Fatima around to White Farm, Lindsay. I'll walk through the glen." His thought was, "I might as well see what like is Alexander's inamorata!" It was true that he had seen her quite long ago, but time had overlaid the image, or perhaps he had never paid especial note.

Peter Lindsay stooped to catch the reins that the other tossed him. "There's weather in thae clouds, sir!"

"Not before night, I think. They're moving very slowly."

Lindsay turned with the horses. Ian, light of step, resilient, "magnificent," turned from the purple moor into the shade of birches. A few moments and he was near the cot of Mother Binning. A cock crowed, a feather of blue smoke went up from her peat fire.

He came to her door, meaning to stay but for a good-natured five minutes of gossip. She had lived here forever, set in the picture with ash-tree and boulder. But when he came to the door he found sitting with her, in the checkered space behind the opening, Glenfernie's inamorata.

Now he remembered her.... He wondered if he had truly ever forgotten her.

When he had received his welcome he sat down upon the door-step. He could have touched Elspeth's skirt. When she lowered her eyes they rested upon his gold-brown head, upon his hand in a little pool of light.

"Eh, laddie!" said Mother Binning, "but ye grow mair braw each time ye come!"

Elspeth thought him braw. The wishing-green where they danced, hand in hand!... Now she knew—now she knew —why her heart had lain so cold and still—for months, for years, cold and still! That was what hearts did until the sun came.... Definitely, in this hour, for her now, upon this stretch of the mortal path, Ian became the sun.

Ian sat daffing, talking. The old woman listened, her wheel idle; the young woman listened. The young woman, sitting half in shadow, half in light, put up her hand and drew farther over her face the brim of her wide hat of country weave. She wished to hide her eyes, her lips. She sat there pale, and through her ran in fine, innumerable waves human passion and longing, wild courage and trembling humility.

The sunlight that flooded the door-stone and patched the cottage floor began to lessen and withdraw. Low and distant there sounded a roll of thunder. Jock Binning came upon his crutches from the bench by the stream where he made a fishing-net.

"A tempest's daundering up!"

Elspeth rose. "I must go home—I must get home before it comes!"

"If ye'll bide, lassie, it may go by."

"No, I cannot." She had brought to Mother Binning a basket heaped with bloomy plums. She took it up and set it on the table. "I'll get the basket when next I come. Now I must go! Hark, there's the thunder again!"

Ian had risen also. "I will go with you. Yes! It was my purpose to walk through to White Farm. I sent Fatima around with Peter Lindsay."

As they passed the ash-tree there was lightning, but yet the heavens showed great lakes of blue, and a broken sunlight lay upon the path.

"There's time enough! We need not go too fast. The path is rough for that."

They walked in silence, now side by side, now, where the way was narrow, one before the other. The blue clouded over, there sprang a wind. The trees bent and shook, the deep glen grew gray and dark. That wind died and there was a breathless stillness, heated and heavy. Each heard the other's breathing as they walked.

"Let us go more quickly! We have a long way."

"Will you go back to Mother Binning's?"

"That, too, is far."

They had passed the cave a little way and were in mid-glen. It was dusk in this narrow pass. The trees hung, shadows in a brooding twilight; between the close-set pillars of the hills the sky showed slate-hued, with pallid feathers of cloud driven across. Lightning tore it, the thunder was loud, the trees upon the hilltops began to move. Some raindrops fell, large, slow, and warm. The lightning ran again, blindingly bright; the ensuing thunderclap seemed to shake the rock. As it died, the cataract sound of the wind was heard among the ranked trees. The drops came faster, came fast.

"It's no use!" cried Ian. "You'll be drenched and blinded! There's danger, too, in these tall trees. Come back to the cave and take shelter!"

He turned. She followed him, breathless, liking the storm—so that no bolt struck him. In every nerve, in every vein, she felt life rouse itself. It was like day to old night, summer to one born in winter, a passion of revival where she had not known that there was anything to revive. The past was as it were not, the future was as it were not; all things poured into a tremendous present. It was proper that there should be storm without, if within was to be this enormous, aching, happy tumult that was pain indeed, but pain that one would not spare!

Ian parted the swinging briers. They entered the cavern. If it was dim outside in the glen, it was dimmer here. Then the lightning flashed and all was lit. It vanished, the light from the air in conflict with itself. All was dark—then the flash again! The rain now fell in a torrent.

"At least it is dry here! There is wood, but I have no way to make fire."

"I am not cold."

"Sit here, upon this ledge. Alexander and I cleared it and widened it."

She sat down. When he spoke of Alexander she thought of Alexander, without unkindness, without comparing, without compunction, a thought colorless and simple, as of one whom she had known and liked a long time ago. Indeed, it might be said that she had little here with which to reproach herself. She had been honest—had not said "Take!" where she could not fulfil.... And now the laird of Glenfernie was like a form met long ago—long ago! It seemed so long and far away that she could not even think of him as suffering. As she might leave a fugitive memory, so she turned her mind from him.

Ian thought of Alexander ... but he looked, by the lightning's lamp, at the woman opposite.

She was not the first that he had desired, but he desired now with unwonted strength. He did not know why—he did not analyze himself nor the situation—but all the others seemed gathered up in her. She was fair to him, desirable!... He thirsted, quite with the mortal honesty of an Arab, day and night and day again without drink in the desert, and the oasis palms seen at last on the horizon. In his self-direction thitherward he was as candid, one-pointed, and ruthless as the Arab might be. He had no deliberate thought of harm to the woman before him—as little as the Arab would have of hurting the well whose cool wave seemed to like the lip touch. Perhaps he as little stopped to reason as would have done the Arab. Perhaps he had no thought of deeply injuring a friend. If there were two desert-traversers, or more than two, making for the well, friendship would not hold one back, push another forward. Race!—and if the well was but to one, then let fate and Allah approve the swiftest! Under such circumstances would not Alexander outdo him if he might? He was willing to believe so. Glenfernie said himself that the girl did not know if she cared for him. If, then, the well was not for him, anyway?... *Where was the wrong?* Now Ian believed in his own power and easy might and pleasantness and, on the whole, goodness—believed, too, in the love of Alexander for him, love that he had tried before, and it held. *And if he made love to Elspeth Barrow need old Steadfast ever know it?* And, finally, and perhaps, unacknowledged to himself, from the first, he turned to that cabinet of his heart where was the vial made of pride, that held the drop of malice. The storm continued. They looked through the portcullis made by the briers upon a world of rain. The lightning flashed, the thunder rolled; in here was the castle hold, dim and safe. They were as alone as in a fairy-tale, as alone as though around the cave beat an ocean that boat had never crossed.

They sat near each other; once or twice Ian, rising, moved to and fro in the cave, or at the opening looked into the turmoil without. When he did this her eyes followed him. Each, in every fiber, had consciousness of the other. They were as conscious of each other as lion and lioness in a desert cave.

They talked, but they did not talk much. What they said was trite enough. Underneath was the potent language, wave meeting wave with shock and thrill and exultation. These would not come, here and now, to outer utterance. But sooner or later they would come. Each knew that—though not always does one acknowledge what is known.

When they spoke it was chiefly of weather and of country people....

The lightning blazed less frequently, thunder subdued itself. For a time the rain fell thick and leaden, but after an hour it thinned and grew silver. Presently it wholly stopped.

"This storm is over," said Ian.

Elspeth rose from the ledge of stone. He drew aside the dripping curtain of leaf and stem, and she stepped forth from the cave, and he followed. The clouds were breaking, the birds were singing. The day of creation could not have seen the glen more lucent and fragrant. When, soon, they came to its lower reaches, with White Farm before them, they saw overhead a rainbow.

*　*　*　*　*

The day of the storm and the cave was over, but with no outward word their inner selves had covenanted to meet again. They met in the leafy glen. It was easy for her to find an errand to Mother Binning's, or, even, in the long summer afternoons, to wander forth from White Farm unquestioned. As for him, he came over the moor, avoided the cot at the glen head, and plunged down the steep hillside below. Once they met Jock Binning in the glen. After that they chose for their trysting-place that green hidden arm that once she and the laird of Glenfernie had entered.

Elspeth did not think in those days; she loved. She moved as one who is moved; she was drawn as by the cords of the sun. The Ancient One, the Sphinx, had her fast. The reflection of a greater thing claimed her and taught her, held her like a bayadere in a temple court.

As for Ian, he also held that he loved. He was the Arab bound for the well for which he thirsted, single-minded as to that, and without much present consciousness of tarnish or sin.... But what might arise in his mind when his thirst was quenched? Ian did not care, in these blissful days, to think of that.

He had come on the day of the storm, the cave, and the rainbow to a fatal place in his very long life. He was upon very still, deep water, glasslike, with only vague threads and tremors to show what might issue in resistless currents. He had been in such a place, in his planetary life, over and over and over again. This concatenation had formed it, or that concatenation; the surrounding phenomena varied, but essentially it was always the same, like a dream place. The question was, would he turn his boat, or raft, or whatever was beneath him, or his own stroke as swimmer, and escape from this glassy place whose currents were yet but tendrils? He could do it; it was the Valley of Decision.... But so often, in all those lives whose bitter and sweet were distilled into this one, he had not done it. It had grown much easier not to do it. Sometimes it had been illusory love, sometimes ambition, sometimes towering pride and self-seeking, sometimes mere indolent unreadiness, dreamy self-will. On he had gone out of the lower end of the Valley of Decision,

where the tendrils became arms of giants and decisions
might no longer be made.

CHAPTER XV

The laird of Glenfernie stayed longer from home than, riding away, he had expected to do. It was the latter half of August when he and Black Alan, Tam Dickson and Whitefoot, came up the winding road to Glenfernie door. Phemie it was, at the clothes-lines, who noted them on the lowest spiral, who turned and ran and informed the household. "The laird's coming! The laird's coming!" Men and women and dogs began to stir.

Strickland, looking from the window of his own high room, saw the riders in and out of the bronzing woods. Descending, he joined Mrs. Grizel upon the wide stone step without the hall door. Davie was in waiting, and a stable-boy or two came at a run.

"Two months!" said Mrs. Grizel. "But it used to be six months, a year, two years, and more! He grows a home body, as lairds ought to be!"

Alexander dismounted at the door, took her in his arms and kissed her twice, shook hands with Strickland, greeted Davie and the men. "How good it is to get home! I've pined like a lost bairn. And none of you look older— Aunt Grizel hasn't a single white hair!"

"Go along with you, laddie!" said Aunt Grizel. "You haven't been so long away!"

The sun was half-way down the western quarter. He changed his riding-clothes, and they set food for him in the hall. He ate, and Davie drew the cloth and brought wine and glasses. Some matter or other called Mrs. Grizel away, but Strickland stayed and drank wine with him.

Questions and answers had been exchanged. Glenfernie gave in detail reasons for his lengthened stay. There had been a business postponement and complication—in London Jamie's affairs; again, in Edinburgh, insistence of kindred with whom Alice was blooming, "growing a fine lady, too!" and at the last a sudden and for a while dangerous sickness of Tam Dickson's that had kept them a week at an inn a dozen miles this side of Edinburgh.

"Each time I started up sprang a stout hedge! But they're all down now and here I am!" He raised his wine-glass. "To home, and the sweetness thereof!" said Alexander.

"I am glad to see you back," said Strickland, and meant it.

The late sunlight streamed through the open door. Bran, the old hound, basked in it; it wiped the rust from the ancient weapons on the wall and wrote hieroglyphics in among them; it made glow the wine in the glass. Alexander turned in his chair.

"It's near sunset.... Now what, just, did you hear about Ian Rullock's going?"

"We supposed that he would be here through the autumn—certainly until after your return. Then, three days ago, comes Peter Lindsay with the note for you, and word that he was gone. Lindsay thought that he had received letters from great people and had gone to them for a visit."

Alexander spread the missive that had been given him upon the table. "It's short!" He held it so that Strickland might read:

GLENFERNIE,—Perhaps the leaf is not yet wholly sere. Be that as it may be, I'm leaving Black Hill for a time.

IAN RULLOCK.

"That's a puzzling billet!" said Alexander. "'*Glenfernie— Ian Rullock!*'"

"What does he mean by the leaf not dead?"

"That was a figure of speech used between us in regard to a certain thing.... Well, he also has moods! It is my trust that he has not answered to some one's piping that the leaf's not dead! That is the likeliest thing—that he answered and has gone. I'll ride to Black Hill to-morrow." The sun set, twilight passed, candles were lighted. "Have you seen any from White Farm?"

"I walked there from Littlefarm with Robin Greenlaw. Jarvis Barrow was reading Leviticus, looking like a listener in the Plain of Sinai. They expected Gilian home from Aberdeen. They say the harvest everywhere is good."

Alexander asked no further and presently they parted for the night. The laird of Glenfernie looked from his chamber window, and he looked toward White Farm. It was dark, clear night, and all the autumn stars shone like worlds of hope.

The next morning he mounted his horse and went off to Black Hill. He would get this matter of Ian straight. It was early when he rode, and he came to Black Hill to find Mr. Touris and his sister yet at the breakfast-table. Mrs. Alison, who might have been up hours, sat over against a dour-looking master of the house who sipped his tea and crumbled his toast and had few good words for anything. But he was glad and said that he was glad to see Glenfernie.

"Now, maybe, we'll have some light on Ian's doings!"

"I came for light to you, sir."

"Do you mean that he hasn't written you?"

"Only a line that I found waiting for me. It says, simply, that he leaves Black Hill for a while."

"Well, you won't get light from me! My light's darkness. The women found in his room a memorandum of ships and two addresses, one a house in Amsterdam, and one, if you please, in Paris—*Faubourg Saint-Germain!*"

"Do you mean that he left without explanation or good-by?"

Mrs. Alison spoke. "No, Archibald does not mean that. One evening Ian outdid himself in bonniness and golden talk. Then as we took our candles he told us that the wander-fever had him and that he would be riding to Edinburgh. Archibald protested, but he daffed it by. So the next day he went, and he may be in Edinburgh. It would seem nothing, if these Highland chiefs were not his kin and if there wasn't this round and round rumor of the Pretender and the French army! There may be nothing— he may be riding back almost to-morrow!"

But Mr. Touris would not shake the black dog from his shoulders. "He'll bring trouble yet—was born the sort to do it!"

Alexander defended him.

"Oh, you're his friend—sworn for thick and thin! As for Alison, she'd find a good word for the fiend from hell!— not that my sister's son is anything of that," said the Scotchman. "But he'll bring trouble to warm, canny, king-and-kirk-abiding folk! He's an Indian macaw in a dove-cote."

They rose from table. Out on the terrace they walked up and down in the soft, bright morning light. Mr. Touris seemed to wish company; he clung to Glenfernie until the latter must mount his horse and ride home. Only for a moment did Alexander and Mrs. Alison have speech together.

"When will you be seeing Elspeth?"

"I hope this afternoon."

"May joy come to you, Alexander!"

"I want it to come. I want it to come."

He and Black Alan journeyed home. As he rode he thought now and again of Ian, perhaps in Edinburgh according to his word of mouth, but perhaps, despite that word, on board some ship that should place him in the Low Countries, from which he might travel into France and to Paris and that group of Jacobites humming like a byke of bees around a prince, the heir of all the Stewarts. He thought with old affection and old concern. Whatever Ian did—intrigued with Jacobite interest or held aloof like a sensible man—yet was he Ian with the old appeal. *Take me or leave me—me and my dusky gold!* Alexander drew a deep breath, shook his shoulders, raised his head. "Let my friend be as he is!"

He ceased to think of Ian and turned to the oncoming afternoon—the afternoon rainbow-hued, coming on to the sound of music.

Again in his own house, he and Strickland worked an hour or more upon estate business. That over and dinner past, he went to the room in the keep. When the hour struck three he passed out of the opening in the old wall, clambered down the bank, and, going through the wood, took his way to White Farm.

Just one foreground wish in his mind was granted. There was an orchard strip by White Farm, and here, beneath a red-apple tree, he found Elspeth alone. She was perfectly direct with him.

"Willy told us that you were home. I thought you might come now to White Farm. I was watching. I wanted to speak to you where none was by. Let us cross the burn and walk in the fields."

The fields were reaped, lay in tawny stubble. The path ran by this and by a lichened stone wall. Overhead, swallows were skimming. Heath and bracken, rolled the colored hills. The air swam cool and golden, with a smell of the harvest earth.

"Elspeth, I stayed away years and years and years, and I stayed away not one hour!"

She stopped; she stood with her back to the wall. The farm-house had sunk from sight, the sun was westering, the fields lay dim gold and solitary. She had over her head a silken scarf, the ends of which she drew together and held with one brown, slender hand against her breast. She wore a dark gown; he saw her bosom rise and fall.

"I watched for you to tell you that this must not go on any longer. I came to my mind when you were gone, Mr. Alexander—I came to my mind! I think that you are braw and noble, but in the way of loving, as love is between man and woman, I have none for you—I have none for you!"

The sun appeared to dip, the fields to darken. Pain came to Glenfernie, wildering and blinding. He stood silent.

"I might have known before you went—I might have known from that first meeting, in May, in the glen! But I was a fool, and vague, and willing, I suppose, to put tip of tongue to a land of sweetness! If, mistaken myself, I helped you to mistake, I am bitter sorry and I ask your forgiveness! But the thing, Glenfernie, the thing stands! It's for us to part."

He stared at her dumbly. In every line of her, in every tone of her, there was finality. He was tenacious of purpose, capable of long-sustained and patient effort, but he seemed to know that, for this life, purpose and effort here might as well be laid aside. The knowledge wrapped him, quiet, gray, and utter. He put his hands to his brow;

he moved a few steps to and fro; he came to the wall and leaned against it. It seemed to him that he regarded the clay-cold corpse of his life.

"O the world!" cried Elspeth. "When we are little it seems so little! If you suffer, I am sorry."

"Present suffering may be faced if there's light behind."

"There's not this light, Glenfernie.... O world! if there is some other light—"

"And time will do naught for me, Elspeth?"

"No. Time will do naught for you. It is over! And the day goes down and the world spins on."

They stood apart, without speaking, under their hands the heaped stones of the wall. The swallows skimmed; a tinkling of sheep-bells was heard; the stubble and the moor beyond the fields lay in gold, in sunken green and violet; the hilltops met the sky in a line long, clean, remote, and still. Elspeth spoke.

"I am going now, back home. Let's say good-by here, each wishing the other some good in, or maybe out of, this carefu' world!"

"You, also, are unhappy. Why?"

"I am not! Do I seem so? I am sorry for unhappiness— that is all! Of course we grow older," said Elspeth, "older and wiser. But you nor no one must think that I am unhappy! For I am not." She put out her hands to him. "Let us say good-by!"

"Is it so? Is it so?"

"Never make doubt of that! I want you to see that it is clean snapped—clean gone!"

She gave him her hands. They lay in his grasp untrembling, filled with a gathered strength. He wrung them, bowed his head upon them, let them go. They fell at her sides; then she raised them, drew the scarf over her head and, holding it as before, turned and went away up the path between the yellow stubble and the wall. She walked quickly, dark clad; she was gone like a bird into a wood, like a branch of autumn leaves when the sea fog rolls in.

The laird of Glenfernie turned to his ancient house on the craggy hill.... That night he made him a fire in his old loved room in the keep. He sat beside it; he lighted candles and opened books, and now and then he sat so still before them that he may have thought that he read. But the books slipped away, and the candles guttered down, and the fire went out. At last, in the thick darkness, he spread his arms upon the table and bowed his head in them, and his frame shook with a man's slow weeping.

CHAPTER XVI

The bright autumn sank into November, November winds and mists into a muffled, gray-roofed, white-floored December. And still the laird of Glenfernie lived with the work of the estate and, when that was done, and when the long, lonely, rambling daily walk or ride was over, with books. The room in the keep had now many books. He sat among them, and he built his fire higher, and his candles burned into late night. Whether he read or did not read, he stayed among them and drew what restless comfort he might. Strickland, from his own high room, waking in the night, saw the loophole slit of light.

He felt concern. The change that had come to his old pupil was marked enough. Strickland's mind dwelt on the old laird. Was that the personality, not of one, but of two, of the whole line, perhaps, developing all the time, step by step with what seemed the plastic, otherwise, free time of youth, appearing always in due season, when its hour struck? Would Alexander, with minor differences, repeat his father? How of the mother? Would the father drown the mother? In the enormous all-one, the huge blend, what would arrive? Out of all fathers and mothers, out of all causes?

It could not be said that Alexander was surly. Nor, if the

weather was dark with him, that he tried to shake his darkness into others' skies. Nor that he meanly succumbed to the weight, whatever it was, that bore upon him. He did his work, and achieved at least the show of equanimity. Strickland wondered. What was it that had happened? It never occurred to him that it had happened here in this dale. But in all that life of Alexander's in the wider world there must needs have been relationships of lands established. Somewhere, something had happened to overcloud his day, to uncover ancestral resemblances, possibilities. Something, somewhere, and he had had news of it this autumn.... It happened that Strickland had never seen Glenfernie with Elspeth Barrow.

Mrs. Grizel was not observant. So that her nephew came to breakfast, dinner, and supper, so that he was not averse to casual speech of household interests, so that he seemed to keep his health, so that he gave her now and then words and a kiss of affection, she was willing to believe that persons addicted to books and the company of themselves had a right to stillness and gravity. Alice stayed in Edinburgh; Jamie soldiered it in Flanders. Strickland wrote and computed for and with the laird, then watched him forth, a solitary figure, by the fir-trees, by the leafless trees, and down the circling road into the winter country. Or he saw firelight in the keep and knew that Alexander walked to and fro, to and fro, or sat bowed over a book. Late at night, waking, he saw that Glenfernie still watched.

It was not Ian Rullock nor anything to do with him that had helped on this sharp alteration, this turn into some Cimmerian stretch of the mind's or the emotions' vast landscape. If Strickland had at first wondered if this might be the case, the thought vanished. Glenfernie, free to speak of Ian, spoke freely, with the relief of there, at least, a sunny day. It somewhat amazed and disquieted, even while it touched, the older man of quiet passions and even ways, the old strength of this friendship. Glenfernie seemed to brood with a mother-passion over Ian. To an extent here he confided in Strickland. The latter knew of the worry about Jacobite plots and the drawing of Ian into that vortex—Ian known now to be in Paris, writing thence twice or thrice during this autumn and early winter, letters that came to Glenfernie's hand by unusual channels, smacking all of them of Jacobite or High Tory transmissals. Strickland did not see these letters. Of them Alexander said only that Ian wrote as usual, except that he made no reference to sere leaves turning green or a dead staff budding.

In the room with only the loophole windows, by the firelight, Alexander read over again the second of these letters. "So you have loved and lost, old Steadfast? Let it not grieve you too much!" And that was all of that. And it pleased Alexander that it was all. Ian was too wise to touch and finger the heart. Ian, Ian, rich and deep and himself almost! Ten thousand Ian recollections pressed in upon Alexander. Let Ian, an he would, go a-lusting after old dynasties! Yet was he Ian! In these months it was Ian memories that chiefly gave Alexander comfort.

They gave beyond what, at this time, Mrs. Alison could give. At considerable intervals he went to Black Hill. But his old friend lived in a rare, upland air, and he could not yet find rest in her clime. She saw that.

"It's for after a while, isn't it, Alexander? Oh, after a while you'll see that it is the breathing, living air! But do not feel now that you are in duty bound to come here. Wait until you feel like coming, and never think that I'll be hurt—"

"I am a marsh thing," he said. "I feel dull and still and cold, and over me is a heavy atmosphere filled with motes. Forgive me and let me come to you farther on and higher up."

He went back to the gray crag, Glenfernie House and the room in the keep, the fire and his books, and a brooding traveling over the past, and, like a pool of gold in a long arctic night, the image, nested and warm, of Ian. Love was lost, but there stayed the ancient, ancient friend.

Two weeks before Christmas Alice came home, bright as a rose. She talked of a thousand events, large and small. Glenfernie listened, smiled, asked questions, praised her, and said it was good to have brightness in the house.

"Aye, it is!" she answered. "How grave and old you and Mr. Strickland and the books and the hall and Bran look!"

"It's heigho! for Jamie, isn't it?" asked Alexander. "Winter makes us look old. Wait till springtime!"

That evening she waylaid Strickland. "What is the matter with Alexander?"

"I don't know."

"He looks five years older. He looks as though he had been through wars."

"Perhaps he has. I don't know what it is," said Strickland, soberly.

"Do you think," said Alice—"do you think he could have had—oh, somewhere out in the world!—a love-affair, and it ended badly? She died, or there was a rival, or something like that, and he has just heard of it?"

"You have been reading novels," said Strickland. "And yet—!"

That night, seeing from his own window the light in the keep, he turned to his bed with the thought of the havoc of love. Lying there with open eyes he saw in procession Unhappy Love. He lay long awake, but at last he turned and addressed himself to sleep. "He's a strong climber! Whatever it is, maybe he'll climb out of it."

But in the keep, Alexander, sitting by the fire with lowered head and hanging hands, saw not the time when he would climb out of it....

He went no more to White Farm. He went, though not every Sunday, to kirk and sat with his aunt and with Strickland in the laird's boxlike, curtained pew. Mr. M'Nab preached of original sin and ineffable condemnation, and of the few, the very, very few, saved as by fire. He saw Jarvis Barrow sitting motionless, sternly agreeing, and beyond him Jenny Barrow and then Elspeth and Gilian. Out of kirk, in the kirkyard, he gave them good day. He studied to keep strangeness out of his manner; an onlooker would note only a somewhat silent, preoccupied laird. He might be pondering the sermon. Mr. M'Nab's sermons were calculated to arouse alarm and concern—or, in the case of the justified, stern triumph— in the human breast. White Farm made no quarrel with the laird for that quietude and withdrawing. In the autumn he had told Jarvis Barrow of that hour with Elspeth in the stubble-field. The old man listened, then, "They are strange warks, women!" he said, and almost immediately went on to speak of other things. There seemed no sympathy and no regret for the earthly happening. But he liked to debate with the laird election and the perseverance of the saints.

Jenny Barrow, only, could not be held from exclamation over Glenfernie's defection. "Why does he na come as he used to? Wha's done aught to him or said a word to gie offense?" She talked to Menie and Merran since Elspeth and Gilian gave her notice that they were wearied of the subject. Perhaps Jenny's concern with it kept her from the perception that not Glenfernie only was changing or had changed. Elspeth—! But Elspeth had been always a dreamer, rather silent, a listener rather than a speaker. Jenny did not look around corners; the overt sufficed for a bustling, good-natured life. Gilian's arrival, moreover, made for a diversion of attention. By the time novelty subsided again into every day an altered Elspeth had so fitted into the frame of life that Jenny was unaware of alteration.

But Gilian was not Jenny.

Each of Jarvis Barrow's granddaughters had her own small bedroom. Three nights after Gilian's home-coming she came, when the candles were out, into Elspeth's room. It was September and, for the season, warm. A great round moon poured its light into the little room. Elspeth was seated upon her bed. Her hair was loosened and fell over her white gown. Her feet were under her; she sat like an Eastern carving, still in the moonlight.

"Elspeth!"

Elspeth took a moment to come back to White Farm. "What is it, Gilian?"

Gilian moved to the window and sat in it. She had not

undressed. The moon silvered her, too. "What has happened, Elspeth?"

"Naught. What should happen?"

"It's no use telling me that.—We've been away from each other almost a year. I know that I've changed, grown, in that time, and it's natural that you should do the same. But it's something besides that!"

Elspeth laughed and her laughter was like a little, cold, mirthless chime of silver bells. "You're fanciful, Gilian!... We're no longer lassies; we're women! So the colors of things get a little different—that's all!"

"Don't you love me, Elspeth?"

"Yes, I love you. What has that to do with it?"

"Has it not? Has love naught to do with it? Love at all— all love?"

Elspeth parted her long dark hair into two waves, drew it before her, and began to braid it, sitting still, her limbs under her, upon the bed. "I saw you on the moor walking and talking with grandfather. What did he say to you?"

"You are changed and I said that you were changed. He had not noticed—he would not be like to notice! Then he told me about the laird and you."

"Yes. About the laird and me."

"You couldn't love him? They say he is a fine man."

"No, I couldn't love him. I like him. He understands. No

one is to blame."

"But if it is not that, what is it—what is it, Elspeth?"

"It's naught—naught—naught, I tell you!"

"It's a strange naught that makes you like a dark lady in a ballad-book!"

Elspeth laughed again. "Didn't I say that you were fanciful? It's late and I am sleepy."

That had been while the leaves were still upon the trees. The next morning and thenceforward Elspeth seemed to make a point of cheerfulness. It passed with her aunt and the helpers in the house. Jarvis Barrow appeared to take no especial note if women laughed or sighed, so long as they lived irreproachably.

The leaves bronzed, the autumn rains came, the leaves fell, the trees stood bare, the winds began to blow, there fell the first snowflakes. Gilian, walking home from the town, was overtaken on the moor by Robin Greenlaw.

"Where is Elspeth?"

"We are making our winter dresses. She would not leave her sewing."

The cousins walked upon the moor path together. Gilian was fairer and more strongly made than Elspeth. They walked in silence; then said Robin:

"You're the old Gilian, but I'm sure I miss the old Elspeth!"

"I think, myself, she's gone visiting! I rack and rack my brains to find what grief could have come to Elspeth. She will not help me."

"Gilian, could it be that, after all, her heart is set on the laird?"

"Did you know about that?"

"In part I guessed, watching them together. And then I saw how Glenfernie oldened in a night. Then, being with my uncle one day, he let drop a word that I followed up. I led him on and he told me. Glenfernie acted like a true man."

"If there's one thing of which I'm sure it is that she hardly thinks of him from Sunday to Sunday. She thinks then for a little because she sees him in kirk—but that passes, too!"

"Then what is it?"

"I don't know. I don't know of anybody else. Maybe no outer thing has anything to do with it. Sometimes we just have drumlic, dreary seasons and we do not know why.... She loves the spring. Maybe when spring comes she'll be Elspeth once more!"

"I hope so," said Greenlaw. "Spring makes all the world bonny again."

That was in November. On Christmas Eve Elspeth Barrow drowned herself in the Kelpie's Pool.

CHAPTER XVII

There had been three hours of light on Christmas Day when Robin Greenlaw appeared at Glenfernie House and would see the laird.

"He's in his ain room in the keep," said Davie, and went with the message.

Alexander came down the stair and out into the flagged court. The weather had been unwontedly clement, melting the earlier snows, letting the brown earth forth again for one look about her. To-day there was pale sunlight. Greenlaw sat his big gray. The laird came to him.

"Get down, man, and come in for Christmas cheer!"

"Send Davie away," said Greenlaw.

Alexander's gray eyes glanced. "You're bringing something that is not Christmas cheer!—Davie, tell Dandie Saunderson to saddle Black Alan at once.—Now, Robin!"

"Yesterday," said Greenlaw, "Elspeth Barrow vanished from White Farm. They wanted to send Christmas fare to old Skene the cotter. She said she would take a basket there, and so she went away, down the stream—about ten of the morning they think it was. It was not for hours that they grew at all anxious. She's never come back. She did not go to Skene's. We can hear no word of her from any. Her grandfather and I and the men at White Farm looked for her through the night. This morning there's an alarm sent up and down the dale."

"What harm could happen—"

"She might have strayed into some lonely place—fallen—hurt herself. There were gipsies seen the other day over by Windyedge. Or she might have walked on and on upon what road she took, and somehow none chanced to notice her. I am going now to ride the Edinburgh way."

"Have you gone up the glen?"

"That was tried this morning at first light. But that is just opposite to Skene's and the way she certainly took at first. She would have to turn and go about through the woods, or White Farm would see her." His voice had a haunting note of fear and trouble.

Glenfernie caught it. "She was not out of health nor unhappy?"

"She is changed from the old Elspeth. When you ask her if she is unhappy she says that she is not.... I do not know. Something is wrong. With the others, I am seeking about as though I expected each moment to see her sitting or standing by the roadside. But I do not expect to see her. I do not know what I expect. We have sent to Windyedge to apprehend those gipsies."

"Let me speak one moment to Mr. Strickland to send the men forth and go himself. Then I am ready."

On Black Alan he rode with Robin down the hill and through the wood and upon the White Farm way. The earth was mainly bare of snow, but frozen hard. The hoofs rang out but left no print. The air hung still, light and dry; the sun, far in the south, sent slanting, pale-gold beams. The two men made little speech as they rode. They passed men and youths, single figures and clusters.

"Ony news, Littlefarm? We've been—or we're going—seeking here, or here—"

A woman stopped them. "It was thae gipsies, sirs! I had a dream about them, five nights syne! A lintwhite was flying by them, and they gave chase. Either it's that or she made away with herself! I had a dream that might be read that way, too."

When they came to White Farm it was to find there only Jenny and Menie and Merran.

"Somebody maun stay to keep the house warm gin the lassie come stumbling hame, cauld and hungry and half doited! Eh, Glenfernie, ye that are a learned man and know the warld, gie us help!"

"I am going up the glen," said Alexander to Greenlaw. "I do not know why, but I think it should be tried again. And I know it, root and branch. I am going afoot. I will leave Black Alan here."

They wasted no time. He went, while Robin Greenlaw on his gray took the opposed direction. Looking back, he saw the great fire that Jenny kept, dancing through the open door and in the pane of the window. Then the trees and the winding of the path shut it away, shut away house and field and all token of human life.

He moved swiftly to the mouth of the glen, but then more slowly. The trees soared bare, the water rushed with a hoarse sound, snow lay in clefts. So well he knew the place! There was no spot where foot might have climbed, no ledge nor opening where form might lay, huddled or outstretched, that lacked his searching eye or hand. Here was the pebbly cape with the thorn-tree where in May he had come upon Elspeth, sitting by the water, singing.... Farther on he turned into that smaller, that fairy glen, bending like an arm from the main pass. Here was the oak beneath which they had sat, against which she had leaned. It wrapt him from himself, this place. He stood, and space around seemed filled with forms just beyond visibility. What were they? He did not know, but they seemed to breathe against his heart, to whisper.... He searched this place well, but there were only the winter banks and trees, the little burn, the invisible presences. Back in the deep glen a hawk sailed overhead, across the stripe of pale-blue sky. Alexander went on by the stream and the projecting rock and the twisted roots. There was no sound other than the loud voice of the water, talking only of its return to the sea. When he came to the cave he pushed aside the masking growth and entered. Dark and barren here, with the ashes of an old fire! For one moment, as it were distinctly, he saw Ian. He stood so clear in the mind's eye that it seemed that one intense effort might have set him bodily in the cavern. But the central strength let the image go. Alexander moved the ashes of the fire with his foot, shuddered in the place of cold and shadow, and, stooping, went out of the cave and on upon his search for Elspeth Barrow.

He sought the glen through, and at last, at the head, he came to Mother Binning's cot. Her fire was burning; she was standing in the door looking toward him.

"Eh, Glenfernie! is there news of the lassie?"

"None. You've got the sight. Can you not *see*?"

"It's gane from me! When it gaes I'm just like ony bird with a broken wing."

"If you cannot see, what do you think?"

"I dinna want to think and I dinna want to say. Whaur be ye gaeing now?"

"On over the moor and down by the Kelpie's Pool."

"Gae on then. I'll watch for ye coming back."

He went on. Something strange had him, drawing him. He came out from the band of trees upon the swelling open moor, bare and brown save where the snow laced it. Gold filtered over it; a pale sky arched above; it was wide, still, and awful—a desert. He saw the light run down and glint upon the pool. Searchers had ridden across this moor also, he had been told. He went down at once to the pool and stood by the kelpie willow. He was not thinking, he was not keenly feeling. He seemed to stand in open, endless, formless space, and in unfenced time. A clump of dry reeds rose by his knee, and upon the other side of these he noticed that a stone had been lifted from its bed. He stooped, and in the reeds he found an inch-long fragment of ribbon—of a snood.

He stepped back from the willow. He took off and dropped upon the moor hat and riding-coat and boots, inner coat and waistcoat. Then he entered the Kelpie's Pool. He searched it, measure by measure, and at last he found the body of Elspeth. He drew it up; he loosened and let fall the stone tied in the plaid that was wrapped around it; he bore the form out of the pool and laid it upon the bank beyond the willow. The sunlight showed the whole, the face and figure. The laird of Glenfernie, kneeling beside it, put back the long drowned hair and saw, pinned upon the bosom of the gown, the folded letter, wrapped twice in thicker paper. He took it from her and opened it. The writing was yet legible.

I hope that I shall not be found. If I am, let this answer for me. I was unhappy, more unhappy than you can think. Let no one be blamed. It was one far from here and you will not know his name. Do not think of me as wicked nor as a murderess. The unhappy should have pardon and rest. Good-by to all—good-by!

In the upper corner was written, "For White Farm." That was all.

Glenfernie put this letter into the bosom of his shirt. He then got on again the clothing he had discarded, and, stooping, put his arms beneath the lifeless form. He lifted it and bore it from the Kelpie's Pool and up the moor. He was a man much stronger than the ordinary; he carried it as though he felt no weight. The icy water of the pool upon him was as nothing, and as he walked his face was still as a stone face in a desert. So he came with Elspeth's body back to the glen, and Mother Binning saw him coming.

"Hech, sirs! Hech, sirs! Will it hae been that way—will it hae been that way?"

He stopped for a moment. He laid his burden down upon the boards just within the door and smoothed back the streaming hair. "Even the shell flung out by the ocean is beautiful!"

"Eh, man! Eh, man! It's wae sometimes to be a woman!"

"Give me," he said, "a plaid, dry and warm, to hap her in."

"Will ye na leave her here? Put her in my bed and gae tell White Farm!"

"No, I will carry her home."

Mother Binning took from a chest a gray plaid. He lifted again the dead woman, and she happed the plaid about her. "Ah, the lassie—the lassie! Come to me, Glenfernie, and I will scry for you who it was!"

He looked at her as though he did not hear her. He lifted the body, holding it against his shoulder like a child, and went forth. He knew the path so absolutely, he was so strong and light of foot, that he went without difficulty through the glen, by the loud crying water, by the points of crag and the curving roots and the drifts of snow, by the green patches of moss and the trees great and small. He did not hasten nor drag, he did not think. He went like a bronze Talus, made simply to find, to carry home.

Known feature after known feature of the place rose before him, passed him, fell away. Here was the arm of the glen, and here was the pebbled cape and the thorn-tree. The winter water swirled around it, sang of cold and a hateful power. Here was the mouth of the glen. Here were the fields which had been green and then golden with ripe corn. Here were the White Farm roof and chimneys and windows, and blue smoke from the chimney going straight up like a wraith to meet blue sky. Before him was the open door.

He had thought of there being only Jenny and the two servant lasses. But in the time he had been gone there had regathered to White Farm, for learning each from each, for consultation, for mere rest and food, a number of the searchers. Jarvis Barrow had returned from the northward-stretching moor, Thomas and Willy from the southerly fields. Men who had begun to drag deep places in the stream were here for some provision. A handful of women, hooded and wrapped, had come from neighboring farms or from the village. Among them talked Mrs. Macmurdo, who kept the shop, and the hostess of the Jardine Arms. And there was here Jock Binning, who, for all his lameness and his crutches, could go where he wished.... But it was Gilian, crossing upon the stepping-stones, who saw Glenfernie coming by the stream with the covered form in his arms. She met him; they went up the bank to the house together. She had uttered one cry, but no more.

"The Kelpie's Pool," he had answered.

Jarvis Barrow came out of the door. "Eh! God help us!"

They laid the form upon a bed. All the houseful crowded about. There was no helping that, and as little might be helped Jenny's lamentations and the ejaculations of others. It was White Farm himself who took away the plaid. It lay there before them all, the drowned form. The face was very quiet, strangely like Elspeth again, the Elspeth of the springtime. All looked, all saw.

"Gude guide us!" cried Mrs. Macmurdo. "And I wadna be some at the Judgment Day when come up the beguiled, self-drownit lassies!"

Jock Binning's voice rose from out the craning group.

"Aye, and I ken—and I ken wha was the man!"

White Farm turned upon him. He towered, the old man. A winter wrath and grief, an icy, scintillant, arctic passion, marked two there, the laird of Glenfernie and the elder of the kirk. Gilian's grief stood head-high with theirs, but their anger, the old man's disdaining and the young man's jealousy, was far from her. In Jarvis Barrow's hand was the paper, taken from Elspeth, given him by Glenfernie. He turned upon the cripple. "Wha, then? Wha, then? Speak out!"

He had that power of command that forced an answer. Jock Binning, crutched and with an elfish face and figure and voice, had pulled down upon himself the office of revelator. The group swayed a little from him and he was left facing White Farm and the laird of Glenfernie. He had a wailing, chanting, elvish manner of speech. Out streamed this voice:

"'Twere the last of June, twa-three days after the laird rode to Edinburgh, and she brought my mither a giftie of plums and sat doon for a crack with her. By he came and stood and talked. Syne the clouds thickened and the thunder growlit, and he wad walk with her hame through the glen—"

"Wha wad? Wha?"

"Captain Ian Rullock."

"*Ian Rullock!*"

"Aye, Glenfernie! And after that they never came to my mither's again. But I marked them aft when they didna mark me, in the glen. Aye, and I marked them ance in the little glen, and there they were lovers surely—gin kisses and clasped arms mak lovers! She wad come by herself to their trysting, and he wad come over the muir and down the crag-side. It was na my business and I never thocht to tell. But eh! all ill will out, says my mither!"

CHAPTER XVIII

The early sunlight fell soft and fine upon the river Seine and the quays and buildings of Paris. The movement and buzz of people had, in the brightness, something of the small ecstasy of bees emerging from the hive with the winter pall just slipped. Distant bells were ringing, hope enticed the grimmest poverty. Much, after all, might be taken good-naturedly!

A great, ornate coach, belonging to a person of quality, crossed the Seine from the south to the north bank. Three gentlemen, seated within, observed each in his own fashion the soft, shining day. One was Scots, one was English, and the owner of the coach, a Frenchman. The first was Ian Rullock.

"Good weather for your crossing, monsieur!" remarked the person of quality. He was so markedly of position that the two men whom he had graciously offered to bring a mile upon their way, and who also were younger men, answered with deference and followed in their speech only the lines indicated.

"It promises fair, sir," said Ian. "In three days Dunkirk, then smooth seas! Good omens everywhere!"

"You do not voyage under your own name?"

"After to-morrow, sir, I am Robert Bonshaw, a Scots physician."

"Ah, well, good fortune to you, and to the exalted person you serve!"

The coach, cumbrous and stately, drawn by four white horses, left the bridge and came under old palace walls, and thence by narrow streets advanced toward the great house of its owner. Outside was the numerous throng, the scattering to this side and that of the imperiled foot travelers. The coach stopped.

"Here is the street you would reach!" said the helpful person of quality.

A footman held open the door; the Scot and the English-man gave proper expression of gratitude to their benefactor, descended to earth, turned again to bow low, and waited bareheaded till the great machine was once more in motion and monseigneur's wig, countenance, and velvet coat grew things of the past. Then the two turned into a still and narrow street overhung by high, ancient structures and roofed with April sky.

The one was going from Paris, the other staying. Both were links in a long chain of political conspiring. They walked now down the street that was dark and old, underfoot old mire and mica-like glistening of fresher rain. The Englishman spoke:

"Have you any news from home?"

"None. None for a long while. I had it conveyed to my

kindred and to an old friend that I had disappeared from Paris—gone eastward, Heaven knew where—probably Crim Tartary! So my own world at least, as far as I am concerned, will be off the scent. That was in the winter. I have really heard nothing for months.... When the dawn comes up and we are all rich and famed and gay, *my-lorded* from John o' Groat's House to Land's End—then, Warburton, then—"

"Then?"

"Then we'll be good!" Ian laughed. "Don't you want, sometimes, to be good, Warburton? Wise—and simple. Doesn't it rise before you in the night with a most unearthly beauty?"

"Oh, I think I am so-so good!" answered the other. "So-so bad, so-so good. What puts you in this strain?"

"Tell me and I will tell you! And now I'm going to Scotland, into the Highlands, to paint a prince who, when he's king, will, no manner of doubt, wear the tartan and make every thane of Glamis thane of Cawdor likewise!... One half the creature's body is an old, childish loyalty, and the other half's ambition. The creature's myself. There are also bars and circles and splashes of various colors, dark and bright. Sometimes it dreams of wings—wings of an archangel, no less, Warburton! The next moment there seems to be an impotency to produce even beetle wings!... What a weathercock and variorum I am, thou art, he is!"

"We're no worse than other men," said Warburton, comfortably. "We're all pretty ignorant, I take it!"

They came to a building, old and not without some lingering of strength and grace. It stood in the angle of

Mary Johnston

two streets and received sunshine and light as well as cross-tides of sound. The Scot and the Englishman both lodged here, above a harness-maker and a worker in fine woods. They passed into the court and to a stair that once had known a constant, worldly-rich traffic up and down. Now it was still and twilight, after the streets. Both men had affairs to put in order, business on hand. They moved now abstractedly, and when Warburton reached, upon the first landing, the door of his rooms, he turned aside from Ian with only a negligent, "We'll sup together and say last things then."

The Scot went on alone to the next landing and his own room. These were not his usual lodgings in Paris. Agent now of high Jacobite interests, shuttle sent from conspirers in France to chiefs in Scotland, on the eve of a departure in disguise, he had broken old nest and old relations, and was now as a stranger in a city that he knew well, and where by not a few he was known. The room that he turned into had little sign of old, well-liked occupancy; the servant who at his call entered from a smaller chamber was not the man to whom he was used, but a Highlander sent him by a Gordon then in Paris.

"I am back, Donal!" said Ian, and threw himself into a chair by the table. "Come, give an account of your errands!"

Donal, middle-aged, faithful, dour and sagacious, and years away from loch and mountain, gave account. Horses, weapons, clothing, all correct for Dr. Robert Bonshaw and his servant, riding under high protection from Paris to Dunkirk, where a well-captained merchant-vessel stayed for them in port. Ian nodded approval.

"I'm indebted, Donal, to my cousin Gordon!"

Donal let a smile come to within a league of the surface. "Her ainself has a wish to hear the eagle scream over Ben Nevis!"

Rullock's hand moved over a paper, checking a row of figures. "Did you manage to get into my old lodging?"

"Aye. None there. All dusty and bare. But the woman who had the key gave me—since I said I might make a guess where to find you, sir—these letters. They came, she said, two weeks ago." Donal laid them upon the table.

"Ah!" said Ian, "they must have gotten through before I shut off the old passageway." He took them in his hand. "There's nothing more now, Donal. Go out for your dinner."

The man went. Ian added another column of figures, then took the letters and with them moved to a window through which streamed the sun of France. The floor was patched with gold; there was warmth as well as light. He pushed a chair into it, sat down, and opened first the packet that he knew had come from his uncle. He broke the seal and read two pages of Mr. Touris in a mood of anger. There were rumors—. True it was that Ian had now his own fortune, had it at least until he lost it and his life together in some mad, unlawful business! But let him not look longer to be heir of Archibald Touris! Withdraw at once from ill company, political or other, and return to Scotland, or at least to England, or take the consequences! The letter bore date the first week of December. It had been long in passing from hand to hand in a troubled, warring world. Ian Rullock, fathoms deep in the present business, held in a web made by many lines of force, both thick and thin, refolded the paper and made to put it into his pocketbook, then bethinking himself, tore it instead

Mary Johnston

into small pieces and, rising, dropped these into a brazier where burned a little charcoal. He would carry nothing with his proper name upon it. Coming back to the chair in the sunshine, he sat for a moment with his eyes upon a gray huddle of roofs visible through the window. Then he broke the seal and unfolded the letter superscribed in Alexander's strong writing.

There were hardly six lines. And they did not tell of how discovery had been made, nor why, nor when. They said nothing of death nor life—no word of the Kelpie's Pool. They carried, tersely, a direct challenge, the ground Ian Rullock's conception of friendship, a conception tallying nicely with Alexander Jardine's idea of a mortal enmity. Such a fishing-town, known of both, back of such a sea beach in Holland—such a tavern in this place. Meet there—wait there, the one who should reach it first for the other, and—to give all possible ground to delays of letters, travel, arrangements generally—in so late a month as April. "Find me there, or await me there, my one-time friend, henceforth my foe! I—or Justice herself above me—would teach you certain things!"

The cartel bore date the 1st of January—later by a month than the Black Hill letter. It dropped from Ian's hand; he sat with blankness of mind in the sunlight. Presently he shivered slightly. He leaned his elbows on his knees and his forehead in his hands and sat still. Alexander! He felt no hot straining toward meeting, toward fighting, Alexander. Perversely enough, after a year of impatient, contemptuous thought in that direction, he had lately felt liking and an ancient strong respect returning like a tide that was due. And he could not meet Alexander in April—that was impossible! No private affair could be attended to now.

... Elspeth, of whom the letter carried no word, Elspeth from whom he had not heard since in August he left that countryside, Elspeth who had agreed with him that love of man and woman was nobody's business but their own, Elspeth who, when he would go, had let him go with a fine pale refusal to deal in women's tears and talk of injury, who had said, indeed, that she did not repent, much bliss being worth some bale—Elspeth whom he could not be sure that he would see again, but whom at times before his eyes at night he saw.... Immediately upon his leaving Black Hill she had broken with Glenfernie. She was clear of him—the laird could reproach her with nothing!

What had happened? He had told her how, at need, a letter might be sent. But one had never come. He himself had never written. Writing was set in a prickly ring of difficulties and dangers. What had happened? Strong, secret inclination toward finding least painful things for himself brought his conclusion. Sitting there in the sunshine, his will deceiving him, he determined that it was simply that Elspeth had at last told Glenfernie that she could not love him because she loved another. Probably—persistence being markedly a trait of Old Steadfast's—he had been after her once and again, and she had turned upon him and said much more than in prudence she should have said! So Alexander would have made his discovery and might, if he pleased, image other trysts than his own in the glen! Certainly he had done this, and then sat down and penned his challenge!

Elspeth! He was unshakably conscious that Glenfernie would tell none what Elspeth might have been provoked into giving away. Old Steadfast, there was no denying, had that knightliness. Three now knew—no more than three. If, through some mischance, there had been wider discovery, she would have written! The Black Hill letter, too, would have had somewhat there to say.

Then, behind the challenge, stood old and new relations between Ian Rullock and Alexander Jardine! It was what Glenfernie might choose to term the betrayal of friendship—a deep scarification of Old Steadfast's pride, a severing cut given to his too imperial confidence, poison dropped into the wells of domination, "No!" said to too much happiness, to any surpassing of him, Ian, in happiness, "No!" to so much reigning!

Ian shook himself, thrust away the doubtful glimmer of a smile. That way really did lie hell....

He came back to a larger if a much perplexed self. He could not meet Glenfernie on that sea beach, fight him there. He did not desire to kill Old Steadfast, though, as the world went, pleasure was to be had in now and then giving superiority pain. Face to face upon those sands, some blood shed and honor satisfied, Alexander would be reasonable—being by nature reasonable! Ian shook himself.

"Now he draws me like a lodestone, and now I feel Lucifer to his Michael! What old, past mountain of friendship and enmity has come around, full wheel?"

But it was impossible for him to go to that sea strand in Holland.

Elspeth! He wondered what she was doing this April day. Perhaps she walked in the glen. It was colder there than here, but yet the trees would be budding. He saw her face again, and all its ability to show subtle terror and subtle joy, and the glancing and the running of the stream between. Elspeth.... He loved her again as he sat there, somewhat bowed together in the sunlight, Alexander's challenge upon the floor by his foot. There came creeping to him an odd feeling of long ago having loved her—long ago and more than once, many times more than once. Name and place alone flickered. There might be something in Old Steadfast's contention that one lived of old time and all time, only there came breaking in dozing and absent-mindedness! Elspeth—

He saw her standing by him, and it seemed as though she had a basket on her arm, and she looked as she had looked that day of the thunder-storm and the hour in the cave behind the veil of rain. Without warning there welled into his mind broken lines from an old tale in verse of which he was fond:

"Me dreamed al this night, pardie,
An elf-queen shall my leman be ...
An elf-queen wil I have, I-wis,
For in this world no woman is
Worthy to be my mate ...
Al other women I forsake
And to an elf-queen I me take
By dale and eke by down."

Syllable and tone died. With his hand he brushed from his eyes the vision that he knew to be nothing but a heightened memory. Might, indeed, all women be one woman, one woman be all women, all forms one form, all times one time, like event fall softly, imperceptibly, upon like event until there was thickness, until there was made a form of all recurrent, contributory forms? Events, tendencies, lives— unimaginable continuities! Repetitions and repetitions and repetitions—and no one able to leave the trodden road that ever returned upon itself—no one able to take one step from the circle into a new dimension and thence see the form below....

Ian put his hands over his eyes, shook himself, started up and stood at the window. Sky, and roofs on roofs, and in the street below toy figures, pedestrians. "Come back— come back to breathable air! Now what's to be done— what's to be done?" After some moments he turned and picked up the letter upon the floor and read it twice. In memory and in imagination he could see the fishing-town, the inn there, the dunes, the ocean beach fretted by the long, incoming wave. Perhaps and most probably, this very bright afternoon, the laird of Glenfernie waited for him there, pacing the sands, perhaps, watching the comers to the inn door.... Well, he must watch in vain. Ian Rullock would one day give him satisfaction, but certainly not now. Vast affairs might not be daffed aside for the laird of Glenfernie's convenience! Ian stood staring out of window at those huddled roofs, the challenge still in his hand. Then, slowly, he tore the paper to pieces and committed it to the brazier where was already consumed Black Hill's communication.

That evening he supped with Warburton, and the next morning saw him and Donal riding forth from Paris, by St.-Denis, on toward Dunkirk. From this place, four days later, sailed the brig *Cock of the North*, destination the Beauly Firth. Dr. Robert Bonshaw and his man experienced, despite the prediction of the Frenchman of quality, a rough and long voyage. But the *Cock of the North* weathered tumultuous sea and wind and came, in the northern spring, to anchor in a great picture of firth and green shore and dark, piled mountains. Dr. Robert Bonshaw and his man, going ashore and into Inverness, found hospitality there in the house of a certain merchant. Thence, after a day or so, he traveled to the castle of a

Highland chief of commanding port. Here occurred a gathering; here letters and asseverations brought from France were read, listened to, weighed or taken without much weighing, so did the Highland desire run one way. An old net added to itself another mesh.

Dr. Robert Bonshaw, a very fit, invigorating agent, traveled far and near through the Highlands this May, this June, this July. It was to him an interesting, difficult, intensely occupied time; he was far from Lowland Scotland and any echoes therefrom, saving always political echoes. He had no leisure for his own affairs, saving always that background consideration that, if the Stewarts really got back the crown, Ian Rullock was on the road to power and wealth. This consideration was not articulate, but diffused. It interfered not at all with the foreground activities and hard planning—no more than did the fine Highland air. It only spurred him as did the winy air. The time and place were electric; he worked hard, many hours on end, and when he sought his bed he dropped at once to needed sleep. From morn till late at night, whether in castle or house or journeying from clan to clan, he was always in company. There was no time for old thoughts, memories, surmises. That was one world and he was now in another.

Upon the eleventh day of May, the year 1745, was fought in Flanders the battle of Fontenoy. The Duke of Cumberland, Koenigsegge the Austrian, and the Dutch Prince of Waldeck had the handling of something under fifty thousand English. Marshal Saxe with Louis XV at his side wielded a somewhat larger number of French. The English and their allies were beaten. French spirits rode on high, French intentions widened.

The Stewart interest felt the blood bound in its veins. The

bulk of the British army was on the Continent and shaken by Fontenoy; King George himself tarried in Hanover. Now was the time—now was the time for the heir of all the Stewarts to put his fortune to the touch—to sail from France, to land in Scotland, to raise his banner and draw his sword and gather Highland chief and Lowland Jacobite, the while in England rose for him and his father English Jacobites and soon, be sure, all English Tories! France would send gold and artillery and men to her ancient ally, Scotland. Up at last with the white Stewart banner! reconquer for the old line and all it meant to its adherents the two kingdoms! In the last week of July Prince Charles Edward, somewhat strangely and meagerly attended, landed at Loch Sunart in the Highlands. There he was joined by Camerons, Macdonalds, and Stewarts, and thence he moved, with an ever-increasing Highland *tail*, to Perth. A bold stream joined him here—northern nobles of power, with their men. He might now have an army of two thousand. Sir John Cope, sent to oppose him with what British troops there were in Scotland, allowed himself to be circumvented. The Prince, having proclaimed his father, still at Rome, James III, King of Great Britain, and produced his own commission as Regent, marched from Perth to Edinburgh. The city capitulated and Charles Edward was presently installed in Holyrood, titularly at home in his father's kingdom, in his ancient palace, among his loyal subjects, but actually with far the major moiety of that kingdom yet to gain.

The gracious act of rewarding must begin. Claim on royal gratitude is ever a multitudinous thing! In the general manifoldness, out of the by no means yet huge store of honey Ian Rullock, for mere first rung of his fortune's ladder, received the personally given thanks of his Prince and a captaincy in the none too rapidly growing army.

CHAPTER XIX

The castle, defiant, untakable save by long siege and famine, held for King George by a garrison of a few hundreds, spread itself like a rock lion in a high-lifted rock lair. Bands of Highlanders watched its gates and accesses, guarding against Hanoverian sallies. From the castle down stretched Edinburgh, heaped upon its long, spinelike hill, to the palace of Holyrood, and all its tall houses, tall and dark, and all its wynds and closes, and all its strident voices, and all its moving folk, seemed to have in mind that palace and the banner before it. The note of the having rang jubilation in all its degrees, or with a lower and a muffled sound distaste and fear, or it aimed at a middle strain neither high nor low, a golden mean to be kept until there might be seen what motif, after all, was going to prevail! It would never do, thought some, to be at this juncture too clamorous either way. But to the unpondering ear the jubilation carried it, as to the eye tartans and white cockades made color, made high light, splashed and starred and redeemed the gray town. There was one thing that could not but appeal. A Scots royal line had come into its home nest at Holyrood. Not for many and many and many a year had such a thing as that happened! If matters went in a certain way Edinburgh might regain ancient pomp and circumstance. That was a consideration that every hour arranged a new plea in the citizen heart.

Excitement, restless movement, tendency to come together in a crowd, were general, as were ejaculation, nervous laughter, declamation. The roll of drum, call of trumpet, skirl of pipes, did not lack. Charles Edward's army encamped itself at Duddingston a little to the east of the city. But its units came in numbers into the town. The warlike hue diffused itself. Horsemen were frequent, and a continual entering of new adherents, men in small or large clusters, marching in from the country, asking the way to the Prince. For all the buzzing and thronging, great order prevailed. Women sat or stood at windows, or passed in and out of dark wynds, or, escorted, picked their way at street crossings. Now and then went by a sedan-chair. Many women showed in their faces a truly religious fervor, a passionate Jacobite loyalty, lighting like a flame. Many sewed white cockades. All Scotland, all England, would surely presently want these! Men of all ranks, committed to the great venture, moved with a determined gaiety and *elan*. "This is the stage, we are the actors; the piece is a great piece, the world looks on!" The town of Edinburgh did present a grandiose setting. Suspense, the die yet covered, the greatness of the risk, gave, too, its glamour of height and stateliness. All these men might see, in some bad moment at night, not only possible battle death—that was in the counting—but, should the great enterprise fail, scaffolds and hangmen. Many who went up and down were merely thoughtless, ignorant, reckless, or held in a vanity of good fortune, yet to the eye of history all might come into the sweep of great drama. Place and time rang and were tense. Flare and sonorousness and a deep vibration of the old massive passions, and through all the outward air a September sea mist creeping.

Ian Rullock, walking down the High Street, approaching St. Giles, heard his name spoken from a little knot of well-dressed citizens. As he turned his head a gentleman detached himself from the company. It proved to be Mr. Wotherspoon the advocate, old acquaintance and adviser of Archibald Touris, of Black Hill.

"Captain Rullock—"

"Mr. Wotherspoon, I am glad to see you!"

Mr. Wotherspoon, old moderate Whig, and the Jacobite officer walked together down the clanging way. The mist was making pallid garlands for the tall houses, a trumpet rang at the foot of the street, Macdonald of Glengarry and fifty clansmen, bright tartan and screaming pipes, poured by.

"Auld Reekie sees again a stirring time!" said the lawyer.

"I am glad to have met you, sir," said Rullock. "I fancy that you can tell me home news. I have heard none for a long time."

"You have been, doubtless," said Mr. Wotherspoon, "too engaged with great, new-time things to be fashed with small, old-time ones."

"One of our new-time aims," said Ian, "is to give fresh room to an old-time thing. But we won't let little bolts fly! I am anxious for knowledge."

Mr. Wotherspoon seemed to ponder it. "I live just here. Perhaps you will come up to my rooms, out of this Mars' racket?"

"In an hour's time I must wait on Lord George Murray. But I have till then."

They entered a close, and climbed the stair of a tall, tall house, dusky and old. Here, half-way up, was the lawyer's lair. He unlocked a door and the two came, through a small vestibule, into a good-sized, comfortable, well-furnished room. Rullock glanced at the walls.

"I was here once or twice, years ago. I remember your books. What a number you have!"

"I recall," said Mr. Wotherspoon, "a visit that you paid me with the now laird of Glenfernie."

The window to which they moved allowed a glimpse of the colorful street. Mr. Wotherspoon closed it against the invading noise and the touch of chill in the misty air. He then pushed two chairs to the table and took from a cupboard a bottle and glasses.

"My man is gadding, with eyes like saucers—like the rest of us, like the rest of us, Captain Rullock!" They sat down. "My profession," said the lawyer, "can be made to be narrow and narrowing. On the other hand, if a man has an aptitude for life, there is much about life to be learned with a lawyer's spy-glass! A lawyer sees a variety of happenings in a mixed world. He quite especially learns how seldom black and white are found in anything like a pure condition. A thousand thousand blends. Be wise and tolerant—or to be wise be tolerant!" He pushed the bottle.

Ian smiled. "I take that, sir, to mean that you find *God save King James!* not wholly harsh and unmusical—"

"Perhaps not wholly so," said the lawyer. "I am Whig and

Presbyterian and I prefer *God save King George!* But I do not look for the world to end, whether for King George or King James. I did not have in mind just this public occasion."

His tone was dry. Ian kept his gold-brown eyes upon him. "Tell me what you have heard from Black Hill."

"I was there late in May. Mr. Touris learned at that time that you had quitted France."

"May I ask how he learned it?"

"The laird of Glenfernie, who had been in the Low Countries, told him. Apparently Glenfernie had acquaintances, agents, who traced it out for him that you had sailed from Dunkirk for Beauly Firth, under the name of Robert Bonshaw."

"*So he was there, pacing the beach*," thought Ian. He lifted his glass and drank Mr. Wotherspoon's very good wine. That gentleman went on.

"It was surmised at Black Hill that you were helping on the event—the great event, perhaps—that has occurred. Indeed, in July, Mr. Touris, writing to me, mentioned that you had been seen beyond Inverness. But the Highlands are deep and you traveled rapidly. Of course, when it was known that the Prince had landed, your acquaintance assumed your joining him and becoming, as you have become, an officer in his army." He made a little bow.

Ian inclined his head in return. "All at Black Hill are well, I hope? My aunt—"

"Mrs. Alison is a saint. All earthly grief, I imagine, only

quickens her homeward step."

"What grief has she had, sir, beyond—"

"Beyond?"

"I know that my aunt will grieve for the break that has come between my uncle and myself. I have, too," said Ian, with deliberation, "been quarreled with by an old friend. That also may distress her."

The lawyer appeared to listen to sounds from the street. Rising, he moved to the window, then returned. "Bonnet lairds coming into town! You are referring now to Glenfernie?"

"Then he has made it common property that he chose to quarrel with me?"

"Oh, chose to—" said Mr. Wotherspoon, reflectively.

There was a silence. Ian set down his wine-glass, made a movement of drawing together, of determination.

"I am sure that there is something of which I have not full understanding. You will much oblige me by attention to what I now say, Mr. Wotherspoon. It is possible that I may ask you to see that its substance reaches Black Hill." He leaned back in his chair and with his gold-brown eyes met the lawyer's keen blue ones. "Nothing now can be injured by telling you that for a year I have acted under responsibility of having in keeping greater fortunes than my own. That kind of thing, none can know better than you, binds a man out of his own path and his own choices into the path and choices of others. Secrecy was demanded of me. I ceased to write home, and presently I removed from old lodgings and purposely blurred indications of where I was or might be found. In this way—the warring, troubled time aiding—it occurred that there practically ceased all communication between me and those of my blood and friendship whose political thinking differs from mine.... I begin to see that I know little indeed of what may or may not have occurred in that countryside. Early in April, however, there came to my hand in Paris two letters—one from my uncle, written before Christmas, one from Alexander Jardine, written a month later. My uncle's contained the information that, lacking my immediate return to this island and the political faith of his side of the house, I was no longer his nephew and heir. The laird of Glenfernie, upon an old quarrel into which I need not enter, chose to send me a challenge simply. *Meet him, on such a sands in Holland....* Well, great affairs have right of way over small ones! Under the circumstances, he might as well have appointed a plain in the moon! The duel waits.... I tell you what I know of home affairs. I shall be obliged for any information you may have that I have not."

Mr. Wotherspoon's sharp blue eyes seemed to consider it. He drummed on the table. "I am a much older man than you, Captain Rullock, and an old adviser of your family. Perhaps I may speak without offense? That subject of quarrel, now, between you and the laird of Glenfernie—"

The other made a movement, impatient and imperious. "It is not likely, sir, that he divulged that!"

"He? No! But fate—fortune—the unrolling course of things—plain Providence—whatever you choose to call it—seems at times quite below or above that reticence which we others so naturally prize and exhibit!"

"You'll oblige me, sir, by not speaking in riddles."

The irony dropped from Mr. Wotherspoon's tone. He faced the business squarely. "Do you mean to say that you do not know of the suicide of Elspeth Barrow?"

The chair opposite made a grating sound, pushed violently back upon the bare, polished floor. Down the street, through the window, came the sound of Cluny Macpherson's pipers, playing down from the Lawnmarket. Rullock seemed to have thrust his chair back into the shadow. Out of it came presently his voice, low and hoarse:

"No."

"They found her on Christmas Day—drowned in the Kelpie's Pool. Self-murder—murder also of a child that would have been."

Again silence. The lawyer found that he must go through with it, having come so far. "It seems that there is a cripple fellow of the neighborhood who had stumbled, unseen, upon your trysts. He told—spoke it all out to the crowd gathered. There was a letter, too, upon her which gave a clue. But she never named you and evidently meant not to name you.... Poor child! She may have thought herself strong, and then things have come over her wave on wave. Her grandfather—that dark upbringing on tenets harsh and wrathful—certainty of disgrace. Pitiful!"

There came a sound from the chair pushed back from the light. Mr. Wotherspoon measured the table with his fingers.

"It seems that the countryside was searching for her. It was the laird of Glenfernie who, alone and coming upon some trace, entered the Kelpie's Pool and found her there. They say that he carried her, dead, in his arms through the glen to White Farm."

Some proclamation or other was being made at the Cross of Edinburgh. A trumpet blew and the street was filled with footsteps.

"The laird of Glenfernie," said the lawyer, "has joined, I hear, Sir John Cope at Dunbar. It is not impossible that you may have speech together from opposing battle-lines." He poured wine. "My bag of news is empty, Captain Rullock."

Ian rose from his seat. His face was gray and twisted, his voice, when he spoke, hollow, low, and dry. "I must go now to Lord George Murray.... It was all news, Mr. Wotherspoon. I—What are words, anyhow? Give you good day, sir!"

Mr. Wotherspoon, standing in his door, watched him down the stair and forth from the house. "He goes brawly! How much is night, and how much streak of dawn?"

* * * * *

Sir John Cope, King George's general in Scotland, had but a small army. It was necessary in the highest degree that Prince Charles Edward should meet and defeat this force before it was enlarged, before from England came more and more regular troops.... A battle won meant prestige gained, the coming over of doubting thousands, an echo into England that would bring the definite accession of great Tory names. Cope and his twenty-five hundred men, regulars and volunteers, approaching Edinburgh from the east, took position near the village of Prestonpans. On the morning of the 20th of September out moved to meet him the Prince and Lord George Murray, behind them less than two thousand men.

By afternoon the two forces confronted each the other; but Cope had chosen well, the right position. The sea guarded one flank, a deep and wide field ditch full of water the other. In his rear were stone walls, and before him a wide marsh. The Jacobite strength halted, reconnoitered, must perforce at last come to a standstill before Cope's natural fortress. There was little artillery, no great number of horse. Even the bravest of the brave, Highland or Lowland, might draw back from the thought of trying to cross that marsh, of meeting the moat-like ditch under Cope's musket-fire. Sunset came amid perturbation, a sense of check, impending disaster.

Ian Rullock, acting for the moment as aide-de-camp, had spent the day on horseback. Released in the late afternoon, lodged in a hut at the edge of the small camp, he used the moment's leisure to climb a small hill and at its height to throw himself down beside a broken cairn. He shut his eyes, but after a few moments opened them and gazed upon the camp of Cope, covering also but a little space, so small were the armies. His lips parted.

"Well, Old Steadfast, and what if you are there, waiting?..."

The sun sank. A faint red light diffused itself, then faded into brown dusk. He rose and went down into the camp. In the brows of many there might be read depression, uncertainty. But in open places fires had been built, and about several of these Highlanders were dancing to the screaming of their pipes. Rullock bent his steps to headquarters. An officer whom he knew, coming forth, drew him aside in excitement.

"We've got it—we've got it, Rullock!"

"What? The plan?"

"The way through! Here has come to the Prince the man who owns the marsh! He knows the firm ground. Cope does not know that it is there! Cope thinks that it is all slough! This man swears that he can and will take us across, one treading behind another. It's settled. When sleep seems to wrap us, then we'll move!"

That was what was done, and done so perfectly, late at night, Sir John Cope sleeping, thinking himself safe as in a castle. File after file wound noiselessly, by the one way through the marsh, and upon the farther side, so near to Cope, formed in the darkness into battle-lines.... Ian Rullock, passing through the marsh, saw in imagination Alexander lying with eyes closed.

The small force, the Stewart hope, prepared for onslaught. The dawn was coming, there was a smell of it in the air, far away a cock crowed. There stood, in the universal dimness, a first and strongest line, a second and weaker, badly armed line. The mass of this army were Highlanders, alert, strong, accustomed to dawn movements, dreamlike in the heather, along the glen-sides, in the crooked pass. They knew the tactics of surprise. They had claymores and targes, and the most muskets. But the second line had inadequate provision of weapons. Many here bore scythes fastened to staves. As they carried these over their shoulders Ian, looking back, saw them against the palest light like Death in replica.

The two lines hung motionless, on stout ground, now within the defense to which Cope had trusted, very close to the latter's sleeping camp. There were sentries, but the night was dark, the marsh believed to be unpassable, the crossing carried out with stealthy skill. But now the night was going.

In the most uncertain, the faintest light, there seemed to Cope's watchers, looking that way, a line of bushes not noted the day before. Officers were awakened. A movement ran through the camp like the shiver of water under dawn wind. The light thickened. A trumpet rang with a startled, emphatic note. Drums rolled. *To arms! To arms!* King George's army started up in the dawning. Infantry hastened into ranks, cavalrymen ran to their horses. The line of bushes moved, began to come forward with great rapidity.

The Highlanders flung themselves upon Cope's just-forming cavalry. With their claymores they slashed at the faces of horses. The hurt beasts wheeled, broke for the rear. Their fellows were wounded. Amid a whirlwind of blows, screams, shouts, with a suddenness that appalled, disorder became general. The Highlanders seemed to fight with a demoniac strength and ferocity and after methods of their own. They used their claymores, their dirks, their scythes fastened upon poles, against the horses, then, springing up, put long arms about the horsemen and, regardless of sword or pistol, dragged them down. They shouted their Gaelic slogans; their costume, themselves, seemed out of a fiercer, earlier world. A strangeness overclouded the senses; mist wreaths were everywhere, and an uncertainty as to the numbers of demons.... The cavalry broke. Officers tried to save the situation, to rally the units, to save all from being borne back. But there was no helping. Befell a panic flight, and at its heels the

Highland rush streamed into and had its way with Cope's infantry. The battle was won with a swift and horrible completeness and became a massacre. Not much quarter was given; much that was horrible was done and seen. Immoderate victory sat and sang to the white-cockaded army.

Out of the mist-bank before Captain Ian Rullock grew a great horse with a man upon it of great stature and frame. It came to the Jacobite like a vision, with a startling and intense reality. He was standing with his sword drawn; there was a drift of mist, and then there was the horse and rider—there was Alexander.

He looked down at Ian, and his face was not pale but set. He made a gesture that seemed full of satisfaction, and would have dismounted and drawn his sword. But there came a dash of maddened horses and their riders and a leaping stream of tartaned men. These drove like a wedge between; his horse wheeled, would leave no more its fellows; the tide of brute and man bore him away with it. Ian watched all go fighting by, a moving frieze, out of the mist into the mist.

CHAPTER XX

A triumphant Stewart went back to Holyrood, an exultant army, calling itself, now with some good show of bearing it through, the "royal" army, carried into Edinburgh its confident step and sanguine hue. Victory was with the old line, the magnificent attempt! The erstwhile doubting throng began, stage by stage, to mount toward enthusiasm. It was the quicker done that Charles Edward, or his wisest advisers, put forth a series of judicious civic and public measures. And, now that Cope had fled, King George had in Scotland no regular troops. Every day there came open accessions to the Prince's strength. The old Stewarts up again became a magnet, drawing more and more the filings. The Prince had presently between five and six thousand troops. The north was his, Edinburgh, the Jacobites scattered through the Lowlands. The moderate Whig and Presbyterian might begin to think of compounding, of finding virtues in necessity. The irreconcilables felt great alarm and saw coming upon them a helplessness.

But the Stewarts, with French approval behind, aimed at the recovery of England no less than Scotland. Windsor might well overdazzle Holyrood. This interest had received many and strong protestations of support from a wide swathe of English nobility and gentry. Lift the victorious army over the border, set it and the young Prince bodily upon English ground, would not great family after great family rouse its tenants, arm them, join the Prince? So at least it seemed to the flushed Stewart hope. King George was home from Hanover, British troops being brought back from the Continent. Best to fan high the fire of the rising while it might with most ease be fanned—best to march as soon as might be into England!

On the 1st of November they marched, three detachments by three roads, and the meeting-place Carlisle. All went most merrily well. On the 10th of November began the siege of Carlisle. The Prince had cannon now, some taken at Prestonpans, some arrived, no great time before, from France, first fruits of French support. The English General Wade was at Newcastle with a larger army than that of the Jacobites. But the siege of Carlisle was not lifted by Wade. After three days city and castle surrendered. Charles Edward and his army entered England.

From Carlisle they marched to Penrith—to Kendal, Lancaster, Preston, Manchester—clear, well-conducted marches, the army held well together and in hand, here and there handfuls of recruits. But no flood of loyally-shouting gentry, no bearers of great names drawing the sword for King James III and a gallant, youthful Regent! Each dawn said they will come! Each eve said they have not come! One month from leaving Edinburgh found this army of Highland chiefs and their clans, Lowland Scots, a few Englishmen, a few Irishmen, and a few Frenchmen, led by skilful enough generals and by a Prince the great-grandson of Charles I, deep in England, but little advanced in bulk for all that. Old cavalier England stayed upon its acres. Other times, other manners! And how to know when an old vortex begins to disintegrate and a mode of action becomes antiquated, belated?

Wade was to one side with his army, and now there loomed ahead the Duke of Cumberland and ten thousand English troops. Battle seemed imminent, yet again the Scots force pushed by. The 4th of December found this strange wedge, of no great mass, but of a tested, rapier-like keenness and hardness, at the town of Derby, with London not a hundred and thirty miles away. And still no English rising for the rightful King! Instead Whig armies, and a slow Whiggish buzzing beginning through all the country.

The Duke of Cumberland and Marshal Wade, two jaws opening for Jacobite destruction, had between them twenty thousand men. Spies brought report of thirty thousand drawn up before London, on Finchley Common. The Prince might have so many lions of the desert in his Highlanders, but multitude will make a net that lions cannot break. At Derby also they had news from that Scotland now so dangerously far behind them. Royal Scots had landed from France, the Irish brigade from the same country was on the seas, and French regiments besides. Lord John Drummond had in Scotland now at least three thousand men and good promise of more. The Prince held council with the Duke of Perth, Lord George Murray, Lord Nairn, the many chiefs and leading voices. Return to Scotland, make with these newly gathered troops and with others a greater army, expect aid from France, stand in a gained kingdom the onslaught from Hanoverian England? Or go on—go on toward London? Encounter, defeat, with half his number, the Duke of Cumberland's ten thousand, keep Wade from closing in behind them, meet the Finchley Common thousands, come to the enemy's capital of half a million souls? Return where there were friends? Go on where false-promising friends hugged safety? Go on to London, still hoping, trusting still to the glamour and outcry that ran before them, to extraordinary events called miracles? Hot was the debate! But on the 6th of December the Jacobite army turned back toward Scotland.

It began its homeward march long before dawn. Not all nor most had been told the decision. Even the changed direction, eyes upon slow-descending not upon climbing stars, did not at first enlighten. It might mean some detour, the Duke being out-maneuvered. But at last rose the winter dawn and lit remembered scene after scene. The news ran. The army was in retreat.

Ian Rullock, riding with a kinsman, Gordon, heard, up and down, an angry lamenting sound. "Little do the clans like turning back!"

"Hark! The chieftains are telling them it is for the best."

"Is it for the best? I do not like this month or aught that is done in it!"

A week later they were at Lancaster; three days after that at Kendal. Here Wade might have fallen upon them, but did not. A day or two and the main column approached Penrith. The no great amount of artillery was yet precious. Heavy to drag over heavy roads, the guns and straining horses were left in the rear. Four companies of Lowland infantry, Macdonald of Glengarry and his five hundred Highlanders, a few cavalrymen, and Lord George Murray himself tarried with the guns. The main column disappeared, lost among mountains and hills; this detached number had the wild country, the forbidding road, the December day to themselves. To get the guns and ammunition-wagons along proved a snail-and-tortoise business. Guns and escort fell farther and farther behind.

Ian Rullock, acting still as aide, rode from the Prince nearing Penrith to Lord George Murray, now miles to the rear. Why was the delay? and 'ware the Duke of Cumberland, certainly close at hand! The delay was greater, the distance between farther, than the Prince had supposed. Rullock rode through the late December afternoon by huge frozen waves of earth, under a roof of pallid blue, in his ears a small complaining wind like a wailing child. He rode till nightfall, and only then came to his objective, finding needed rest in the village of Shap. Here he sought Lord George Murray, gave information and was given it in turn, ate, drank, and then turned back through the December night to the Prince.

He rode and the huge winter stars seemed to watch him with at once a glittering intentness and a disdain of his pygmy being. Once he looked up to them with a gesture of his head. "Are we so far apart and so different?" he asked of Orion.

He was several miles upon his way to Penrith. Before him appeared a crossroad, noted by him in the afternoon. A great salient of a hill overhung it, and on the near side a fir wood crept close. He looked about him, and as he rode kept his hand upon his pistol. He did not think to meet an enemy in strength, but there might be lurkers, men of the countryside ready to fall upon stragglers from the army that had passed that way. He had left behind the crossroad when from in front, around the jut of the hill, came four horsemen. He turned his head. Others had started from the wood. He made to ride on as though he were of their kindred and cause, but hands were laid upon his bridle.

"Courier, no doubt—"

All turned into the narrow road. Half an hour's riding

brought in sight a substantial farm-house and about it the dimly flaring lights of a considerable camp, both cavalry and infantry. Rullock supposed it to be a detachment of Wade's, though it was possible that the Duke of Cumberland might have thrust advance troops thus far. He wished quite heartily that something might occur to warn Lord George Murray, the Macdonalds and the Prince's guns, asleep at Shap. For himself, he might, if he chose, pick out among the glittering constellations a shape like a scaffold.

When he dismounted he was brought past a bivouac fire and a coming and going of men afoot and on horseback, into the farm-house, where two or three officers sat at table. Questioned, threatened, and re-questioned, he had of course nothing to divulge. The less pressure was brought in that these troops were in possession of the facts which the moment desired. His name and rank he gave, it being idle to withhold them. In the end he was shut alone into a small room of the farm-house, behind a guarded door. He saw that there was planned an attack upon the detachment that with dawn would move from Shap. But this force of Wade's or of the Duke's was itself a detachment and apparently of no great mass. He could only hope that Lord George and the Macdonalds would move warily and when the shock came be found equal. All that was beyond his control. In the chill darkness he turned to the consideration of his own affair, which seemed desperate enough. He found, by groping, a bench against the wall. Wrapping himself in his cloak, he lay down upon this and tried to sleep, but could not. With all his will he closed off the future, and then as best he might the immediately environing present. After all, these armies—these struggles—these eery ambitions.... The feeling of *out of it* crept over him. It was an unfamiliar perception, impermanent. Yet it might leave a trace to work in the under-consciousness, on a far day to emerge, be revalued and added to.

This December air! Fire would be good—and with that thought he seemed to catch a gleam through the small-paned, small window, and in a moment through the opening door. He rose from the bench. A man in a long cloak entered the room, behind him a soldier bearing a lantern which he set upon a shelf above a litter of boards and kegs. Dismissed by a gesture, he went out, shutting the door behind him. The first man dropped his cloak, drew a heavy stool from the thrust-aside lumber, and sat down beneath the lantern. He spoke:

"Of all our many meeting-places, this looks most like the old cave in the glen!"

Ian moistened his lips. He resumed his seat against the wall. "I wondered, after Prestonpans, if you went home."

"Did you?"

"No, you are right. I did not."

"At all times it is the liar's wont still to lie. Small things or great—use or no use!"

"I am a prisoner and unarmed. You are the captor. To insult lies in your power."

"That is a jargon that may be dropped between us. Yet I, too, am bound by conventions! Seeing that you are a prisoner, and not my prisoner only, I cannot give you your sword or pistols, and we cannot fight.... The fighting, too, is a convention. I see that, and that it is not adequate. Yet so do I hold you in hatred that I would destroy you in this poor way also!"

The two sat not eight feet apart. Time was when either, finding himself in deadly straits, would have seen in the other a sure rescuer, or a friend to perish with him. One would have come to the other in a burst of light and warmth. So countless were the associations between them, so much knowledge, after all, did they have of each other, that even now, if they hated and contended, it must be, as it were, a contention within an orb. To each hemisphere, repelling the other, must yet come in lightning flashes the face of the whole.

Glenfernie, under the lantern-light, looked like the old laird his father. "No long time ago," he said, "'revenge,' 'vengeance,' seemed to me words of a low order! It was not so in my boyhood. Then they were often to me passionate, immediate, personal, and vindicated words! But it grew to be that they appeared words of a low order. It is not so now. As far as that goes I am younger than I was a year ago. I stand in a hot, bright light where they are vindicated. If fate sets you free again, yet I do not set you free! I shall be after you. I entered this place to tell you that."

"Do as you will!" answered Ian. Scorn mounted in his voice. "I shall withstand the shock of you!"

The net of name and form hardened, grew more iron and closer meshed. Each *I* contracted, made its carapace thicker. Each *I* bestrode, like Apollyon, the path of the other.

"Why should I undertake to defend myself?" said Ian. "I do not undertake to do so! So at least I shall escape the hypocrite! It is in the nature of man to put down other kings and be king himself!"

"Aye so? The prime difficulty in that is that the others, too, are immortal." Glenfernie rising, his great frame seemed to fill the little room. "Sooner may the Kelpie's Pool sink into the earth than I forego to give again to you what you have given! What is now all my wish? It is to seem to you, here and hereafter, the avenger of blood and fraud! Remember me so!"

He stood looking at the sometime friend with a dark and working face. Then, abruptly turning, he went away. The door of the small room closed behind him. Ian heard the bolt driven.

The night went leadenly by. At last he slept, and was waked by trumpets blowing. He saw through the window that it was at faintest dawn. Much later the door opened and a man brought him a poor breakfast. Rullock questioned him, but could gain nothing beyond the statement that to-day at latest the "rebels" would be wiped from the face of the earth. When he was gone Ian climbed to the small window that, even were it open and unguarded, was yet too small for his body to pass. But, working with care, he managed to loosen and draw inward without noise one of the round panes. Outside lay a trampled farm-yard. A few soldiers, apparently invalided, lounged about, but there was no such throng such as he had passed through when they brought him here. He supposed that the attack upon the force at Shap might be in progress. If the Duke of Cumberland's whole power was at hand the main column might be set upon. All around him the hills, the farm inclosure, and these petty walls cut off the outer world. The hours, the day, limped somehow by. He walked to keep himself warm.

Back and forth and to and fro. December—December—December! How cold was the Kelpie's Pool? Poisoned love—poisoned friendship—ambition in ruin—bells ringing for executions! To and fro—to and fro. He had always felt life as sensuous, rich, and warm, with garlands and colors. It had been large and aglow, with a profusion of arabesques of imagination and emotion. Thought had not lacked, but thought, too, bore a personal, passional cast, and was much interested in a golden world of sense. Just this December day the world seemed the ocean-bed of life, where dull creatures moved slowly in cold, thick ooze, and annihilation was much to be desired.... The day went by. The same man brought him supper. There seemed to be triumph in his face. "They'll be bringing in more prisoners—unless we don't make prisoners!" Nothing more could be gained from that quarter. In the night it began to rain. He listened to its dash against the window. Black Hill came into mind, and the rain against his windows there. He was cold, and he tried, with the regressive sense, to feel himself in that old, warm nest. His Black Hill room rose about him, firelit. The fire lighted that Italian painting of a city of refuge and a fleeing man, behind whom ran the avenger of blood.... Then it was July, and he was in the glen with Elspeth Barrow. He fought away from the recollection of that, for it involved a sickness of the soul.... Italy! Think of Italy. Venice, and a month that he had spent there alone—Old Steadfast being elsewhere. It had been a warm season, warm and rich, sun-kissed and languorous, like the fruit, like the Italian women.... Leave out the women, but try to feel again the sun of Venice!

He tried, but the cold of his prison fought with the sun. Then suddenly sprang clamor without. The uproar increased. He rose, he heard the bolts open, the door open. In came light and voices. "Captain Rullock! We beat them at Clifton! We learned that you were here! Lord George sent us back for you...."

Three days later Scotch earth was again beneath their feet. They marched to Glasgow; they marched to Stirling; they fought the battle of Falkirk and again there was Jacobite victory. And now there was an army of eight thousand.... And then began a time of poor policy, mistaken moves. And in April befell the battle of Culloden and far-resounding ruin.

CHAPTER XXI

The green May rolled around and below the Highland shelter where Ian lay, fugitive, like thousands of others, after Culloden. The Prince had stayed to give an order to his broken army. *Sauve qui peut!* Then he, too, became a fugitive, passing from one fastness to another of these glens and the mountains that overtowered them. The Stewart hope was sunk in the sea of dead hopes. Cumberland, with for the time and place a great force and with an ugly fury, hunted all who had been in arms against King George.

Ian Rullock couched high upon a mountain-side, in a shelter of stone and felled tree built in an angle of crag, screened by a growth of birch and oak, made long ago against emergencies. A path, devious and hidden, connected it first with a hut far below, and then, at several miles' distance, with the house of a chieftain, now a house of terror, with the chieftain in prison and his sons in hiding, and the women watching with hard-beating hearts. Ian, a kinsman of the house, had been given, *faute de mieux*, this old, secret hold, far up, where at least he could see danger if it approached. Food had been stored for him here and sheepskins given for bedding. He was so masked by splintered and fallen pieces of rock that he might, with great precautions, kindle a fire. A spring like a fairy cup gave him water. More than one rude comfort had been provided. He had even a book or two, caught up from his kinsman's small collection. He had been here fourteen days.

At first they were days and nights of vastly needed rest. Bitter had been the fatigue, privation, wandering, immediately after Culloden! Now he was rested.

He was by nature sanguine. When the sun had irretrievably blackened and gone out he might be expected at least to attempt to gather materials and ignite another. He was capable of whistling down the wind those long hopes of fame and fortune that had hung around the Stewart star. And now he was willing to let go the old half-acknowledged boyish romance and sentiment, the glamour of the imagination that had dressed the cause in hues not its own. Two years of actual contact with the present incarnations of that cause had worn the sentiment threadbare.

Seated or lying upon the brown earth by the splintered crag, alone save for the wheeling birds and the sound of wind and water and the sailing clouds, he had time at last for the rise into mind, definitely shaped and visible, of much that had been slowly brewing and forming. He was conscious of a beginning of a readjustment of ideas. For a long time now he had been pledged to personal daring, to thought forced to become supple and concentrated, to hard, practical planning, physical hardship and danger. In the midst of this had begun to grow up a criticism of all the enterprises upon which he was engaged. Scope—in many respects the Jacobite character, generally taken, was amiable and brave, but its prime exhibit was not scope! Somewhat narrow, somewhat obsolete; Ian's mind now saw Jacobitism in that light. As he sat without his rock fortress, in the shadow of birch-trees, with lower hills and glens at his feet, he had a pale vision of Europe, of the world. Countries and times showed themselves contiguous. "Causes," dynastic wars, political life, life in other molds and hues, appeared in chords and sequences and strokes of the eye, rather than in the old way of innumerable, vivid, but faintly connected points. "I begin to see," thought Ian, "how things travel together, like with like!" His body was rested, recovered, his mind invigorated. He had had with him for long days the very elixir of solitude. Relations and associations that before had been banked in ignorance came forth and looked at him. "You surely have known us before, though you had forgotten that you knew us!" He found that he was taking delight in these expansions of meaning. He thought, "If I can get abroad out of this danger, out of old circles, I'll roam and study and go to school to wider plans!" He suddenly thought, "This kind of thing is what Old Steadfast meant when he used to say that I did not see widely enough." He moved sharply. A hot and bitter flood seemed to well up within him. "He himself is seeing narrowly now—Alexander Jardine!"

He left the crag and went for a scrambling and somewhat dangerous walk along the mountain-side. There was peril in leaving that one rock-curtained place. Two days before he had seen what he thought to be signs of red-coated soldiers in the glen far below. But he must walk—he must exercise his body, note old things, not give too much time to new perceptions! He breathed the keen, sweet mountain air; with a knife that he had he fell to making a staff from a young oak; he watched the pass below and the shadows of the clouds; he climbed fairly to the mountain-top and had a great view; he sang an old song, not aloud, but under his breath; and at last he must come back with solitude to his fastness. And here was brooding thought again!

Two more days passed. The man from the hut below in the pass came at dusk with food carefully sent from the chieftain's hall. Redcoats had gone indeed through the glen, but they could never find the path to this place! They might return or they might not; they were like the devil who rose by your side when you were most peaceful! Angus went down the mountain-side. The sound of his footstep died away. Ian had again Solitude herself.

Another day and night passed. He watched the sun climb toward noon, and as the day grew warm he heard a step upon the hidden path. With a pistol in either hand he moved, as stealthily, as silently as might be, to a platform of rock that overhung the way of the intruder. In another moment the latter was in sight—one man climbing steadily the path to the old robber fastness. He saw that it was Glenfernie. No one followed him. He came on alone.

Rullock put by his pistols and, moving to a chair of rock, sat there. The other's great frame rose level with him, stepped upon the rocky floor. Ian had been growing to feel an anger at solitude. When he saw Alexander he had not been able to check an inner movement of welcome. He felt an old—he even felt a new—affection for the being upon whom, certainly, he had leaned. There flowed in, in an impatient wave, the consideration that he must hate....

But Glenfernie hated. Ian rose to face him.

"So you've found your way to my castle? It is a climb! You had best sit and rest yourself. I have my sword now, and I will give you satisfaction."

Glenfernie nodded. He sat upon a piece of fallen rock. "Yes, I will rest first, thank you! I have searched since dawn, and the mountain is steep. Besides, I want to talk to you."

Ian brought from his cupboard oat-cake and a flask of brandy. The other shook his head.

"I had food at sunrise, and I drank from a spring below."

"Very good!"

The laird of Glenfernie sat looking down the mountain-sides and over to far hills and moving clouds, much as he used to sit in the crook of the old pine outside the broken wall at Glenfernie. There was a trick of posture when he was at certain levels within himself. Ian knew it well.

"Perhaps I should tell you," said Alexander, "that I came alone through the pass and that I have been alone for some days. If there are soldiers near I do not know of them."

"It is not necessary," answered Ian. While he spoke he saw in a flash both that his confidence was profound that it was not necessary, and that that incapacity to betray that might be predicated of Old Steadfast was confined to but one of the two upon this rock. The enlightenment stung, then immediately brought out a reaction. "To each some specialty in error! I no more than he am monstrous!" There arose a desire to defend himself, to show Old Steadfast certain things. He spoke. "We are going to fight presently—"

"Yes."

"That's understood. Now listen to me a little! For long years we were together, friends near and warm! You knew that I saw differently from you in regard to many things—in regard, for instance, to women. I remember old discussions.... Well, you differed, and sometimes you were angry. But for all that, friendship never went out with violence! You knew the ancient current that I swam in—that it was narrower, more mixed with earth, than your own! But you were tolerant. You took me as I was.... What has developed was essentially there then, and you knew it. The difference is that at last it touched what you held to be your own. Then, and not till then, the sinner became *anathema!*"

"In some part you say truth. But my load of inconsistency does not lighten yours of guilt."

"Perhaps not. We were friends. Five-sixths of me made a fair enough friend and comrade. We interlocked. You had gifts and possessions I had not. I liked the oak-feeling of you—the great ship in sail! In turn, I had the key, perhaps, to a few lands of bloom and flavor that you lacked. We interchanged and thought that we were each the richer. Five-sixths.... Say, then, that the other sixth might be defined as no-friend, or as false friend! Say that it was wilful, impatient of superiorities, proud, vain, willing to hurt, betray, and play the demon generally! Say that once it gave itself swing it darkened some of the other sixths.... Well, it is done! Yet there was gold. Perhaps, laird of Glenfernie, there is still gold in the mine!"

"You are mistaken in your proportions. Gold! You are to me the specter of the Kelpie's Pool!"

Silence held for a minute or two. The clouds, passing between earth and sun, made against the mountain slopes impalpable, dark, fantastic shapes. An eagle wheeled above its nest at the mountain-top. Ian spoke again. His tone had altered.

"If I do not decline remorse, I at least decline the leaden cope of it you would have me wear! There is such a thing as fair play to oneself! Two years ago come August Elspeth Barrow and I agreed to part—"

"Oh, 'agreed'—"

"Have it so! I said that we must part. She acquiesced— and that without the appeals that the stage and literature show us. Oh, doubtless I might have seen a pierced spirit, and did not, and was brute beast there! But one thing you have got to believe, and that is that neither of us knew what was to happen. Even with that, she was aware of how a letter might be sent, with good hope of reaching me. She was not a weak, ignorant girl.... I went away, and within a fortnight was deep in that long attempt that ends here. I became actively an agent for the Prince and his father. A hundred names and their fates were in my hands. You can fill in the multitude of activities, each seeming small in itself, but the whole preoccupying every field.... If Elspeth Barrow wrote I never received her letter. When my thought turned in that direction, it saw her well and not necessarily unhappy. Time passed. For reasons, I ceased to write home, and again for reasons I obliterated paths by which I might be reached. For months I heard nothing, as I said nothing. I was on the very eve of quitting Paris, under careful disguise, to go into Scotland. Came suddenly your challenge—and still, though I knew that to you at least our relations must have been discovered, I knew no more than that! I did not know that she was dead.... I could not stay to fight you then. I left you to brand me as you pleased in your mind."

Mary Johnston

"I had already branded you."

"Later, I saw that you had. Perhaps then I did not wonder. In September—almost a year from that Christmas Eve—I yet did not know. Then, in Edinburgh, I came upon Mr. Wotherspoon. He told me.... I had no wicked intent toward Elspeth Barrow—none according to my canon, which has been that of the natural man. We met by accident. We loved at once and deeply. She had in her an elf queen! But at last the human must have darkened and beset her. Had I known of those fears, those dangers, I might have turned homeward from France and every shining scheme...."

"Ah no, you would not—"

"... If I would not, then certainly I should have written to Jarvis Barrow and to others, acknowledging my part—"

"Perhaps you would have done that. Perhaps not. You might have found reasons of obligation for not doing so. 'Loved deeply'! You never loved her deeply! You have loved nothing deeply save yourself!"

"Perhaps. Yet I think," said Ian, "that I would have done as much as that. But Alexander Jardine, of course, would not have taken one erring step!"

"Have you done now?"

"Yes."

Glenfernie rose to his feet. He stood against the gulf of air and his great frame seemed enlarged, like the figure of the Brocken. He was like his father, the old laird, but there glowed an extremer dark anger and power. The old laird had made himself the dream-avenger of injuries adopted, not felt at first hand. The present laird knew the wounding, the searing. "All his life my father dreamed of grappling with Grierson of Lagg. My Grierson of Lagg stands before me in the guise of a false friend and lover!... What do I care for your weighing to a scruple how much the heap of wrong falls short of the uttermost? The dire wrong is there, to me the direst! Had I deep affection for you once? Now you speak to me of every treacherous morass, every *ignis fatuus*, past and present! The traveler through life does right to drain the bogs as they arise—put it out of their power to suck down man, woman, and child! It is not his cause alone. It is the general cause. If there be a God, He approves. Draw your sword and let us fight!"

They fought. The platform of rock was smooth enough for good footing. They had no seconds, unless the shadows upon the hills and the mountain eagles answered for such. Ian was the highly trained fencer, adept of the sword. Glenfernie's knowledge was lesser, more casual. But he had his bleak wrath, a passion that did not blind nor overheat, but burned white, that set him, as it were, in a tingling, crackling arctic air, where the shadows were sharp-edged, the nerves braced and the will steel-tipped. They fought with determination and long—Ian now to save his own life, Alexander for Revenge, whose man he had become. The clash of blade against blade, the shifting of foot upon the rock floor, made the dominant sound upon the mountain-side. The birds stayed silent in the birch-trees. Self-service, pride, anger, jealousy, hatred— the inner vibrations were heavy.

The sword of Ian beat down his antagonist's guard, leaped, and gave a deep wound. Alexander's sword fell from his hand. He staggered and vision darkened. He came to his knees, then sank upon the ground. Ian bent over him. He felt his anger ebb. A kind of compunction seized him. He thought, "Are you so badly hurt, Old Steadfast?"

Alexander looked at him. His lips moved. "Lo, how the wicked prosper! But do you think that Justice will have it so?" The blood gushed; he sank back in a swoon.

On this mountain-side, some distance below the fastness, a stone, displaced by a human foot, rolled down the slope with a clattering sound. The fugitive above heard it, thought, too, that he caught other sounds. He crossed to the nook whence he had view of the way of approach. Far down he saw the redcoats, and then, much nearer, coming out from dwarf woods, still King George's men.

Ian caught up his belt and pistols. He sheathed his sword. "They'll find you and save you, Glenfernie! I do not think that you will die!" Above him sprang the height of crag, seemingly unscalable. But he had been shown the secret, just possible stair. He mounted it. Masked by bushes, it swung around an abutment and rose by ledge and natural tunnel, perilous and dizzy, but the one way out to safety. At last, a hundred feet above the old shelter, he dipped over the crag head to a saucer-like depression walled from all redcoat view by the surmounted rock. With a feeling of triumph he plunged through small firs and heather, and, passing the mountain brow, took the way that should lead him to the next glen.

CHAPTER XXII

The laird of Glenfernie, rising from the great chair by the table, moved to the window of the room that had been his father's and mother's, the room where both had died. He remembered the wild night of snow and wind in which his father had left the body. Now it was August, and the light golden upon the grass and the pilgrim cedar. Alexander walked slowly, with a great stick under his hand. Old Bran was dead, but a young Bran stretched himself, wagged his tail, and looked beseechingly at the master.

"I'll let you out," said the latter, "but I am a prisoner; I cannot let myself out!"

He moved haltingly to the door, opened it, and the dog ran forth. Glenfernie returned to the window. "Prisoner." The word brought to his strongly visualizing mind prisoners and prisons through all Britain this summer— shackled prisoners, dark prisons, scaffolds.... He leaned his head against the window-frame.

"O God that my father and my grandfather served—God of old times—of Israel in Egypt! I think that I would release them all if I could—*all but one! Not him!*" He looked at the cedar. "Who was he, in truth, who planted that, perhaps for a remembrance? And he, and all men, had and have some one deep wrong that shall not be brooked!"

He stood in a brown study until there was a tap at the door. "Come in!"

Alice entered, bearing before her a bowl of flowers of all fair hues and shapes. She herself was like a bright, strong, winsome flower. "To make your room look bonny!" she said, and placed the bowl upon the table. To do so she pushed aside the books. "What a withered, snuff-brown lot! Won't you be glad when you are back in the keep with all the books?"

Glenfernie, wrapped in a brown gown, came with his stick back to the great chair before the books. "Bonny— they are bonny!" he said and touched the flowers. "I've set a week from to-day to be dressed and out of this and back to the keep. Another week, and I shall ride Black Alan."

"Ah," said Alice. "You mustn't determine that you can do it all yourself! There will be the doctor and the wound!"

Alexander took her hands and held them. "You are a fine philosopher! Where is Strickland?"

"Helping Aunt Grizel with accounts. Do you want him?"

"When you go. But not for a long while if you will stay."

Alice regarded him with her mother's shrewdness. "Oh, Glenfernie, for all you've traveled and are so learned, it's not me nor Mr. Strickland, but the moon now that you're wanting! I don't know what your moon is, but it's the moon!"

Alexander laughed. "And is not the moon a beautiful thing?"

"The books say that it is cold and almost dead, wrinkled and ashen. But I've got to go," said Alice, "and I'll send you Mr. Strickland."

Strickland came presently. "You look much stronger this morning, Glenfernie. I'm glad of that! Shall I read to you, or write?"

"Read, I think. My eyes dazzle still when I try. Some strong old thing—the Plutarch there. Read the *Brutus*."

Strickland read. He thought that now Alexander listened, and that now he had traveled afar. The minutes passed. The flowers smelled sweetly, murmuring sounds came in the open windows. Bran scratched at the door and was admitted. Far off, Alice's voice was heard singing. Strickland read on. The laird of Glenfernie was not at Rome, in the Capitol, by Pompey's statue. He walked with Elspeth Barrow the feathery green glen.

Davie appeared in the door. "A letter, sir, come post." He brought it to Glenfernie's outstretched hand.

"From Edinburgh—from Jamie," said the latter.

Strickland laid down his book and moved to the window. Standing there, his eyes upon the great cedar, massive and tall as though it would build a tower to heaven, his mind left Brutus, Caesar, and Cassius, and played somewhat idly over the British Isles. He was recalled by an exclamation, not loud, but so intense and fierce that it startled like a meteor of the night. He turned. Glenfernie sat still in his great chair, but his features were changed, his mouth working, his eyes shooting light. Strickland advanced toward him.

"Not bad news of Jamie!"

"Not of Jamie! From Jamie." He thrust the letter under the other's eyes. "Read—read it out!"

Strickland read aloud.

> "Here is authoritative news. Ian Rullock, after lying two months in the tolbooth, has escaped. A gaoler connived, it is supposed, else it would seem impossible. Galbraith tells me he would certainly have been hanged in September. It is thought that he got to Leith and on board a ship. Three cleared that day—for Rotterdam, for Lisbon, and Virginia."

Alexander took the letter again. "That is all of that import." Strickland once more felt astonishment. Glenfernie's tone was quiet, almost matter-of-fact. The blood had ebbed from his face; he sat there collected, a great quiet on the heels of storm. It was impossible not to admire the power that could with such swiftness exercise control. Strickland hesitated. He wished to speak, but did not know how far he might with wisdom. The laird forestalled him.

"Sit down! This is to be talked over, for again my course of life alters."

Strickland took his chair. He leaned his arm upon the table, his chin upon his hand. He did not look directly at the man opposite, but at the bowl of flowers between them.

"When a man has had joy and lost it, what does he do?" Glenfernie's voice was almost contemplative.

"One man one thing, and one another," said Strickland. "After his nature."

"No. All go seeking it in the teeth of death and horror. That's universal! Joy must be sought. But it may not wear the old face; it may wear another."

"I suppose that true joy has one face."

"When one platonizes—perhaps! I keep to-day to earth, to the cave. Do you know," said Alexander, "why I sit here wounded?"

"Of outward facts I do not know any more than is, I think, pretty generally known through this countryside."

"As—?"

Strickland looked still at the bowl of flowers. "It is known, I think, that you loved Elspeth Barrow and would have wedded her. And that, while you were from home, the man who called himself, and was called by you, your nearest friend, stepped before you—made love to her, betrayed her—and left her to bear the shame.... I myself know that he kept you in ignorance, and that, away from here, he let you still write to him in friendship and answered in that tone.... All know that she drowned herself because of him, and that you knew naught until you yourself entered the Kelpie's Pool and found her body and carried her home.... After that you left the country to find and fight Ian Rullock. Folk know, too, that he evaded you then. You returned. Then came this insurrection, and news that he was in Scotland with the Pretender. You joined the King's forces. Then, after Culloden, you found the false friend in hiding, in the mountains. The two of you fought, and, as is often the way, the injurer seemed again to win. You were dangerously wounded. He fled. Soldiers upon his track found you lying in your blood. You were carried to Inverness. Dickson and I went to you, brought you at last home. In the mean time came news that the man you fought had been taken by the soldiers. I suppose that we have all had visions of him, in prison, expecting to suffer with other conspirators."

"Yes, I have had visions ... outward facts!... Do you know the inner, northern ocean, where sleep all the wrecks?"

"As I have watched you since you were a boy, it is improbable that I should not have some divining power. In Inverness, too, while you were fevered, you talked and talked.... You have walked with Tragedy, felt her net and her strong whip." Strickland lifted his eyes from the bowl, pushed back his chair a little, and looked full at the laird of Glenfernie. "What then? Rise, Glenfernie, and leave her behind! And if you do not now, it will soon be hard for you to do so! Remember, too, that I watched your father—"

"After I find Ian Rullock in Holland or Lisbon or America—"

Strickland made a movement of deep concern. "You have met and fought this man. Do you mean so to nourish vengeance—"

"I mean so to aid and vindicate distressed Justice."

"Is it the way?"

"I think that it is the way."

Strickland was silent, seeing the uselessness. Glenfernie was one to whom conviction must come from within. A stillness held in the room, broken by the laird in the voice that was growing like his father's. "Nothing lacks now but strength, and I am gaining that—will gain it the faster now! Travel—travel!... All my travel was preparatory to this."

"Do you mean," asked Strickland, "to kill him when you find him?"

"I like your directness. But I do not know—I do not know!... I mean to be his following fiend. To have him ever feel me—when he turns his head ever to see me!"

The other sighed sharply. He thought to himself, "Oh, mind, thy abysses!"

Indeed, Glenfernie looked at this moment stronger. He folded Jamie's letter and put it by. He drew the bowl of flowers to him and picked forth a rose. "A week—two at most—and I shall be wholly recovered!" His voice had fiber, decision, even a kind of cheer.

Strickland thought, "It is his fancied remedy, at which he snatches!"

Glenfernie continued: "We'll set to work to-morrow upon long arrangements! With you to manage here, I will not be missed." Without waiting for the morrow he took quill and paper and began to figure.

Strickland watched him. At last he said, "Will you go at once in three ships to Holland, Portugal, and America?"

"Has the onlooker room for irony, while to me it looks so simple? I shall ship first to the likeliest land.... In ten days—in two weeks at most—to Edinburgh—"

Strickland left him figuring and, rising, went to the window. He saw the great cedar, and in mind the pilgrim who planted it there. All the pilgrims—all the crusaders— all the men in Plutarch; the long frieze of them, the full ocean of them ... all the self-search, dressed as search of another. "I, too, I doubt not—I, too!" Buried scenes in his own life rose before Strickland. Behind him scratched Glenfernie's pen, sounded Glenfernie's voice:

"I am going to see presently if I can walk as far as the keep. In two or three days I shall ride. There are things that I shall know when I get to Edinburgh. He would take, if he could, the ship that would land him at the door of France."

CHAPTER XXIII

Alexander rode across the moors to the glen head. Two or three solitary farers that he met gave him eager good day.

"Are ye getting sae weel, laird? I am glad o' that!"

"Good day, Mr. Jardine! I rejoice to see you recovered. Well, they hung more of them yesterday!"

"Gude day, Glenfernie! It's a bonny morn, and sweet to be living!"

At noon he looked down on the Kelpie's Pool. The air was sweet and fine, bird sounds came from the purple heather. The great blue arch of the sky smiled; even the pool, reflecting day, seemed to have forgotten cold and dread. But for Glenfernie a dull, cold, sick horror overspread the place. He and Black Alan stood still upon the moor brow. Large against the long, clean, horizon sweep, they looked the sun-bathed, stone figures of horse and man, set there long ago, guarding the moor, giving warning of the kelpie.

"None has been found to warn. There is none but the kelpie waits for.... But punish—punish!"

Mary Johnston

He and Black Alan pushed on to the head of the glen. Here was Mother Binning's cot, and here he dismounted, fastening the horse to the ash-tree. Mother Binning was outdoors, gathering herbs in her apron.

*   *   *   *   *

She straightened herself as he stepped toward her. "Eh, laird of Glenfernie, ye gave me a start! I thought ye came out of the ground by the ash-tree!... Wound is healed, and life runs on to another springtime?"

"Yes, it's another springtime.... I do not think that I believe in scrying, Mother Binning. But I'm where I pick up all straws with which to build me a nest! Sit down and scry for me, will you?"

"I canna scry every day, nor every noon, nor every year. What are you wanting to see, Glenfernie?"

"Oh, just my soul's desire!"

Mother Binning turned to her door. She put down the herbs, then brought a pan of water and set it down upon the door-step, and herself beside it. "It helps—onything that's still and clear! Wait till the ripple's gane, and then dinna speak to me. But gin I see onything, it will na be sae great a thing as a soul's desire."

She sat still and he stood still, leaning against the side of her house. Mother Binning sat with fixed gaze. Her lips moved. "There's the white mist. It's clearing."

"Tell me if you see a ship."

"Yes, I see it...."

"Tell me if you see its port."

"Yes, I see."

"Describe it—the houses, the country, the dress and look of the people—"

Mother Binning did so.

"That's not Holland—that would be Lisbon. Look at the ship again, Mother. Look at the sailors. Look at the passengers if there are any. Whom do you see?"

"Ah!" said Mother Binning. "There's a braw wrong-doer for you, sitting drinking Spanish wine!"

"Say his name."

"It's he that once, when you were a lad, you brought alive from the Kelpie's Pool."

"Thank you, Mother! That's what I wanted. *Scrying!* Who gives to whom—who gives back to whom? The underneath great I, I suppose. Left hand giving to right—and no brand-new news! All the same, other drifts concurring, I think that he fled by the Lisbon ship!"

Mother Binning pushed aside the pan of water and rubbed her hand across her eyes. She took up her bundle of herbs. "Hoot, Glenfernie! do ye think that's your soul's desire?"

Jock came limping around the house. Alexander could not now abide the sight of this cripple who had spied, and had not shot some fashion of arrow! He said good-by and loosed Black Alan from the ash-tree and rode away. He would not tread the glen. His memory recoiled from it as from some Eastern glen of serpents. He and Black Alan went over the moors. And still it was early and he had his body strength back. He rode to Littlefarm.

Robin Greenlaw was in the field, coat off in the gay, warm weather. He came to Glenfernie's side, and the latter dismounted and sat with him under a tree. Greenlaw brought a stone jug and tankard and poured ale.

The laird drank. "That's good, Robin!" He put down the tankard. "Are you still a poet?"

"If I was so once upon a time, I hope I am so still. At any rate, I still make verses. And I see poems that I can never write."

"'Never'—how long a word that is!"

Greenlaw gazed at the workers in the field. "I met Mr. Strickland the other day. He says that you will travel again."

"'Travel'—yes."

"The Jardine Arms gets it from the Edinburgh road that Ian Rullock made a daring escape."

"He had always ingenuity and a certain sort of physical bravery."

"So has Lucifer, Milton says. But he's not Lucifer."

"No. He is weak and small."

"Well, look Glenfernie! I would not waste my soul chasing him!"

"How dead are you all! You, too, Greenlaw!"

Robin flushed. "No! I hate all that he did that is vile! If all his escaping leads him to violent death, I shall not find it in me to grieve! But all the same, I would not see you narrowed to the wolf-hunter that will never make the wolf less than the wolf! I don't know. I've always thought of you as one who would serve Wisdom and show us her beauty—"

"To me this is now wisdom—this is now beauty. Poets may stay and make poetry, but I go after Ian Rullock!"

"Oh, there's poetry in that, too," said Greenlaw, "because there's nothing in which there isn't poetry! But you're choosing the kind you're not best in, or so it seems to me."

Glenfernie rode from Littlefarm homeward. But the next day he and Black Alan went to Black Hill. Here he saw Mr. Touris alone. That gentleman sat with a shrunken and shriveled look.

"Eh, Glenfernie! I am glad to see that you are yourself again! Well, my sister's son has broken prison."

"Yes, one prison."

"God knows they were all mad! But I could not wish to see him in my dreams, hanging dark from the King's gallows!"

"From the King's gallows and for old, mad, Stewart hopes? I find," said Glenfernie, "that I do not wish that, either. He would have gone for the lesser thing—and the long true, right vengeance been delayed!"

"What is that?" asked Mr. Touris, dully.

"His wrong shall be ever in his mind, and I the painter's brush to paint it there! Give me, O God, the power of genius!"

"Are you going to follow him and kill him?"

"I am going to follow him. At first I thought that I would kill him. But my mind is changing as to that."

Mr. Touris sighed heavily. "I don't know what is the matter with the world.... One does one's best, but all goes wrong. All kinds of hopes and plans.... When I look back to when I was a young man, I wonder.... I set myself an aim in life, to lift me and mine from poverty. I saved for it, denied for it, was faithful. It came about and it's ashes in my mouth! Yet I took it as a trust, and was faithful. What does the Bible say, 'Vanity of vanities'? But I say that the world's made wrong."

Glenfernie left him at last, wrinkled and shrunken and shriveled, cold on a summer day, plying himself with wine, a serving-man mending the fire upon the hearth. Alexander went to Mrs. Alison's parlor. He found her deep chair placed in the garden without, and she herself sitting there, a book in hand, but not read, her form very still, her eyes upon a shaft of light that was making vivid a row of flowers. The book dropped beside her on the grass; she rose quickly. The last time they had met was before Culloden, before Prestonpans.

She came to him. "You're well, Alexander! Thanks be! Sit down, my dear, sit down!" She would have made him take her chair, but he laughed and brought one for himself from the room. "I bless my ancestors for a physical body that will not keep wounds!"

She sank into her chair again and sat in silence, gazing at him. Her clear eyes filled with tears, but she shook them away. At last she spoke: "Oh, I see the other sort of wounds! Alexander! lay hold of the nature that will make them, too, to heal!"

"Saint Alison," he answered, "look full at what went on. Now tell me if those are wounds easy to heal. And tell me if he were not less than a man who pocketed the injury, who said to the injurer, 'Go in peace!'"

She looked at him mournfully. "Is it to pocket the injury? Will not all combine—silently, silently—to teach him at last? Less than man—man—more than man, than to-day's appearing man?... I am not wise. For yourself and the ring of your moment you may be judging inevitably, rightly.... But with what will you overcome—and in overcoming what will you overcome?"

He made a gesture of impatience. "Oh, friend, once I, too, could be metaphysical! I cannot now."

Speech failed between them. They sat with eyes upon the garden, the old tree, the August blue sky, but perhaps they hardly saw these. At last she turned. She had a slender, still youthful figure, an oval, lovely, still young face. Now there was a smile upon her lips, and in her eyes a light deep, touching, maternal.

"Go as you will, hunt him as you will, do what you will! And he, too—Ian! Ian and his sins. Grapes in the wine-press—wheat beneath the flail—ore in the ardent fire, and over all the clouds of wrath! Suffering and making to suffer—sinning and making to sin.... And yet will the dawn come, and yet will you be reconciled!"

"Not while memory holds!"

"Ah, there is so much to remember! Ian has so much and you have so much.... When the great memory comes you will see. But not now, it is apparent, not now! So go if you will and must, Alexander, with the net and the spear!"

"Did he not sin?"

"Yes."

"I also sin. But my sin does not match his! God makes use of instruments, and He shall make use of me!"

"If He 'shall,' then He shall. Let us leave talk of this. Where you go may love and light go, too—and work it out, and work it out!"

He did not stay long in her garden. All Black Hill oppressed him now. The dark crept in upon the light. She saw that it was so.

"He can be friends now with none. He sees in each one a partisan his own or Ian's." She did not detain him, but when he rose to say good-by helped him to say it without delay.

He went, and she paced her garden, thinking of Ian who had done so great wrong, and Alexander who cried, "My enemy!" She stayed in the garden an hour, and then she turned and went to play piquet with the lonely, shriveled man, her brother.

CHAPTER XXIV

Two days after this Glenfernie rode to White Farm. Jenny Barrow met him with exclamations.

"Oh, Mr. Alexander! Oh, Glenfernie! And they say that you are amaist as weel as ever—but to me you look twelve years older! Eh, and this warld has brought gray into *my* hair! Father's gane to kirk session, and Gilian's awa'."

He sat down beside her. Her hands went on paring apples, while her eyes and tongue were busy elsewhere.

"They say you're gaeing to travel."

"Yes. I'm starting very soon."

"It's na *said oot*—but a kind of whisper's been gaeing around." She hesitated, then, "Are you gaeing after him, Glenfernie?"

"Yes."

Jenny put down her knife and apple. She drew a long breath, so that her bosom heaved under her striped gown. A bright color came into her cheeks. She laughed.

"Aweel, I wadna spare him if I were you!"

He sat with her longer than he had done with Mrs. Alison. He felt nearer to her. He could be friends with her, while he moved from the other as from a bloodless wraith. Here breathed freely all the strong vindications! He sat, sincere and strong, and sincere and strong was the countrywoman beside him.

"Oh aye!" said Jenny. "He's a villain, and I wad gie him all that he gave of villainy!"

"That is right," said Alexander, "to look at it simply!" He felt that those were his friends who felt in this as did he.

On the moor, riding homeward, he saw before him Jarvis Barrow. Dismounting, he met the old man beside a cairn, placed there so long ago that there was only an elfin story for the deeds it commemorated.

"Gude day, Glenfernie! So that Hieland traitor did not slay ye?"

"No."

Jarvis Barrow, white-headed, strong-featured, far yet, it seemed, from incapacitating old age, took his seat upon a great stone loosened from the mass. He leaned upon his staff; his collie lay at his feet. "Many wad say a lang time, with the healing in it of lang time, since a fause lover sang in the ear of my granddaughter, in the glen there!"

"Aye, many would say it."

"I say 'a fause lover.' But the ane to whom she truly listened is an aulder serpent than he ... wae to her!"

"No, no!"

"But I say 'aye!' I am na weak! She that worked evil and looseness, harlotry, strife, and shame, shall she na have her hire? As, Sunday by Sunday, I wad ha' set her in kirk, before the congregation, for the stern rebuking of her sin, so, mak no doubt, the Lord pursues her now! Aye, He shakes His wrath before her eyes! Wherever she turns she sees 'Fornicatress' writ in flames!"

"No!"

"But aye!"

"Where she was mistaken—where, maybe, she was wilfully blind—she must learn. Not the learning better, but the old mistake until it is lost in knowledge, will clothe itself in suffering! But that is but a part of her! If there is error within, there is also Michael within to make it of naught! She releases herself. It is horrible to me to see you angered against her, for you do not discriminate—and you are your Michael, but not hers!"

"Adam is speaking—still the woman's lover! I'm not for contending with you. She tore my heart working folly in my house, and an ill example, and for herself condemnation!"

"Leave her alone! She has had great unhappiness!" He moved the small stones of the cairn with his fingers. "I am going away from Glenfernie."

"Aye. It was in mind that ye would! You and he were great friends."

"The greater foes now."

"I gie ye full understanding there!"

"With my father, those he hated were beyond his touch. So he walked among shadows only. But to me this world is a not unknown wood where roves, alive and insolent, my utter enemy! I can touch him and I will touch him!"

"Not you, but the Lord Wha abides not evil!... How sune will ye be gaeing, Glenfernie?"

"As soon as I can ride far. As soon as everything is in order here. I know that I am going, but I do not know if I am returning."

"I haud na with dueling. It's un-Christian. But mony's the ancient gude man that Jehovah used for sword! Aye, and approved the sword that he used—calling him faithful servant and man after His heart! I am na judging."

From the moor Glenfernie rode through the village. Folk spoke to him, looked after him; children about the doors called to others, "It's tha laird on Black Alan!" Old and young women, distaff or pan or pot or pitcher in hand, turned head, gazed, spoke to themselves or to one another. The Jardine Arms looked out of doors. "He's unco like tha auld laird!" Auld Willy, that was over a hundred, raised a piping voice, "Did ye young things remember Gawin Elliot that was his great-grandfather ye'd be saying, 'Ye might think it was Gawin Elliot that was hangit!'" Mrs. Macmurdo came to her shop door. "Eh, the laird, wi' all the straw of all that's past alight in his heart!"

Alexander answered the "good days," but he did not draw rein. He rode slowly up the steep village street and over the bare waste bit of hill until here was the manse, with the kirk beyond it. Coming out of the manse gate was the minister. Glenfernie checked his mare. All around spread a bare and lonely hilltop. The manse and the kirk and the minister's figure buttressed each the others with a grim strength. The wind swept around them and around Glenfernie.

Mr. M'Nab, standing beside the laird, spoke earnestly. "We rejoice, Glenfernie, that you are about once more! There is the making in you of a grand man, like your father. It would have been down-spiriting if that son of Belial had again triumphed in mischief. The weak would have found it so."

"What is triumph?"

"Ye may well ask that! And yet," said M'Nab, "I know. It is the warm-feeling cloak that Good when it hath been naked wraps around it, seeing the spoiler spoiled and the wicked fallen into the pit that he digged!"

"Aye, the naked Good."

The minister looked afar, a dark glow and energy in his thin face. "They are in prison, and the scaffolds groan— they who would out with the Kirk and a Protestant king and in with the French and popery!"

"Your general wrong," said Glenfernie, "barbed and feathered also for a Scots minister's own inmost nerve! And is not my wrong general likewise? Who hates and punishes falsity, though it were found in his own self, acts for the common good!"

"Aye!" said the minister. "But there must be assurance that God calls you and that you hate the sin and not the sinner!"

"Who assures the assurances? Still it is I!"

Glenfernie rode on. Mr. M'Nab looked after him with a darkling brow. "That was heathenish—!"

Alexander passed kirk and kirkyard. He went home and sat in the room in the keep, under his hand paper upon which he made figures, diagrams, words, and sentences. When the next day came he did not ride, but walked. He walked over the hills, with the kirk spire before him lifting toward a vast, blue serenity. Presently he came in sight of the kirkyard, its gravestones and yew-trees. He had met few persons upon the road, and here on the hilltop held to-day a balmy silence and solitude. As he approached the gate, to which there mounted five ancient, rounded steps of stone, he saw sitting on one of these a woman with a basket of flowers. Nearer still, he found that it was Gilian Barrow.

She waited for him to come up to her. He took his place upon the steps. All around hung still and sunny space. The basket of flowers between them was heaped with marigolds, pinks, and pansies.

"For Elspeth," said Gilian.

"It is almost two years. You have ceased to grieve?"

"Ah no! But one learns how to marry grief and gladness."

"Have you learned that? That is a long lesson. But some are quicker than others or had learned much beforehand.... Where is Elspeth?"

"Oh, she is safe, Glenfernie!"

"I wanted her body safe—safe, warm, in my arms!"

"Spirit and spirit. Meet spirit with spirit!"

"No! I crave and hunger and am cold. Unless I warm myself—unless I warm myself—with anger and hatred!"

"I wish it were not so!"

"I had a friend.... I warm myself now in the hunt of a foe—in his look when he sees me!"

Gilian smote her hands together. "So Elspeth would have loved that! So the smothered God in you loves that!"

"It is the God in me that will punish him!"

"Is it—is it, Glenfernie?"

He made a wide gesture of impatience. "Cold—languid—pithless! You, Robin, Strickland, Alison Touris—"

Gilian looked at her basket of marigolds, pinks, and pansies. "That word death.... I bring these here, but Elspeth is with me everywhere! There is a riddle—there is a strange, huge mistake. She must solve it, she must make that port of all ports—and you and I must make it.... It is a hard, heroic, long adventure!"

"I speak of the pine-tree in the blast, and such as you would give me pansies! I speak of the eagle at the crag-top in the storm, and you offer butterflies!"

"Ah, then, go and kill her lover and the man who was your friend!"

Glenfernie rose from the step, in his face strong anger and denial. He stood, seeking for words, looking down upon the seated woman and her flowers. She met him with parted lips and a straight, fearless look.

"Will you take half the flowers, Glenfernie, and put them for Elspeth?"

"No. I cannot go there now!"

"I thought you would not. Now I am Elspeth. I love her. I would give her gladness—serve her. She says, 'Let him alone! Do you not know that his own weird will bring him into dark countries and light countries, and where he is to go? Is your own tree to be made thwart and misshapen, that his may be reminded that there is rightness of growth? He is a tree—he is not a stone, nor will he become a stone. There is a law a little larger than your fretfulness that will take care of him! I like Glenfernie better when he is not a busybody!'"

Alexander stared at her in anger. "Differences where I thought to find likeness—likenesses where I thought to find differences! He deceived me, fooled me, played upon me as upon a pipe; took my own—"

"Ha!" said Gilian. "So you are going a-hunting for more reasons than one?—Elspeth, Elspeth! come out of it!—for Glenfernie, after all, avenges himself!"

Alexander, looking like his father, spoke slowly, with laboring breath. "Had one asked me, I should have said that you above all might understand. But you, too, betray!" With a sweep of his arms abroad, a gesture abrupt and desolate, he turned. He quitted the sunny bare space, the kirkyard and the woman sitting with her basket of marigolds and pansies.

But two nights later he came to this place alone.

The moon was full. It hung like a wonder lantern above the hill and the kirk; it made the kirkyard cloth of silver. The yews stood unreal, or with a delicate, other reality. It was neither warm nor cold. The moving air neither struck nor caressed, but there breathed a sense of coming and going, unhurried and unperplexed, from far away to far away. The laird of Glenfernie crossed long grass to where, for a hundred years, had been laid the dead from White Farm. There was a mound bare to the sunlight thrown from the moon. He saw the flowers that Gilian had brought.

The flowers were colorless in the moonlight—and yet they could be, and were, clothed with a hue of anger from himself. They lay before him purple-crimson. They were withered, but suddenly they had sap, life, fullness—but a distasteful, reminding life, a life in opposition! He took them and threw them away.

Now the mound rested bare. He lay down beside it. He stretched his arms over it. "Elspeth!"—and "Elspeth!"— and "Elspeth!" But Elspeth did not answer—only the cool sunlight thrown back from the moon.

CHAPTER XXV

Ian traveled toward a pass through the Pyrenees. Behind him stretched difficult, hazardous, slow travel—weeks of it. Behind those weeks lay the voyage to Lisbon, and from Lisbon in a second boat north to Vigo. From Vigo to this day of forested slopes and brawling streams, steadily worsening road, ruder dwellings, more primitive, impoverished folk, rolled a time of difficulties small and great, like the mountain pebbles for number. It took will and wit at strain to dissolve them all, and so make way out of Spain into France—through France—to Paris, where were friends.

Spanish travel was difficult at best—Spanish travel with scarcely any gold to travel on found the "best" quite winnowed out. Slow at all times, it grew, lacking money, to be like one of those dreams of retardation. Ian gathered and blew upon his philosophy, and took matters at last with some amusement, at times, even, with a sense of the enjoyable.

He was not quite penniless. Those who had helped in his escape from Edinburgh had provided him gold. But, his voyage paid for, he must buy at Vigo fresh apparel and a horse. When at last he rode eastward and northward he was poor enough! Food and lodging must be bought for himself and his steed. Inns and innkeepers, chance folk applied to for guidance, petty officials in perennially suspicious towns—twenty people a day stood ready to present a spectral aspect of leech and gold-sucker! He was expert in traveling, but usually he had borne a purse quite like that of Fortunatus. Now he must consider that he might presently have to sell his horse—and it was not a steed of Roland's, to bring a great price! He might be compelled to go afoot into France. He might be sufficiently blessed if the millennium did not find him yet living by his wits in Spain. It was Spanish, that prospect! Turn what? Ian asked himself. Bull-fighter—fencing-master— gipsy—or brigand? He played with the notion of fencing-master. But he would have to sell his horse to provide room and equipment, and he must turn aside to some considerable town. Brigand would be easier, in these wild forests and rock fortresses that climbed and stood upon the sky-line. Matter enough for perplexity! But the sweep of forest and mountain wall was admirable—admirable the air, the freedom from the Edinburgh prison. Except occasionally, in the midst of some intensification of annoyance, he rode and maneuvered undetected.

Past happenings might and did come across him in waves. He remembered, he regretted; he pursued a dialectic with various convenient divisions of himself. But all that would be lost for long times in the general miraculous variety of things! On the whole, going through Spain in the autumn weather, even with poverty making mouths alongside, was not a sorry business! Zest lived in pitting vigor and wit against mole hills threatening an aggregation into mountains! As for time, what was it, anyhow, to matter so much? He owned time and a wide world.

Delay and delay and delay. In one town the alcalde kept

Mary Johnston

him a week, denying him the road beyond while inquiries were made as to his identity or non-identity with some famed outlaw escaping from justice. Further on, his horse fell badly lame and he stayed day after day in a miserable village, lounging under a cork-tree, learning patois. There was a girl with great black eyes. He watched her, two or three times spoke to her. But when she saw how he must haggle over the price of food and lodging she laughed, and returned to the side of a muleteer with a sash and little bells upon his hat.

All along the road fell these retardations. Then as the mountains loomed higher, the spirit of contradiction apparently grew tired and fell behind. For several days he traveled quite easily. "My Lady Fortune," asked Ian, "what is up your sleeve?"

The air stayed smiling and sweet. In a town half mountain, half plain, he made friends at the inn with Don Fernando, son of an ancient, proud, decaying house, poor as poverty. Don Fernando had been in Paris, knew by hearsay England, and had heard Scotland mentioned. Spaniard and Scot drank together. The former was drawn into almost love of Ian. Here was a help against boundless ennui! Ian and his horse, and the small mail strapped behind the saddle, finally went off with Don Fernando to spend a week in his old house on the hillside just without the town. Here was poverty also, but yet sufficient acres to set a table and pour good wine and to make the horse forget the famine road behind him. Here were lounging and siesta, rest for body and mind, sweet "do well a very little!" Don Fernando would have kept the guest a second week and then a third.

But Ian shook his head, laughed, embraced him, promised a return of good when the great stream made it possible, and set forth upon his further travel. The horse looked sleek, almost fat. The Scot's jaded wardrobe was cleaned, mended, refreshed. Living with Don Fernando were an elder sister and an ancient cousin who had fallen in love with the big, handsome Don, traveling so oddly. These had set hand-maidens to work, with the result that Ian felt himself spruce as a newly opened pink. And Don Fernando gave him a traveling-cloak—very fine—a last year's gift, it seemed, from a grandee he had obliged. Cold weather was approaching and its warmth would be grateful. Ian's great need was for money in purse. These new friends had so little of that that he chose not to ask for a loan. After all, he could sell the cloak!

The day was fine, the country mounting as it were by stairs toward the mountains. Before him climbed a string of pack-mules. The merchant owning them and their lading traveled with a guard of stout young men. For some hours Ian had the merchant for companion and heard much of the woes of the region and the times, the miseries of travel, the cursed inns, bandits licensed and unlicensed, craft, violence, and robbery! The merchant bewailed all life and kept a hawk eye upon his treasure on the Spanish road. At last he and his guard, his mules and muleteers, turned aside into a skirting way that would bring him to a town visible at no great distance. Left alone, Ian viewed from a hilltop the roofs of this place, with a tower or two starting up like warning fingers. But his road led on through a mountain pass.

The earth itself seemed to be climbing. The mountain shapes, little and big, gathered in herds. Cliffs, ravines, the hoarse song of water, the faces of few human folk, and on these written "Mountains, mountains! Live as we can! Catch who catch can!" After a time the road was deprived of even these faces. The Scot thought of home mountains. He thought of the Highlands. Above him and at some distance to the right appeared a distribution of cliffs that reminded him of that hiding-place after Culloden. He looked to see the birchwood, the wheeling eagle. The sun was at noon. Riding in a solitude, he almost dozed in the warm light. The Highlands and the eagle wheeling above the crag.... Black Hill and Glenfernie and White Farm and Alexander.... Life generally, and all the funny little figures running full tilt, one against another....

His horse sprang violently aside, then stood trembling. Forms, some ragged, some attired with a violent picturesqueness, had started from without a fissure in the wood and from behind a huge wayside rock. Ian knew them at a glance for those brigands of whom he had heard mention and warning enough. Don Fernando had once described their practices.

Resistance was idle. He chose instead a genial patience for his tower, and within it keen wits to keep watch. With his horse he was taken by the fierce, bedizened dozen up a gorge to so complete and secure a robber hold that Nature, when she made it, must have been in robber mood. Here were found yet others of the band, with a bedecked and mustached chief. He was aware that property, not life, answered to their desires. His horse, his fine cloak, his weapons, the small mail and its contents, with any article of his actual wearing they might fancy, and the little, little, little money within his purse—all would be taken. All in the luck! To-day to thee, to-morrow to me. What puzzled him was that evidently more was expected.

When they condescended to direct speech he could understand their language well enough. Nor did they indulge in over-brutal handling; they kept a measure and reminded him sufficiently of old England's own highwaymen. Of course, like old England's own, they would become atrocious if they thought that circumstances indicated it. But they did not seem inclined to go out of their way to be murderous or tormenting. The only sensible course was to take things good-naturedly and as all in the song! The worst that might happen would be that he must proceed to France afoot, without a penny, lacking weapons, Don Fernando's cloak—all things, in short, but the bare clothing he stood in. To make loss as small as possible there were in order suavity, coolness, even gaiety!

And still appeared the perplexing something he could not resolve. The over-fine cloak, the horse now in good condition, might have something to do with it, contrasting as they certainly did with the purse in the last stages of emaciation. And there seemed a studying of his general appearance, of his features, even. Two men in especial appeared detailed to do this. At last his ear caught the word "ransom."

Now there was nobody in Spain knowing enough or caring enough of or for Ian Rullock to entertain the idea of parting with gold pieces in order to save his life. Don Fernando might be glad to see him live, but certainly had not the gold pieces! Moreover, it presently leaked fantastically out that the bandits expected a large ransom. He began to suspect a mistake in identity. That assumption, increasing in weight, became certainty. They looked him all around, they compared notes, they regarded the fine cloak, the refreshed steed. "English, senor, English?"

"Scots. You do not understand that? Cousin to English."

"English. We had word of your traveling—with plenty of gold."

"It is a world of mistakes. I travel, but I have no gold."

"It is a usual lack of memory of the truth. We find it often. You are traveling with escort—with another of your nation, your brother, we suppose. There are servants. You are rich. For some great freak you leave all in the town down there and ride on alone. Foreigners often act like madmen. Perhaps you meant to return to the town. Perhaps to wait for them in the inn below the pass. You have not gold in your purse because there is bountiful gold just behind you. Why hurt the beautiful truth? Sancho and Pedro here were in the inn-yard last night."

Sancho's hoarse voice emerged from the generality. "It was dusk, but we saw you plainly enough, we are sure, senor! In your fine cloak, speaking English, discussing with a big tall man who rode in with you and sat down to supper with you and was of your rank and evidently, we think, your brother or close kinsman!"

The chief nodded. "It is to him that we apply for your ransom. You, senor, shall write the letter, and Sancho and Pedro shall carry it down. It will be placed, without danger to us, in your brother's hand. We have our ways.... Then, in turn, your brother shall ride forth, with a single companion, from the town, and in a clear space that we shall indicate, put the ransom beneath a certain rock, turning his horse at once and returning the way he came. If the gold is put there, as much as we ask, and according to our conditions, you shall go free as a bird, senor, though perhaps with as little luggage as a bird. If we do not receive the ransom—why, then, the life of a bird is a little thing! We shall put you to death."

Ian combated the profound mistake. What was the use? They did not expect him to speak truth, but they were convinced that they had the truth themselves. At last it came, on his part, to a titanic whimsicalness of assent. At least, assenting, he would not die in the immediate hour! Stubbornly refuse to do their bidding, and his thread of life would be cut here and now.

"All events grow to seem unintelligible masks! So why quarrel with one mask more? Pen, ink, and paper?"

All were produced.

"I must write in English?"

"That is understood, senor. Now this—and this—is what you are to write in English."

The captive made a correct guess that not more than one or two of the captors could read Spanish, and none at all English.

"Nevertheless, senor," said the chief, "you will know that if the gold is not put in that place and after that fashion that I tell you, we shall let you die, and that not easily! So we think that you will not make English mistakes any more than Spanish ones."

Ian nodded. He wrote the letter. Sancho put it in his bosom and with Pedro disappeared from the dark ravine. The situation relaxed.

"You shall eat, drink, sleep, and be entirely comfortable, senor, until they return. If they bring the gold you shall pursue your road at your pleasure even with a piece for yourself, for we are nothing if not generous! If they do not bring it, why, then, of course—!"

Ian had long been bedfellow of wild adventure. He thought that he knew the mood in which it was best met. The mood represented the grist of much subtle effort, comparing, adjustment, and readjustment. He cultivated it now. The banditti admired courage, coolness, and good humor. They had provision of food and wine, the sun still shone warm. The robber hold was set amid dark, gipsy beauty.

The sun went down, the moon came up. Ian, lying upon shaggy skins, knew well that to-morrow night—the night after at most—he might not see the sun descend, the moon arise. What then?

Alexander Jardine, sailing from Scotland, came to Lisbon a month after Ian Rullock. He knew the name of the ship that had carried the fugitive, and fortune had it that she was yet in this port, waiting for her return lading. He found the captain, learned that Ian had transhipped north to Vigo. He followed. At Vigo he picked up a further trace and began again to follow. He followed across Spain on the long road to France. He had money, horses, servants when he needed them, skill in travel, a tireless, great frame, a consuming purpose. He made mistakes in roads and rectified them; followed false clues, then turned squarely from them and obtained another leading. He squandered upon the great task of dogging Ian, facing Ian, showing Ian, again and again showing Ian, the wrong that had been done, patience, wealth of kinds, a discovering and prophetic imagination. He traveled until at last here was the earth, climbing, climbing, and before him the forested slopes, the mountain walls, the great partition between Spain and France. An eagle would fly over it, and another eagle would follow him, for a nest had been robbed and a friendship destroyed!

As the mountains enlarged he fell in with an Englishman of rank, a nobleman given to the study of literature and peoples, amateur on the way to connoisseurship, and now traveling in Spain. He journeyed *en prince* with his secretary and his physician, servants and pack-horses, and, in addition, for at least this part of Spain, an armed escort furnished by the authorities, at his proper cost, against just those banditti dangers that haunted this strip of the globe. This noble found in the laird of Glenfernie a chance-met gentleman worth cultivating and detaining at his side as long as might be. They had been together three or four days when at eve they came to the largest inn of a town set at a short distance from the mountain pass through which ran their further road. Here, at dusk, they dismounted in the inn-yard, about them a staring, commenting crowd. Presently they went to supper together. The Englishman meant to tarry a while in this town to observe certain antiquities. He might stay a week. He urged that his companion of the last few days stay as well. But the laird of Glenfernie could not.

"I have an errand, you see. I am to find something. I must go on."

"Two days, then. You say yourself that your horses need rest."

"They do.... I will stay two days."

But when morning came the secretary and the physician alone appeared at table. The nobleman lay abed with a touch of fever. The physician reported that the trouble was slight—fatigue and a chill taken. A couple of days' repose and his lordship would be himself again.

Glenfernie walked through the town. Returning to the inn, he found that the Englishman had asked for him. For an hour or two he talked or listened, sitting by the nobleman's bed. Leaving him at last, he went below to the inn's great room, half open to the courtyard and all the come and go of the place. It was late afternoon. He sat by a table placed before the window, and the river seemed to flow by him, and now he looked at it from a rocky island, and now he looked elsewhere. The room grew ruddy from the setting sun. An inn servant entered and busied himself about the place. After him came an aged woman, half gipsy, it seemed. She approached the seat by the window. Her worn mantle, her wide sleeve, seemed to touch the deep stone sill. She was gone like a moth. Glenfernie's eye discovered a folded paper lying in the window. It had not been there five minutes earlier. Now it lay before him like a sudden outgrowth from the stone. He put out a hand and took it up. The woman was gone, the serving-man was gone. Outside flowed the river. Alexander unfolded the paper. It was addressed to *Senor Nobody*. It lay upon his knee, and it was Ian's hand. His lips moved, his vision blurred. Then came steadiness and he read.

What he read was a statement, at once tense and whimsical, of the predicament of the writer. The latter, recognizing the confusion of thought among his captors, wrote because he must, but did not truly expect any aid from Senor Nobody. The writing would, however, prolong life for two days, perhaps for three. If at the end of that time ransom were not forthcoming death would forthcome. Release would follow ransom. But Senor Nobody truly could not be expected to take interest! Most conceivably the stranger's lot must remain the stranger's lot. In that case pardon for the annoyance! If, miraculously, the bearer did find Senor Nobody—if Senor Nobody read this letter—if strangers were not strangers to

Senor Nobody—if gold and mercy lay alike in Senor Nobody's keeping—then so and so must be done. Followed three or four lines of explicit directions. Did all the above come about, then truly would the undersigned, living, and pursuing his journey into France, and making return to Senor Nobody when he might, rest the latter's slave! Followed the signature, *Ian Rullock*.

Alexander sat by the window, in the rocky island, and the Spanish river flowed by. It was dusk. Then came lights, and the English secretary and physician, with servants to lay the table and bring supper. Glenfernie ate and drank with the two men. His lordship was reported better, would doubtless be up to-morrow. The talk fell upon Greece, to which country the nobleman was, in the end, bound. Greek art, Greek literature, Greek myth. Here the secretary proved scholar and enthusiast, a liker especially of the byways of myth. He and Alexander voyaged here and there among them. "And you remember, too," said the secretary, "the Cranes of Ibycus—"

They rose at last from table. Secretary and physician must return to their patron. "I am going to hunt bed and sleep," said Glenfernie. "To-morrow, if his lordship is recovered, we'll go see that church."

In the rude, small bedchamber he found his Spanish servant. Presently he would dismiss him, but first, "Tell me, Gil, of the banditti in these mountains."

Gil told. The foreigner who employed him asked questions, referred intelligently from answer to answer, and at last had in hand a compact body of information. He bade Gil good night. Ways of banditti in any age or place were much the same!

The room was small, with a rude and narrow bed. There was a window, small, too, but open to the night. Pouring through this there entered a vagrant procession of sound, with, in the interstices, a silence that had its own voice. As the night deepened the procession thinned, at last died away.

When he undressed he had taken the letter to Senor Nobody and put it upon the table. Now, lying still and straight upon the bed in the dark room, there seemed a blacker darkness where it lay, four feet from him, a little above the level of his eyes. There it was, a square, a cube, of Egyptian night, hard, fierce, black, impenetrable.

For a long time he kept a fixed gaze upon it. Beyond and above it glimmered the window. The larger square at last drew his eyes. He lay another long while, very still, with the window before him. Lying so, thought at last grew quiet, hushed, subdued. Very quietly, very sweetly, like one long gone, loved in the past, returning home, there slipped into view, borne upon the stream of consciousness, an old mood of stillness, repose, dawn-light by which the underneath of things was seen. Once it had come not infrequently, then blackness and hardness had whelmed it and it came no more. He had almost forgotten the feel of it.

Presently it would go.... It did so, finding at this time a climate in which it could not long live. But it was powerfully a modifier.... Glenfernie, dropping his eyes from the window, found the square that was the letter, a square of iron gray.

A part of the night he lay still upon the narrow bed, a part he spent in slow walking up and down the narrow room, a part he stood motionless by the window. The dawn was faintly in the sky when at last he took from beneath the pillow his purse and a belt filled with gold pieces and sat down to count them over and compare the total with the figures upon a piece of paper. This done, he dressed, the light now gray around him. The letter to Senor Nobody lay yet upon the table. At last, dressed, he took it up and put it in the purse with the gold. Leaving the room, he waked his servant where he lay and gave him directions. A faint yellow light gleamed in the lowest east.

He waited an hour, then went to the room where slept the secretary and the physician. They were both up and dressing. The physician had been to his patron's room. "Yes, his lordship was better—was awake—meant after a while to rise." Glenfernie would send in a request. Something had occurred which made him very desirous to see his lordship. If he might have a few minutes—? The secretary agreed to make the inquiry, went and returned with the desired invitation. Glenfernie followed him to the nobleman's chamber and was greeted with geniality. Seated by the Englishman's bed, he made his explanation and request. He had so much gold with him—he showed the contents of the belt and purse—and he had funds with an agent in Paris and again funds in Amsterdam. Here were letters of indication. With a total unexpectedness there had come to him in this town a call that he could not ignore. He could not explain the nature of it, but a man of honor would feel it imperative. But it would take nicely all his gold and so many pieces besides. He asked the loan of these, together with an additional amount sufficient to bring him through to Paris. Once there he could make repayment. In the mean time his personal note and word—The Englishman made no trouble at all.

"I'll take your countenance and bearing, Mr. Jardine. But I'll make condition that we do travel together, after all, as far, at least, as Tours, where I mean to stop awhile."

"I agree to that," said Glenfernie.

The secretary counted out for him the needed gold. In the narrow room in which he had slept he put this with his own in a bag. He put with it no writing. There was nothing but the bare gold. Carrying it with him, he went out to find the horses saddled and waiting. With Gil behind him, he went from the inn and out of the town. The letter to Senor Nobody had given explicit enough direction. Clear of all buildings, he drew rein and took bearings. Here was the stream, the stump of a burned mill, the mountain-going road, narrower and rougher than the way of main travel. He followed this road; the horses fell into a plodding deliberateness of pace. The sunshine streamed warm around, but there was little human life here to feel its rays. After a time there came emergence into a bare, houseless, almost treeless plain or plateau. The narrow, little-traveled road went on upon the edge of this, but a bridle-path led into and across the bareness. Alexander followed it. Before him, across the waste, sprang cliffs with forest at their feet. But the waste was wide, and in the sun they showed like nothing more than a burnished, distant wall. His path would turn before he reached them. The plain's name might have been Solitariness. It lay naked of anything more than small scattered stones and bushes. There upgrew before him the tree to which he was bound. A solitary, twisted oak it shot out of the plain, its protruding roots holding stones in their grasp. Around was shelterless and bare, but the heightening wall of cliff seemed to be watching. Alexander rode nearer, dismounted, left Gil with the two horses, and, the bag of gold in his hand, walked to the tree. Here was the stone shaped like a closed hand. He put the ransom between the stone fingers and the stone palm.

There was no word with it. Senor Nobody had no name. He turned and strode back to the horses, mounted, and with Gil rode from the naked, sunny plain.

CHAPTER XXVI

The Peace of Aix-la-Chapelle lay a year in the future. Yet in Paris, under certain conditions and auspices, Scot or Englishman might dwell in security enough. The Jacobite remnant, foe to the British government, found France its best harbor. A quietly moving Scots laird, not Jacobite, yet might be lumped by the generality with those forfeited Scots gentlemen who, having lost all in a cause urged and supported by France, now, without scruple, took from King Louis a pension that put food in their mouths, coats on their backs, roofs over their heads. Alexander Jardine, knowing the city, finding quiet lodgings in a quiet street, established himself in Paris. It was winter now, cold, bright weather.

In old days he had possessed not a few acquaintances in this city. A circle of thinkers, writers, painters, had powerfully attracted him. Circumstances brought him now again into relation with one or two of this group. He did not seek them as formerly he had done. But neither could he be said to avoid companionship when it came his way. It was not his wish to become singular or solitary. But he was much alone, and while he waited for Ian he wandered in the rich Paris of old, packed life. Street and Seine-side and market knew him; he stood in churches, and before old altarpieces smoked by candles. Booksellers

remarked him. Where he might he heard music; sometimes he would go to the play. He carried books to his
lodging. He sat late at night over volumes new and old.
The lamp burned dim, the fire sank; he put aside reading
and knowledge gained through reading, and sat, sunk
deep into a dim desert within himself; at last got to bed
and fell to sleep and to dreams that fatigued, that took him
nowhere. When the next day was here he wandered again
through the streets.

One of his old acquaintances he saw oftener than he did
others. This was a scholar, a writer, an encyclopedist of
to-morrow who liked the big Scot and to be in his
company. One day, chance met, they leaned together
upon the parapet of a bridge, and watched the crossing
throng. "One's own particles in transit! Can you grasp
that, Deschamps?"

"I have heard it advanced. No. It is hard to hold."

"It is like a mighty serpent. You would think you had it
and then it is gone.... If one could hold it it would
transform the world."

"Yes, it would. At what are you staring?"

"The serpent is gone. I thought that I saw one whom I do
not hold to be art and part with me." He gazed after a
crossing horseman. "No! There was merely a trick of him.
It is some other."

"The man for whom you are waiting?"

"Yes."

Deschamps returned to the subject of a moment before.

"It is likely that language bewrays much more than we think it does. I say 'the man.' You echo it. And I am 'man.' And you are 'man.' 'Man'—'Man'! Every instant it is said. Yet the identity that we state we never assume!"

"I said that we could not hold the serpent."

Ten days afterward he did see Ian. The latter, after a slow and difficult progress through France, came afoot into Paris. He sought, and was glad enough to find, an old acquaintance and sometime fellow-conspirator— Warburton.

"Blessed friendship!" he said, and warmed himself by Warburton's fire. Something within him winced, and would, if it could, have put forward a different phrase.

Warburton poured wine for him. "Now tell your tale! For months those of us who remained in Paris have heard nothing but Trojan woes!"

Ian told. Culloden and after—Edinburgh—Lisbon—Vigo —travel in Spain—Senor Nobody—

"That was a curious adventure! And you don't know the ransomer's name?"

"Not I! Scnor Nobody he rests."

"Well, and after that?"

Ian related his wanderings from the Pyrenees up to Paris. Scotland, Spain, and France, the artist in him painted pictures for Warburton—painted with old ableness and abandon, and, Warburton thought, with a new subtlety. The friend hugged his knees and enjoyed it like a well-done play. Here was Rullock's ancient spirit, grown more richly appealing! Trouble at least had not downed him. Warburton, who in the past year had been thrown in contact with a number whom it had downed, and who had suffered depression thereby, felt gratitude to Ian Rullock for being larger, not smaller, than usual.

At last, the fire still burning, Ian warmed and refreshed, they wheeled from retrospect into the present. Warburton revealed how thoroughly shattered were Stewart hopes.

"I begin to see, Rullock, that we've simply passed those things by. We can't go back to that state of mind and affairs."

"I don't want to go back."

"I like to hear you say that. I hear so much whining the other way! Well, as a movement it's over.... And the dead are dead, and the scarred and impoverished will have to pick themselves up."

"Quite so. Is there any immediate helping hand?"

"King Louis gives a pension. It's not much, but it keeps one from starving. And as for you, I've in keeping a packet for you from England. It reached me through Goodworth, the India merchant. I've a notion that your family will manage to put in your hand some annual amount. Of course your own fortune is sequestered and you can return neither to England nor to Scotland."

"My aunt may have had faith that I was living. She would do all that she could to help.... No, I'll not go back."

"Your chance would lie in some post here. Take up old

acquaintances where they have power, and recommend yourself to new ones with power. Great ladies in especial," said Warburton.

"We haven't passed that by?"

"Not yet, Rullock, not yet!"

Ian dreamed over the fire. At last he stretched his arms. "Let us go sleep, Warburton! I have come miles...."

"Yes, it is late. Oh, one thing more! Alexander Jardine is in Paris."

"Alexander!"

"I don't know what he is doing here. In with the writing, studying crew, I suppose. I came upon him by accident, near the Sorbonne. He did not see me and I did not speak."

"I'll not avoid him!"

"I remember your telling me that you had quarreled. That was the eve of your leaving Paris in the springtime, before the Prince went to Scotland. You haven't made it up?"

"No. I suppose we'll never make it up."

"What was it over?"

"I can't tell you that.... It had a double thread. Did he come to Paris, I wonder, because he guessed that I would bring up here?" He rose and stood staring down into the fire. "I think that he did so. Well, if he means to follow me through the world, let him follow! And now no more to-night, Warburton! I want sleep—sleep—sleep!"

The next day and the next and the next began a new French life. He had luck, or he had the large momentum of a personality not negligible, an orb covered with a fine network of enchanter's symbols. The packet from England held money, with an engagement to forward a like sum twice a year. It was not a great sum, but such as it was he did not in the least scorn it. It had come, after all, from Archibald Touris—but Ian knew the influence behind that.

Warburton presented his name to the Minister who dispensed King Louis's fund for Scots gentlemen concerned in the late attempt, losers of all, and now destitute in France. So much would come out of that! The two together waited upon monseigneur in whose coach they had once crossed the Seine. He had blood ties with Stewart kings of yesterday, and in addition to that evidenced a queer, romantic fondness for lost causes, and a willingness to ferry across rivers those who had been engaged in them. Now he displayed toward the Englishman and the Scot a kind of eery, distant graciousness. Ah yes! he would speak here and there of Monsieur Ian Rullock—he would speak to the King. If there were things going *ces messieurs* might as well have some good of them! Out of old acquaintances in Paris Ian gathered not a few who were in position to further new fortunes. Some of these were men and some were women. He took a lodging, neither so good nor so bad. Warburton found him a servant. He obtained fine clothes, necessary working-garb where one pushed one's fortune among fine folk. The more uncertain and hazardous looked his fortunes the more he walked and spoke as though he were a golden favorite of the woman with the wheel.

All this moved rapidly. He had not been in Paris a week ere again, as many times before, he had the stage all set for Success to walk forth upon it! But it had come December—December—December, and he looked forward to that month's passing.

He had not seen Alexander. Then, in the middle of the month he found himself one evening in a peacock cluster of fine folk, at the theater—a famous actress to be viewed in a comedy grown the rage. The play was nearly over when he saw Alexander in the pit, turned from the stage, gazing steadily upon him. Ian placed himself where he might still see him, and returned the gaze.

Going out when the play was over, the two met face to face in the lighted space between the doors. Each was in company of others—Ian with a courtier, decked and somewhat loudly laughing group, Glenfernie with a painter of landscape, Deschamps, and an Oriental, member of some mission to the West. Meeting so, they stopped short. Their nostrils dilated, there seemed to come a stirring over their bodies. Inwardly they felt a painful constriction, a contraction to something hard, intent, and fanged. This was the more strongly felt by Alexander, but Ian felt it, too. Did Glenfernie mean to dog him through life—think that he would be let to do so? Alone in a forest, very far back, they might, at this point, have flown at each other's throat. But they had felled many forests since the day when just that was possible.... The thing conventionally in order for such a moment as the present was to act as though that annihilation which each wished upon the other had been achieved. All that they had shared since the day when first they met, boys on a heath in Scotland, should be instantaneously blotted out. Two strangers, jostled face to face in a playhouse, should turn without sign that there had ever been that heath. So, symbolically, annihilation might be secured! For a moment each sought for the blank eyes, the unmoved stone face.

As from a compartment above sifted down a dry light with great power of lighting. It came into Alexander's mind, into that, too, of Ian.... How absurd was the human animal! All this saying the opposite left the truth intact. They were not strangers, each was quite securely seated in the other. Self-annihilation—self-oblivion!... All these farcical high horses!... Men went to see comedies and did not see their own comedy.

The laird of Glenfernie and Ian Rullock each very slightly and coldly acknowledged the other's presence. No words passed. But the slow amenity of life bent by a fraction the head of each, just parted the lips of each. Then Alexander turned with an abrupt movement of his great body and with his companions was swallowed by the crowd.

On his bed that night, lying straight with his hands upon his breast, he had for the space of one deep breath an overmastering sense of the suaveness of reality. Crudity, angularity, harshness, seemed to vanish, to dissolve. He knew dry beds of ancient torrents that were a long and somewhat wide wilderness of mere broken rock, stone piece by stone piece, and only the more jagged edges lost and only the surface worn by the action, through ages, of water. It was as though such a bed grew beneath his eyes meadow smooth—smoother than that—smooth as air, air that lost nothing by yielding—smooth as ether that, yielding all, yielded nothing.... The moment went, but left its memory. As the moment was large so was its memory.

He fought against it with tribes of memories, lower and dwarfish, but myriads strong. The bells from some convent rang, the December stars blazed beyond his window, he put out his arms to the December cold.

Ian, despite that moment in the playhouse, looked for the arrival of a second challenge from Glenfernie. For an instant it might be that they had seen that things couldn't be so separate, after all! That there was, as it were, some universal cement. But instants passed, and, indubitably, the world was a broken field! Enmity still existed, full-veined. It would be like this Alexander, who had overshot another Alexander, to send challenge after challenge, never to rest satisfied with one crossing of weapons, with blood drawn once! Or if there was no challenge, no formal duel, still there would be duel. He would pursue—he would cry, "Turn!"—there would be perpetuity of encounter. To the world's end there was to be the face of menace, of old reproach—the arrows dropped of pain of many sorts. "In short, vengeance," said Ian. "Vengeance deep as China! When he used to deny himself revenge in small things it was all piling up for this!... What I did slipped the leash for him! Well, aren't we evened?"

What he looked for came, brought by Deschamps. The two met in a field outside Paris, with seconds, with all the conventionally correct paraphernalia. The setting differed from that of their lonely fight on a Highland mountain-side. But again Ian, still the better swordsman, wounded Alexander. This time he gave—willed perhaps to give—a slight hurt.

"That is nothing!" said Glenfernie. "Continue—" But the seconds, coming between them, would not have it so. It was understood that their principals had met before, and upon the same count. Blood had been drawn. It was France—and mere ugly tooth-and-claw business not in favor. Blood had flowed—now part!

"'Must' drives then to-day," said Alexander. "But it is December still, Ian Rullock!"

"Turn the world so, if you will, Glenfernie!" answered the other. "And yet there is June somewhere!"

They left the field. Alexander, going home in a hired coach with Deschamps, sat in silence, looking out of the window. His arm was bandaged and held in a sling.

"They breed determined foes in Scotland," said Deschamps.

"That Scotland is in me," Glenfernie answered. "That Scotland and that December."

Three days later he wandered alone in Paris, came at last to old stone steps leading down to the river, in an unpopulous quarter. A few boats lay fastened to piles, but the landing-place hung deserted in the winter sunlight. There lacked not a week of Christmas. But the season had been mild. To-day was not cold, and stiller than still. Glenfernie, his cloak about him, sat upon the river steps and watched the stream. It went by, and still it stood there before him. It came from afar, and it went to afar, and still it shone where his hand might touch it. It turned like a wheel, from the gulf to the height and around again. He followed its round—ocean and climbing vapor, cloud, rain, and far mountain springs, descent and the mother sea. The mind, expanding, ceased to examine radius by radius, but held the whole wheel. Alexander sat in inner quiet, forgetting December.

Turning from that contemplation, he yet remained still, looking now at the sunshine on the steps.... There seemed to reach him, within and from within, rays of color and fragrance, the soul of spice pinks, marigolds, and pansies.... Then, within and from within, Elspeth was with him.

Dead! She was not dead.... Of all idle words—!

It was not as a shade—it was not as a memory, or not as the poor things that were called memory! But she came in the authority and integrity of herself, that was also, most dearly, most marvelously, himself as well—permeative, penetrative, real, a subtle breath named Elspeth! So subtle, so wide and deep, elastic, universal, with no horizons that he could see.... To and fro played the tides of knowledge.

Elspeth all along—sunshines and shadows—Elspeth a wide, living life—not crushed into the two moments upon which he had brooded—not the momentary Elspeth who had walked the glen with him, not the momentary Elspeth lifted from the Kelpie's Pool, borne in his arms, cold, rigid, drowned, a long, long way! But Elspeth, integral, vibrant, living—Elspeth of centillions of moments— Elspeth a beautiful power moving strongly in abundant space....

His form stayed moveless upon the river steps while the wave of realization played.

The experience linked itself with that of the other night when the stony bed of existence, broken, harsh, irregular, had suddenly dissolved into connections myriad wide, deep, and fine.... He had prated with philosophers of oneness. Then what he had prated of had been true! There was a great difference between talking of and touching truth....

But he could not hold the touch. The wings flagged, he fell into the jungle of words. His body turned upon the steps. The caves and dens of his being began to echo with cries and counter-cries.

Hurt? Had she not been hurt at all? But she *was* hurt—poisoned, ruined, drawn to death! Had she long and wide and living power to heal her own harm? Still was it not there—he would have it there!

Ian Rullock! With a long, inward, violent recoil Alexander shrank into the old caves of himself. All, the magic web of color and fragrance dwindled, came to be a willow basket filled with White Farm flowers placed upon the kirkyard steps.

Ian Rullock had stolen her—Ian, not Alexander, had been her lover, kissed her, clasped her, there in the glen! Ian, the Judas of friendship—thief of a comrade's bliss—cheat, murderer, mocker, and injurer!

The wave of oneness fled.

Glenfernie, looking like the old laird his father, his cloak wrapped around him, feeling the December air, left the river steps, wandered away through Paris.

But when he was alone with the night he tried to recover the wave. It had been so wonderful. Even the faint, faint echo, the ghostly afterglow, were exquisite; were worth more than anything he yet had owned. He tried to recover the earlier part of the wave, separating it from the later flood that had seemed critical of righteous wrath, just punishment. But it would not come back on those terms.... But yet he wanted it, wanted it, longed for it even while he warred against it.

CHAPTER XXVII

That was one December. The year made twelve steps and here was December again. With it came to Ian a proffer from the nobleman of the coach across the Seine. Some ancient business, whether of soul or sense, carried him to Rome. Monsieur Ian Rullock—said to be for the moment banished from a certain paradise—might find it in his interest to come with him—say as traveling companion. Ian found it so. Monseigneur was starting at once. Good! let us start.

Ian despatched his servant to the lodging known to be occupied by the laird of Glenfernie. The man had a note to deliver. Alexander took it and read:

> GLENFERNIE, I am quitting Paris with the Duc de—, for Rome.—IAN RULLOCK.

The man gone, Alexander put fire to the missive and burned it, after which he walked up and down, up and down the wide, bare room. When some time had passed he came back to chair and table, inkwell and pen, and a half-written letter. The quill drove on:

> ... None could do better by the estate than you—not I nor any other. So I beg of you to stay, dear Strickland,

who have stayed by us so long!

There followed a page of business detail—inquiries—
expressed wishes. Glenfernie paused. Before him,
propped against a volume of old lore, stood a small
picture;—Orestes asleep in the grove of the Furies. He sat
leaning back in his chair, regarding it. He had found it and
purchased it months before, and still he studied it. His
eyes fell to the page; he wrote on:

You ask no questions, and yet I know that you
question. Well, I will tell you—knowing that you will
strain out and give to others only what should be
given.... He has been, and I have been, in Paris a year.
He and I have fought three times—fought, that is, as
men call fighting. Once upon that mountain-side at
home, twice here. Now he is going—and I am going—
to Rome. Shall I fight him again—with metal digged
from the earth, fashioned and sharpened in some red-
lighted shop of the earth? I am not sure that I shall—
rather, I think that I shall not.... Is there ever a place
where a kind of growth does not go on? There is a
moonrise in me that tells me that that fighting is to be
scorned. But what shall I do, seeing that he is my
foe?... Ah, I do not know—save haunt him, save bring
and bring again my inner man, to clinch and wrestle
with and throw, if may be, his inner man. And to see
that he knows that I do this—that it tells back upon
him—through and through tells back!... It has been a
strange year. Now and then I am aware of curious far
tides, effects from some giant orb of being. But I go
on.... For my daily life in Paris—here it is, your open
page!... You see, I still seek knowledge, for all your
gibe that I sought darkness. And now, as I go to
Rome—

He wrote on, changing now to details as to communication, placing of moneys, and such matters. At length came references to the last home news, expressions of trust and affection. He signed his name, folded, superscribed and sealed the letter, then sat on, studying the picture before him.

Monseigneur, with gold, with fine horses, with an eery, swooping, steadiness of direction, journeyed fast. He and his traveling companion reached Rome early in February. There was a villa, there were attendants, there was the Frenchman's especial circle, set with bizarre jewels, princes of the Church, Italian nobles of his acquaintance, exiles, a charlatan of immense note, certain ladies. He only asked of his guest, Monsieur Rullock, that he help him to entertain the whole chaplet, giving to his residence in Rome a certain splendid virility.

February showed skies like sapphire. There drew on carnival week. Masks and a wildness of riot—childish, too—

Ian leaned against the broken base of an ancient statue, set in the villa garden, at a point that gave a famous view. Around, the almond-trees were in bloom. The marble Diana had gazed hence for so many years, had seen so much that might make the dewy greenwood forgotten! It was mid-afternoon and flooding light. Here Rome basked, half-asleep in a dream of sense; here the ant city worked and worked.

Ian stood between tides, behind him a forenoon, before him an evening of carnival participation. In the morning he had been with a stream of persons; presently, with the declining sun, would be with another. Here was an hour or two of pause, time of day for rest with half-closed eyes.

He looked over the pale rose wave of the almonds, he saw Peter's dome and St. Angelo. He was conscious of a fatigue of his powers, a melancholy that they gave him no more than they did. "How it is all tinsel and falsetto!... I want a clean, cold, searching wave—desert and night— not life all choked with wax tapers and harlequins! I want something.... I don't know what I want. I only know I haven't got it!"

His arm moved upon the base of the statue. He looked up at the white form with the arrow in its hands. "Self-containment.... What, goddess, you would call chastity all around?... All the spilled self somehow centered. But just that is difficult—difficult—more difficult than anything Hercules attempted. Oh me!" He sat down beneath the cypress that stood behind the statue and rested his head within his hands. From Rome, on all sides, broke into the still light trumpets and bell-ringing, pipes and drums, shout and singing. It sounded like a thousand giant cicadae. A group of masks went through the garden, by the Diana figure. They threw pine cones and confetti at the gold-brown foreigner seated there. One wore an ass's head, another was dressed as a demon with horns and tail, a third rolled as Bacchus, a fourth, fifth, and sixth were his maenads. All went wildly by, the clamor of the city swelled.

This was first day of carnival. Succeeding days, succeeding nights, mounted each a stage to heights of folly. Starred all through was innocent merrymaking, license held in leash. But the gross, the whirling, and the sinister elements came continuously and more strongly into play. Measured sound grew racket, camaraderie turned into impudence. Came at last pandemonium. All without Rome—Campagna and mountains—were in Rome. Peasant men and women slept, when they slept, in and beneath carts and huge wine-wagons camped and parked in stone forests of imperial ruins. Artisan, mechanic, and merchant Rome lightened toil and went upon the hunt for pleasure, dropping servility in the first ditch. Foreigners, artists, men from everywhere, roved, gazed, and listened, shared. The great made displays, some with beauty, some of a perverted and monstrous taste. The lords of the Church nodded, looked sleepily or alertly benevolent. At times all alike turned mere populace. Courtesans thronged, the robber and the assassin found their prey. All men and women who might entertain, ever so coarsely, ever so poorly, were here at market. Mummers and players, musicians, dancers, jugglers, gipsies, and fortune-tellers floated thick as May-flies. Voices, voices, and every musical instrument—but all set in a certain range, and that not the deep nor the sweet. So it seemed, and yet, doubtless, by searching might have been found the deep and the sweet. Certainly the air of heaven was sweet, and it went in and between.

All who might or who chose went masked. So few did not choose that street and piazza seemed filled with all orders of being and moments of time. Terrible, grotesque, fantastic, pleasing, went the rout, and now the hugest crowd was here and now it was there, and now there were moments of even diffusion. At night the lights were in multitude, and in multitude the flaring and strange decorations. Day and night swung processions, stood spectacles, huge symbolic movements and attitudes, grown obscure and molded to the letter, now mere stage effects. Day by day through carnival week the noise increased, restraint lessened.

At times Ian was in company with monseigneur and those who came to the villa; at times he sought or was sought by others that he knew in Rome, fared into carnival with them. Much more rarely he dipped into the swirl alone.

The saturnalia drew toward its close. Ash Wednesday, like a great gray-sailed ship, was seen coming large into port. The noise grew wild, license general. All available oil must be poured into the fire of the last day of pleasures. Ian was to have been with monseigneur's party gathered to view a pageant lit by torches of wax, then to drink wine, then, in choice masks, to break in upon a dance of nymphs, whirl away with black or brown eyes.... It was the program, but at the last he evaded it, slipped from the villa, chose solitary going. Why, he did not know, save that he felt aching satiety.

Here in the streets were half-lights, afterglow from the sunken sun and smoky torches. The latter increased in number, the oil-lamps, great and small, were lit, the tapers of various qualities and thicknesses. Where there were open spaces vast heaps of seasoned wood now flaming caused processions of light and shadow among ruins, against old triumphal arches, against churches and dwellings old, half-old, and new, lived in, chanted in still, intact and usable. Above was star-sown night, but Rome lay under a kobold roof of her own lighting. Noise held grating sway, mere restless motion enthroned with her. Worlds of drunken grasshoppers in endless scorched plains! The masks seemed now demoniac, less beauty than ugliness.

Ian found himself on the Quirinal, in the great ragged space dominated by the Colossi. Here burned a bonfire huge enough to make Plutonian day, and here upon the fringes of that light he encountered a carnival brawl, and became presently involved in it. He wore a domino striped black and silver, and a small black mask, a black hat with wide brim and a long, curling silver feather. He was tall, broad-shouldered, noticeable.... The quarrel had started among unmasked peasants, then had swooped in a numerous band dressed as ravens. Light-fingered gentry, inconspicuously clad, aided in provoking misunderstanding that should shake for them the orchard trees. A company of wine-bibbers with monstrous, leering masks, staggering from a side-street, fell into the whirlpool. With vociferation and blows the whole pulled here and there, the original cause of the falling out buried now in a host of new causes. Ian, caught in an eddy, turned to make way out of it. A peasant woman, there with a group from some rock village, received a chance buffet, so heavy that she cried out, staggered, then, pushed against in the melee, fell upon the earth. The raven crew threatened trampling. "*Jesu Maria!*" she cried, and tried to raise herself, but could not. Ian, very near her, took a step farther in and, stooping, lifted her. But now the ravens chose to fall foul of him. The woman was presently gone, and her peasant fellows.... He was beating off a drunken Comus crew, with some of active ill-will. His dress was rich—he was not Roman, evidently—the surge had foamed and dragged across from the bonfire and the open place to the dark mouth of a poor street. Many a thing besides light-hearted gaieties happened in carnival season.

He became aware that a friendly person had come up, was with him beating off raven, gorgon, and satyr. He saw that this person was very big, and caught an old, oft-noted trick in the swing of his arm. To-night, in carnival time, when there was trouble, it seemed quite natural and with a touch of home that Old Steadfast should loom forth.

A clang of music, shouting, and an oncoming array of lights helped to daunt band of ravens and drunken masks. A procession of fishermen with nets and monsters of the sea approached, went by. The attackers merged in the throng that attended or followed, went away with innocent shouts and songs. A second push followed the first, a great crowd of masks and spectators bound for a piazza through which was to pass one of the final large pageants. This wave carried with it Ian and Alexander. On such a night, where every sea was tumult, one indication, one propelling touch, was as good as another. The two went on in company. Alexander was not masked. Ian was, but that did not to-night hide him from the other. They came into the flaringly lighted place. Around stood old ruins, piers, broken arches and columns, and among these modern houses. For the better viewing of the spectacle banks of seats had been built, tier upon tier rising high, propped against what had been ancient bath or temple. The crowd surged to these, filling every stretch and cranny not yet seized upon. There issued that the tiers were packed; dark, curving, mounting rows where foot touched shoulder. The piazza turned amphitheater.

Still, in this carnival night, Ian and Alexander found themselves together. They were sitting side by side, a third of the way between pavement and the topmost row. They sat still, broodingly, in a cloud of things rememberable, no distinct images, but all their common past, good and bad, and the progress from one to the other, making as it were one chord, or a mist of one color. They did not reason about this momentary oneness, but took it as it came. It was carnival season.

Yet the cloud dripped honey, the color was clear and not unrestful, the chord sweet and resounding.

The pageant, fantastic, towering, red and purple lighted, passed by. The throng upon the seats moved, rose, struck heavily with their feet, going down the narrow ways. Many torches had been extinguished, many that were carried had gone on, following the last triumphal car. Here were semi-darkness, great noise and confusion—weight, too, pressing upon ground that long ago had been honeycombed; where the crypt of a three-hundred-year-old church touched through an archway old priest paths beneath a vanished temple, that in turn gave into a mixed ruin of dungeons and cellars opening at last to day or night upon a hillside at some distance from the place of raised benches. Now, the crowd pressing thickly, the earth crust at one point trembled, cracked, gave way. Scaffolding and throng came with groans and cries into a very cavern. Those that were left above, high on narrow, overswaying platforms, with shouts of terror pushed back from the pit mouth, managed with accidents, injuries enough, to get to firmer earth. Then began, among the braver sort, rescue of those who had gone down with soil and timbers. What with the darkness and the confused and sunken ruin, this was difficult enough.

Ian and Alexander, unhurt, clambered down the standing part and by the light of congregated and improvised torches helped in that rescue, and helped strongly. Many were pinned beneath wood, smothered by the caving earth. The rent was wide and in places the ruin afire. Groans, cries, appeals shook the hearts of the carnival crowd. All would now have helped, but it was not possible for many. There must be strength to descend into the pit and work there.

A beam pinned a man more than near a creeping flame. The two Scots beat out that fire. Glenfernie heaved away the beam, Ian drew out the man, badly hurt, moaning of wife and child. Glenfernie lifted him, mounted with him, over heaped debris, by uncertain ledge and step, until other arms, outstretched, could take him. Turning back, he took from Ian a woman's form, lifted it forth. Down again, the two worked on. Others were with them, there was made a one-minded ring, folly forgot.

At last it seemed that all were rescued. A few men only moved now in the hollow, peering here and there. The fire had taken headway; the gulf, it was evident, would presently be filled with flame. The heat beat back those at the rim. "Come out! Come out, every one!" The rescuers began to clamber forth.

Came down a roaring pile of red-lit timbers, with smoke and sparks. It blocked the way for Alexander and Ian. Turning, here threatened a pillar of choking murk, red-tongued. Behind them was a gaping, narrow archway. Involuntary recoil before that stinging push of smoke brought them in under this. They were in a passageway, but when again they would have made forth and across to the side of the pit, and so, by climbing, out of it, they found that they could not. Before them lay now a mere field of fire, and the blowing air drove a biting smoke against them.

"Move back, until this burns itself out! The earth gave into some kind of underground room. This is a passage."

It stretched black behind them. Glenfernie caught up a thick, arm-long piece of lighted wood that would answer for brand. They worked through a long vaulted tunnel, turned at right angles, and came into what their torch showed to have been an ancient chapel. In a niche stood a broken statue, on the wall spread a painting of St. Christopher in midstream.

"Shall we go on? There must be a way out of this maze."

"If the torch will last us through."

They passed out of the chapel into a place where of old the dead had been buried. They moved between massy pillars, by the shelves of stone where the bones lay in the dust. It seemed a great enough hall. At the end of this they discovered an upward-going stair, but it was old and broken, and when they mounted it they found that it ended flat against thick stone, roof to it, pavement, perhaps, to some old church. They saw by a difference in the flags where had been space, the stair opening into the hollow of the church; but now was only stone, solid and thick. They struck against it, but it was moveless, and in the church, if church there were above, none in the dead night to hear them. They came down the stair, and through a small, half-blocked doorway stumbled into a labyrinth of passages and narrow chambers. They found old pieces of wood—what had been a wine-cask, what might have had other uses. They broke these into torch lengths, lighting one from another as that burned down. These underways did not seem wholly neglected, buried, and forgotten. There lacked any total blocking or demolition, and there was air. But intricacy and uncertainty reigned.

The mood of the amphitheater when they had sat side by side claimed them still. There had been a reversion or a coming into fresh space where quarrel faded like a shadow before light. The light was a golden, hazy one, made up of myriads of sublimed memories, associations, judgments, conclusions. Nothing defined emerged from it; it was simply somewhat golden, somewhat warm light, as from a sun well under the horizon—a kind of dreamy well-being as of old Together, unquestioning Acceptance. Suddenly aroused, each might have cried, "For the moment—it was for a moment only!" Then, for the moment, there was return, with addition. It came like a winged force from the bounds of doing or undoing. While it lasted it imposed upon them quieted minds, withdrew any seeming need for question. They sought for egress from this place where their bodies moved, explanation of this material labyrinth. But they did not seek explanation of this mood, fallen among pride and anger, wrong and revenge. It came from at large, with the power of largeness. They were back, "for the moment," in a simplicity of ancient, firm companionship.

They spoke scarcely at all. It had been a habit of old, in their much adventuring together, to do so in long silences. Alexander had set the pace there, Ian learning to follow.... It was as if this were an adventure of, say, five years ago, and it was as if it were a dream adventure. Or it was as if some part of themselves, quietly and with a hidden will separating itself, had sailed away from the huge storm and cloud and red lightnings.... What they did say had wholly and only to do with immediate exigencies. Behind, in pure feeling, was the unity.

Down in this underground place the air began to come more freshly.

"Look at the flame," said Ian. "It is bending."

They had left behind rooms and passages lined with unbroken masonry. Here were newer chambers and excavations, softer walled.

"They have been opening from this side. That was dug not so long ago."

Another minute and they came into a ragged, cavern-like space filled with fresh night air. Presently they were forth upon a low hillside, and at their feet Tiber mirrored the stars. Rome lay around. The carnival lights yet flared, the carnival noise beat, beat. This was a deserted strip, an islet between restless seas.

Ian and Alexander stood upon trodden earth and grass, about them the yet encumbering ruins of an ancient building, pillars and architraves and capitals, broken friezes and headless caryatids. Here was the river, here the ancient street. They breathed in the air, they looked at the sky, but then at Rome. Somewhere a trumpet was fiercely crying. Like an impatient hand, like a spurred foot, it tore the magician's fabric of the past few hours.

Ian laughed. "We had best rub our eyes!" To the fine hearing there was a catch of the breath, a small dancing hope in his laughter. "*Or, Glenfernie, shall we dream on?*"

But the other opened his eyes upon things like the Kelpie's Pool and the old room in the keep where a figure like himself read letters that lied. He saw in many places a figure like himself, injured and fooled, stuck full of poisoned arrows. The figure grew as he watched it, until it overloomed him, until he was passionately its partisan. He said no word, but he flung the smoking torch yet held in hand among the ruins, and, leaving Ian and his black and silver, plunged down the slope to the old, old street along which now poured a wave of carnival.

CHAPTER XXVIII

The laird of Glenfernie lay in the flowering grass, beneath a pine-tree, rising lonely from the Roman Campagna. The grass flowed for miles, a multitudinous green speculating upon other colors, here and there clearly donning a gold, an amethyst, a blue. The pine-tree looked afar to other pine-trees. Each seemed solitary. Yet all had the oneness of the great stage, and if it could comprehend the stage might swim with its little solitariness into a wider uniqueness. In the distance lay Rome. He could see St. Peter's dome. But around streamed the ocean of grass and the ocean of air. Lifted from the one, bathed in the other, strewed afar, appeared the wreckage of an older Rome. There was no moving in Rome or its Campagna without moving among time-cleansed bones and vestiges. Rome and its Campagna were like Sargasso Seas and held the hulks of what had been great galleons. The air swam above endless grass, endless minute flowers. In long perspective traveled the arches of an Aqueduct.

He lay in the shadow of a broken tomb. It was midspring. The bland stillness of this world was grateful to him, after long inner storm. He lay motionless, not far from the skirts of Contemplation.

The long line of the Aqueduct, arch after arch, succession

fixed, sequence which the gaze made unitary, toled on his thought. He was regarding span after span of imagery held together, a very wide and deep landscape of numerous sequences, more planes than one. He was seeing, around the cells, the shadowy force lines of the organ, around the organ the luminous mist of the organism. He passed calmly from one great landscape to another.

Rome. To-day and yesterday and the day before, and to-morrow. The "to-morrow" put in the life, guaranteeing an endless present, endless breathing. He saw Rome the giant, the stone and earth of her, the vast animal life of her, the vast passional, the mental clutch and hammer-blow. The spiritual Rome? He sought it—it must be there. At last, among the far arches, it rose, a light, a leaven, an ether.... Rome.

If there were boundaries in this ocean of air they were gauze-thin and floating. He looked here and there, into landscapes Rome led to. Like and like, and synthesis of syntheses! Images, finding that of which they were images, lost their grotesqueness or meaninglessness of line, their quality of caricature, lost unripeness, lost the dull annoy of riddles never meant to be answered.... He had a great fund of images, material so full that it must begin to build higher. Building higher meant arrival in a fluid world where all aggregates were penetrable.

He lay still among the grasses, and it was as though he lay also amid the wide, simple, first growths of a larger, more potent living. Now and again, through years, he had been aware of approaches, always momentary, to this condition, to a country that lay behind time and space, cause and effect, as he ordinarily knew them. The lightning went—but always left something transforming. And then for three years all gleams stopped, a leaden wall that they could not pierce rearing itself.

Latterly they had begun to return.... The proud will might rise against them, but they came. Then it must be so, he would have said of another, that the will was divided. Part of it must still have kept its seat before the door whence the lights came, stayed there with its face in its hands, waiting its season. And a part that had said no must be coming to say yes, going and taking its place beside the other by the door. And together they were strong enough to bring the gleaming back, watching the propitious moment. But still there was the opposed will, and it was strong.... When the light came it sought out old traces of itself, and these became revivified. Then all joined together to make a flood against the abundant darkness. A day like this joined itself through likeness to others on the other side of the three years, and also to moments of the months just passed and passing. Union was made with a sleepless night in an inn of Spain, with the hours after his encounter with Ian in the Paris theater, with that time he sat upon the river steps and saw that the dead were living and the prisoners free, with the hour in the amphitheater and after, in carnival.

He saw and heard, felt and tasted, life in greater lengths and breadths. He comprehended more of the pattern. The tones and semi-tones fell into the long scale. Such moments brought always elevation, deep satisfaction.... More of the will particles traveled from below to the center by the door.

The soul turned the mind and directed it upon Alexander Jardine's own history. It spread like a landscape, like a continent viewed from the air, and here it sang with attainment and here it had not attained; and here it was light, and here there were darknesses; right-doing here and wrong-doing there and every shade between. He saw that there was right- and wrong-doing quite outside of conventional standards.

Where were frontiers? The edges of the continent were merely spectral. Where did others end and he begin, or he end and others begin? He saw that his history was very wide and very deep and very high. Through him faintly, by nerve paths in the making, traveled the touch of oneness.

Alexander Jardine—Elspeth Barrow—Ian Rullock. And all others—and all others.

There swam upon him another great perspective. He saw Christ in light, Buddha in light. The glorified—the unified. *Union.*

Alexander Jardine—Elspeth Barrow—Ian Rullock. And all others—and all others. *For we are members, one of another.*

The feathered, flowered grass, miles of it, and the sea of air.... By degrees the level of consciousness sank. The splendid, steadfast moment could not be long sustained. Consciousness drew difficult breath in the pure ether, it felt weight, it sank. Alexander moved against the old tomb, turned, and buried his face in his arms. The completer moment went by, here was the torn self again. But he strove to find footing on the thickening impressions of all such moments.

Moving back to Rome, along the old way where had marched all the legions, by the ruins, under the blue sky, he had a sense of going with Caesar's legions, step by step, targe by targe, and then of his footstep halting, turning out, breaking rhythm.... From this it was suddenly a winter night and at Glenfernie, and he sat by the fire in his father's death-room. His father spoke to him from the bed and he went to his side and listened to dying words, distilled from a wide garden that had relaxed into bitterness, growths, and trails of ideal hatred.... *What was it, setting one's foot upon an adder?... What was the adder?*

He entered the city. His lodging was above the workroom and shop of a recoverer of ancient coins and intaglios, skilful cleanser and mender of these and merchant to whom would buy. The man was artist besides, maker of strange drawings whom few ever understood or bought.

Glenfernie liked him—an elderly, fine, thin, hook-nosed, dark-eyed, subtle-lipped, little-speaking personage. No great custom came to the shop in front; the owner of it might work all day in the room behind, with only two or three peals of a small silvery summoning bell. The lodger acquired the habit of sitting for perhaps an hour out of each twenty-four in this workroom. He might study at the window gem or coin and the finish of old designs, or he might lift and look at sheet after sheet of the man's drawings, or watch him at his work, or have with him some talk.

The drawings had a fascination for him. "What did you mean behind this outward meaning? Now here I see this, and I see that, but here I don't penetrate." The man laid down his mending a broken Eros and came and stood by the table and spoke. Glenfernie listened, the wood propping elbow, the hand propping chin, the eyes upon the drawing. Or he leaned back in the great visitor's chair and looked instead at the draftsman. They were strange drawings, and the draftsman's models were not materially visible.

To-day Glenfernie came from the noise of Rome without into this room. His host was sitting before a drawing-board. Alexander stood and looked.

"Are you trying to bring the world of the plane up a dimension? Then you work from an idea above the world of the solid?"

"*Si.* Up a dimension."

"What are these forms?"

"I am dreaming the new eye, the new ear, the new hand."

Glenfernie watched the moving and the resting hand. Later in the day he returned to the room.

"It has been a fertile season," said the artist. "Look!"

At the top of a sheet of paper was written large in Latin, LOVE IS BLIND. Beneath stood a figure filled with eyes. "It is the same thing," said the man.

The next day, at sunset, going up to his room after restless wandering in this city, he found there from Ian another intimation of the latter's movements:

GLENFERNIE,—I am going northward. There will be a month spent at monseigneur's villa upon the Lake of Como. Then France again.—IAN RULLOCK.

Alexander laid the paper upon the table before him, and now he stared at it, and now he gazed at space beyond, and where he gazed seemed dark and empty. It was deep night when finally he dipped quill into ink and wrote:

IAN RULLOCK,—Stay or go as you will! I do not follow you now as I did before. I come to see the crudeness, the barrenness, of that. But within—oh, are you not my enemy still? I ask Justice that, and what can she do but echo back my words? "Within" is a universe.—ALEXANDER JARDINE.

Five days later he knew that Ian with the Frenchman in whose company he was had departed Rome. On that morning he went again without the city and lay among the grasses. But the sky to-day was closed, and all dead Rome that had been proud or violent or a lover of self seemed to move around him multitudinous. He fought the shapes down, but the sea in storm then turned sluggish, dead and weary.... What was he going to do? Scotland? Was he going back to Scotland? The glen, the moor, White Farm and the kirk, Black Hill and his own house—all seemed cold and without tint, gray, small, and withered, and yet oppressive. All that would be importunate, officious. He cried out, "O my God, I want healing!" For a long time he lay there still, then, rising, went wandering by arches and broken columns, choked doorways, graved slabs sunken in fairy jungles. Into his mind came a journey years before when he had just brushed a desert. The East, the Out-of-Europe, called to him now.

CHAPTER XXIX

Ian guided the boat to the water steps. Above, over the wall, streamed roses, a great, soundless fall of them, reflected, mass and color, in the lake. Above the roses sprang deep trees, shade behind shade, and here sang nightingales. Facing him sat the Milanese song-bird, the singer Antonia Castinelli. She had the throat of the nightingale and the beauty of the velvety open rose.

"Why land?" she said. "Why climb the steps to the chatter in the villa?"

"Why indeed?"

"They are not singing! They are talking. There is deep, sweet shadow around that point."

The boat turned glidingly. Now it was under tall rock, parapeted with trees.

"Let Giovanni have the boat. Come and sit beside me! You are too far away for singing together."

Old Giovanni at the helm, boatman upon this lake since youth, used long since to murmuring words, to touching hands, stayed brown and wrinkled and silent and unspeculative as a walnut. Perhaps his mind was sunk in his own stone hut behind vine leaves. The two under the rose-and-white-fringed canopy leaned toward each other.

"Tell me of your strange, foreign land! Have you roses there—roses—roses? And nightingales that sing out your heart under the moon?"

"I will tell you of the heather, the lark, and the mavis."

She listened. "Oh, it does not taste as tastes this lake! Give me pain! Tell me of women you have loved.... Oh, hear! The nightingales stop singing."

"Do you ever listen to the silence?"

"Of course ... when a friend dies—or I go to Mass—and sometimes when I am singing very passionately. But this lake—"

She began to sing. The contralto throbbed, painted, told, brought delight and melancholy. He sat with his hand loosened from hers, his eyes upon the lake's blue-green depths. At last she stopped.

"Oh—h!... Let us go back to the talking shore and the chattering villa! Somebody else is singing—somebody or something! I hear silence—I hear it in the silence.... Some things I can sing against, and some things I can't."

They went underneath the wall of roses. Her arm, sleeved as with mist, touched his; her low, wide brow and great liquid eyes were at his shoulder, at his breast. "O foreigner—and yet not at all foreign! Tell me your English words for roses—walls of roses—and music that never ceases in the night—and pleasing, pleasing,

pleasing love!"

The boat came to the water steps. The two left it, climbing between flowers. Down to them came a wave of laughter and hand-clapping.

"Celestina recites—but I do not think she does it so well!... That is my window—see, where the roses mount!"

The company, flowing forth, caught them upon the terrace. "Lo, the truants!"

But that night, instead of climbing where the roses climbed, he took a boat from the number moored by the steps and rowed himself across the lake to a piece of shore, bare of houses, lifting by steep slope and crag into the mountain masses. He fastened the boat and climbed here. The moon was round, the night merely a paler day. He went up among low trees and bushes until he came to naked rock. He climbed here as far as he might, found some manner of platform, and threw himself down, below him the lake, around him the mountains.

He lay still until the expended energy was replaced. At last the mind moved and, apprentice-bound to feeling, began again a hot and heavy and bitter work, laid aside at times and then renewed. It was upon the vindication to himself of Ian Rullock.

It was made to work hard.... Its old task used to be to keep asleep upon the subject. But now for a considerable time this had been its task. Old feeling, old egoism, awakened up and down, drove it hard! It had to make bricks without straw. It had to fetch and carry from the ends of the earth.

Emotion, when it must rest, provided for it a dull place of

listlessness and discontent. But the taskmaster now would have it up at all hours, fashioning reasons and justifications. The soonest found straw in the fields lay in the faults of others—of the world in general and Alexander Jardine in particular. Feeling got its anodyne in gloating over these. It had the pounce of a panther for such a bitter berry, such a weed, such a shameful form. It did not always gloat, but it always held up and said, *Who could be weaker here—more open to question?* It made constant, sore comparison.

The lake gleamed below him, the herded mountains slept in a gray silver light. How many were the faults of the laird of Glenfernie! Faults! He looked at the dark old plains of the moon. That was a light word! He saw Alexander pitted and scarred.

Pride! That had always been in the core of Glenfernie. That has been his old fortress, walled and moated against trespass. Pride so high that it was careless—that its possessor could seem peaceable and humble.... But find the quick and touch it—and you saw! What was his was his. What he deemed to be his, whether it was so or not! Touch him there and out jumped jealousy, hate, and implacableness—and all the time one had been thinking of him as a kind of seer!

Ian turned upon the rock above Como. And Glenfernie was ignorant! The seer had seen very little, after all. His touch had not been precisely permeative when it came to the world, Ian Rullock. If liking meant understanding, there had not been much understanding—which left liking but a word. If liking was a degree of love, where then had been love, where the friend at all? After all, and all the time, Glenfernie's notion of friendship was a sieve. The notion that he had held up as though it were the

North Star!

The world, Ian Rullock, could not be so contemned....

He felt with heat and pain the truth of that. It was a wrong that Glenfernie should not understand! The world, Ian Rullock, might be incomplete, imperfect—might have taken, more than once, wrong turns, left its path, so to speak, in the heavens. But what of the world, Alexander Jardine? Had it no memories? He brooded over what these memories might be—must be; he tried to taste and handle that other's faults in time and space. But he could not plunge into Alexander's depths of wrath. As he could not, he made himself contemptuous of all that—of Old Steadfast's power of reaction!

A star shot across the moon-filled night, so large a meteor that it made light even against that silver. A mass within Ian made a slow turn, with effort, with thrilling, changed its inclination. He saw that disdain, that it was shallow and streaked with ebony. He moved with a kind of groan. "Was there—is there—wickedness?... What, O God, is wickedness?"

He pressed the rock with his hand—sat up. The old taskmaster, alarmed, gathered his forces. "I say that it is just that—pride, vengefulness, hard misunderstanding!"

A voice within him answered. "Even so, is it not still yourself?"

He stared after the meteor track. There was a conception here that he had not dreamed of.

It seemed best to keep still upon the rock. He sat in inner wonder. There was a sense of purity, of a fresh coolness not physical, of awe. He was in presence of something comprehensive, immortal.

"Is it myself? Then let it pour out and make of naught the old poison of myself!"

The perception could not hold. It flagged and sank, echoing down into the caves. He sat still and felt the old taskmaster stir. But this time he found strength to resist. There resulted, not the divine novelty and largeness of that one moment, but a kind of dim and bare desert waste of wide extent. And as it ate up all width, so it seemed timeless. Across this, like a person, unheralded, came and went two lines from "Richard III"

> Clarence is come—false, fleeting, perjured Clarence,
> That stabbed me in the field by Tewksbury.

It went and left awareness of the desert. "False— fleeting—perjured...."

He saw himself as in mirrors.

The desert ached and became a place of thorns and briers and bewilderment. Then rose, like Antaeus, the task- master. *"And what of all that—if I like life so?"*

Sense of the villa and the roses and the nightingales in the coverts—sense of wide, mobile sweeps and flowing currents inwashing, indrawing, pleasure-crafts great and small—desire and desire for desire—lust for sweetness, lust for salt—the rose to be plucked, the grapes to be eaten—and all for self, all for Ian....

He started up from the rock above Como, and turned to descend to the boat. That within him that set itself to make thin cloud of the taskmaster pulled him back as by the hair of the head and cast him down upon the rocky floor.

He lay still, half upon his face buried in the bend of his arm. He felt misery.

"My soul is sick—a beggar—like to become an outcast!"

How long he lay here now he did not know. The nadir of night was passed, but there was cold and voidness, an abyss. He felt as one fallen from a great height long ago. "There is no help here! Let me only go to an eternal sleep—"

A wind began. In the east the sky grew whiter than elsewhere. There came a sword-blow from an unseen hand, ripping and tearing veils. *Elspeth—Elspeth Barrow!*

In a bitterness as of myrrh he came into touch with cleanness, purity, wholeness. Henceforth there was invisible light. Its first action was not to show him scorchingly the night of Egypt, but with the quietness of the whitening east to bring a larger understanding of Elspeth.

CHAPTER XXX

The caravan, having spent three days in a town the edge of the desert, set forth in the afternoon. The caravan was a considerable one. Three hundred camels, more than a hundred asses, went heavily laden. Twenty men rode excellent horses; ten, poorer steeds; the company of others mounted with the merchandise or, staff in hand, strode beside. In safe stretches occurred a long stringing out, with lagging at the rear; in stretches where robber bands or other dangers might be apprehended things became compact. Besides traders and their employ, there rode or walked a handful of chance folk who had occasion for the desert or for places beyond it. These paid some much, some little, but all something for the advantage of this convoy. The traders did not look to lose, whoever went with them. Altogether, several hundred men journeyed in company.

The elected chief of the caravan was a tall Arab, Zeyn al-Din. Twelve of the camels were his; he was a merchant of spices, of wrought stuff, girdles, and gems—a man of forty, bold and with scope. He rode a fine horse and kept usually at the head of the caravan. But now and again he went up and down, seeing to things. Then there was talking, loud or low, between the head man and units of the march.

Mary Johnston

Starting from its home city, this caravan had been for two days in good spirits. Then had become to creep in disaster, not excessive, but persistent. One thing and another befell, and at last a stealing sickness, none knew what, attacking both beast and man. They had made the town at the edge of the desert. Physicians were found and rest taken. Recuperation and trading proceeded amicably together. The day of departure wheeling round, the noontide prayer was made with an especial fervor and attention. Then from the *caravanserai* forth stepped the camels.

The sun descending, the caravan threw a giant shadow upon the sand. Ridge and wave of sterile earth broke it, confused it, made it an unintelligible, ragged, moving, and monstrous shade. The sun was red and huge. As it lowered to the desert rim Zeyn al-Din gave the order for the seven-hour halt. The orb touched the sand; prayer carpets were spread.

Night of stars unnumbered, the ineffable tent, arched the desert. The caravan, a small thing in the world, lay at rest. The meal was over. Here was coolness after heat, repose after toil. The fires that had been kindled from scrub and waste lessened, died away. Zeyn al-Din appointed the guards for the night, went himself the rounds.

Where one of the fires had burned he found certain of those men who were not merchants nor servants of merchants, yet traveled with the caravan. Here were Hassan the Scribe, and Ali the Wanderer, and the dervish Abdallah, and others. Here was the big Christian from some outlandish far-away country, who had dwelt for the better part of a year in the city whence the caravan started, who had money and a wish to reach the city toward which the caravan journeyed. In the first city he had become, it seemed, well liked by Yusuf the Physician, that was the man that Zeyn al-Din most admired in life. It was Yusuf who had recommended the Christian to Zeyn, who did not like infidel sojourners with caravans. Zeyn himself was liberal and did not so much mind, but he had had experience with troubles created along the way and in the column itself. The more ignorant or the stiffer sort thought it unpleasing to Allah. But Zeyn al-Din would do anything really that Yusuf the Physician wanted. So in the end the big Christian came along. Zeyn, interpreting fealty to Yusuf to mean care in some measure for this infidel's well-being, began at once with a few minutes' riding each day beside him. These insensibly expanded to more than a few. He presently liked the infidel. "He is a man!" said Zeyn and that was the praise that he considered highest. The big Christian rode strongly a strong horse; he did not fret over small troubles nor apparently fear great ones; he did not say, "This is my way," and infer that it was better than others; he liked the red camel, the white, and the brown. "Who dances with the sand is not stifled," said Zeyn.

Now he found the Christian with Hassan, listening at ease, stretched upon the sand, to Ali the Wanderer. The head man, welcomed, listened, too, to Ali bringing his story to a close. "That is good, Ali the Wanderer! Just where grows the tree from which one gathers that fruit?"

"It can't be told unless you already know," said Ali.

"Allah my refuge! Then I would not be asking you!" answered Zeyn. "I should have shaken the tree and gathered the diamonds, rubies, and emeralds, and been off with them!"

"You did not hear what was said. Ibn the Happy found

that they could not be taken from the tree. He had tried what you propose. He broke off a great number and ran away with them. But they turned to black dust in his bosom. He put them all down, and when he looked back he saw them still shining on the tree."

"What did Ibn the Happy do?"

"He climbed into the tree and lived there."

In the distance jackals were barking. "I like nothing better than listening to stories," said Zeyn al-Din. "But, Allah! Just now there are more important things to do! Yusuf the Red, I name you watcher here until moonrise. Then waken Melec, who already sleeps there!"

His eyes touched in passing the big Christian. "Oh yes, you would be a good watcher," thought Zeyn. "But there's a folly in this caravan! Wait till good fortune has a steadier foot!"

But good fortune continued a wavering, evanishing thing. Deep in the night, from behind a stiffened wave of earth, rose and dashed a mounted band of Bedouin robbers. Yusuf the Red and other watchers had and gave some warning. Zeyn al-Din's voice was presently heard like a trumpet. The caravan repelled the robbers. But five of its number were lost, some camels and mules driven off. The Bedouins departing with wild cries, there were left confusion and bewailing, slowly straightening, slowly sinking. The caravan, with a pang, recognized that ill luck was a traveler with it.

The dead received burial; the wounded were looked to, at last hoisted, groaning, upon the camels, among the merchandise. Unrested, bemoaning loss, the trading company made their morning start three hours behind the set time. For stars in the sky, there was the yellow light and the sun at a bound, strewing heat. In the melee the robbers had thrust lance or knife into several of the water-skins. Yet there was, it was held, provision enough. The caravan went on. At midday the Bedouins returned, reinforced. Zeyn al-Din and his mustered force beat them off. No loss of goods or life, but much of time! The caravan went on, that with laden beasts must move at best much like a tortoise. That night the rest was shortened. Two hours after midnight and the strings of camels were moving again, the asses and mules so monstrously misshapen with bales of goods, the horses and horsemen and those afoot. At dawn, not these Bedouins, but another roving band, harassed them. Time was running like water from a cracked pitcher.

This day they cleared the robber bands. There spread before them, around them, clean desert. Then returned that sickness.

"O Zeyn al-Din, what could we expect who travel with him who denies Allah?"

The stricken caravan crept under the blaze across the red waste. Camels fell and died. Their burdens were lifted from them and added to the packs of others; their bodies were left to light and heat and moving air.... It grew that an enchantment seemed to hold the feet of the caravan. Evils came upon them, sickness of men and beasts. And now it was seen that there was indeed little water.

"O Zeyn al-Din, rid us of this infidel!"

"The infidel is in you!" answered Zeyn al-Din. "Much speaking makes for thirst and impedes motion. Let us cross this desert."

"O Zeyn al-Din, if you be no right head man we shall choose another!"

"Choose!" said Zeyn al-Din, and went to the head of a camel who would not rise from the sand.

Ill luck clung and clung. Twelve hours and there began to be cabals. These grew to factions. The larger of these swallowed the small fry, swelled and mounted, took the shape of practically the whole caravan. "Zeyn al-Din, if you do not harken to us it will be the worse for you! Drive away the Christian dog!"

"Abu al-Salam, are you the chief, or I?—Now, companions, listen! These are the reasons in nature for our troubles—"

But no! It was the noon halt. The desert swam in light and silence. The great majority of the traders and their company undertook to play divining, judging, determining Allah. The big Christian stood over against them and looked at them, his arms folded.

"It is no such great matter!... Very good then! What do you want me to do?"

"Turn your head and your eyes from us, and go to what fate Allah parcels out to you!"

There arose a buzzing. "Better we slay him here and now! So Allah will know our side!"

Zeyn al-Din stepped forth. "This is the friend of my friend and I am pledged. Slay, and you will have two to slay! O

Allah! what a thing it is to stare at the west when the riders are in the east!"

"Zeyn al-Din, we have chosen for head man Abu al-Salam."

"Allah with you! I should say you had chosen well. I have twelve camels," said Zeyn al-Din. "I make another caravan! Mansur, Omar, and Melec, draw you forth my camels and mules!"

With a weaker man there might have been interference, stoppage. But Zeyn's mass and force acquired clear space for his own movements. He made his caravan. He had with him so many men. Three of these stood by him; the others cowered into the great caravan, into the shadow of Abu al-Salam.

Zeyn threw a withering look. "Oh, precious is the skin!"

The big infidel came to him. "Zeyn al-Din, I do not want all this peril for me. I have ridden away alone before to-day. Now I shall go in that direction, and I shall find a garden."

"Perhaps we shall find it," said Zeyn. "Does any other go with my caravan?"

It seemed that Ali the Wanderer went, and the dervish Abdallah.... There was more ado, but at last the caravan parted.... The great one, the long string of beads, drew with slow toil across the waste, along the old track. The very small one, the tiny string of beads, departed at right angles. Space grew between them. The dervish Abdallah turned upon his camel.

"It seems that we part. But, O Allah! around 'We part' is drawn 'We are together!'"

Zeyn al-Din made a gesture of assent. "O I shall meet in bazaars Abu al-Salam! 'Ha! Zeyn al-Din!'—'Ha! Abu al-Salam!'"

The sun sank lower. The vastly larger caravan drew away, drew away, over the desert rim. Between the two was now a sea of desert waves. Where the great string of camels, the asses, the riders, the men could be seen, all were like little figures cut from dark paper, drawn by some invisible finger, slowly, slowly across a wide floor. Before long there were only dots, far in the distance. Around Zeyn al-Din's caravan swept a great solitude.

"Halt!" said Zeyn. "Now they observe us no longer, and this is what we do!"

All the merchant lading was taken from the camels. The bales of wealth strewed the sand. "Wealth is a comfortable garment," said Zeyn, "but life is a richer yet! That which gathers wealth is wealth. Now we shall go thrice as fast as Abu al-Salam!"

"Far over there," said Ali the Wanderer, and nodded his head toward the quarter, "is the small oasis called the Garland."

"I have heard of it, though I have not been there," answered Zeyn. "Well, we shall not rest to-night; we shall ride!"

They rode in the desert beneath the stars, going fast, camels and horses, unencumbered by bales and packs unwieldy and heavy. But there were guarded, as though they were a train of the costliest merchandise, the shrunken water-skins....

The laird of Glenfernie, riding in silence by Zeyn al-Din, whom he had thanked once with emphasis, and then had accepted as he himself was accepted, looked now at the desert and now at the stars and now at past things. A year and more—he had been a year and more in the East. If you had it in you to grow, the East was good growing-ground.... He looked toward the stars beneath which lay Scotland.

The night passed. The yellow dawn came up, the sun and the heat of day. And they must still press on.... At last the horses could not do that. At eve they shot the horses, having no water for them. They went on upon camels. Great suffering came upon them. They went stoically, the Arabs and the Scot. The eternal waste, the sand, the arrows of the sun.... The most of the camels died. Day and night and morn, and, almost dead themselves, the men saw upon the verge the palms of the desert oasis called the Garland.

* * * * *

Seven men dwelt seven days in the Garland. Uninhabited it stood, a spring, date-palms, lesser verdure, a few birds and small beasts and winged insects. It was an emerald set in ashy gold.

The dervish Abdallah sat in contemplation under a palm. Ali the Wanderer lay and dreamed. Zeyn al-Din and his men, Mansur, Omar, and Melec, were as active as time and place admitted. The camels tasted rich repose. Day went by in dry light, in a pleasant rustling and waving of palm fronds. Night sprang in starshine, wonderful soft lamps orbed in a blue vault. Presently was born and grew a white moon.

Alexander Jardine, standing at the edge of the emerald, watched it. He could not sleep. The first nights in the Garland he with the others had slept profoundly. But now there was recuperation, strength again. Around swept the circle of the desert. Above him he saw Canopus.

He ceased to look directly at the moon, or the desert, or Canopus. He stretched himself upon the clear sand and was back in the inner vast that searched for the upper vast. Since the grasses of the Campagna there had been a long search, and his bark had encountered many a wind, head winds and favoring winds, and had beaten from coast to coast.

"O God, for the open, divine sea and Wisdom the compass—"

He lay beneath the palm; he put his arm over his eyes. For an hour he had been whelmed in an old sense, bitter and stately, of the woe, the broken knowledge, the ailing and the pain of the world. All the world.... That other caravan, where was it?... Where were all caravans? And all the bewilderment and all the false hopes and all the fool's paradises. All the crying in the night. Children....

Little by little he recognized that he was seeing it as panorama.... None saw a panorama until one was out of the plane of its components—out of the immediate plane. Gotten out as all must get out, by the struggling Thought, which, the thing done, uses its eyes....

He looked at his past. He did not beat his breast nor cry out in repentance, but he saw with a kind of wonder the plains of darkness. Oh, the deserts, and the slow-moving caravans in them!

He lay very still beneath the palm. All the world.... *All.*

"*All is myself.*"

"Ian? Myself—myself—myself!"

He heard a step upon the sand—the putting by of a branch. The Sufi Abdallah stood beside him. Alexander made a movement.

"Lie still," said the other, "I will sit here, for sweet is the night." He took his place, white-robed, a gleaming upon the sand. Silent almost always, it was nothing that he should sit silent now, quiet, moveless, gone away apparently among the stars.

The moments dropped, each a larger round. Glenfernie moved, sat up.

"I've felt you and your calm in our caravaning. Let me see if my Arabic will carry me here!—What have you that I have not and that I long for?"

"I have nought that you have not."

"But you see the having, and I do not."

"You are beginning to see."

The wind breathed in the oasis palms. The earth turned, seeking the sun for her every chamber, the earth made pilgrimage around the sun, eying point after point of that excellence, the earth journeyed with the sun, held by the invisible cords.

"I wish new sight—I wish new touch—I wish comprehension!"

"You are beginning to have it."

"I have more than I had.... Yes, I know it—"

"There is birth.... Then comes the joy of birth. At last comes the knowledge of why there is joy. Strive to be fully born."

"And if I were so—?"

"Then life alters and there is strong embrace."

A great stillness lay upon the oasis and the desert around. Men and beasts were sleeping, only these two waking, just here, just now. After a moment the dervish spoke again. "The holder-back is the sense of disunity. Sit fast and gather yourself to yourself.... Then will you find how large is your brood!"

He rose, stood a moment above Glenfernie, then went away. The man whom he left sat on, struck from within by fresh shafts. Perception now came in this way, with inner beam. How huge was the landscape that it lighted up!... Alexander sat still. He bent his head—there was a sense, extending to the physical, of a broken shell, of escape, freedom.... He found that he was weeping. He lay upon the sand, and the tears came as they might from a young boy. When they were past, when he lifted himself again, the morning star was in the sky.

CHAPTER XXXI

Strickland, in the deep summer glen, saw before him the feather of smoke from Mother Binning's cot. The singing stream ran clearly, the sky arched blue above. The air held calm and fine, filled as it were with golden points. He met a white hen and her brood, he heard the slow drone of Mother Binning's wheel. She sat in the doorway, an old wise wife, active still.

"Eh, mon, and it's you!—Wish, and afttimes ye'll get!" She pushed her wheel aside. "I've had a feeling a' the day!"

Strickland leaned against her ash-tree. "It's high summer, Mother—one of the poised, blissful days."

"Aye. I've a feeling.... Hae ye ony news at the House?"

"Alice sings beautifully this summer. Jamie is marrying down in England—beauty and worth he says, and they say."

"Miss Alice doesna marry?"

"She's not the marrying kind, she says."

Mary Johnston

"Eh, then! She's bonny and gude, juist the same! Did ye come by White Farm?"

"Yes. Jarvis Barrow fails. He sits under his fir-tree, with his Bible beside him and his eyes on the hills. Littlefarm manages now for White Farm."

"Robin's sunny and keen. But he aye irked Jarvis with his profane sangs." She drew out the adjective with a humorous downward drag of her lip.

Strickland smiled. "The old man's softer now. You see that by the places at which his Bible opens."

"Oh aye! We're journeyers—rock and tree and Kelpie's Pool with the rest of us."

She seemed to catch her own speech and look at it. "That's a word I hae been wanting the morn!—The Kelpie's Pool, with the moor sae green and purple around it." She sat bent forward, her wrinkled hands in her lap, her eyes, rather wide, fixed upon the ash-tree.

"We have not heard from the laird," said Strickland, "this long time."

"The laird—now there! What ye want further comes when the mind strains and then waits! I see in one ring the day and Glenfernie and yonder water. Wherever the laird be, he thinks to-day of Scotland."

"I wish that he would think to returning," said Strickland. He had been leaning against the doorpost. Now he straightened himself. "I will go on as far as the pool."

Mother Binning loosed her hands. "Did ye have that

thought when ye left hame?"

"No, I believe not."

"Gae on, then! The day's bonny, and the Lord's gude has a wide ring!"

Strickland walking on, left the stream and the glen head. Now he was upon the moor. It dipped and rose like a Titan wave of a Titan sea. Its long, long unbroken crest, clean line against clean space, brought a sense of quiet, distance, might. Here solitude was at home. Now Strickland moved, and now he stood and watched the quiet. Turning at last a shoulder of the moor, he saw at some distance below him the pool, like a small mirror. He descended toward it, without noise over the springy earth.

A horse appeared between him and the water. Strickland felt a most involuntary startling and thrill—then half laughed to think that he had feared that he saw the water-steed, the kelpie. The horse was fastened to a stake that once had been the bole of an ancient willow. It grazed around—somewhere would be a master.... Presently Strickland's eye found the latter—a man lying upon the moorside, just above the water. Again with a shock and thrill—though not like the first—it came to him who it was.

The laird of Glenfernie lay very still, his eyes upon the Kelpie's Pool. His old tutor, long his friend, quiet and stanch, gazed unseen. When he had moved a few feet an outcropping of rock hid his form, but his eyes could still dwell upon the pool and the man its visitor. He turned to go away, then he stood still.

"What if he means a closer going yet?" Strickland settled

back against the rock. "He would loose his horse first—he would not leave it fastened here. If he does that then I will go down to him."

Glenfernie lay still. There was no wind to-day. The reeds stood straight, the willow leaves slept, the water stayed like dusky glass. The air, pure and light, hung at rest in the ether. Minutes went by, an hour. He might, Strickland thought, have lain there a long time. At last he sat up, rose, began to walk around the pool. He went around it thrice. Then again he sat down, his arms upon his knees, watching the dusk water. He did not go nor sit like one overwrought or frenzied or despairing. His great frame, his bearing, the air of him, had quietude, but not listlessness; there seemed at once calm and intensity as of a still center that had flung off the storm. Time flowed. Thought Strickland:

"He is as far as I am from death in that water. I'll cease to spy."

He moved away, moss and ling muffling step, gained and dipped behind the shoulder of the moor. The horse grazed on. The laird sat still, his arms upon his knees, his head a little lifted, his eyes crossing the Kelpie's Pool to the wave-line against the sky.

Strickland went to where the moor path ran by the outermost trees of the glen head. Here he sat down beneath an oak and waited. Another hour passed; then he heard the horse's hoofs. He rose and met Glenfernie home-returning.

"It is good to see you, Strickland!"

"I found you yonder by the Kelpie's Pool. Then I came

here and waited."

"I have spent hours there.... They were not unhappy. They were not at all unhappy."

They moved together along the moor track, the horse following.

"I am glad and glad again that you have come—"

"I have been coming a good while. But there were preventions."

"We have heard nothing direct for almost a year."

"Then my letters did not reach you. I wrote, but knew that they might not. There is the smoke from Mother Binning's cot." He stood still to watch the mounting feather. "I remember when first I saw that, a six-year-old, climbing the glen with my father, carried on his shoulder when I was tired. I thought it was a hut in a fairy-tale.... So it is!"

To Strickland the remarkable thing lay in the lack of strain, the simplicity and fullness. Glenfernie was unfeignedly glad to see him, glad to see home shapes and colors. The blue feather among the trees had simply pleased him as it could not please a heart fastened to rage and sorrow. The stream of memories that it had beckoned—many others, it must be, besides that of the six-year-old's visit—seemed to have washed itself clear, to have disintegrated, dissolved venom and stinging. Strickland, pondering even while he talked, found the word he wanted: "Comprehensiveness.... He always tended to that."

Said Glenfernie, "I've had another birth, Strickland, and

all things are the same and yet not the same." He gave it as an explanation, but then left it. They were going the moorland way to Glenfernie House. He was looking from side to side, recovering old landscape in sweep and in detail. Bit by bit, as they came to it, Strickland gave him the country news. At last there was the house before them, among the firs and oaks, topping the crag. They came into the wood at the base of the hill. The stream—the trees—above, the broken, ancient wall, the roofs of the new house that was not so new, the old, outstanding keep. The whole rested, mellowed, lifted, still, against a serene and azure sky. Alexander stood and gazed.

"The keep. The pine still knots and clings there by the school-room. Do you remember, Strickland, a day when you set me to read 'The Cranes of Ibycus'?"

"I remember."

"Life within life, and sky above sky!—I hear Bran!"

*   *   *   *   *

They mounted the hill. It seemed to run before them that the laird had come home. Bran and Davie and the men and maids and Alice, a bonny woman, and Mrs. Grizel, very little withered, exclaimed and ran. Tibbie Ross was there that day, and Black Alan neighed from his stall. Even the waving trees—even the flowers in the garden—Home, and its taste and fragrance—its dear, close emanations....

That evening at supper Mrs. Grizel made a remark. She leaned back in her chair and looked at Glenfernie. "I never thought you like your mother before! Oh aye! there's your father, too, and a kind of grand man he was, for all that he saw things dark. But will you look, Mr. Strickland, and see Margaret—"

Much later, from his own room, Strickland, gazing forth, saw light in the keep. Alexander would be sitting there among the books and every ancient memorial. Strickland felt a touch of doubt and apprehension. Suppose that to-morrow should find not this Alexander, at once old and new, but only the Alexander who had ridden from Glenfernie, who had shipped to Lisbon, nearly three years ago? To-day's deep satisfaction only a dream! Strickland shook off the fear.

"He breathed lasting growth.... O Christ! the help for all in winged men!"

He turned to his bed. Lying awake he went in imagination to the desert, to the Eastern places, that in few words the laird had painted.

And in the morning he found still the old-new Alexander. He saw that the new had always been in the old, the oak in the acorn.... There was a great, sane naturalness in the alteration, in the advance. Strickland caught glimpses of larger orders.

"*I will make thee ruler over many things.*"

The day was deep and bright. The laird fell at once into the old routine. For none at Glenfernie was there restlessness; there was only ache gone, and a feeling of fulfilling. Mrs. Grizel pattered to and fro. Alice sang like a lark, gathering pansy seed from her garden. Phemie and Eppie sang. The men whistled at their work. Davie discoursed to himself. But Tibbie Ross was wild to get away early and to the village with the news. By the foot of the hill she began to meet wayfarers.

"Oh, aye, this is the real weather! Did ye know—"

Alexander did not leave home that day. In their old work-room he listened to Strickland's account of his stewardship.

"Strickland, I love you!" he said, when it was all given.

He wrote to Jamie; he sat in the garden seat built against the garden wall and watched Alice as she moved from plant to plant.

"You do not say much," thought Alice, "but I like you—I like you—I like you!"

In the afternoon Strickland met him coming from the little green beyond the school-room.

"I have been out through the wall, under the old pine. I seemed to hold many things in the palm of the hand.... I believe that you know what it is to make essences."

After bedtime Strickland saw again the light in the keep. But he had ceased to fear. "Oh All-Being, how rich and stately and various and surprising you are!" In the morning, outside in the court, he found Black Alan saddled.

"The laird will be riding to Black Hill," said Tam Dickson.

CHAPTER XXXII

Mr. Archibald Touris put out a wrinkled hand to his wineglass. "You have been in warm countries. I envy you! I wish that I could get warm."

"Black Hill is looking finely. All the young trees—"

"Yes. I took pride in planting.—But what for—what for—what for?" He shivered. "Glenfernie, please close that window!"

Alexander, coming back, stood above the master of Black Hill. "Will you tell me, sir, where Ian is now?"

Mr. Touris twitched back a little in his chair. "Don't you know? I thought perhaps that you did."

"I ceased to follow him two years ago. I dived into the East, and I have been long where you do not hear from the West."

The other fingered his wine-glass. "Well, I haven't heard myself, for quite a while.... You would think that he might come back to England now. But he can't. Doubtless he would never wish to come again to Black Hill. But England, now.... But they are ferocious yet against every head great and small of the attempt. And I am told there are aggravating circumstances. He had worn the King's coat. He was among the plotters and instigators. He broke prison. Impossible to show mercy!" Mr. Touris twitched again. "That's a phrase like a gravestone! If the Almighty uses it, then of course he can't be Almighty.... Well, the moral is that none named Ian Rullock can come again to Scotland or England."

"Have you knowledge that he wishes to do so?"

Mr. Touris moved again. "I don't know.... I told you that we hadn't heard. But—"

He stopped and sat staring into his wine-glass. Alexander read on as by starlight: "*But I did hear—through old channels. And there is danger of his trying to return.*"

The master of Black Hill put the wine to his lips. "And so you have been everywhere?"

"No. But in places where I had not been before."

"The East India has ways of gathering information. Through Goodworth I can get at a good deal when I want to.... There is Wotherspoon, also. I am practically certain that Ian is in France."

"When did he write?"

"Alison has a letter maybe twice a year. One's overdue now."

"How does he write?"

"They are very short. He doesn't touch on old

things—except, perhaps, back into boyhood. She likes to get them. When you see her, don't speak of anything save his staying in France, as he ought to." He dragged toward him a jar of snuff. "There are informers and seekers out everywhere. Do you remember a man in Edinburgh named Gleig?"

"Yes."

"Well, he's one of them. And for some reason he has a personal enmity toward Ian. So, you see—"

He lapsed into silence, a small, aging, chilly, wrinkled, troubled man. Then with suddenness a wintry red crept into his cheek, a brightness into his eyes. "You've changed so, Glenfernie, you've cheated me! You are his foe yourself. Perhaps even—"

"Perhaps even—?"

The other gave a shriveled response to the smile. "No. I certainly did not mean that." He took his head in his hands and sighed. "What a world it is! As I go down the hill I wish sometimes that I had Alison's eyes.... Well, tell me about yourself."

"The one thing that I want to tell you just now, Black Hill, is that I am not any longer bloodhound at the heels of Ian. What was done is done. Let us go on to better things. So at last will be unknit what was done."

Black Hill both seemed and did not seem to pay attention. The man who sat before him was big and straight and gave forth warmth and light. He needed warmth and light; he needed a big tree to lean against. He vaguely hoped that Glenfernie was home to stay. He rubbed his hands and drank more wine.

"No one has known for a long time where you were....
Goodworth has an agent in Paris who says that Ian tried
once to find out that."

"To find out where I was?"

"Yes."

Alexander gazed out of window, beyond the terrace and
the old trees to the long hill, purple with heath, sunny and
clear atop.

A servant came to the door. "Mrs. Alison has returned,
sir."

Glenfernie rose. "I will go find her then.—I will ride over
often if I may."

"I wish you would!" said Black Hill. "I was sorry about
that quarrel with your father."

The old laird's son walked down the matted corridor. The
drawing-room door stood open; he saw one panel of the
tall screen covered with pagodas, palms, and macaws.
Further on was the room, clean and fragrant, known as
Mrs. Alison's room. This door, too, was wide. He stood
by his old friend. They put hands into hands; eyes met,
eyes held in a long look.

She said, "O God, I praise Thee!"

They sat within the garden door, on one side the clear,
still room, on the other the green and growing things, the
great tree loved by birds. The place was like a cloister. He

stayed with her an hour, and in all that time there was not a great deal said with the outer tongue. But each grew more happy, deeper and stronger.

He talked to her of the Roman Campagna, of the East and the desert....

As the hour closed he spoke directly of Ian. "That is myself now, as Elspeth is myself now. I falter, I fail, but I go on to profounder Oneness."

"Christ is born, then he grows up."

"May I see Ian's last letters?"

She put them in his hands. "They are very short. They speak almost always of external things."

He read, then sat musing, his eyes upon the tree. "This last one—You answered that it was not known where I was?"

"Yes. But he says here at the last, 'I feel it somewhere that he is on his way to Scotland.'"

"I'll have to think it out."

"Every letter is objective like this. But for all that, I divine, in the dark, a ferment.... As you see, we have not heard for months."

The laird of Glenfernie rode at last from Black Hill. It was afternoon, white drifts of clouds in the sky, light and shadow moving upon field and moor and distant, framing mountains. He rode by Littlefarm and he called at the house gate for Robin Greenlaw. It seemed that the latter was away in White Farm fields. The laird might meet him riding home. A mile farther on he saw the gray horse crossing the stream.

Glenfernie and Greenlaw, meeting, left each the saddle, went near to embracing, sat at last by a stone wall in the late sunshine, and felt a tide of liking, stronger, not weaker, than that of old days.

"You are looking after White Farm?"

"Yes. The old man fails. Jenny has become a cripple. Gilian and I are the rulers."

"Or servers?"

"It amounts to the same.... Gilian has a splendid soul."

"The poems, Robin. Do you make them yet?"

"Oh yes! Now and then. All this helps.... And you, Glenfernie, I could make a poem of you!"

The laird laughed. "I suppose you could of all men.... Gilian and you do not marry?"

"We are not the marrying kind. But I shouldn't love beauty inside if I didn't love Gilian.... I see that something big has come to you, Glenfernie, and made itself at home. You'll be wanting it taken as a matter of course, and I take it that way.... No matter what you have seen, is not this vale fair?"

"Fair as fair! Loved because of child and boy and man.... Robin, something beyond all years as we count them can be put into moments.... A moment can be as sizable as a sun."

"I believe it. We are all treading toward the land of wonders."

When he parted from Robin it was nearly sunset. He did not mean to stop to-day at White Farm, but he turned Black Alan in that direction. He would ride by the house and the shining stream with the stepping-stones. Coming beneath the bank thick with willow and aspen, he checked the horse and sat looking at the long, low house. It held there in a sunset stillness, a sunset glory, a dream of dawn. He dismounted, left the horse, and climbed to the strip of green before the place. None seemed about, all seemed within. Here was the fir-tree with the bench around—so old a tree, watching life so long!... Now he saw that Jarvis Barrow sat here. But the old man was asleep. He sat with closed eyes, and his Bible was under his hand. Beside him, tall and fair, wide-browed, gray-eyed, stood Gilian. Her head was turned toward the fringed bank; when she saw Alexander she put her finger against her lips. He made a gesture of understanding and went no nearer. For a moment he stood regarding all, then drew back into shadow of willow and aspen, descended the bank, and, mounting Black Alan, rode home through the purple light.

CHAPTER XXXIII

The countryside, the village—the Jardine Arms—Mrs. Macmurdo in her shop to all who entered—talked of the laird's homecoming. "He's a strange sort!"

"Some do say he's been to America and found a gold-mine."

"Na! He's just been journeying around in himself."

"I am na spekalative. He's contentit, and sae am I. It's a mair natural warld than ye think."

"Three year syne when he went away, he lookit like ane o' thae figures o' tragedy—"

"Aweel, then, he's swallowed himself and digested it."

"I ca' it fair miracle! The Lord touched him in the night."

"Do ye haud that he'll gang to kirk the morn?"

"I dinna precisely ken. He micht, and he micht not."

He went, entering with Mrs. Grizel, Alice, and Strickland, sitting in the House pew. How many kirks he thought of, sitting there—what cathedrals, chapels; what rude, earnest places; what temples, mosques, caves, ancient groves; what fanes; what worshiped gods! One, one! Temple and image, worshiped and worshiper. Self helping self. "O my Self, daily and deeply help myself!"

The little white stone building—the earnest, strenuous, narrow man in the pulpit, the Scots congregation—old, old, familiar, with an inner odor not unpungent, not unliked! Life Everlasting—Everlasting Life....

"That ye may have life and have it more abundantly."

White Farm sat in the White Farm place. Jarvis Barrow was there. But he did not sit erect as of yore; he leaned upon his staff. Jenny was missed. Lame now, she stayed at home and watched the passing, and talked to herself or talked to others. Gilian sat beside the old man. Behind were Menie and Merran, Thomas and Willy. Glenfernie's eyes dwelt quietly upon Jarvis and his granddaughter. When he willed he could see Elspeth beside Gilian.

The prayers, the sermon, the hymns.... All through the world-body the straining toward the larger thing, the enveloping Person! As he sat there he felt blood-warmth, touch, with every foot that sought hold, with every hand that reached. He saw the backward-falling, and he saw that they did not fall forever, that they caught and held and climbed again. He saw that because he had done that, time and time again done that.

Mr. M'Nab preached a courageous, if harsh, sermon. The old words of commination! They were not empty—but in among them, fine as ether, now ran a gloss.... The sermon ended, the final psalm was sung.

"When Zion's bondage God turned back,
As men that dreamed were we.
Then filled with laughter was our mouth.
Our tongue with melody—"

But the Scots congregation went out, to the eye sober, stern, and staid. Glenfernie spoke to Jarvis Barrow. He meant to do no more than give a word of greeting. But the old man put forth an emaciated hand and held him.

"Is it the auld laird? My eyes are na gude.—Eh, laird, I remember the sermons of your grandfather, Gawin Elliot! Aye, aye! he was a lion against sinners! I hae seen them cringe!... It is the auld laird, Gilian?"

"No, Grandfather. You remember that the old laird was William. This is Mr. Alexander."

"He that was always aff somewhere alane?" White Farm drew his mind together. "I see now! You're right. I remember."

"I am coming to White Farm to-morrow, Mr. Barrow."

"Come then.... Is Grierson slain?"

"He's away in past time," said Gilian. "Grandfather, here's Willy to help you.—Don't say anything more to him now, Glenfernie."

The next day he rode to White Farm. Jenny, through the window, saw him coming, but Jarvis Barrow, old bodily habits changing, lay sleeping on his own bed. Nor was Gilian at hand. The laird sat and talked with Jenny in the clean, spare living-room. All the story of her crippling was to be told, and a packed chest of country happenings gone over. Jenny had a happy, voluble half-hour. At last, the immediate bag exhausted, she began to cast her mind in a wider circle. Her words came at a slower pace, at last halted. She sat in silence, an apple red in her cheeks. She eyed askance the man over against her, and at last burst forth:

"Gilian said I should na speir—but, eh, Glenfernie, I wad gie mair than a bawbee to ken what you did to him!"

"Nothing."

"Naething?"

"Nothing that you would call anything."

Jenny sat with open mouth. "They said you'd changed, even to look at—and sae you have!—*Naething!*"

Jarvis Barrow entered the room, and with him came Gilian. The old man failed, failed. Now he knew Glenfernie and spoke to him of to-day and of yesterday—and now he addressed him as though he were his father, the old laird, or even his grandfather. And after a few minutes he said that he would go out to the fir-tree. Alexander helped him there. Gilian took the Bible and placed it beside him.

"Open at eleventh Isaiah," he said. "'*And there shall come forth a rod out of the stem of Jesse, and a Branch shall grow out of his roots*—'"

Gilian opened the book. "You read," and she sat down beside him.

"I wish to talk to you," said Alexander to her. "When—?"

"I am going to town to-morrow afternoon. I'll walk back over the moor."

When he came upon the moor next day it was bathed by a sun half-way down the western quarter. The colors of it were lit, the vast slopes had alike tenderness and majesty. He moved over the moor; then he sat down by a furze-bush and waited. Gilian came at last, sat down near him in the dry, sweet growth. She put her arms over her knees; she held her head back and drank the ineffable rich compassion of the sky. She spoke at last.

"Oh, laird, life's a marvel!"

"I feel the soul now," he said, "of marigolds and pansies. That is the difference to me."

"What shall you do? Stay here and grow—or travel again and grow?"

"I do not yet know.... It depends."

"It depends on Ian, does it not?"

"Yes.... Now you speak as Gilian and now you speak as Elspeth."

"That is the marvel of the world.... That Person whom we call Being has also a long name.—My name, her name, your name, his name, its name, all names! Side by side, one over another, one through another.... Who comes out but just that Person?"

They sat and watched the orb that itself, with its members the planets, went a great journey. Gilian began to talk about Elspeth. She talked with quietness, with depth, insight, and love, sitting there on the golden moor. Elspeth—childhood and girlhood and womanhood. The sister of Elspeth spoke simply, but the sifted words came from a poet's granary. She made pictures, she made melodies for Alexander. Glints of vision, fugitive strains of music, echoes of a quaint and subtle mirth, something elemental, faylike—that was Elspeth. And lightning in the south in summer, just shown, swiftly withdrawn—power and passion—sudden similitudes with great love-women of old story—that also was Elspeth. And a crying and calling for the Star that gathers all stars—that likewise was Elspeth. Such and such did Elspeth show herself to Gilian. And that half-year that they knew about of grief and madness—it was not scanted nor its misery denied! It, too, was, or had been, of Elspeth. Deep through ages, again and again, something like that might have worked forth. But it was not all nor most of that nature—had not been and would not be—would not be—would not be. The sister of Elspeth spoke with pure, convinced passion as to that. Who denied the dark? There were the dark and the light, and the million million tones of each! And there was the eternal space where differences trembled into harmony.

With the sunset they moved over the great, clean slope to where it ran down to fields and trees. Before them was White Farm, below them the glistening stream, coral and gold between and around the stepping-stones. They parted here, Gilian going on to the house, the laird turning again over the moor.

He passed the village; he came by the white kirk and the yew-trees and the kirkyard. All were lifted upon the hilltop, all wore the color of sunset and the color of dawn. The laird of Glenfernie moved beside the kirkyard wall. He seemed to hold in his hand marigolds, pinks, and pansies. He saw a green mound, and he seemed to put the flowers there, out of old custom and tenderness. But no longer did he feel that Elspeth was beneath the mound. A wide tapering cloud, golden-feathered, like a wing of glory, stretched half across the sky. He looked at it; he looked at that in which it rested. His lips moved, he spoke aloud.

"O Death! where is thy sting? O grave! where is thy victory?"

CHAPTER XXXIV

Days and weeks went by. Autumn came and stepped in russet toward winter. Yet it was not cold and the mists and winds delayed. The homecoming of the laird of Glenfernie slipped into received fact—a fact rather large, acceptable, bringing into the neighborhood situation of things in general a perceptible amount of expansion and depth, but settling now, for the general run, into comfortable every-day. They were used—until these late years—to seeing a laird of Glenfernie about. When he was not there it was a missed part of the landscape. When he was in presence Nature showed herself correctly filled out. This laird was like and not like the old lairds. Big like the one before him in outward frame and seeming, there were certainly inner differences. Dale and village pondered these differences. It came at last to a judgment that this Glenfernie was larger and kinder. The neighborhood considered that he would make a good home body, and if he was a scholar, sitting late in the old keep over great books, that harmed no one, redounded, indeed, to the dale's credit. His very wanderings might so redound now that they were over. "That's the laird of Glenfernie," the dale might say to strangers.

It was dim, gray, late November weather. There poured rain, shrieked a wind. Then the sky cleared and the air stilled. There came three wonderful days, one after the other, and between them wonderful nights with a waxing moon. Alexander, riding home from Littlefarm, found waiting for him in the court Peter Lindsay, of Black Hill. This was a trusted man.

"I hae a bit letter frae Mistress Alison, laird." Giving it to him, Peter came close, his eye upon the approaching stable-boy. "Dinna look at it here, but when ye're alone. I'll bide and tak the answer."

Alexander nodded, turned, and crossed to the keep. Within its ancient, deep entrance he broke seal and opened the paper superscribed by Mrs. Alison. Within was not her handwriting. There ran but two lines, in a hand with which he was well acquainted:

"*Will you meet one that you know in the cave to-night four hours after moonrise?*"

He went back to the messenger. "The answer is, 'Yes.' Say just that, Peter Lindsay."

The day went by. He worked with Strickland. The latter thought him a little absent, but the accounts were checked and decisions made. At the supper-table he was more quiet than usual.

"Full moon to-night," said Alice. "What does it look like, Alexander, when it shines in Rome and when it comes up right out of the desert?"

"It lights the ruins and it is pale day in the desert. What makes you think to-night of Rome and the desert?"

"I do not know. I see the rim now out of window."

The moon climbed. It shone with an intense silver behind leafless boughs and behind the dark-clad boughs of firs. It came above the trees. The night hung windless and deeply clear. A fire burned upon the hearth of the room in the keep. Alexander sat before it and he sat very still, and vast pictures came to the inner eye, and to the inner ear meanings of old words....

He rose at last, took a cloak, and went down the stone stair into a night cold, still, and bright. The path by the school-house, the hand's-breadth of silvered earth, the broken, silvered wall, the pine, the rough descent.... He went through the dark wood where the shining fell broken like a shattered mirror. Beyond held open country until he came to the glen mouth. The moon was high. He heard faint sounds of the far night-time, and his own step upon the silver earth. He came to the glen and the sound of water streaming to the sea.

How well he knew this place! Thick trees spread arms above, rock that leaned darkened the narrow path. But his foot knew where to tread. In some more open span down poured the twice-broken light; then came darkness. There was a great checkering of light and darkness and the slumbrous sound of water. The path grew steeper and rougher. He was approaching the middle of the place.

At last he came to the cave mouth and the leafless briers that curtained it. Just before it was reached, the moon-beams struck through clear air. There was a silver lightness. A form moved from where it had rested against the rock. Ian's voice spoke.

"Alexander?"

"Yes, it is I."

"The night is so still. I heard you coming a long way off. I have lighted a fire in the cave."

They entered it—the old boyhood haunt. All the air was moted for them with memories. Ian had made the fire and had laid fagots for mending. The flame played and murmured and reddened the walls. The roof was high, and at one place the light smoke made hidden exit. It was dead night. Even in the daytime the glen was a solitary place.

Alexander put down his cloak. He looked about the place, then, squarely turning, looked at Ian. Long time had passed since they had spoken each to other in Rome. Now they stood in that ancient haunt where the very making of the fire sang of the old always-done, never-to-be-omitted, here in the cave. The light was sufficient for each to study the other's face. Alexander spoke:

"You have changed."

"And you. Let us sit down. There is much that I want to say."

They sat, and again it was as they used to do, with the fire between them, but out of plane, so that they might fully view each other. The cave kept stillness. Subtly and silently its walls became penetrable. They crumbled, dissolved. Around now was space and the two were men.

Ian looked worn, with a lined face. But the old brown-gold splendor, though dusked over, drew yet. No one might feel him negligible. And something was there, quivering in the dusk.... He and Alexander rested without speech—or rather about them whirled inaudible speech— intuitions, divinations. At last words formed themselves. Ian spoke:

"I came from France on the chance that you were here....
For a long time I have been driven, driven, by one with a
scourge. Then that changed to a longing. At last I
resolved.... The driving was within—as within as longing
and determination. I have heard Aunt Alison say that
every myth, all world stories, are but symbols, figures, of
what goes on within. Well, I have found out about the
Furies, and about some other myths."

"Yes. They tried to tell inner things."

"I came here to say that I wronged folk from whom a man
within me cannot part. One is dead, and I have to seek her
along another road. But you are living, breathing there! I
made myself your foe, and now I wish that I could
unmake what I made.... I was and am a sinful soul.... It is
for you to say if it is anything to you, what I confess." He
rose from the fire and moved once or twice the length of
the place. At last he came and stood before the other. "It is
no wonder if it be not given," he said. "But I ask your
forgiveness, Alexander!"

"Well, I give it to you," said Alexander. His face worked.
He got to his feet and went to Ian. He put his hands upon
the other's shoulders. "*Old Saracen!*" he said.

Ian shook. With the dropping of Alexander's hands he
went back a step; he sat down and hid his head in his
arms.

Said Alexander: "You did thus and thus, obeying inner
weakness, calling it all the time strength. And do I not
know that I, too, made myself a shadow going after
shadows? My own make of selfishness, arrogance, and
hatred.... Let us do better, you and I!" He mended the fire.
"By understanding the past may be altered. Already it is

altered with you and me.... I was here the other day. I stayed a long time. There seemed two boys in the cave and there seemed a girl beside them. The three felt with and understood and were one another." He came and knelt beside Ian. "Let us forge a stronger friendship!"

Ian, face to the rock, was weeping, weeping. Alexander knelt beside him, lay beside him, arm over heaving shoulders. Old Steadfast—Old Saracen—and Elspeth Barrow, also, and around and through, pulsing, cohering, interpenetrating, healing, a sense of something greater....

It passed—the torrent force, long pent, aching against its barriers. Ian lay still, at last sat up.

"Come outside," said Alexander, "into the cold and the air."

They left the cave for the moonlight night. They leaned against the rock, and about them hung the sleeping trees. The crag was silvered, the stream ran with a deep under-sound. The air struck pure and cold. The large stars shone down through all the flooding radiance of the moon. The familiar place, the strange place, the old-new place.... At last Ian spoke, "Have you been to the Kelpie's Pool?"

"Yes. The day I came home I lay for hours beside it."

"I was there to-night. I came here from there."

"It is with us. But far beside it is also with us!"

"The carnival at Rome. When I left Rome I went to the Lake of Como. I want to tell you of a night there—and of nights and days later, elsewhere—"

"Come within, as we used to do, and talk the heart out."

They went back to the fire. It played and sang. The minutes, poignant, full, went by.

"So at last prison and scaffold risks ceased to count. I took what disguise I could and came."

"All at Black Hill know?"

"Yes. But they are not betrayers. I do not show myself and am not called by my name. I am Senor Nobody."

"Senor Nobody."

"When I broke Edinburgh gaol I fled to France through Spain. There in the mountains I fell among brigands. I had to find ransom. Senor Nobody provided it. I never saw him nor do I know his name.... Alexander!"

"Aye."

"Was it you?"

"Aye. I hated while I gave.... But I don't hate now. I don't hate myself. Ian!"

The fire played, the fire sang.

Alexander spoke: "Now your bodily danger again— You've put your head into the lion's mouth!"

"That lion weighs nothing here."

"I am glad that you came. But now I wish to see you go!"

"Yes, I must go."

"Is it back to France?"

"Yes—or to America. I do not know. I have thought of that. But here, first, I thought that I should go to White Farm."

"It would add risk. I do not think that it is needed."

"Jarvis Barrow—"

"The old man lies abed and his wits wander. He would hardly know you, I think—would not understand. Leave him now, except as you find him within."

"Her sister?"

"I will tell Gilian. That is a wide and wise spirit. She will understand."

"Then it is come and gone—"

"Disappear as you appeared! None here wants your peril, and the griefs and evils were you taken."

"I expected to go back. The brig *Seawing* brought me. It sails in a week's time."

"You must be upon it, then."

"Yes, I suppose so." He drew a long, impatient breath. "Let us leave all that! Sufficient to the day—I wander and wander, and there are stones and thorns—and Circe, too!... You have the steady light, but I have not! The wind blows it—it flickers!"

"Ah, I know flickering, too!"

"Is there a great Senor Somebody? Sometimes I feel it—and then there is only the wild ass in the desert! The dust blinds and the mire sticks."

"Ah, Old Saracen—"

The other pushed the embers together. "This cave—this glen.... Do you remember that time we were in Amsterdam and each dreamed one night the same dream?"

"I remember."

The fire was sinking for the night. The moon was down in the western sky. Around and around the cave and the glen and the night the inner ear heard, as it were, a long, faint, wordless cry for help. Alexander brooded, brooded, his eyes upon the lessening flame. At last, with a sudden movement, he rose. "I smell the morning air. Let us be going!"

The two covered the embers and left the cave. The moon stood above the western rim of the glen, the sound of the water was deep and full, frost hung in the air, the trees great and small stood quiet, in a winter dream. Ian and Alexander climbed the glen-side, avoiding Mother Binning's cot. Now they were in open country, moving toward Black Hill.

The walk was not a short one. Daybreak was just behind the east when they came to the long heath-grown hill that faced the house, the purple ridge where as boys they had met. They climbed it, and in the east was light. Beneath them, among the trees, Black Hill showed roof and chimney. Then up the path toward them came Peter Lindsay.

He seemed to come in haste and a kind of fear. When he saw the two he threw up his hands, then violently gestured to them to go back upon their path, drop beneath the hilltop. They obeyed, and he came to them himself, panting, sweat upon him for all the chill night. "Mr. Ian— Laird! Sogers at the house—"

"Ah!"

"Twelve of them. They rade in an hour syne. The lieutenant swears ye're there, Mr. Ian, and they search the house. Didna ye see the lights? Mrs. Alison tauld me to gae warn ye—"

CHAPTER XXXV

The soldiers, having fruitlessly searched Black Hill, for the present set up quarters there, and searched the neighborhood. They gave a wide cast to that word. It seemed to include all this part of Scotland. Before long they appeared, not unforeseen, at Glenfernie.

The lieutenant was a wiry, wide-nostriled man, determined to please superiors and win promotion. He had now men at the Jardine Arms no less than men at Black Hill. Face to face with the laird of Glenfernie in the latter's hall, he explained his errand.

"Yes," said Glenfernie. "I saw you coming up the hill. Will you take wine?"

"To your health, sir!"

"To your health!"

The lieutenant set down the glass and wiped his lips. "I have orders, Mr. Jardine, which I may not disobey."

"Exactly so, Lieutenant."

"My duty, therefore, brings me in at your door—though

of course I may say that you and your household are hardly under suspicion of harboring a proscribed rebel! A good Whig"—he bowed stiffly—"a volunteer serving with the Duke in the late trouble, and, last but not least, a personal enemy of the man we seek—"

"The catalogue is ample!" said Glenfernie. "But still, having your orders to make no exception, you must search my house. It is at your service. I will show you from room to room."

Lieutenant and soldiers and laird went through the place, high and low and up and down. "Perfunctory!" said the lieutenant twice. "But we must do as we are told!"

"Yes," said the laird. "This is my sister's garden. The small building there is an old school-room."

They met Alice walking in the garden, in the winter sunshine. Strickland, too, joined them here. Presentations over, the lieutenant again repeated his story.

"Perfunctory, of course, here—perfunctory! The only trace that we think we have we found in a glen near you. There is a cave there that I understand he used to haunt. We found ashes, still warm, where had been a fire. Pity is, the ground is so frozen no footstep shows!"

"You are making escape difficult," said Strickland.

"I flatter myself that we'll get him between here and the sea! I am going presently," said the lieutenant, "to a place called White Farm. But I am given to understand that there are good reasons—saving the lady's presence—why he'll find no shelter there."

"Over yonder is the old keep," said Glenfernie. "When that is passed, I think you will have seen everything."

They left Strickland and Alice and went to the keep. Their footsteps and those of the soldiers behind them rang upon the stone stairs.

"Above is the room," said the laird of Glenfernie, "where as a boy I used to play at alchemy. I built a furnace. I had an intention of making lead into gold. I keep old treasures there still, and it is still my dear old lair—though with a difference as I travel on, though with a difference, Lieutenant, as we travel on!"

They came into the room, quiet, filled with books and old apparatus, with a burning fire, with sunlight and shadow dappling floor and wall. "Well, he would hardly hide here!" said the lieutenant.

"Not by received canons," answered Glenfernie.

The lieutenant spoke to the soldiers. "Go about and look beneath and behind matters. There are no closets?"

"There are only these presses built against the stone." The laird opened them as he spoke. "You see—blank space!" He moved toward a corner. "This structure is my ancient furnace of which I spoke. I still keep it fuel-filled for firing." As he spoke he opened a sizable door.

The lieutenant, stooping, saw the piled wood. "I don't know much of alchemy," he said. "I've never had time to get around to those things. It's bringing out sleeping values isn't it?"

"Something like that." He shut the furnace door, and they

stood watching the soldiers search the room. In no long time this stood a completed process.

"Perfunctory!" said again the lieutenant. "Now men, we'll to White Farm!"

"There is food and drink for them below, on this chilly day," said the laird, "and perhaps in the hall you'll drink another glass of wine?"

All went down the stairs and out of the keep. Another half-hour and the detail, lieutenant and men, mounted and rode away. Glenfernie and Strickland watched them down the winding road, clear of the hill, out upon the highway.

Alexander went back alone to the keep that, also, from its widened loopholes, might watch the searchers ride away. He mounted the stair; he came into his old room. Ian stood beside the table. The sizable furnace door hung open, the screen of heaped wood was disarranged.

"It was a good notion, that recess behind my old furnace!" said Glenfernie. "You took no harm beyond some cobwebs and ashes?"

"None, Senor Nobody," said Ian.

That day went by. The laird and Strickland talked together in low voices in the old school-room. Davie, too, appeared there once, and an old, trusted stableman. At sunset came Robin Greenlaw, and stayed an hour. The stars shone out, around drew a high, windy crystal night.

Mrs. Grizel went to bed. Alexander, with Alice and Strickland, sat by the fire in the hall. There was much that the laird wished to say that he said. They spoke in low voices, leaning toward the burning logs, the light playing over their faces, the light laughing upon old armor, crossed weapons, upon the walls. Alice, a bonny woman with sense and courage, sat beside Glenfernie. Strickland, from his corner, saw how much she looked like her mother; how much, to-night, Alexander looked like her.

They talked until late. They came to agreement, quiet, moved, but thorough. Glenfernie rose. He took Alice in his arms and kissed her thrice. Moisture was in the eyes of both.

"Sleep, dear, sleep! So we understand, things grow easy!"

"I think that you are right, and that is a long way to comfort," said Alice. "Good night, good night, Alexander!"

When she was gone the two men talked yet a little longer, over the dying fire. Then they, too, wished each other good night. Strickland went to his room, but Alexander left the house and crossed the moon-filled night to the keep. It was now he and Ian.

There was no strain. "Old Steadfast" and "Old Saracen," and a long pilgrimage together, and every difference granted, yet, in the background, a vast, an oceanic unity.... Ian rose from the settle. He and the laird of Glenfernie sat by the table and with pen and paper made a diagram of escape. They bent to the task in hand, and when it was done, and a few more words had been said, they turned to the pallets which Davie had spread on either side of the hearth. The moon and the low fire made a strange half-light in the room. The two lay still, addressed to sleep. They spoke and answered but once.

Said Ian: "I felt just then the waves of the sea!—The waves of the sea and the roads of France.... The waves and roads of the days and nights and months and years. I there and you here. There is an ether, doubtless, that links, but I don't tread it firmly.... Be sure I'll turn to you, call to you, often, over the long roads, from out of the trough of the waves! *Senor Nobody! Senor Nobody!*" He laughed, but with a catch of the breath. "Good night!"

"Good night, Old Saracen!" said Alexander.

Morn came. That day Glenfernie House heard still that all that region was searched. The day went by, short, gray, with flurries of snow. By afternoon it settled to a great, down-drifting pall of white. It was falling thick and fast when Alexander Jardine and Ian Rullock passed through the broken wall beyond the school-room. The pine branches were whitening, the narrow, rugged path ran a zigzag of white.

Strickland had parted from them at the wall, and yet Strickland seemed to be upon the path, following Glenfernie. Ian wore a dress of Strickland's, a hat and cloak that the countryside knew. He and Strickland were nearly of a height. Keeping silence and moving through a dimness of the descending day and the shaken veil of the snow, almost any chance-met neighbor would have said, in passing, "Good day, Mr. Strickland!"

The path led into the wood. Trees rose about them, phantoms in the snowstorm. The snow fell in large flakes, straight, undriven by wind. Footprints made transient shapes. The snow obliterated them as in the desert moving sand obliterated. Ian and Alexander, leaving the wood, took a way that led by field and moor to Littlefarm.

The earth seemed a Solitary, with no child nor lover of hers abroad. The day declined, the snow fell. Ian and Alexander moved on, hardly speaking. The outer landscape rolled dimmed, softened, withdrawn. The inner world moved among its own contours. The day flowed toward night, as the night would flow toward day.

They came to the foot of the moor that stretched between White Farm and Littlefarm.

"There is a woman standing by that tree," said Ian.

"Yes. It is Gilian."

They moved toward her. Tall, fair, wide-browed and gray-eyed, she leaned against the oak stem and seemed to be at home here, too. The wide falling snow, the mystic light and quietness, were hers for mantle. As they approached she stirred.

"Good day, Glenfernie!—Good day, Ian Rullock!— Glenfernie, you cannot go this way! Soldiers are at Littlefarm."

"Did Robin—"

"He got word to me an hour since. They are chance-fallen, the second time. They will get no news and soon be gone. He trusted me to give you warning. He says wait for him at the cot that was old Skene's. It stands empty and folk say that it is haunted and go round about." She left the tree and took the path with them. "It lies between us and White Farm. This snow is friendly. It covers marks—it keeps folk within-doors—nor does it mean to fall too long or too heavily."

They moved together through the falling snow.

It was a mile to old Skene's cot. They walked it almost in silence—upon Ian's part in silence. The snow fell; it covered their footprints. All outlines showed vague and looming. The three seemed three vital points moving in a world dissolving or a world forming.

The empty cot rose before them, the thatch whitened, the door-stone whitened. Glenfernie pushed the door. It opened; they found a clean, bare place, twilight now, still, with the falling snow without.

Gilian spoke. "I'll go on now to White Farm. Robin will come. In no long time you'll be upon the farther road.... Now I will say Fare you well!"

Alexander took her hands. "Farewell, Gilian!"

Gray eyes met gray eyes. "Be it short time or be it long time—soon home to Glenfernie, or long, long gone—farewell, and God bless you, Glenfernie!"

"And you, Gilian!"

She turned to Ian. "Ian Rullock—farewell, too, and God bless you, too!"

She was gone. They watched through the door her form moving amid falling snow. The veil between thickened; she vanished; there were only the white particles of the dissolving or the forming world. The two kept silence.

Twilight deepened, night came, the snow ceased to fall for a time, then began again, but less thickly. One hour went by, two, three. Then came Robin Greenlaw and

Peter Lindsay, riding, and with them horses for the two who waited at Skene's cot.

Four men rode through the December night. At dawn they neared the sea. The snow fell no longer. When the purple bars came into the east they saw in the first light the huddled roofs of a small seaport. Beyond lay gray water, with shipping in the harbor.

At a crossroads the party divided. Robin Greenlaw and Peter Lindsay took a way that should lead them far aside from this port, and then with circuitousness home. Before they reached it they would separate, coming singly into their own dale, back to Black Hill, back to Littlefarm. The laird of Glenfernie and Littlefarm, dismounting, moving aside, talked together for a few moments. Ian gave Peter Lindsay a message for Mrs. Alison.... Good-bys were said. Greenlaw remounted; he and Peter Lindsay moved slowly from the two bound to the port. A dip of the earth presently hid them. Alexander and Ian were left in the gray dawn.

"Alexander, I know the safe house and the safe man and the safe ship. Why should you run further danger? Let us say good-by now!"

"No, not now."

"You have come to the edge of Scotland. Say farewell here, and danger saved, rather than on the water stairs in a little while—"

"No. I will go farther, Ian. There is Mackenzie's house, over there."

They rode through the winter dawn to the house at the

edge of the port, where lived a quiet man and wife, under obligations to the Jardines. There visited them now the laird of Glenfernie and his secretary, Mr. Strickland.

The latter, it seemed, was not well—kept his room that day. The laird of Glenfernie went about, indeed, but never once went near the waterside.... And yet, at eve, the master of the *Seawing*, riding in the harbor, took the resolution to sail by cockcrow.

The sun went down with red and gold, in a winter splendor. Dark night followed, but, late, there rose a moon. Alexander and Ian, coming down to the harbor edge at a specified place, found there the waiting boat with two rowers. It hung before them on the just-lit water. "Now, Old Steadfast, farewell!" said Ian.

"I am going a little farther. Step in, man!"

The boat drove across, under the moon, to the *Seawing*. The two mounted the brig's side and, touching deck, found the captain, known to Ian, who had sailed before upon the *Seawing*, and known since yesterday to Glenfernie. The captain welcomed them, his only passengers, using not their own names, but others that had been chosen. In the cabin, under the swinging lantern, there followed a few words as to weather, ports, and sailing. The tide served, the *Seawing* would be forth in an hour. The captain, work calling, left them in the small lighted place.

"The boat is waiting. Now, Old Steadfast—Senor Nobody—"

"Old Saracen, we used to say that we'd go one day to India—"

"Yes—"

"Well, let us go!"

"*Us*—"

"Why not?"

They stood with the table between them. Alexander's hands moved toward Ian's. They took hands; there followed a strong, a convulsive pressure.

"We sin in differing ways and at differing times," said Alexander, "but we all sin. And we all struggle with it and through it and onward! And there must be some kind of star upon our heights. Well, let us work toward it together, Old Saracen!"

They went out of the cabin and upon the deck. The boat that had brought them was gone. They saw it in the moonlight, half-way back to the quay. On the *Seawing*, sailors were lifting anchor. They stood and watched. The moon was paling; there came the scent of morning; far upon the shore a cock crew. The *Seawing's* crew were making sail. Out and up went her pinions, filled with a steady and favoring wind. She thrilled; she moved; she left the harbor for a new voyage, fresh wonder of the eternal world.

Choose from Thousands of 1stWorldLibrary Classics By

A. M. Barnard
Ada Leverson
Adolphus William Ward
Aesop
Agatha Christie
Alexander Aaronsohn
Alexander Kielland
Alexandre Dumas
Alfred Gatty
Alfred Ollivant
Alice Duer Miller
Alice Turner Curtis
Alice Dunbar
Allen Chapman
Alleyne Ireland
Ambrose Bierce
Amelia E. Barr
Amory H. Bradford
Andrew Lang
Andrew McFarland Davis
Andy Adams
Angela Brazil
Anna Alice Chapin
Anna Sewell
Annie Besant
Annie Hamilton Donnell
Annie Payson Call
Annie Roe Carr
Annonaymous
Anton Chekhov
Archibald Lee Fletcher
Arnold Bennett
Arthur C. Benson
Arthur Conan Doyle
Arthur M. Winfield
Arthur Ransome
Arthur Schnitzler
Arthur Train
Atticus
B.H. Baden-Powell
B. M. Bower
B. C. Chatterjee
Baroness Emmuska Orczy
Baroness Orczy
Basil King
Bayard Taylor
Ben Macomber
Bertha Muzzy Bower
Bjornstjerne Bjornson

Booth Tarkington
Boyd Cable
Bram Stoker
C. Collodi
C. E. Orr
C. M. Ingleby
Carolyn Wells
Catherine Parr Traill
Charles A. Eastman
Charles Amory Beach
Charles Dickens
Charles Dudley Warner
Charles Farrar Browne
Charles Ives
Charles Kingsley
Charles Klein
Charles Hanson Towne
Charles Lathrop Pack
Charles Romyn Dake
Charles Whibley
Charles Willing Beale
Charlotte M. Braeme
Charlotte M. Yonge
Charlotte Perkins Stetson
Clair W. Hayes
Clarence Day Jr.
Clarence E. Mulford
Clemence Housman
Confucius
Coningsby Dawson
Cornelis DeWitt Wilcox
Cyril Burleigh
D. H. Lawrence
Daniel Defoe
David Garnett
Dinah Craik
Don Carlos Janes
Donald Keyhoe
Dorothy Kilner
Dougan Clark
Douglas Fairbanks
E. Nesbit
E. P. Roe
E. Phillips Oppenheim
E. S. Brooks
Earl Barnes
Edgar Rice Burroughs
Edith Van Dyne
Edith Wharton

Edward Everett Hale
Edward J. O'Biren
Edward S. Ellis
Edwin L. Arnold
Eleanor Atkins
Eleanor Hallowell Abbott
Eliot Gregory
Elizabeth Gaskell
Elizabeth McCracken
Elizabeth Von Arnim
Ellem Key
Emerson Hough
Emilie F. Carlen
Emily Bronte
Emily Dickinson
Enid Bagnold
Enilor Macartney Lane
Erasmus W. Jones
Ernie Howard Pie
Ethel May Dell
Ethel Turner
Ethel Watts Mumford
Eugene Sue
Eugenie Foa
Eugene Wood
Eustace Hale Ball
Evelyn Everett-green
Everard Cotes
F. H. Cheley
F. J. Cross
F. Marion Crawford
Fannie E. Newberry
Federick Austin Ogg
Ferdinand Ossendowski
Fergus Hume
Florence A. Kilpatrick
Fremont B. Deering
Francis Bacon
Francis Darwin
Frances Hodgson Burnett
Frances Parkinson Keyes
Frank Gee Patchin
Frank Harris
Frank Jewett Mather
Frank L. Packard
Frank V. Webster
Frederic Stewart Isham
Frederick Trevor Hill
Frederick Winslow Taylor

Friedrich Kerst
Friedrich Nietzsche
Fyodor Dostoyevsky
G.A. Henty
G.K. Chesterton
Gabrielle E. Jackson
Garrett P. Serviss
Gaston Leroux
George A. Warren
George Ade
Geroge Bernard Shaw
George Cary Eggleston
George Durston
George Ebers
George Eliot
George Gissing
George MacDonald
George Meredith
George Orwell
George Sylvester Viereck
George Tucker
George W. Cable
George Wharton James
Gertrude Atherton
Gordon Casserly
Grace E. King
Grace Gallatin
Grace Greenwood
Grant Allen
Guillermo A. Sherwell
Gulielma Zollinger
Gustav Flaubert
H. A. Cody
H. B. Irving
H.C. Bailey
H. G. Wells
H. H. Munro
H. Irving Hancock
H. R. Naylor
H. Rider Haggard
H. W. C. Davis
Haldeman Julius
Hall Caine
Hamilton Wright Mabie
Hans Christian Andersen
Harold Avery
Harold McGrath
Harriet Beecher Stowe
Harry Castlemon
Harry Coghill
Harry Houidini

Hayden Carruth
Helent Hunt Jackson
Helen Nicolay
Hendrik Conscience
Hendy David Thoreau
Henri Barbusse
Henrik Ibsen
Henry Adams
Henry Ford
Henry Frost
Henry James
Henry Jones Ford
Henry Seton Merriman
Henry W Longfellow
Herbert A. Giles
Herbert Carter
Herbert N. Casson
Herman Hesse
Hildegard G. Frey
Homer
Honore De Balzac
Horace B. Day
Horace Walpole
Horatio Alger Jr.
Howard Pyle
Howard R. Garis
Hugh Lofting
Hugh Walpole
Humphry Ward
Ian Maclaren
Inez Haynes Gillmore
Irving Bacheller
Isabel Cecilia Williams
Isabel Hornibrook
Israel Abrahams
Ivan Turgenev
J.G.Austin
J. Henri Fabre
J. M. Barrie
J. M. Walsh
J. Macdonald Oxley
J. R. Miller
J. S. Fletcher
J. S. Knowles
J. Storer Clouston
J. W. Duffield
Jack London
Jacob Abbott
James Allen
James Andrews
James Baldwin

James Branch Cabell
James DeMille
James Joyce
James Lane Allen
James Lane Allen
James Oliver Curwood
James Oppenheim
James Otis
James R. Driscoll
Jane Abbott
Jane Austen
Jane L. Stewart
Janet Aldridge
Jens Peter Jacobsen
Jerome K. Jerome
Jessie Graham Flower
John Buchan
John Burroughs
John Cournos
John F. Kennedy
John Gay
John Glasworthy
John Habberton
John Joy Bell
John Kendrick Bangs
John Milton
John Philip Sousa
John Taintor Foote
Jonas Lauritz Idemil Lie
Jonathan Swift
Joseph A. Altsheler
Joseph Carey
Joseph Conrad
Joseph E. Badger Jr
Joseph Hergesheimer
Joseph Jacobs
Jules Vernes
Julian Hawthrone
Julie A Lippmann
Justin Huntly McCarthy
Kakuzo Okakura
Karle Wilson Baker
Kate Chopin
Kenneth Grahame
Kenneth McGaffey
Kate Langley Bosher
Kate Langley Bosher
Katherine Cecil Thurston
Katherine Stokes
L. A. Abbot
L. T. Meade

L. Frank Baum
Latta Griswold
Laura Dent Crane
Laura Lee Hope
Laurence Housman
Lawrence Beasley
Leo Tolstoy
Leonid Andreyev
Lewis Carroll
Lewis Sperry Chafer
Lilian Bell
Lloyd Osbourne
Louis Hughes
Louis Joseph Vance
Louis Tracy
Louisa May Alcott
Lucy Fitch Perkins
Lucy Maud Montgomery
Luther Benson
Lydia Miller Middleton
Lyndon Orr
M. Corvus
M. H. Adams
Margaret E. Sangster
Margret Howth
Margaret Vandercook
Margaret W. Hungerford
Margret Penrose
Maria Edgeworth
Maria Thompson Daviess
Mariano Azuela
Marion Polk Angellotti
Mark Overton
Mark Twain
Mary Austin
Mary Catherine Crowley
Mary Cole
Mary Hastings Bradley
Mary Roberts Rinehart
Mary Rowlandson
M. Wollstonecraft Shelley
Maud Lindsay
Max Beerbohm
Myra Kelly
Nathaniel Hawthrone
Nicolo Machiavelli
O. F. Walton
Oscar Wilde

Owen Johnson
P.G. Wodehouse
Paul and Mabel Thorne
Paul G. Tomlinson
Paul Severing
Percy Brebner
Percy Keese Fitzhugh
Peter B. Kyne
Plato
Quincy Allen
R. Derby Holmes
R. L. Stevenson
R. S. Ball
Rabindranath Tagore
Rahul Alvares
Ralph Bonehill
Ralph Henry Barbour
Ralph Victor
Ralph Waldo Emmerson
Rene Descartes
Ray Cummings
Rex Beach
Rex E. Beach
Richard Harding Davis
Richard Jefferies
Richard Le Gallienne
Robert Barr
Robert Frost
Robert Gordon Anderson
Robert L. Drake
Robert Lansing
Robert Lynd
Robert Michael Ballantyne
Robert W. Chambers
Rosa Nouchette Carey
Rudyard Kipling
Saint Augustine
Samuel B. Allison
Samuel Hopkins Adams
Sarah Bernhardt
Sarah C. Hallowell
Selma Lagerlof
Sherwood Anderson
Sigmund Freud
Standish O'Grady
Stanley Weyman
Stella Benson
Stella M. Francis

Stephen Crane
Stewart Edward White
Stijn Streuvels
Swami Abhedananda
Swami Parmananda
T. S. Ackland
T. S. Arthur
The Princess Der Ling
Thomas A. Janvier
Thomas A Kempis
Thomas Anderton
Thomas Bailey Aldrich
Thomas Bulfinch
Thomas De Quincey
Thomas Dixon
Thomas H. Huxley
Thomas Hardy
Thomas More
Thornton W. Burgess
U. S. Grant
Upton Sinclair
Valentine Williams
Various Authors
Vaughan Kester
Victor Appleton
Victor G. Durham
Victoria Cross
Virginia Woolf
Wadsworth Camp
Walter Camp
Walter Scott
Washington Irving
Wilbur Lawton
Wilkie Collins
Willa Cather
Willard F. Baker
William Dean Howells
William le Queux
W. Makepeace Thackeray
William W. Walter
William Shakespeare
Winston Churchill
Yei Theodora Ozaki
Yogi Ramacharaka
Young E. Allison
Zane Grey